*Santa Claws is Coming to*

Deathlehem

Santa Claws is Coming to Deathlehem

Edited by
Michael J. Evans
and
Harrison Graves

A
Grinning Skull Press
Publication

DEDICATION

As always, to all those who enjoy embrace
all things Christmas, light and dark.
And to all those living with HIV/AIDS.

ACKNOWLEDGMENTS

As always, we would like to thank Jeffrey Kosh for another stunning cover, and to all the authors who make this anthology series possible.

TABLE OF CONTENTS

Best Wishes for a Haunted Holiday

Some folks have asked me why horror stories for Christmas. My answer is usually why not (the real reason behind this anthology series is explained in the very first volume). What many folks, especially those asking this question, don't know, however, is that Christmas and horror stories go hand in hand. Well, not necessarily horror stories, but ghost stories. It was a tradition during Victorian times for folks to gather together on Christmas Eve to smoke, drink, and tell ghost stories. They didn't necessarily have to take place on Christmas, but it was a nice touch if they did. When you ask them about Christmas ghost stories, *A Christmas Carol* by Charles Dickens, but they're at a loss to come up with any others, which is why, this year, we included another classic Dickens Christmas story, "The Story of the Goblins who Stole a Sexton." But Dickens isn't the only one to have penned tales of holiday ghost. M.R. James wrote many of his ghost stories around Christmas time; E.F. Benson, A.M. Burrage, and Jerome K. Jerome all wrote spooky winter tales, some of which actually take place on Christmas Eve/Day. Wouldn't it be nice to see this tradition return?

There are other holiday traditions that seem to be making

a comeback within recent years. Take Elf on the Shelf, for example. Personally, I don't remember the Elf on the Shelf. I know we had one... Well, more than one. I do remember seeing them on the tree and being strategically placed around the house, and I do remember my grandmother having them, but I don't recall them ever moving around like they do now. That might be because I was a good kid, especially when you look at kids today. I didn't need threats of coal in the stocking to be good. I was more or less a bookworm, even back then. What kind of trouble can one get into while reading a book? But I guess it's just as well, given how creepy that could be for a little kid. This little perv elf watching everything you do. He only makes himself known around Christmas time, but the little guy must be skulking around the house all year long, especially if he's supposed to report back to Santa on a regular basis. Talk about a nightmare. I mean, I would've gotten zero sleep because he'd probably haunt my dreams like a Yule-tide Freddy Kreuger. No wonder he's the subject of so many horror stories. I shudder to think what nightmarish visions my older brothers would have created just to torment me. And speaking of evil children, my brothers would fit the mold. Well, at least two of them, and as the years went by, that dwindled down to one. Yeah, he was the bad apple, rotten to the core. Still is, as far as I know. There's not enough coal in the world to fill his stocking. I don't think Krampus and Grýla would have been able to handle him. Hell, they'd probably send him back.

And now that I think about it, I don't remember ever hearing anything about any of the evil icons of Christmas— Perchta, Jólakötturinn (the Yule Cat), Belsnickel, Krampus, and many others. I lived a sheltered life in good ol' Brooklyn, NY, where we were told Christmas was all about family, love, giving, and the birth of Christ. As I got older, commercialism of the holiday all but wiped out everything we were taught. My heart, like the Grinch's, became a shriveled black thing. Deathlehem, as you may know, is my attempt to rekindle the warmth of the Christmas Spirit, but until such time, Krampus and Hans Trapp and the Yule Lads would be my new holiday heroes.

What? Hans Trapp? You've never hear of him? Just wait. You'll make his acquaintance in this volume. That's right, Scott Chaddon's "The Monster in the Mirror" will introduce you to Mr. Trapp. You'll be praying Christmas passes you by. In fact, you'll be introduced to a slew of bad guys here, from the aforementioned Hans Trapp, to Nathan D. Ludwig's weresantas or Santamen, from pi_rational's yule-tide witch, to the wicked little children, without whom these Christmas bad guys would be hitting the unemployment line. Or like the Winter Warlock in the animated Christmas program, *Santa Claus is Coming to Town*, they'd lose their power and mystery and become normal people. But "normal" people can be just as scary, as Jacqueline Morgan Meyer can attest to in "The Seventh Christmas." There's also the impish little demon from Evan Baughfman's "Home Sweet Home." I really don't think a "No Vacancy" sign would have worked in this case.

As for the wicked children… There are plenty of those. Norma in Dan Foley's "Norma and the Elf" just might have you running to the hospital for vasectomies or tubal ligations. And then there's the evil little urchin in Mike Marcus's "Bait," who just might bring an end to Christmas. And in "The N in Santa," Greg Sisco poses the question, can a normally good child be considered naughty because of one wish made while under extreme emotional duress? And what about those kids who Santa disappoints? You know, good kids who turn bad because the fat man didn't deliver. Take the little girl who asks Santa for pony for Christmas and gets a Barbie Dream

House instead. Or the little boy who wants a new iPhone and ends up with a bunch of socks and underwear (well, at least he won't have to worry about the Yule Cat). That can make for plenty of animosity toward the jolly, old elf. If I was Santa, I'd be sleeping with one eye open and take plenty of backup when visiting the houses of certain children.

But that's life in Deathlehem, the home of killer Christmas trees, haunted forests, and marauding reindeer. So don't let me delay you any longer. Turn the page and let the journey begin. Enjoy your stay in Deathlehem.

Michael J. Evans
and the staff at
Grinning Skull Press,
Best Wishes for a Happy Helliday
and a frightful New Year!

S*ACRIFICE

Pi_Rational Writer

It was the North wind that was to blame, for it was he that carried me away from where I had lain for many years and woke me out of my deep, restful sleep. There was an oddness to this wind, a soft touch that had never been there before, and my eyes opened, my body awoke, as if from a nightmare at that change. What could that softness mean in the North wind? My limbs were frozen and creaked from the cold. The air around me was sharp, like a blade of a knife against the skin. Around me was darkness, as deep as it was vast, and only the silver light of the moon shone through the clouds in that sinister way it has.

The wind returned and picked me up harshly, its cold, dead fingers gripping me and tossing me around like a leaf.

"From whence have you come, witch?" the North wind whispered to me, but I remained silent and pensive, enjoying its immense power over me. Why should an old witch like me complain when the wind chose me as its passenger? A rare treat that was. So the wind carried me, its arms against my body a pair of icicles, which my frozen bones enjoyed in their ancient state. I was a North witch, after all, and cold did not scare me, but only made me stronger. So we traveled this way, high, high up in the sky, ignoring the annoying glow of eager stars and the shy, bewildered silver light of the moon.

First, we had passed reindeer herds that had turned their graceful heads up at us, celebrating the power of the great North wind. As I passed, they bowed their antlers at my presence, knowing full well that I could destroy their kind with a single spell. It was good to be awake, and my eyes shone brighter with their icy glow as the wind carried me further, further down.

It was large fields that we passed next, followed by deep, dark forests, where the trees sang to us with their grand branches moving, shaking snow off their cold, numb limbs. At the sound of them, I woke up even more, and a frigid breath came from within me. The trees stopped at once, frozen solid in their places. I saw animals and birds drop from their branches, chilled to the core, hard and solid as rock, and quite dead. A roar of laughter came out of my throat and hung above the now-dead forest, its sound spreading where the tree song had been only a moment ago. That roar of mine rings there still, and nobody dares go around that forest of death. Satisfied, I looked for my next prey. That is when the North wind, offended at my trickery and sorry to have brought me over this land, shook his limbs violently, and threw me off his back. My body flowed through the cold thin air until I landed in a pile of hard, old, icy snow.

I whistled at the wind, knowing it would annoy him and stalk him through many lands. Yet, the wind kept going, seemingly untouched and still gaining strength.

It was anyone's guess where I was dropped, and all I could see were endless trees and the same silver moonlight as it wrapped itself around snow-covered trees and frozen valleys. Nothing stirred at the sight of me, terrified to be noticed by the frozen North witch. I moved slowly, floating right above icy snow, my dark robes dragging behind me, my long nails leaving their marks in the snow. My eyes shone brighter and brighter, freezing to death anything they happened to touch with their unnatural light. Even the stars turned from me as I passed underneath them, utterly terrified to lose their precious glow. I was glad of their fear, for it is precisely that which sustained me and grew my vile powers. I bared my sharp teeth in a smile as I floated on, a dark messenger of death on her long, spiteful journey.

There was a road I had spotted, and the snow was trampled by many feet. I got on my fours and squatted at the footsteps, smelling them with my nose, which had rotted off many centuries ago but still worked as good as if it was there. Oh, that warm smell of life! It was intoxicating, and I was eager to make my way over to whence it came from. So I followed the footsteps, bright and sweet, until I came upon a farm. The North Star sparked in the sky above the farm, and I knew it was going to be a season of renewal. Christmas was near; I could hear it like a dull ringing of a thousand bells in my ears.

What a lovely sight this little farm was. I rejoiced, knowing that I could feed on it for a whole year, until another Christmas should come. Inside, I could sniff out a family, and saliva dripped down my chin and onto the snow at the thought of them. The snow bubbled and melted where my saliva hit, for I was a volcano on the inside despite being frozen as a corpse. The farm animals smelled me then and screamed and kicked at each other, trying to escape their awful fates. The horses foamed at the mouth, and the cows would bear nothing but stillborn calves from this time forth. I grinned and turned into a cat. The animals were no fools and would always avoid me like the plague that I was, but the humans... Those humans thought themselves the most significant of beings, and their egos would not let them see that they were ruled by the same laws of nature as all the rest. The humans would never know who I was and would always think that I was only a stray cat, same as on any other farm. The only way to know who I really was, was to look at my tongue, which was not at all like a cat's, but sharp and forked, like that of a snake.

So I jumped up on the windowsill and looked inside the house. It was dark, and only a single candle glowed timidly in the corner. In the middle of the large room, a Christmas tree was set up, only a few drab presents below it, for it was obvious that the farm was small and most likely hard up. Well, it did not matter, and I hissed happily before I climbed under the structure of the house to hide myself during the day. My work here, on this night, was done.

As the last light of the day slipped away, my ancient eyes opened again, and I rubbed my dry, empty sockets as I crouched under the house. Nobody had noticed a thing, except for the farm animals, but nobody had paid them much attention. Their distress was dismissed simply as the weather, a rather convenient excuse. I took my cat form and slipped into the house through the floorboards that have come loose. Once inside, I made my way through the rooms.

The house was small and quite broken down. The rooms were tiny, dark, and few. The parents, who had a room of their own, were old and worn, abused by the years of hardship and hard labor. I came closer to the sleeping wife, for she smelled sweet and new. At once, my ears perked up, for I could tell she was with child and would give birth any day now. A Christmas baby... What a miracle! That was a special child, no doubt, for all the creatures know what kind are born then. My eyes sparked with joy, and I licked my dry lips, excitement building within me. This special baby would be mine, I decided, for a soul this bright and special will have the power to cast a million of the strongest, vilest spells. I smiled my crooked smile and retreated into the darkness.

The children slept in the next room. They were still young and tender, and my eyes shone as bright as ever at their innocent young faces. There was a boy, who was about five, and a girl, around three, sleeping together in a single bed, huddled together for warmth. I blew at them slowly and gently and saw them get colder and sadder; nightmares found a way into their dreams. Pleased, I turned to the crib. Soon, a baby would be inside this crib. My frozen bones tingled with excitement, and my forked tongue extended all the way to the crib, licking the edges as carefully as ever.

In all my excitement, I must have made the house much colder, for now the children had their breaths visible and very frozen. The fire died, and their father stirred in the next room. I lowered myself and crawled away, hiding out under that large Christmas tree. It took only a moment for the parents to wake and shiver under the heavy blanket of ice that I, in all my excitement, had laid so thickly on their house. They wrapped themselves in old rags to no relief and got busy building the fire again. I, in turn, was busy making a spell. I took my normal form and whispered under that tree until a golden box materialized out of my old, haggard limbs. I dropped it under the Christmas tree, unable to grip it, for I was ancient and battered and my limbs were like old stumps now.

But my spell worked. The box shone bright and quite festive under that tree of theirs. A present from me. I smiled, and my forked tongue slipped out through the gap in my decayed teeth.

When the morning approached, I crawled under the broken floorboards underneath the house, where the smell of soil was such a comfort, and the heat did not travel. I already knew how it would all play out. At Christmas, the children would be eager to open the small presents they had, and surely mine would not be missed. The family would marvel at its beauty, the delicate ribbon wrapped around the box, the brightness of the color. The children would fight over who got to open it, and the mother would scold them, holding on to her swollen belly, that fresh little thing inside her almost ready. The room would be charged and full of something thick and uncomfortable; they would fight. Still, that would be nothing, for once they opened my present, they would be mine.

Outside, the winds blew, running through the fields and bringing with them snows and blizzards, sorrows and discomforts of that season. Winter was the best time for evil, for the darkness hung above the land like a veil and refused to let go, gripping tighter and tighter until all living things were almost at the edge of exhaustion. Like this, Christmas Eve had come, bringing with it cruel snows and punishing winds, stripping houses of their warmth with its twelve north winds, freezing everything around it to dead, solid rock.

I slept, gaining my strength and bidding my time. I only woke when I heard that unmistakable sharp sound I've been waiting on. Every witch knows it, and I lifted my head as I heard a piercing bell ring through the cold, stiff air of the house. A baby's cry.

It was time.

I climbed out and took the form of a cat, making my way slowly into the house. The family was there, still awake and arguing. A new, fresh baby cried in its tiny cradle, terrified at the voices and harsh words. I leaned over him. It would be imprudent to touch the baby. Him I wanted to be fresh and unscathed when I got to receive him. That baby was the only one who could truly see me, knew all my tricks and colors, and it cried harder at the sight of me.

"You are so very young," I whispered to him, "but already I know your fate."

In the corner, my Christmas present lay discarded and forgotten. It was as I planned it. The spell was out, covering this house as thick as rancid butter. It would recede and free them next Christmas, but it would be too late then. Only a witch can tell when someone is under a spell, so the family looked just as they always had been. They themselves did not notice how anger spilled out of each of them, and where empathy had once lived, only self-interest and envy could find a way in.

I walked among them, unseen and unnoticed. I started with small spells. In the morning, I would see a pot of coffee start to boil, and I would push it over slowly, my long nails scraping the floor. The pot would fall and spill its hot contents, and a moment later, the husband would scream out his insults, fling them like stones at his wife for spilling the coffee. She, in turn, would blame her husband for the crop that failed a year ago or the cow that fell over last night, dead and riddled with disease. Like this the humans would quarrel, and their children, scared of the rising tide of anger in the house, would hide under the bed or the table, hoping to escape the wrath of their parents. I fed on that anguish and bitterness, growing stronger by the day. My menacing spells grew with me.

In the night, I hovered above the baby's crib, licking my dry lips at the sight of him, and mimicked its cries. The mother would run into the room only to find her baby sleeping and well. She would go back to sleep, exhausted by the day, but as soon as her mind slipped into a dream, I would cry again, summoning her once more to her child's side. Again and again I repeated my torment, feeding on her frustration, which grew so large that I felt quite strong again, as fit as I have been hundreds of years before.

Only their animals could see me and feel my constant suffocating presence. They screamed and dropped dead; they refused to be fed and starved themselves; they escaped and ran down a frozen field, only to fall over from mere exhaustion. It was not long until that was noticed by the neighbors. They came to the family, their faces sullen and dark, demanding to know what disease had befallen the household. But the family was under my spell, and they refused to listen. Instead, they blamed their neighbors for their troubles. So I helped them in their delusions.

Under the darkness of night, under the guise of a cat, I ran to their Northern neighbor and bit one of their piglets. What a noise the animals there had caused that night at the sight of me! I was proud of the evil I had released on them. The next day, the piglet was found black as tar, its eyes bulging with blood and pus, the noise emanating from its lungs not that of an animal, but of a beast. What was even more terrifying was that it developed a taste for human flesh. Again and again it would lunge at a human, its teeth sharp and menacing. All the neighbors came to see, and fearing disease, they killed the piglet. But I put my spell on that unfortunate animal, and every man that visited the farm came back to his own only to find the same disease spreading within his walls. It was a disaster, of course. All the farms destroyed their piglets that year, and the dead, gray bodies of the pigs burned for days at each farm. But I made sure my family had none of the disease; I made sure their pigs were as pink and healthy as a picture. The arguments with the neighbors were unavoidable. The family did not want to kill their piglets, but the neighbors demanded it, fearing the disease would spread anyway. And besides, isn't it always a consolation to have another go through the same hardship as yourself? Unpleasant words were exchanged, and it was not long until the family found itself alone and hated by everyone around them. The visitors stopped coming, and not one person even so much as passed by their gate.

This was some of my best work, and I loved the feel of their isolation, anger, and despair. Oh, how they blamed everyone, how they told most unfair stories of their recent friends, not even once thinking to stop and consider that perhaps the blame was with them instead. But that was the way of humans, and I love to use that to my advantage where I can.

What I wanted most of these humans was their fresh, little baby. Rosy-cheeked and still very small, he was the only one I could not touch, for his innocence was too much even for me. No evil can work on a being who had not as much as thought an ill thought all its life. Instead, the baby stared out into the world with a curiosity that sparked in its eyes, dark as the frozen waters in the ocean. I could not bear to make eye contact with him, for they were so pure I knew they would tear me down where I stood. It was not long until I would have him.

Despair had settled on the house and the family like never before. It gripped their souls and muddied their hearts, turning them on each other. No neighbor would come to help them, and no friend would stop by to calm their fears. I smiled to myself, satisfied by the chaos I had created. Christmas was fast approaching, and I only had so much time left to me before my spell wore off.

The farm was in decay. The animals dropped like flies, and there was not much that could keep the family from starvation. The anger and fear made way for more frustration—it grew like a wildfire ignited by the spark of hostility—and the fighting intensified. I walked like the master of the house among the darkness that now clung to the walls, blowing the icy winds through the rooms, quite satisfied with what I had done.

One day I came upon the husband kneeling by the candle. He had grown gaunt and looked aged by at least ten years. I saw that the dark circles under his eyes had widened and grew, like a bitter plague spreading through him. He thought he was alone, and after all, they could never feel me in the room. It took me some time to understand that he was praying. It was charming, really, him thinking his words could escape my spell and reach whatever God they were meant for. Gods may be close to people in need, but I was much, much closer. I leaned in and entered his mind, bored with the desperation of his thoughts. His mind was like an instrument, made of strings that were strung so tight they were bound to break. So I helped them; one by one, I pulled at each string, snapping one or two with my frozen, dead fingers until the melody was quite ruined, and when I was done, the man's mind broke.

He stood up and had to steady himself against the weight of what had transpired. His eyes were dark and dead now, unable to feel anything at all. With something like excitement, he ran out of the room and to his wife's side. The wife looked skinny and haggard. She drove herself mad over the family, and it was not long until she, too, lost her mind. I smiled when I saw them, their last, pitiful moments together brought joy to my dark soul.

"Mary, I know what we must do at last!" The husband spoke quickly, for he was brimming with excitement. His wife stared at him, apathetic to his words. Her baby was at her chest, clinging desperately to her warm flesh, as if seeing into the future. Her baby son was the only bright beam of light in that entire place.

"I know how to fix it, I do." The husband waved his hands

in his wife's face, but she paid him no attention. The world had ground her down, it seemed, and I was pleased to see her let go so easily, without so much as a fight.

"What do you want, Joseph?" A flat voice, barely there, but how delicious this whole thing was. I grew as her anger spread through the room.

"God spoke to me, Mary," the husband insisted, "and I know how we can improve our situation at last. If I do it right, we won't starve come winter."

She looked up at him then, a long, uneasy look full of disgust. "Christmas is approaching," was all she said. And then she turned to him, accepting what he had to say at once.

"Give me that baby," his whisper rang through the room; the words felt heavy and cold, really cold. Even I shivered, enjoying every moment of their trauma, pulling at the strings of his mind still, leading him deeper and deeper into the darkness. I smiled and felt something warm bubble up inside the volcano of me.

"What do you want with him?" The wife hesitated because I suspect she could see the kind of a madman her husband had become.

"Give me the baby," Joseph said softly, but his words tumbled out clumsily and harshly, falling between the two people like a corpse.

There was a pause, and I grew stronger in it. Oh yes, the time was fast approaching, and I will have him at last, my ultimate reward.

"We must sacrifice him, don't you see?" Joseph stepped closer to his wife. "This is what we must do to end this, to prosper and grow. Mary, do you trust me?"

But his wife backed away, the child in her hands still, not quite a year old he was. Joseph approached.

"All this bad luck, all this doom, all gone. I know you want that, Mary, and besides, what is just one child? One less mouth to feed."

Tears rolled down Mary's thin face, tears as large as the biggest jewels, and for a moment, even I felt for this pathetic little woman. Still, I had to have her son. The power in him was great and ripe. Only a parent can decide such fate, and it was the ultimate present to the darkness that I was. So I blew in their direction and they shivered, uncomfortable under my icy gaze. The wife looked up at her husband, and as the light flickered, I revealed myself to them at once.

What a picture of beauty I was for them! Silver wrapped around me, and my hair was bright as a golden thread. My eyes shone as bright as the Northern star, and the parents gave quite a gasp when they saw me emerge from the darkness.

I extended my arm towards them, smiling my most pleasant smile. The woman drew back the child, but there was hesitation in her movements. To them, I looked a perfect picture of an angel. The man's features had darkened, and he grabbed the child out of his wife's hands and hurriedly placed the baby into mine.

"Do you sacrifice this child to me?" I asked in my softest whisper, trying really hard to cover up my creaking, old voice.

The woman cried, but the man was calm. "We do," he replied.

"Very well then." I licked my lips and stared for the first time into the child's eyes. My tongue was still thin and forked, like a snake's, and the woman screamed when she saw it. I crouched and took my usual form, clutching the little thing close to my cold, disfigured form. Now both of them screamed, but it was too late. I jumped out the window and onto the roof, laughing my terrible, screeching laugh. The animals went wild, and I heard the last of them drop dead.

It started to snow, and the wind had picked up its power.

Christmas Eve was rolling in, and I could feel the spell thin out and fall away from this house like layers of dirt that had dried up at last and could no longer hold on. The North wind was once again at it, blowing through the land, sending shivers into every living thing.

"Pick me up," I cried up to him, my voice powerful now and carrying quite a distance.

But the North wind knew what I was up to and refused to take me away. It blew past me in disgust, smelling the fresh decay, the innocence gone of the child who will not make it past his first birthday. Yet, I was too powerful for the wind to escape. I muttered a spell under my breath, dark and menacing, and my spell managed to cling on to the tail of the wind. He had no choice but to pick me up.

Like this I traveled back to my frozen, cursed lair, up to a place that no human can reach, clutching a tiny child in my arms, a sacrifice. The sacrifice was growing colder and colder by the moment, shedding life as he made his only journey through these barren arctic lands.

T⸱HE N⸱ IN S⸱ANTA
Greg Sisco

The whole way home from school at the start of winter break, I can't stop thinking about Santa and Satan.

Dad says they're the same guy. Dressed in red. Flying animals. The whole world in one night. All that sorcery. He says it's obvious if you think about it. Take the seven deadly sins, for example.

Gluttony and sloth, right off the bat. A fat guy who only works one day a year, can't be bothered to shave, tells every house in the world to leave out milk and cookies. Then he brings you candy canes and chocolates on top of that. And everybody eats dinners so big they have to lie down and fall asleep for two hours after. Oh yeah. Lord of the gluttons and sloths, that Santa. That's two sins right there.

Greed and envy? You betcha. That's his *modus appendectomy*, Dad says. Or *modem operatic*—I forget the phrase. *Motor apparatus*? Anyway, it means it's his "whole deal." Get every-body addicted to material possessions; coveting their neigh-bors' goods; begging for this, that, and the other. Big check-marks in those boxes. So now we're at four sins easy.

Pride? Ooh, boy. Think about it. He's got his picture on every can of Coca-Cola this time of year. He's on billboards, in commercials, he's got kids singing songs about him in schools, or even door to door, trying to stay in his good graces. Santa's proud. You better believe Santa's proud. Five sins.

Lust? Well, Dad says there's more than one kind of lust. Mostly people think of it as sex, but you can lust for power or fame just as easily as women or men, and Santa wouldn't have come this far without a lust for power. Heck, Dad says even if you do think of lust as strictly sex, Santa's got that list of bad girls. You think he never pops over to one of those houses? Indulges in *her* milk and cookies? Shows her *his* candy cane? Sin number six.

And that only leaves wrath. Dad says wrath always comes at the end.

"A ping-pong table, three Transformers, um... Did I say Animal Crossing?" Next to me on the school bus, Jaden is still rattling off presents he got from his Mom last night.

"Why did you already get presents?" I ask. "Jesus wasn't born 'til the twenty-fifth."

"I get two Christmases because my parents are divorced," boasts Jaden. "I'm going to spend the break with my dad, so my mom gave me all my presents early."

"Wait, so your parents don't live together?"

"No, they split up like two years ago. Last year I thought it was gonna be like two half-Christmases where they're both kinda lame but together they're as good as a normal one, but actually, they were both super good. And Santa even came to both. He dropped off my presents early with my mom and got me, like, extra stuff. Then this year with my mom was even bigger, like even bigger than when my parents were still together. And my dad and his girlfriend both said Santa has already been bringing stuff there and they can't believe how much there is. It's crazy. Both Christmases are even better than the one Christmas ever since they split up."

"Hold on. Back up. Your dad has a *girlfriend*?"

"Yeah. Tiffany. She's super nice, actually, which is cool. Last year he had this girlfriend, Laura, who was kind of mean, and I don't think she liked me. But Tiffany cooks these *huge* meals and she works at a candy store, so she always has all this free chocolate she brings home."

I stare out the window. Yeah, that about covers it. Gluttony, sloth, greed, envy, pride, lust… All that's left is wrath. And wrath always comes at the end.

✳ ✳ ✳

Christmas Eve I wake up to Mom and Dad fighting in the living room. I'm trying to sleep, but I can't help half-listening. Something about Dad going out on his motorcycle and not wearing his helmet. Mom thinks it's irresponsible and Dad thinks he's strong enough in Jesus that accidents won't happen to him.

Honestly, sometimes I think Dad's too confident. Everything turns into an argument with him and he never says, "That's a good point," unless you say something he already agreed with.

I know Mom doesn't like the motorcycle at all, and I kind of don't blame her. I accidentally saw part of a movie once where a woman crashed a motorcycle and her head came off. I could barely sleep for three whole nights. Even now, I still have a nightmare about it from time to time. And she was wearing a helmet. Dad says there's no such thing as too much faith, but I don't know. That lady might have had too much.

It's like the Santa thing.

Dad says everybody just accepts that Santa doesn't age and he lives forever, and nobody asks themselves who a man that lives forever might be. "I'll give you a hint," he says. "There's only two of them, and one doesn't sin."

But in Sunday school they told me God flooded the whole world once and killed everybody except Noah's family. And if Santa wanting everybody singing about him makes him proud, well, there are more songs about God than Santa. And every time we go to church, God wants money. So I think God might sin, too. Or maybe it's not sinning when God does it, but he still does it, right?

Plus, my pastor said Enoch and Elijah never died. They were "taken by God," but they're still alive. So God and the devil might not be the only people who never die. There might even be other ones God didn't tell us about.

Sometimes I think things might be a little more complicated than Dad thinks. You know?

And another thing that bothers me.

Dad says if you take the N in SANTA and move it to the end, it becomes SATAN. He says that's the biggest giveaway. The devil isn't even trying to hide it. He put it right there in his name.

But Dad also said, and they even said the same thing at Sunday school, that the devil is the best liar in the world. They say he's so clever he can trick pretty much everybody except God at least some of the time.

So I don't get it. Why couldn't the best liar in the world come up with a better way to hide his name than just moving one letter over? Like, nobody knows who Banksy is. Maybe *he's* the devil. That would make more sense.

I asked Dad about it once and he said, "See, you're starting to doubt it, aren't you? That's how clever the devil is. Sometimes he uses a bad lie to make you think it couldn't be him."

That seemed like a pretty clever answer to my question, but it also seemed like it meant Dad was more clever than the devil. I know for sure Dad isn't God, and the next most clever person he could be is the devil. So I asked him if *he* was the devil and he slapped me.

I'm thinking about all this up in my room, and by the time the fight downstairs ends and Dad slams a door somewhere and I can hear Mom crying, I've spent so much time thinking that I'm not tired anymore. I know I should probably go down and give Mom a hug, but I just feel bad in the house sometimes. So I sneak out my window and get my bike from the side yard and ride away in no particular direction.

I wear my helmet though. I'm not as sure about all this stuff as Dad is.

* * *

I end up riding my bike to the mall. I tell myself it's because I really have to go to the bathroom, but the truth is I could probably hold it until I got home. Even if I couldn't, I know Dad would say God would rather I go behind some bushes than go into a mall on Christmas Eve. But when I look at the parking lot, so full that everybody is driving their cars around and waiting for other people to leave, I have to see what it's like.

For a second, when the automatic doors open, I almost reconsider. I've never seen a place so crowded and loud. Everybody is carrying giant plastic bags stuffed with clothes and toys and electronics. There are kids crying, pulling on their parents' clothes. Here and there, you can hear people yelling and arguing, either with their families or with people who work at the stores. It's scary to look at, and I try to get over the shock and remind myself that everybody else I know except Dad, and *maybe* Mom, is pretty comfortable with all this.

After a minute, it's still freaking me out, and I'm just about to turn around and leave when I hear a voice say, "Hey, how's it going?"

I turn and there's Jaden, standing with his dad and a big, tall woman I assume is Tiffany.

"Oh. Hi," I say.

"We just got popcorn from the place on the second floor. It was *super* good. Are you here with your parents?"

"Um… No. I rode my bike."

"Cool. *My* dad won't let me go to the mall by myself."

"Give it a year or two, Jaden. We'll talk," says Jaden's dad.

"Did you get to open a present on Christmas Eve? I always get the first one on Christmas Eve."

"Um… No. I don't usually get presents," I say as a family of five pushes past me in the doorway.

"On Christmas Eve, you mean? You at least get some from Santa on Christmas, right?"

"Um…"

"Jaden," says Jaden's dad, a hand on his shoulder. "It's not really any of our business how other families celebrate."

"Santa doesn't come to my house," I try to explain.

"That's bullcrap. He's going cheap. Come on. Let's go talk to him."

Jaden grabs my hand and pulls me away from the front doors, around a corner.

"Jaden, you don't get to make this kind of decision for somebody else," says Tiffany.

"Yeah, and you don't get to say *bullcrap* either," says his dad. "Where do you get this shit?"

My mouth drops open and I stand frozen, staring straight ahead.

"Sorry," says Jaden's dad to me. "That's a joke I do with Jaden. I shouldn't have said it in front of a kid I just met. A bit of inappropriate humor. I apologize."

I admit I'm not used to hearing grown-ups use bad words. I've only heard Mom use one once and *never* Dad, but it's not the "s" word that has me frozen. Not even the abominable "f" bomb itself could take my attention away from the sight down the hall where Jaden was starting to pull me. A huge crowd of grown-ups and kids, from babies all the way up to almost teenagers, stands in a long, winding line, and at the front of it all, there is a sleigh and a bag of gifts and a chair. And in the chair...

No.

It can't be real.

"That's... Santa?"

"Of course it is! You've never met him?"

I shake my head no because I'm having trouble talking.

"Okay, okay," says Jaden's dad, pulling Jaden back a step. He kneels in front of me so his face is the same level as mine. "Listen. I don't know what your family believes, but if you're uncomfortable, just say so and I can take you home, or you can leave on your bike, or we can all go do something else. We'd be happy to have you. If you *want* to talk to Santa, I'll wait in line with you and you can, but really, if you're scared or uncomfortable or you just don't want to, you definitely don't have to. No questions asked."

Across the room, even among all these people, somehow Santa catches me staring. He looks back at me with a big, wide smile and waves, slowly, across the mall.

I swallow and make myself breathe.

"I want to talk to him."

* * *

I have to confess one thing. Two Christmases ago, I *did* get a present from Santa.

A few days before, Mom and Dad got into a fight about something or other that I didn't understand. They started yelling and screaming, and that was the only time I ever heard Mom use a bad word. She called Dad an A-hole. He was stunned. He said she was being immature and then he left for a week. Mom and I had Christmas by ourselves.

I don't know if the fight had anything to do with it, but that night Mom said I should try writing a letter to Santa. She even helped me write it because I couldn't spell so good at the time and I had to make the letters really big. I didn't know what to ask for, so I asked him for a game. Just a game. Any kind.

Sure enough, on Christmas, there was a present on the floor. It had a puzzle game in it. A clear ball with a lot of plastic platforms inside and a loose marble. You were supposed to make the marble roll down the platforms without having it fall off.

Mom made me promise not to show Dad when he came back. She said it would be our secret.

The truth is the ball game was kind of fun, but I couldn't really enjoy it all the way because I knew it was from Santa. Even after my birthday, when Mom secretly wrapped it up again and gave it to me so Dad would think it was from her and I didn't have to hide it, I still had a feeling about it. Like Mom and I did something bad.

But again, the truth is, it was still kind of fun.

Normally, even *near* Christmas, let alone *on* Christmas, my parents and I don't go out. Dad doesn't like the atmosphere and says it's not good for me. But that year, Mom took me to see a movie on Christmas, and afterward, we got dinner at a pizza place.

I feel guilty to admit it, but that was my favorite Christmas.

Standing in line to talk to Santa, Jaden jumping up and down and telling his dad all the things he's going to ask for, his dad telling him to remind Santa that some of them coming next year would be okay because he's already been so generous, all these people around us, these kids like Jaden full of excitement, most of the parents smiling, I keep thinking about that year two Christmases ago.

Every other Christmas, we talk a lot about God, and Mom makes dinner, and Dad says how other people are missing out, and I don't want to sound like Mom's not a good cook or that I don't appreciate God or anything, but I'm just not a hundred percent sure everybody else is missing out. Everybody in this line with me looks really happy. All these families look like they love each other and they're having fun, like me and mom at the movie.

And even that devil thing—the most clever liar in the world. The idea of Dad being the devil makes as much sense to me as the one about Santa. They both make good arguments.

When we get to the front of the line, Jaden lets me go first. I have to walk the last few feet very slowly, and I suddenly realize I forgot to go to the bathroom, which was my whole reason for coming into the mall in the first place. I feel so stupid. I stand in front of Santa and he lifts me off the ground and it really starts hitting me how badly I need to go.

"Well, hello there," says Santa with a smile so caring I'd have trouble believing it was real even if I hadn't heard stories about the N in his name. "Who might you be?"

"Are you..." I stutter, not sure how to ask. "Are you really who my dad says you are?"

He laughs hard, tilting his head back. "Of course I am!"

Sitting on the devil's lap with his arm around my shoulder, I'm so scared my bladder feels like it weighs a ton. I push my legs together as hard as I can. I don't know what the devil would do if you peed on him, but I sure as heck don't want to find out.

"Why did..." I inhale hard, making sure I don't cry. "Do you know why God made everything so hard?"

"Ohh," he puts a hand on my back that feels genuinely caring. "It breaks my heart to hear you ask that. You know what? Even I don't have the answer for that one. Somebody told me it's so you can see how strong you are. You are strong, aren't you?"

I look around. Here I am, sitting with the devil, surrounded by gluttony and greed, and I feel that my pants are damp, getting damper. I try to stop going but I can't.

"No," I say, and it's more a realization than an answer.

"Yes, you are," says the devil. "I know you are. Even if you don't see it, I see it. Tell me, because I know it's been a hard year for you, did you still manage to stay good all year?"

I feel my body wanting to cry. I try to swallow it. At home, my parents are probably wondering where I am, never dreaming I'm on the devil's lap, never dreaming I came to ask for what I'm about to ask for.

"No," I say quietly.

"You're really mature for your age," says the devil. "That was an honest answer to a question not many people can answer honestly. Even grown-ups. Let me ask you this one: What do you want for Christmas?"

I look at Jaden, at his dad and Tiffany watching me with excited smiles on their faces, at all these happy families out here enjoying the world with each other. I remember me and Mom at the movies the same way, and at dinner.

"I want my parents to get a..." I choke. I can't say the word. It's such a bad thing to say. Even the devil is looking at me like he's scared I'm going to finish the sentence the way he thinks I am. "I mean... I want them to stop being... you know..." I look down at the floor, back up at him. I force it out. "...married."

The devil stares at me like he's never had anybody ask for this before. "Why do you want that?"

"I just want to be with my mom," I say, and I can't not cry anymore, but I try to at least not be so loud that everyone can tell. "It's happier that way. I am. She is. I think my dad even probably is."

The devil hugs me tight. I put my face in his shoulder and cry louder and he rubs my back the same way Mom does when I'm sad. And for a second, I think maybe he's not the devil at all. Maybe he just misunderstood me when I sat on his lap and asked if he was who my dad said he was. Maybe he just meant he's Santa Claus.

For a *second*, I think that. Until, so quietly I'm the only one who can hear, he whispers, "You got it, kid."

※ ※ ※

When I come home, all teary-eyed and with a huge wet spot on my jeans like a kid half my age, I make up lies. I say I was near the mall and I almost went in to use the bathroom, but I knew I shouldn't, and I crashed my bike trying to get home in time and had an accident.

Dad's still a little annoyed and wants me to explain myself for leaving without telling them, but Mom's all "poor baby." Dad says Mom's babying me too much and I need to take responsibility. Mom thinks if Dad didn't get so dramatic about everything, I wouldn't have felt the need to run off in the first place. Dad thinks me and Mom are the dramatic ones and I'm a wimp because I cried and I'm gross and dumb because I wet my pants. I'd be embarrassed by the whole thing if I wasn't so scared.

I end up going to my room and just lying there, staring at the ceiling. My stomach hurts and I want to throw up, but it never happens. The whole time I just listen to Mom and Dad fighting down there, screaming again. And I wonder if this is it. The big fight. If this is Santa doing his thing. The louder their voices get, the more my stomach hurts, the harder I try not to listen, but they're so loud I can hear every word even with the pillow over my head.

Finally, I hear the front door slam. Then the motorcycle engine. Then it's quiet.

Mom comes up and hugs me and apologizes for Dad. She takes my pants out to wash them.

The rest of the day it's just her and me, but it doesn't feel like it did two Christmases ago. And even if it does feel a little more like that tomorrow, I know it's also going to feel like that puzzle game, where it's sort of fun but where I also know it was flying-reindeer witchcraft that got it for me.

Just before bedtime, I come forward to Mom. I tell her, "I lied to you and Dad. I went to the mall today."

"Oh, it's okay, sweetheart. I don't blame you for being curious. Did you have fun?"

"No. I talked to Santa."

Mom pauses a moment. "Oh yeah? What did you ask him for?"

"Mom, I asked him for something really bad. I wasn't thinking. I didn't mean to. I was talking to him, and I was scared and upset, and I just said it, but I need to write him a letter telling him I don't want it after all."

"Why? What did you ask him for?"

"I can't tell you. But I need to write a letter and you need to help me mail it. It might be the last chance to tell him I take it back."

Mom yawns, but she gets me a pen and paper, and I scribble faster than I've ever written before. I tell Santa thank you for being nice to me and everything, and I love the puzzle game from two years ago, but I wasn't thinking when I asked for the thing I asked for today. I was having a bad day, and I thought I wanted it, but now I realize I don't, so please don't waste your time and energy on it because nobody wants it.

Mom puts it in an envelope for me and, with a little persuasion, even walks out to the mailbox with me to put it in.

"So, just to be clear, you don't want anything at all for Christmas?" she asks.

"No, Mom. Nothing at all."

The butterflies are still there a little bit when she leaves, but not that swarm of them like when Mom and Dad were fighting. That letter in the mailbox is the only reason I sleep at all. In fact, maybe it's the only reason I don't hear Santa come in.

* * *

When I go into the living room the next morning, Mom comes out of the kitchen and says, "I think Dad got you a little present as an apology for being a jerk last night." She indicates a large green gift wrapped in a red ribbon on the living room floor.

"Dad's back?" I ask, and I feel excitement for what seems like the first time in forever.

"Not right now. I think he stopped by in the night."

I go to the package and look down at it. I pick it up and it's heavy, something big and loose rattling around inside. I look at the tag and drop the present on the floor.

"Oh!" says Mom. "What happened?"

"It's not from Dad," I say quietly. "It's from Santa."

Mom's phone rings. She takes it out of her pocket and hangs up without looking.

"What's that, honey?"

"It's from Santa."

"Oh, isn't that something!" she says with a smile, and then she remembers our conversation last night. "Well, you know what? I bet Santa got your letter and decided to get you something else instead."

Mom's phone rings again. She's more annoyed this time, getting it out and hanging up again without looking.

"But he's the devil. Dad said he's the devil."

Mom sighs. "I don't believe that. Do you believe that? Would the devil have gotten you that puzzle game two years ago? And bikes and toys and stuff for all your friends?"

Her phone rings again. She groans loudly and gets it out of her pocket. Before she answers, she says to me, "Why don't you open your present, honey? I bet he got you something you'll like instead." Then she puts the phone to her ear and says, "It is Christmas morning and I am with my child," as she walks into the kitchen.

My hands are shaking as I lean down over the box and untie the red ribbon. I can't bring myself to open the lid. Instead, I take the ribbon to the trash and drop it in.

"Yes," I can hear Mom saying from the kitchen, a slight panic in her voice. "He rides a Honda Shadow. Why?"

I look down at the garbage can and all I can hear is my heart. The letter I wrote to Santa last night sits at the top of the trash, the ribbon on top of it, the envelope still sealed.

Mom screams from the kitchen. Not a scared scream. More like the sound a dog makes when he hurts himself. I hear her phone go sliding across the floor and I hear her whisper, "Oh my God. Oh my God. Oh my God."

But I can't go to her. I can't think about anything except the present. I run across the room and lift the lid off the box, and it's only when I look inside that I run to Mom and fall into her arms.

In the box, staring up with its mouth open in a scream, is Dad's head, a candy cane stuck in each eye.

B*anshee, of the W*ood

Matt Starr

Everybody has their favorite holiday traditions, some more common than others. Setting out candles for ghosts. Huddling shoulder to shoulder on the sidewalk, waiting for the local parade to start. Driving down the stretch of town that's so lit up you wonder how anyone there could get a wink of sleep. Making those candy cane sugar cookies from scratch, the ones that really taste like toothpaste if you're being honest with yourself. Opening a single teaser present on Christmas Eve.

For Lem Carmichael, it was always his yearly pilgrimage to the Choose 'N Cut Christmas Tree Farm in Newland, North Carolina. But it wasn't a tree he was after, nor could he characterize any part of the venture as "favorite." Truth was, he detested the whole season so much that he made the two-hour trip from Winston in complete silence, just on the off-chance he came across a radio station playing that jingle-jangle bullshit. No; he was in search of something that couldn't be so easily cast to the side as soon as the moment had passed. Something with invisible roots that pulled at his guts like teeth.

It was the Saturday after Thanksgiving, his day off, when he dragged the old Subaru Baja deep into the Blue Ridge Mountains again, an open can of beer between his legs. He had developed quite a penchant for gas station sixers and pill mill Roxycontin through the years, and his tolerance for both was elephantine. Functioning while high was as second nature to him as breathing. He was lucky they didn't test at the Conniff & Sons Construction Co. because he knew he would piss hotter than blue blazes if they did.

The woodlands rose in vast, ragged legions of hemlocks, evergreens, red spruces, and dying silverbells as Lem twisted through the narrow roads, the late-morning mountainscape stretching before him, waiting, beguiling and eerie in its growing colorlessness. Smatters of snow already covered the caps in the distance, but down here in the thick of the forest, it was much milder. Almost humid. When he reached the turnoff, Lem eased onto the dirt path with a gentleness that didn't suit a man who lived his life so recklessly. He downed the rest of his beer as he came upon the tin sign about half a mile down, Choose 'N Cut in weather-beaten letters next to the logo of a bizarre, ax-wielding snowman that looked like something a delinquent seventh-grader would doodle on the wall behind the school shitter.

A red single-wide trailer, bedecked in multicolor teardrop lights and a satellite dish, sat just beyond the gate, an observation post for fifty falling acres of Fraser firs. Here and there, families weaved in and out of the rows, shaking limbs and burying their noses in needlelike leaves. There was a claustrophobic quality to it, Lem thought. Like the trees would squeeze the very breath out of your lungs if they caught you not paying attention. The lot was backdropped by a sizable clearing that fed into the mouth of the greater woods, and it was there that the imagination's darkest, most curious fantasies danced out of sight.

Lem parked and killed the engine. He popped the glove box, removed the matte photograph, and studied it for a spell. As if he could ever forget what she looked like. Fat girl with stick legs, a short black and gray merle coat, one brown eye, one blue. A mutt, Aussie mixed with Pointer mixed with God knew what.

"Hold on just a little bit longer," he said.

Then he heard that terrible sound. Saw that flash of the tree-line in his mind's eye.

* * *

Young Lem would be ill if they didn't rise at the crack-ass of dawn on the big day, and so for his tenth Christmas, the three of them rolled out of bed and gathered in the living room before the sun had even come up. The tree lights, which had been left plugged in all night, cast the otherwise dark room in a warm, prismatic glow that gleamed wildly in Lem's gray irises. Every notion of sadness or worry he knew was lost in that magic. His mother smoothed out her robe and kneeled next to a modest yet appreciable display of wrapped packages. His father yawned and put on a record: "Christmas in Dixie" by Alabama.

"Ooo," his mother said. "I just love this one."

Lem could barely contain his excitement as he pored over the gifts, secretly guessing what each of them could be—the same thing he had done for weeks before. He would soon find out as he dove in, making sure not to rip the presents open too fast. He always wanted to savor this part for as long as he could. All told, the haul consisted of a remote control monster truck, a tyrannosaurus rex action figure that he was probably too old for, a new baseball glove for spring, and some CDs for his Walkman. A take that many kids in town would kill for.

"Thank you, Mama, Dad," Lem said, hugging their necks.

"Don't thank us just yet," his mother said. "You've got one more thing coming at your Uncle Simon's house."

Lem's eyes widened. "Really? Why's it over there?"

"Because it's a surprise," his father replied.

Breakfast seemed to last forever, as Lem racked his brain over the mystery gift. He was still too young for a dirt bike, and he couldn't imagine his parents shelling out that kind of money for something that was destined to end in a broken bone and a trip to the ER. Was it a rifle? His uncle had said that it was only a matter of time before Lem was ready to start tagging along for hunting season. It was impossible to tell.

Lem's dad's older brother, Uncle Simon, lived on a good piece of land at the county line. Most of his neighbors were tobacco farmers, but Simon, a cigarette factory foreman by trade, was just the private type who didn't mind cutting a shitload of grass once a week. The family Carmichael crept up the long driveway in the crew cab, stirring motes of dust. Uncle Simon stood on the porch of the two-story farmhouse, having his morning coffee and smoke under the light-clipped eaves. Lem was the first to get out.

"How's it going, Slim Lem?" his uncle asked. At the time, Lem was a gangly sight.

"Good, Uncle Simon. Merry Christmas."

His uncle took a drag, exhaled. "Merry Christmas to you, too, little man."

Lem's parents flanked him, and Uncle Simon flashed a

smile. Was Lem's eagerness that obvious?

"All right," Uncle Simon said, stamping out his cigarette. "Enough's enough. Lemme go get this thing before I worry this kid to death." He disappeared into the house and was gone for a minute or two. Lem found that he couldn't stand still or hold a thought.

What followed was one of those moments that never leaves us, no matter how wide open we leave the door for them to do so. There was a low, dainty jingle, like a tiny sleigh bell, mellifluous to the ears, and the clumsy puppy bounded around the corner of the house with a candy red bow on its head, Uncle Simon trailing closely behind. The dog made a bee-line for Lem, as if it were predetermined, and Lem just knew that his heart had leaped into his throat and got stuck there. Lem crouched down, and the silly animal jumped into his arms, knocking him to his butt as his parents and uncle laughed.

"I think she likes you," Uncle Simon said.

"She's mine?" Lem asked, hardly able to get a word in from the flurry of kisses.

"Yessir. From your mama, daddy, and me."

Lem was able to calm her down enough to give her an honest look-over. Her eyes were heterochromatic, one an earthy brown, the other a glacial blue. She had the softest, kindest face. The face of a thing that needed to be protected. Her body was wriggly and slick, and she shimmied like she still wasn't used to being in it.

"She's a live wire, ain't she?" said Uncle Simon. "Got her at a rescue in the mountains."

"She's perfect," Lem replied, and he realized that his cheeks were wet with tears. It was the first time he had ever cried from happiness. He had never thought it possible before. "What's her name?"

"That's up to you."

Uncle Simon had barely finished his sentence when the puppy belted out a sharp, off-key howl that drew a wince from everyone but Lem. It was almost deafening, a hell of a thing for a creature so small. She licked her chops and did it again. Like she was talking to someone or summoning a storm. Lem's mother plugged her ears.

"This one's got a set of pipes on her," Uncle Simon said.

The puppy continued with her high-pitched yowling. It may have pained everyone else, but it was sweet to Lem. An expression of love.

"How about calling her Merrow after the Irish singing mermaids?" his dad proposed.

"She sounds more like a banshee," his mother said.

"Banshee," Lem repeated, rubbing the scruff of her neck. "I like that."

The dog peered deep into his eyes, recited more of her canticle. She didn't stop until the ride home, which she spent sleeping on his lap.

* * *

Lem made sure no one was looking. The Roxy was already crushed up, so he sprinkled it out on the little square of tinfoil and held the lighter's flame under it with his opposite hand. He sucked the harsh vapors through a glass pipe in long, hungry draws, and in a matter of seconds, his head was bloodless, squeezed to nothing. He collected himself, deposited the paraphernalia into the center console, and got out of the car.

There were four hours of good daylight left, and Lem reckoned he could cover a decent amount of ground in that time. He popped the Baja's bed lid, threw his knapsack over one shoulder, the Mossberg hunting rifle over the other. He fastened the sheathed Bowie knife to his hip. He closed the lid again. The journey across the lot was no Sunday stroll, but he made it without drawing too much attention. In the mountains of North Carolina, nobody batted an eye at the sight of a man with a gun anyhow. The Fraser firs were of high quality, each between six and eight feet tall, round and symmetrical. In all the years since he had moved out of his parents' house, Lem had never allowed one in his own home.

There was joy out here, as evidenced by the laughing families and happy couples, but Lem felt fixed in an atmosphere of building pressure and uneasiness despite the high the pills and booze afforded him. It only increased as he got closer to the woods. Once he reached the clearing, he paused and ran his eyes along the length of the treeline ahead. It glared back, a drab, unwelcoming land. A land of a thousand things that could see you, but you couldn't see them. He adjusted his rifle, took a deep breath, and crossed the flat grass, lumbering, though the concept of his own weight escaped him.

Every step beyond the brush was tenfold its normal volume. The woods were a still place full of things dead or near it, of things prepared to sleep for a season of shadows and longing. The quiet was disorienting, and it made the stirring, falling, and breaking of objects unseen that much more startling. A blueness washed the trees, endless in their ranks, their slender trunks ascending toward God. Lem passed snag after snag and thought it a little funny how something inanimate could look so unkind.

He plunged further into the wild, surveying the undergrowth for signs. A cracking sound called his attention to the left, and he readied his rifle. A fat squirrel. He allowed himself a laugh as it scampered off. He whiffed at the air to see if he could gather any insight from it. One year he had smelled an odor so rotten that it had to have originated from a stage beyond death and decay. He never found the source. This time, all he picked up was a mild wetness, typical for the territory. He pressed on.

The mission was yielding little to write home about when he happened to glance down and catch the woods' equivalent to a needle in a haystack. He squatted for a closer look. An unmistakable short black hair with a white tip lay atop a shriveled brown leaf. The cadence of Lem's heart picked up. He reached into the breast pocket of his field shirt, but it was empty. A sick sensation of freefall rushed through his body.

"Shit," he said, burying his face in his hands.

The peanut butter sandwich cookies were her favorite, and Lem had left them in the car. He would have to go back for them. He scanned the immediate area, not wanting to leave but knowing he didn't have another choice. He would return. He rose to his feet and briskly retraced his steps back toward the lot. He had the whole way to the car to think about how boneheaded he had been for forgetting the bait. But he was in luck: He had all of his fuckups and traumas to keep him company.

Of particular note was the time he had gotten hammered drunk and crashed his old pickup into some poor soul's front-yard winter wonderland. He had staggered out of the cab in nothing but his drawers, hollered, "Merry fucking Christmas," and pissed on the nativity scene as the cops just watched and waited for him to finish. It was shortly thereafter that he had lost contact with his parents and his Uncle Simon, though they assured him that they were praying for him.

Crazy how one event could lead to such chaos and inner turmoil, Lem thought.

* * *

A beautiful thing, a boy and his dog. Lem and Banshee were inseparable from the moment he brought her home. She flopped around the house, teething and tussling discarded wrapping paper, baying at the ceiling with that ridiculous voice. As time passed, the Carmichaels came to realize there was an explanation for it. The reason Banshee screeched so wasn't because she was tone-deaf; it was because she was *actually* deaf. She couldn't hear herself, and so she had no working concept of volume control. Fearing they wouldn't be able to summon her if they needed to, they left the bell attached to her collar permanently. That way, they could always locate her. The music of it preceded her wherever she was, as if to say, *Here comes bow-legged Banshee, jingling, jingling.*

Luckily, Lem didn't have to worry about her wandering too far. She was, by and large, a Velcro dog, and wherever her boy went, she followed. To the ballfield, where she would retrieve whatever Lem tossed up and hit. The quarry on the other side of town. The elementary school, where the playground equipment served as a mock agility course. To his secret place: the abandoned train station that once watched thousands of shipments of tobacco products come and go. He would sit there for hours and think and think, Banshee coiled up next to him, never judging. He had done nothing to earn her affection, her boundless loyalty—save for the occasional peanut butter sandwich cookie—but he had them all the same. Even when he would go away to Boy Scout camp, she waited for him. For Lem, making friends was harder than trapping lightning in a bottle, and Banshee's effortless companionship was the one constant in his life. The only thing that never let him down.

But as much as Banshee loved Lem, she sometimes seemed elsewhere. She had a habit of gazing off at nothing in the distance. There were other quirks, too. Characteristics that some might call "off." For one, she was too expressive for an animal. Not only did she have her own verbal language, but she also spoke with her eyes in ways that were oddly illustrative. She was possessed of an uncanny intuition, always knowing when Lem needed a beckoning paw or a nudging snout. She got bigger but exhibited no other signs of aging, which was perhaps her most puzzling quality. She was unlike any dog Lem had ever met.

When he was thirteen, Lem's parents agreed to let Banshee accompany them on their annual trip to the Choose 'N Cut Christmas Tree Farm. She was wound up from the drive, and when she hopped out of the crew cab, her nose went to the ground, her tail whipping a mile a minute. Lem thought she might pull him from his feet.

"Can I let her off the leash, Dad?" Lem asked as they walked onto the lot.

"Better not," his father said. "Place like this could turn into a maze real quick."

Banshee sniffed at the Fraser firs, marking every so often.

"What do y'all think about this one?" his father asked after a time, gesturing toward a fine-looking tree.

"It's nice," his mother remarked. "Looks like all the others."

"Thank you, Ellery," his dad said.

Banshee seemed hellbent on leading Lem in the opposite direction of his parents. She dug forward into the earth until her collar was pressed firmly against her windpipe. She issued a pitiful bark, muted by the constriction.

"Dad?" Lem said, nodding at the dog.

His father sighed in concession. "Don't go too far. And *don't* let her roam free."

They had barely turned the corner before Lem crouched down and unhooked her leash. "You won't tell anybody, will you, girl?" he asked.

Her eyes said she wouldn't.

Lem and Banshee meandered through the rows of trees at a dizzying pace, the boy surprised at his ability to keep up with the dog. Green blurred into green until there wasn't a fir before them, but rather a broad, open sweep sprawling toward a wooded realm that brought to mind the setting of a grim fairy tale. Lem studied it as he caught his breath. He was intrigued, if not creeped out, by its mysterious nature, but Banshee, on the other hand, was downright spellbound by it. Her hair stood on end down her spine, and her tail, wagging a moment before, became stiff. Lem found it deeply unsettling.

"What is it, girl?" he asked.

She didn't budge at first. But then she cocked her head like she had heard something, and before Lem could think better of it and refasten the leash, she tore off across the clearing in a frantic gallop that nearly brought her to a tumble.

"Banshee!" Lem hollered.

The dog ignored his call, choosing instead to carry on until she had vanished into the woods. Lem felt like he was watching the whole scene play out from somewhere high in the sky, frozen, outside his body. Several beats came and went, with nothing to fill them but paralyzing silence. Then he heard it: the most godawful noise that had ever cursed his ears. It was a yelp that would span a lifetime, a song like Banshee's howl, but where there had been sweetness, there was now the most unimaginable pain and suffering. It sent shockwaves way down into the pit of Lem's stomach. He wanted to throw up. He bolted back through the lot in search of his parents. By the time he had tracked them down, he was in tears.

"What's gotten into you, Lemuel?" his dad asked, dropping to his level. He only broke out the full name when it was serious.

"Banshee," Lem sobbed. "She ran away." And this part he

almost couldn't get out: "I heard her... I heard her scream."

"Ran away?" his mother said. "How?"

Lem tucked his head in shame.

"All right, all right," his father said, disappointed but sympathetic. "Which way did she go?"

Lem got himself together the best he could and took them to where she had left him. The treeline in the distance appeared more brooding than ever. His father squinted at it, hands on his hips, trying to decide what he should make of it. His mother gently rubbed her son's shoulders.

"Banshee!" his dad shouted. "Come on out, girl!" He licked his lips and sighed. "Well, hell, I don't suppose she can hear me, can she?"

"What are we gonna do, Frank?" his mother asked.

Lem's father looked at the woods, then back at him. He repeated this a few more times and tugged up on his belt. "I'll be right back," he said. "She's probably piddling around right there at the edge."

Lem stepped forward. "I'm going with you."

"No, you're not."

"Dad, please!"

Frank Carmichael tapped his toe on the dry earth, breathed out through his nose. "Come on, then. We'll be back, Ellery."

"Frank."

"It'll be all right."

"Be careful," she said.

Lem's father put his arm around him as they traversed the clearing. Lem had always been embarrassed to let anyone see him cry, but he couldn't help it now. It wasn't just that Banshee was lost. It was that horrific squeal he couldn't unhear. The two of them entered through the treeline, navigated through the first string of spruces. They had hoped to stumble upon Banshee getting into some kind of harmless trouble there, but she was nowhere to be found. The trees grew more towering, stalking them as they trooped onward. This was clearly a place no human had business being, and Lem wondered how long it would be until his dad said enough.

After ten minutes or so, they were still on the hunt. That's when they noticed the foul scent. It was sickly sweet and damp, though most everything in sight was dried out. Lem's father held his hand to his son's chest, signaling him to stop, trying to listen for something, anything. Straight ahead, there was a tree unlike the others, short and hollowed out at the base, scars running its trunk. Not right.

"Stay here," Lem's father said, and Lem could see that his forehead was beading sweat.

Frank Carmichael approached the strange tree in little more than a tip-toe as his son looked on. Halfway there, he reached down and picked up a shard of what could only be mirror glass. Lem couldn't see his father's face, but the old man wore that puzzled tension in his shoulders that Lem knew well enough. His father stared at the shard for a moment or two longer before casting it to the side with an unsteady hand. Tiny, jagged stones littered the ground in front of the tree like miniature white stars fallen from the heavens, but Lem's father appeared too engrossed by what was in the hollow of the tree to register them. He became as deathly still as Lem had ever seen him. The boy walked a few paces closer, his skin crawling with gooseflesh. His stomach sank. His father jolted backward and lifted his head.

Lem tracked his father's eyeline until he saw what he was seeing. There were graying pink lengths of matter strung about the branches like heinous party streamers, winding, ropey, and almost balloon-like. A low sheen could be detected on them, even here, deep in the woods. Lem's father raised his hand to his mouth and backpedaled several steps. Then, without much warning, he stormed back toward Lem and started pushing the boy in the direction from which they had come.

"No, wait!" Lem resisted. "What did you see?"

Frank had no time to play games. He threw his son over his shoulder and dragged him out of there kicking and screaming in a fireman's carry.

"Dad, no!" Lem protested. "Banshee! Banshee! We can't leave her, Dad. Please!"

His father disregarded the pleas, left them hanging in the November air as he hurried across the clearing to where Lem's mother was waiting.

"Jesus, Frank," she said. "What happened?"

Rather than answer her, he urged her along the path that led back to the car with a stern expression. It took some doing. Lem was fit to be tied, making such a fuss that people were stopping to stare. His father unloaded him into the crew cab, and then got in after his mother.

"No!" Lem wailed. "Nooo!" He cried so hard that he began to gag, his voice falling hoarse. They had forsaken Banshee. Banshee, who had slept in front of the footboard of his bed every night and climbed into bed with him every morning. Banshee, who had comforted him every time the other kids were cruel. Banshee, who had made like a shield over him in the hallway during the worst hailstorm of his life. Banshee, who had promised him with her eyes that she would never desert him.

"What's going on, Frank?" his mother asked. "For God's sake!"

Lem would not realize until later that the tiny stones he had seen were teeth and the strands in the tree branches were entrails. He would never know what his father saw in the hollow.

"Frank!"

His father managed to cross himself, but he struggled to speak. It was as though an invisible hand had snatched all the air from his lungs. He could only utter two words: "Black mass."

* * *

The peanut butter sandwich cookies were in the storage slot of the car door. Lem had bought a sleeve of them at the gas station that morning and told the clerk no when she tried to upsell him some stocking stuffer candy. He deposited the cookies into the breast pocket of his field shirt and set out all over again.

Lem may have been a little delusional, but he was no fool. He knew that most people thought this was an awful lot of trouble to go through year after year. It was just a dog, after all. But those people didn't know Banshee, and they sure as shit didn't know Lem. They didn't know curling up in a dog bed, hugging a blanket, aching like an exposed tooth root. Trying anything and everything to fill the void that grief digs with the efficiency of an undertaker. They didn't know what it was like to have the luster of Christmas rubbed out of their soul, or if they did, it wasn't for the same reason. They didn't know what it was like to be chained to a memory they could never break free of.

Some things you never get over.

When Lem passed by the red single-wide trailer this time, there was a man standing outside of it, eyeing him down with his arms folded against his chest. He spat at the ground and said, "Every year."

"Pardon?" Lem said.

"You come here every year and don't buy no damn tree," the man said. "What's it going on now? A decade?"

Lem stopped. "What's it to you?" he asked.

The man spat again, uncrossed his arms. "Well, I'm the owner of this here farm is what it is to me. Name's Morrie." He came within an arm's length and extended his hand.

Lem was reluctant to take it. The old fart reeked of garlic powder and weed. He was lean save for a paunch of visceral fat, and he had an untrustworthy face with a mustache like a dirty, white woolly worm. Lem imagined him in that single-wide behind him after all the shoppers had left for the day. Subsisting off chili beans and Facebook memes and satellite internet porn.

"What's your problem?" Morrie asked, acknowledging that Lem wouldn't shake his hand. "Was you raised in a barn?"

The old man talked slick, but he was weak in posture. Probably peacocking to deflect from the fact that he posed no physical threat. Lem knew how he was coming off: spacey but with resting dick face. He was a big, mean-looking, ginger sonofabitch with a bone-sized hole in his heart that leaked an aura of standoffishness at all times. He reckoned there was no harm in letting Morrie know that the malice he had come with was not for him. He finally shook his hand.

"You got a name?" Morrie asked.

"Lem."

"Pleasure to meet you, Lem." He glanced at his new acquaintance's gun and knife. "You gonna buy a tree this year, or are you gonna go to war with the fucking squirrels out yonder?"

"I lost something out there," Lem said. "I'm trying to get it back."

"What'd you lose?"

"My dog."

Morrie squinted hard. Like he was doing complicated math in his head. Then his face lit up in epiphany. "I remember you," he said. "You're the feller what made that scene all them years ago. Got trawled outta here by your daddy like a possessed marlin."

Lem didn't confirm. He opted to look away instead, feeling like a child again.

"Say you're still looking for that same dog?" Morrie asked. "It's been, what, fifteen, twenty years? You gotta know that even if it was a puppy, it'd be long dead by now."

Lem dismissed the claim. He had heard it all before. The year Banshee disappeared was the last year he would come to the Choose 'N Cut with his family, but when he had turned eighteen, he started coming here solo. He was no longer a boy of thirteen but a man of twenty-eight, a grown person who refused to accept a conclusion that everyone else held as gospel. People like them, people like Morrie, didn't understand Banshee. They hadn't seen what Lem had seen.

"You wouldn't get it," Lem said.

"Well, what's that bolt-action on your back for? Ain't even been hunting season for a week."

"Maybe coyotes. Maybe something else."

"Like what?"

"Witches," Lem said, serious as a heart attack.

"Witches?" Morrie asked. "Ain't no witches out there. Maybe some moonshiners and glue sniffers. Witches? Never."

"That's not what I've heard."

Behind the men, a family of three appraised a Fraser fir, full, shimmering, and rich blue-green. They were a jolly if not plain sort, not unlike Lem and his folks had once been. The type you picture going for broke on their decorations every year.

"Ninety, but I'll do eighty," Morrie barked at them, even though he hadn't been asked. He turned his attention back toward Lem. "Look," he said. "They's tall tales in these mountains like you wouldn't believe. Witches and hellhounds and bigfeet and shapeshifting werefolk and whatnot. But I've been here all fifty-seven years of my life, and I can guaran-god-damn-tee you the closest thing you'll get to supernatural out here is the damn kids what wear them robes and fingernail paint. Playing that card game, carrying on, one minute and the next…" He sort of petered off there at the end and spat. "No, sir. I don't know of any tomfuckery on this here land. If something got your dog, which as much as I hate to say it, is likely, it was a bear or a mountain lion."

"All the same," Lem replied.

"Cain't tell you nothing, huh?" Morrie said.

Lem was growing impatient. He was losing daylight by the breath.

"I'll tell you what," Morrie started. "You let me call a buddy of mine to watch the farm for me, and I'll go out there with you."

"I move better alone."

"Hell," Morrie said. "I insist."

Lem sighed. Would an extra set of eyes hurt? He looked at the keeper of Christmas trees, figured a good fart might knock him on his ass. "You might wanna bring a gun if you've got one."

❄ ❄ ❄

They passed a joint of some surprisingly good weed as they cut across the clearing and into the woods, Morrie fiddling with his satchel and mumbling under his breath. The old man had put on a camouflage jacket that was much too large, and he might as well have been floating in it. It was an hour and a half 'til dusk, and Lem intended to use every minute of it. The stray hair from earlier had been promising, but he had gotten his hopes up before, and he didn't want to put himself in that position anymore than he had to. Then again, maybe this all wasn't so much about recovery as it was retribution. But retribution against what?

Lem took the last hit off the joint and disposed of the roach.

"Make sure you stomp that out good," Morrie said. Lem could tell he was higher than fuck. "I'll be damned if the whole western part of the state goes up in flames on my watch."

"It's out, Morrie."

"What'd you say the name of this dog of yours was again? Banjo? Nancy?"

"Banshee," Lem said.

"Aw, right. Banshee," Morrie called. "Here, gal."

"She's deaf," Lem said.

"Well, fuck if that don't complicate things."

Lem supposed that if Banshee could hear, Morrie would have probably scared her off. He was obnoxiously loud, and while she was a friendly pup, she didn't take too well to strangers. Here, in the three o'clock hour, the woods were already beginning to darken. The diminishing light bathed the area in a tranquility that would cool your blood if you weren't used to it. You were never really by yourself out here, and that truth alone was enough to unnerve most anyone. Lem could certainly see that it was enough to disquiet his tagalong. Morrie appeared more agitated and paranoid with each step.

"I thought you said there was no funny stuff out here, Morrie."

"There ain't," Morrie responded, bloodshot eyes darting from one fixed point to the next. "But I don't make it out here all that often. Not as much as I used to, at least."

"Right."

They made it to the spot where Lem had discovered the

hair, and much to his surprise, it was still there. He plucked it, held it up between two fingers.

"That could belong to any number of things," Morrie scoffed.

Lem removed the cookies from his pocket and began tossing them indiscriminately, hoping to lure Banshee in with her favorite treat. The very thought of her licking peanut butter off the roof of her mouth brought a smile to his face.

Morrie huffed. "You're gonna attract something hungry, all right, but it ain't gonna be no damn dog."

Suddenly, a hushed sigh blew through the trees ahead, long-tailed and crisp. Almost euphonious, like a well-spoken, foreign tongue. It couldn't have been the wind because nothing moved.

"Did you hear that?" Lem asked.

Morrie's eyes widened, but he didn't answer.

It came again, still in front of them but from farther away. Lem pursued it, Morrie on his heels. The tree farmer reached into his satchel and came up with an ancient-looking cruiser shotgun that had to have spent the last few years collecting dust.

"What the fuck is that, Morrie?" Lem asked. "A blunderbuss?"

"You poke fun now," Morrie said. "But anybody tries to leave my lot without paying, I'll put a two-foot hole in them."

Lem continued to follow the sound, which fluctuated in closeness and clarity. It didn't feel born from natural origins, but he didn't have anything similar to compare it to. The two men soon found themselves in a leaf-bedded glade the size of a tennis court, and the sound ceased. The air here didn't move around like it did elsewhere; it was stiff and bitter, unpleasant. It gave Lem the willies, and he wasn't the only one.

"You know, I don't actually own that lot," Morrie said.

"My brother does. He lets me live there and run it." He rambled it out like a confession.

"Breathe, Morrie. You can head back if you'd like."

"I'll be fine, long as we make it outta here without me shitting enough bricks to build a house."

Lem paid that last part no mind. He had spotted something protruding through the leaves at the far edge of the glade, and now he was approaching it. A pointy end stuck out maybe two inches. He flicked at it with his boot until it emerged, skipping over the brittle heaps and coming to a rest a few feet away. It was an animal horn, yellowed, fluted, and slightly spiraled. About half a foot long. He swiped at the ground surrounding it and uncovered another, and another. And another. There must have been over a dozen there in that shallow grave of leaves. He didn't know what to make of it, all of them scattered about like fossils at an excavation site.

"You're starting to spook me, my friend," Morrie said. He fetched a flask from inside his camo jacket, unscrewed the cap, and turned it up. "Don't you judge me for having a drink, now. You got no place. You smoked that shit with me back there, and your pupils was as tiny as a pecker hole when I met you."

Lem hadn't said anything to provoke such a defense.

Morrie treated himself to another long drink. As he went to close the flask, he fumbled the cap and it fell to the ground. Bending to pick it up, he noticed something in the dirt next to it. He pinched it with his thumb and pointer, raised it toward the sky. Lem seemed to know what it was before Morrie did. A fingernail.

"Oh, sweet bearded Christ on a cracker," Morrie said.

At that moment, the sighing sounded once more, and its nature was suddenly clear as day. It was a whisper of some kind, beckoning or warning or perhaps both at the same time. What came in the immediate aftermath of that whisper was even more distinctive, and it benumbed Lem in a way that no substance ever had. The soft jingle of a little bell bouncing off the trees. Banshee's bell. Lem was sprinting away like a madman before he even knew it.

"Hey!" Morrie hollered after him. "Fuck this. I'm going back! You're on your own, you sorry sumbitch!"

Lem heard him, but he didn't care. He tore through the snags and the roots and the slumping branches until he couldn't decipher one form from the next. He didn't know where he was going, but he was running there as fast as he could.

* * *

By the time Lem stopped, hands on his knees, gasping for breath, he had no clue where the fuck he was. The jingling had vanished, and so too had nearly every other perceivable sound. This stretch of creation was unremarkable in its geography. Lem reckoned it could have existed anywhere in the western Carolina mountains. Trees, leaves, rocks, sticks, logs, shrubs, repeat. He fished the canteen out of his knapsack and emptied it in a couple of gulps.

"Come on, Banshee," he said, if only to himself. "I know you're out here, girl. I heard you."

He removed the compass from his knapsack next, an artifact from his Boy Scout days. When he popped the cover, the damnedest thing happened: nothing. The needle was paralyzed, refusing to budge, regardless of which way he moved. But that was only the second most alarming reality. The first was that Lem had begun to giggle like he hadn't in years, spittle running down his lips and dripping off his chin. Why was he laughing? It would be night soon, and he was lost in the wilderness without a prayer of being found. Maybe the weight he had lugged around for more than half of his life had gotten the better of him at last.

Lem let the compass slip from his fingers and onto the ground. He chose a direction without rhyme or reason and started walking, not in a hurry. Banshee could be anywhere out here, but if she was still in the area after all this time, she wasn't going anyplace. Lem hummed the melody to "Ring Christmas Bells" of all things, a song that had freaked him out as a kid, and wondered if Morrie had made it back to the trailer at the Choose 'N Cut. Lem imagined he had, the crusty bastard.

The light dimmed rapidly, like a jarred candle being suffocated by its own lid. Lem retrieved the flashlight from his knapsack and switched it on. The funnel-shaped beam slashed through a night as black as starless space. Lem had been out in the country plenty of times at this hour, but he had never felt a darkness so total, so perfect. Like he could take it as his religion if he so desired. He roamed through the abyss for an indeterminate amount of time, humming, thinking at worst he would have to stay put until first light. In some ways, it felt as though Banshee had run away all over again, showing up like she had, and when Lem considered that, it made him want to break down in tears. But he latched onto the smallest glimmer of hope because it was all he had left. He needed it, even if it was wrong and impossible.

Lem contemplated a rest break, fearing he had succumbed to delirium. That was until it returned, appearing from nothing. A whisper in a beautiful, sinister language. But this time it was emanating from more than one source. Lem sought it. He pointed the flashlight toward it. His previous high had worn off over the day, but he sensed a new one coming on, this one strange and potent. The whisper gave way to an angelic chanting, like something Lem imagined would score the battle between the archangel Michael and the forces of evil on the last day. Underneath it all was the jingling.

He came to a tree with a branch that hung low, its limbs scraping the ground. He shined the light on it. A dog's leg, white with black and gray merle, flashed around the base of the tree, and in the blink of an eye, it became the pale leg of a human woman. Lem let out a whimper. There was a rustle to his right, and he turned the flashlight on it. Morrie stumbled toward him, grinning and bumbling in the white glow, a gash across his throat oozing thick paint drips of blood. After a handful of steps, the old man's head rolled clean off his neck like a grotesque piece of fruit falling off the edge of a table. The rest of Morrie collapsed behind it, and before Lem could even react, an apparatus of what looked like meat hooks sank into the headless body and swallowed it into the darkness.

"Shit!" Lem hollered, fumbling the flashlight. He drew the gun, hammering its bolt handle and firing blind three times. He dropped it, hauling ass, shouting into the pitch-black night, chants and whispers chasing after him. But he didn't make it far before he felt the hooks rip into his flesh. A hot, miserable pain.

And he was being dragged through this Hell on Earth for the second time in his life. Dragged on his stomach, clawing at the dirt, trying his damnedest to reach his knife. An invisible tongue was snaking in and out of his ear, and he didn't know if the continuous song of agony pouring out of him was his, Banshee's, or neither. Was it a scream? Was it a wicked laugh? There was a chance that it was a thing entirely new. An evil spawn of both those emotions, echoing through the coming darkness forever and ever. Lem was howling, and the woods were deaf to his cries. She was deaf to his cries.

The Wish

Steven J. Taylor

Peter Wagner looked at his watch for what must have been the fifth time in the last two minutes. It had been a long day, and now he just wanted it to be over. His body ached, despite having sat all day, and the layers of padding that covered his body left him feeling sweaty and uncomfortable. At least he had his own beard. He could not imagine how annoying it would be having to wear a fake beard all day. People were everywhere: crawling along the corridors, weighed down by bulging shopping bags; browsing shopfronts with eager eyes searching for that perfect gift. During his breaks, Peter liked to watch the shoppers. He had sorted them into three distinct groups, which he labeled the "happy shoppers" (those who enjoyed the Christmas shopping experience and wrapped themselves completely in the joy of it), the "forced shoppers" (those who did not enjoy the experience and wanted to get the whole thing over with as quickly as possible), and the "zombies" (those shoppers who milled around aimlessly). He rarely saw a shopper who he could not categorize this way.

But the joy of his watching was becoming tiresome. He checked his watch again. Five minutes left. He looked at his elf helper. She was talking to a woman. One more then. One more child to sit in his lap and detail his Christmas wishes. One more time he would play Santa Claus today.

Peter looked at the boy, who stared back at him with an alarming intensity. The boy's eyebrows were drawn down, and his eyes were practically squinting. His mouth was a thin line. The boy's gaze weighed heavily on Peter, as though he was being judged. He would need to put on a good act. Here was another doubter.

Janine, the elf helper, took the details from the child's mother and surreptitiously whispered the boy's name into a concealed microphone she wore. The earpiece in Peter's ear buzzed with the boy's name. Michael Tirelli.

"Ah, Michael, welcome, welcome," Peter greeted him. The illusion always worked best when he knew their names before being introduced.

Michael stood in front of Peter a moment and looked him up and down. He pursed his lips. Still a doubter. Janine encouraged him to take a seat on Santa's lap. He studied her briefly before taking his place.

"Well, now, Michael, what is it you want Santa to bring you this year?" Peter asked.

Michael stared a moment longer before he began reciting a list of extravagant toys that would be the pride of any ten-year-old's toy collection. As he spoke, Janine scribbled notes hastily on a pad. Peter nodded as he listened, giving the appropriate oohs and ahs where needed. As he listened, he could not help but noticed the boy's lifeless, monotone voice. Did he not want these things?

Then Peter looked at the boy more closely. His faded clothes were practically threadbare at the knees and elbows. His cuffs on his shirt were high above his wrists, and his shoes were heavily scuffed. Perhaps it was not a case of this boy believing in Santa, but rather believing it did not matter what he asked from Santa; he would not get it regardless.

Peter looked up at the mother, who looked down at her nervously fidgeting hands in front of her. Her clothes, too, showed signs of age, and the brightness of her red dress was no longer apparent.

Michael finished reciting his wishes, and Janine went to give the list she had taken down to the mother. Peter was about to engage Michael in small talk to distract him from this when the boy leaned in, placing his face a mere inch from Peter's.

"Now the spy is gone..." Michael whispered in a steely voice that suddenly leaked emotion and venom. "...I'm going to tell you my real wish."

Peter raised his eyebrows but made no move to stop the boy; instead, he listened intently.

"I don't care about those other things," Michael continued. "I only want one thing from you this Christmas. One wish. I want you to kill my stepfather."

Peter blinked slowly, trying hard to keep his face neutral. He looked into the boy's eyes. The stare the boy returned was steely and cold. He was dead serious.

"But why?" was the only words Peter could find.

Michael answered by pulling up the worn sleeve of his shirt to reveal a bruised forearm. "But that's not all," Michael continued. "He drinks and gambles all of our money away so we have nothing."

Michael continued to stare intently at Peter.

Peter glanced up to see Janine in deep conversation with the mother. Janine was probably trying to sell a photo. Everyone liked a picture of their child with Santa. Peter returned his attention to the hard-staring boy, his hopes of escaping this conversation now dashed.

"Killing people is not something I do," Peter stammered.

The boy continued to stare at Peter a moment longer, then looked away. He gazed into the distance, and when he turned back, Peter saw the hardness was no longer there; it had been replaced by tears.

"What kind of man are you?" Michael said, his voice higher than earlier as emotion took hold. "You sit there and judge kids and their behavior, yet do nothing about the adults who do bad things to kids. People call you a saint. How can you be a saint when you watch kids to see if they have been bad or good but not their stepdads?"

"I…" Peter tried to answer but found himself at a loss for words.

"See, you can't even defend yourself. I only ask one thing that would make my life better. You must see what happens. You know who I am. Can you grant me this one wish or not?"

The boy looked at him with tear-filled eyes. Peter wanted anything but to look into those eyes right now. How could he? And what could he say? Should he pull away the veil of childhood innocence? Reveal that he wasn't really Santa? No. The mother would come back screaming and he would lose his job. But he had to say something to the boy.

"I'll…think about it," Peter said, immediately regretting it when he saw the boy's face light up.

"You will?" Michael asked.

No, is what Peter wanted to scream. Yes, is what he said.

＊ ＊ ＊

Peter rode the late bus home that night. After the encounter with Michael, he did not want to go home and be alone with his thoughts. He wanted the company and distraction of others, lest he think further about that poor boy and his heartbreaking request.

He'd stopped in at a small bar that he frequented. He knew a few of the other regular patrons and tried to strike up a conversation with a couple of them, but as soon as there was a break in small talk, he found his mind coming back around to the boy. It haunted him.

Peter arrived home close to eleven that night. The alcohol had gotten the better of him, and putting the key into the slot of his small townhouse was more difficult than usual. The house was cold and dark. He flicked on the light to be greeted by the smiling images of his deceased wife and son in the photo that hung on the wall in the entrance hall. Both had died within a year of each other, one by cancer and the other from a road accident, leaving him a childless widower.

He smiled a greeting at the photo before closing the door behind him. He had lived alone for a decade now. He had not met anyone else, nor did he intend to. Nobody could replace Maria and Carl. That was a hole too deep to fill.

He did not intend to become a sad, lonely old man, but he imagined that is how other people saw him. He spent most of his time at home by himself, puttering around his back garden or reading in his favorite chair by the window. The one opposite his was Maria's chair, the one he kept but in which he never sat.

A friend had suggested he take the role of Santa Claus at the mall. Apart from just looking the part, this friend had said that bringing joy to others, especially kids, would be a way Peter could break his ten-year funk.

Perhaps it had worked. Or perhaps it was better to say it

had been working. But that goodwill shattered like a window pane hit by a flying baseball the moment that young boy made his true wish known. The wish for Santa to kill his stepfather.

But perhaps, Peter thought, this may be the very thing he needed. Not just to bring joy, but to help this boy in some other way. But what way? Kill his stepfather?

Peter slumped into his armchair. He looked at the empty chair across from him. "What should I do, Maria? That poor boy... I just feel so bad for him. When he asked me to kill his stepfather, it affected me so deeply."

Peter looked around the room. He looked at the pictures displaying a once-happy family that hung on the walls. His wedding day. The proud parents holding their baby boy for the first time. His teenage son wearing a broad grin as he displayed his athletics medals. Proud parents with their grown son at his graduation.

Memories. That is all Peter had now.

He wiped a tear from his eye and turned back to the empty chair.

"What is there left for me here, Maria? Without you or Carl, I feel like I am just passing time, waiting to join you." He shifted in his seat, leaning in as if to whisper conspiratorially into the ear of an invisible occupant.

"There is nothing for me now. Nothing here. What if I used my life to improve that of another? What if I saved that boy by killing his father? I am old, and I already feel his mortal coil is a prison. What difference would it make if I lived out my life here or in jail? Would you forgive me if I did it? If I chose to use my life to save another in such a way?"

But the empty chair had nothing to say on the matter. He sat back, and soon Peter drifted off to sleep in his armchair as his thoughts swirled on the poor boy, his demented perception of Santa, and something even wilder that he had never before considered committing in his life. Murder.

As the days and hours passed, Peter began thinking less and less of Michael and the fanciful notion of killing his stepfather. He instead focused on playing a good Santa at the mall. He laughed merrily. He complimented the children on their excellent choices. He drew out promises of good behavior and shared jokes with the children. He was really enjoying his role of Santa Claus, and when thoughts of murder were all but wiped from his mind, Michael came back. Michael's return was like a fire alarm sounding in the middle of the night, and Peter felt all his senses go on high alert.

This time he was alone. Peter checked his watch. It was the middle of the day. Michael was skipping school to visit him.

Michael waited patiently in line for his turn. Peter found it hard to concentrate on the little girl who sat in his lap running through an extensive list of art products she wanted. Michael wore a serious face and stared unflinchingly at him. Peter felt flustered under the boy's baleful eyes. The girl finished, and Peter stammered a quick farewell. Michael was next.

Peter watched a sharp exchange between Michael and his helper, Janine. The discussion seemed achingly long, and Janine gave a huge sigh before approaching Peter.

"He's here without a parent, but he insists on seeing you. It's mall policy he can't be here by himself, but he's being very bullish and wanted me to ask you to let him through anyway."

Janine looked at him expectantly. Every fiber of his being wanted to say no, send this boy away. He wanted to avoid speaking with the boy. Avoid facing the question of murder. But Michael stared intensely at him. A maelstrom of thoughts and emotions crowded Peter's mind as he looked at the boy. Finally, he sighed.

"Let him through," Peter relented.

Janine frowned, then turned to walk back to the entrance and let Michael in. Michael strode forward, his head dipped slightly forward, his eyes staring unflinchingly at Peter. Janine followed in tow, and Peter waved her away.

"You won't be needed; it's just a quick talk."

Janine frowned again before returning to the entrance to start talking with the next customer in line.

Michael pulled himself up into Peter's lap. The hard gaze he cast was beginning to make Peter nervous. Peter's thoughts swirled.

"So," Michael began without any fanfare. "I've given you two days to think. What have you decided?"

Peter had decided nothing. In fact, he was starting to believe he would never see Michael again nor face this moment. But here it was.

"Are you killing my stepdad or not?" Michael asked, a tone of impatience coloring his voice.

"I..." Peter began, but his voice broke. He had no idea what to say.

Michael stared at him for a moment, then seemed to shrink physically. His eyes dropped, and his shoulders slumped. The determined, hard-staring boy was gone, replaced by this soft, vulnerable child instead.

"You're not going to do it, are you?" Michael asked in a soft voice. "You're going to leave me with that monster who abuses me and beats me and spends all my mother's money on gambling and alcohol. I thought if anyone in the world cared, it would be you, Santa Claus. But you're no different than anyone else. My mom. My teachers. Even the cops. None of you are willing to do anything to protect me."

As Michael spoke, Peter felt the words tearing his soul apart. This poor child had felt so trapped and alone he had reached out to Santa Claus and use his Christmas wish to have this man killed. How desolate and desperate must the child be for it to come to this? Something wet hit Peter's hand, and he realized it was one of Michael's tears. Peter came to a decision.

"I'll do it," Peter said.

The boy's demeanor changed immediately. Michael looked up, and hope filled his eyes. He reached out and hugged Peter, thanking him profusely as he did. Peter smiled, embarrassed as heads turned to see the exchange. After a lengthy hug, Michael drew away and pulled an envelope from his pocket and passed it to Peter.

"This has everything you need to know in it. Don't wait for Christmas Eve. I know you're too busy then delivering presents. Do it two nights from now. On the twenty-second."

Peter was unsure of what to say. He went to say something, but Michael again embraced him before dismounting and walking away.

Peter tucked the envelope into coat of his Santa suit as Janine approached him with one eyebrow raised.

"What was that all about?" she asked. "He seemed awfully happy when he left; I hope you haven't made a promise that can't be kept."

No, Peter thought to himself. *No, I have not.*

* * *

"You've been staring at that envelope for an hour now. Are you going to open it, or are you afraid of what might be in it?"

Peter looked up and smiled at the waitress. It wasn't a

real smile; it didn't have any true feeling behind it. The truth was, yes, he was afraid of what was inside.

He watched as she laid down the fresh beer on the bar and took his empty one away.

"Thanks," he muttered as she turned to serve another customer.

He sat alone at the bar. It was busy tonight. All around him, people were sharply dressed and bustling with laughter and good cheer. It was as though the surrounding office towers had tipped all their workers inside just to torment him with their good vibes.

Peter felt morose. He was committed now. He had made a promise to kill a man. He, who had never committed an act of violence in his life, had put himself on a path to becoming a murderer.

Peter sighed and reached for the envelope. Not point in delaying the inevitable. He carefully tore it open and withdrew the contents. A key, a letter, and a drawing of the house layout. He glanced at the schematic, noting that Michael had taken care to list the address on it. The key had no significant markings, so he turned to the letter and read.

Dear Santa,

First, I want to say a big thank you for granting my Christmas wish. I knew deep down you were a good man who cared for children. I can't explain how much of a difference this will make to my life. I will never be on your Naughty List again. That's a promise!

I have put in this envelope a map of my house and a key to the basement. You can get into the basement at the back of the house. I will leave the gate open for you. I will get my stepdad's gun and leave it for you on the desk.

My mom will be working on the night of the twenty-second. My stepdad will probably be drunk and asleep in front of the TV like he always is. He should be easy for you to kill once you have the gun.

Thank you, thank you, thank you. I promise to be good always.

From Michael

Peter read the note twice and studied the home layout before tucking all three items back into the envelope and into his pocket. He then picked up the beer and downed it in one go before ordering something stronger. The merriment continued around him as he set about drinking himself to oblivion.

* * *

Peter walked past the house for the third time. He was stalling, and he knew it. He had committed himself to the act, but he was not quite ready to cross the threshold. Not just yet.

Michael's house had been easy to find. It stood out like a sore thumb on this clean, well-maintained street. The place looked old and battered, and the yard was unkept. Weeds thrived in the uncut lawn and potted plants wilted with disdain. The gate at the front hung at an odd angle, and even the garden gnomes that stood in the garden beds looked dismal and sad.

It was late at night, and there was no traffic on the street. Nothing moved, and the windows of the neighboring houses were dark. Despite this, Peter looked around nervously, afraid he was being watched from the shadows. It was paranoia and he knew it, but he could not shake the feeling that someone was watching him. He could not go on like this. Pacing back and forth along the sidewalk. Someone was bound to look out at some point, if they hadn't already done so. He needed to stop. He needed to commit to action. He stopped at the front of Michael's house and took a deep breath.

The gate squeaked loudly as he pushed it open. He shuddered as though hearing someone drag their fingernails down a blackboard. He again glanced nervously around, but all the windows of the surrounding houses remained ominously dark.

Peter stepped into the front yard. He noticed his breathing had become quicker, and he was sweating despite the coolness of the night. He had naïvely thought he was ready for this. He had bid his home farewell, willing to accept there was a chance he might not return. In his journey here, he felt relatively calm and composed. But now that he had arrived, it all felt completely different.

He paused a moment, then walked swiftly to the side of the house. The gate was slightly ajar, just as Michael had specified in his letter. He pushed through, again shuddering at the sound of another squeaky gate. A dog barked in the distance.

Beyond the gate, a narrow path led along the side of the house. It was a paved path, though here, too, the weeds seemed to be winning out, thrusting themselves between gaps in the paving like proud protesters at a rally. The backyard held a similar story, as weeds had once again won the day amid a scattering of old, broken, and faded toys and a trampoline with a torn and tattered mat.

Peter found the door to the basement where Michael had indicated it would be. He approached the door, fishing into his pocket for the key. Again, he felt the sensation that he was being watched. He glanced along the fence line, then up at the house. There was nothing. No sign that he was anything but alone.

The key slid into the lock and turned easily. The door swung open with a soft groan, and the blackness of the basement below stared back at him like a yawning abyss. Peter shivered and took the steps down into the basement. He felt around the walls, searching for a light switch. Finally, he found it, but when he flicked it, no light came on.

He paused, hoping his eyes would adjust to the gloom. He recalled the layout of the room from Michael's drawing. The gun should be sitting on a table somewhere to his left. He turned his head, but his eyes could not penetrate the blackness ahead. Cursing silently to himself, he stepped to the left, reaching for the table.

There was a sharp snap, and pain shot up his left leg. There was a barbed, steely pressure against both sides of his leg, and he began to feel warm blood flowing down into his shoe. He was about to reach down and feel for the source of the pain when he sensed movement in the room. He stopped, standing dead still, his breathing shallow as he listened. He could hear the pounding of his heart in his ears.

Suddenly, there was a scraping sound, like wood on concrete. Someone or something was definitely in the basement with him. His began sweat nervously, could feel it running soaking into his clothes. Whoever was in the room would have heard the snapping of the trap that held him. He strained his eyes, desperately trying to make out any shape that would help him identify who or what was in the room with him. He hear a slight scuffing sound close by. He dared to speak.

"Michael, is that you?" he hissed between his teeth.

He sensed more movement, then heard the sound of something whooshing through the air. There was a sharp blow to his head. Then there was nothing.

✳ ✳ ✳

Consciousness slowly swam back to Peter.

The first thing he became aware of was that he was sitting

down. Then the pain came. The throbbing of his skull and the aching of his left shin. Then he became aware of other sensations. The stickiness of his blood-soaked sock. The dryness of his mouth that was filled with…what exactly? When he tried spitting it out, he felt a tightness around his mouth and pressure against the back of his head. He had been gagged. He went to pull the gag away when he realized his hands, too, were tied behind his back. He tried to move his feet, but these were also tied.

Peter's breathing accelerated as panic rose. He forced his eyes to focus and looked down. He was tied to a chair in the now-brightly lit basement. On the floor in front of him was a sprung bear trap. Blood stained its blade. *His* blood.

What went wrong with Michael's plan? He had followed the boy's instructions to the word. Had he stumbled into the basement when the stepfather was present? He looked around fearfully, eyes darting about the room, expecting to see the stepfather and police emerge to arrest and detain him. He had failed Michael, had been caught by the stepfather, and now he would go to prison and Michael would still be left at the mercy of his monster stepfather.

Peter's his head fell forward. It had all been in vain. He would go to prison for nothing. And worse, poor Michael would have learned the truth, that Santa wasn't real. Peter had failed the boy miserably.

There was a light cough. Peter looked up to see Michael standing there. The boy was wearing the same hard stare he wore the last time he had visited Peter at the mall. Peter's heart beat faster. Perhaps there was a way out of this after all. He just needed Michael to free him.

Peter tried to speak, but the gag muffled his words.

"You can scream all you want," Michael said as he stepped closer. "There is no one in the house, and the neighbors can't hear you."

Peter furrowed his brow. What did Michael mean by that?

"I see you are confused. I'm not surprised. You clearly didn't do your homework on me, did you, Santa?"

Peter suddenly felt a chill run down his spine. There was a steely edge to Michael's voice, and it was as cold as the arctic winter.

Michael walked over to stand directly in front of Peter, then bent forward so close their noses almost touched. Peter stared deep into Michael's eyes. He saw nothing but fathomless hate.

"It's okay; I get it. There are billions of kids in the world. You're a busy man, especially this time of year. You don't have time to check on every kid. Not *really* check. Do you?"

Michael raised an eyebrow. He was waiting for an answer. Peter shook his head.

"No," Michael continued. "I didn't think so. Because if you had, you would know that my stepfather left my mother six months ago. He took everything. Just emptied the bank account and moved on. Yet here you came to my rescue, thinking to do me a favor when all you had to do was check things out, you lazy, fat bastard."

As Michael spoke, his movements became more animated, and his tone more venomous. Michael pushed away from Peter and began stalking back and forth across the room. He stopped at a table and picked up a large kitchen knife that had been lying there, then continued to pace. Finally, he turned, pointing the knife at Peter.

"Do you have any idea how frustrating and unfair life is? How hard it is for me to go to a school where all the other kids are well off and I am wearing second-hand clothes brought at a charity shop? Can you see how unfair that all is?"

Peter nodded. The boy seemed enraged by this and waved

the knife threateningly.

"Liar!" Michael stepped forward and pressed the tip of the knife against Peter's throat. There was a sharp pain, and Peter felt a slight trickle as blood course down his neck.

"You're a hypocrite, Santa. You only add to this unfairness. Of all the people in the world who could do something about this outrage, you do nothing but continue to add to the problem. You give rich kids the most toys and the fanciest new tech gadgets while you give us poor kids almost nothing. I've been asking for a new bike for years. You gave new bikes to the Murray twins, and what did you give me? A battered, old skateboard. Why do you only give good things to the rich kids? Why? WHY?"

The knife pressed harder into Peter's neck. He could feel the blood flow start to increase. Then Michael pulled away, standing with his back to Peter.

Peter pulled at his bonds. He was held fast. He looked around frantically. He had to get out. This kid was crazy. He could not see anything that would help. He started wrenching at his bonds, ignoring the pain in his hands and wrists.

Michael turned, a look of dismay in his eyes.

"You see now, don't you, Santa?" Michael asked, his voice much softer now. "You see how unfair you have been, giving those rich kids who already have everything even more stuff while leaving the rest of us with nothing. Tell me, if I let you go now, would you change? Would you go back to the North Pole and change everything so the poor kids get the cool stuff for once?"

Peter paused for a second before meeting the boy's eyes and nodding. Michael gave a half-smile in return.

"I'm sorry, Santa, but I don't believe you. I believe there is only one way to make Christmas fair and equal for everyone. Do you know how I can achieve that?"

Sweat prickled Peter's brow, and his eyes widened. Panic began welling uncontrolled inside him, and he started pulling at the ropes more vigorously.

Michael smiled. "You see it now, don't you? The way I make Christmas equal for all? You are right; I do it by killing you. If presents aren't distributed evenly, then they can't be distributed at all. Everyone equal with nothing."

Without another word, Michael stepped forward and thrust the knife into Peter's chest. The blade slid between his ribs, missing Peter's heart but piercing the lung. Michael withdrew the knife, and blood began to gush from the wound. Peter coughed as his lung began filling with the crimson liquid.

"I'm sorry I had to do this, but the world needs to be a fairer place. My mother says I should never stand by when I see injustices. And that's what I'm doing. No Christmas for all is fairer than a great Christmas for those who already have money. Equality has to start somewhere."

Peter had trouble breathing. His lung was filling fast, and soon he would drown on his own blood. There was so much he wished he could say in this moment. So much wisdom he wished he could give this poor, misguided youth. But he could not. He was gagged and dying. He tried coughing, and he could taste blood. He wanted to scream, but he felt his life ebbing fast. He looked up at Michael one last time to see that cold, hard stare before consciousness left him.

✳ ✳ ✳

Michael stared at the dead body of Santa Claus for some time. He could barely believe he'd done it. But he had. He had just killed Santa Claus. He thought for sure the plan would fall through, that Santa's elves would suddenly appear and rescue him. But nothing. Perhaps the "jolly old man" was not as loved as everyone thought.

Finally, Michael stood up and walked over to the table. He picked up his pen and notepad and struck a line through the name "Santa Claus" on his list. He looked at the next. The Tooth Fairy. The bitch that gave some kids ten dollars for their teeth while he earned fifty cents for his. She had to go. He ran his tongue across his teeth. One at the back was starting to come loose. He smiled and pondered it. He needed to start planning. The Tooth Fairy would be tough to kill.

S✱ILVER B✱ELLS
Janine Pipe

Waiting for a train was always a huge pain in the arse, but sometimes, such as today, Cameron didn't have a choice. His car wouldn't start, there was heavy snow due, and public transportation was the only viable option.

Of course, when you are running to someone else's schedule, things never go to plan, and he'd missed all but the last train by the time he returned to the desolate station. Feeling irked due to the lateness, he was also starving. There hadn't even been time to grab a festive-flavored hot chocolate from Costa on the way to this shit-hole. Home was where he wanted to be, to kick back with a beer and watch the footy. And maybe a mince pie. It was nearly Christmas.

Not only was he now forced to board a train hours after he had planned, when it finally deemed to arrive, but it was also the oldest and crappiest looking excuse for an engine he'd seen in a long time.

Dear God, British Transport at its best.

Rolling his eyes and being thankful for at least having the common sense to bring a book, he boarded into one of the three available carriages.

Reminiscent of a scene straight out of a Hitchcock tale, there appeared to be no one else on board the train, not a soul having been present at his stop either.

And he was more than fine with that.

Settling into an uncomfortable seat, he continued reading *The Hound of the Baskervilles*, a story that would likely last well into the regrettably long two-hour journey.

The train was, as usual, freezing. Despite it being mid-December and bloody England, they had failed to install heaters that actually worked. It was bloody typical that the heaters were fucked, yet someone had decided to hang tinsel and a few scabby baubles from the ceiling.

Well done, lads. I feel proper cozy now.

Cameron was positive he was alone on the vessel, save for the driver. He was unsure why there were no other passengers or a guard, but he didn't care. It was better for him to be alone when he felt this way, especially the more his tummy rumbled. He definitely got "hangry" and wished he'd had the forethought to pick up some dinner before heading to the station.

Around the 20-minute mark, Cameron was startled by the carriage door suddenly opening, a man wandering in wrapped up like a snowman and carrying a huge bag of brightly wrapped presents. He had so many layers on he could barely walk. Cameron didn't blame him. He could practically see his breath.

"Hi." Smiling at Cameron, he sat in the seat opposite. Drawing the scarf down so his voice wasn't as muffled, he added, "It was getting pretty boring back there, so I thought I'd walk through the train to see if there was any sign of life."

Cameron, hating small talk with strangers, nodded at the newcomer and hoped he didn't want to make conversation. He'd been happy there was no one else around. Instead of a reply, his stomach growled.

"Hungry?" the man asked, grinning. "Me, too. I'm hoping the route is clear. Not too much snow. I really need to get home and eat before the moon comes out."

Frowning, Cameron thought this was an extremely odd thing to say but shrugged it off.

Sensing he wasn't going to get much out of him, the stranger remained seated but ceased engagement.

The train continued on its way. Every so often, they would rumble past some houses and he could see the tree lights through their front windows.

It's beginning to l—

All of a sudden, the overhead lighting flickered off and then back on again, making Cameron jump. Looking at his watch, he scowled.

It would be pitch black out soon. He really didn't enjoy the walk back from the station to his house when it was like this, even with a full moon high in the night-time sky to guide him.

He cursed the meeting that had made him late again, wishing he'd been able to make an excuse to leave early.

As if somehow sensing his agitation, the engine began to slow, which was curious, since there was no designated stop until Glennville.

Then, with a jerk, it halted entirely.

"What the—"

"Hello," came a muffled, disembodied voice through the speakers. "This is your driver speaking. I am sorry to report that there has been a sighting of something on the tracks. We cannot depart until it's clear. Please stay seated. The doors will remain locked and secure. Do not attempt to leave the carriage. Thank you."

The snowman began to look very nervous.

"This can't be happening. I need to get back; I have to get home... I can't be out when...when it happens!"

Oh, fucking great, Cameron thought. *I'm stuck on a broken-down train with this bell-end.*

As if to amplify his thoughts, the guy started pacing up and down the aisle.

"Need to get home, can't be outside. Need to! Oh shit, no! The moon!"

Feeling somewhat annoyed yet also a touch amused about this behavior, Cameron spoke to the man.

"What's up, mate? You a werewolf or summat, haha?"

It was getting darker by the minute, with no sign of the train restarting. The lights in the carriage began to flicker, as if predicting that something ominous was about to occur.

The man turned slowly and glared at Cameron. "A werewolf? No, you idiot, I'm diabetic. I need to eat or..." He paused and stared at Cameron. "Wh-what, what's wrong with your eyes, mate?"

Beginning to chuckle maniacally at the absurdity of it all, Cameron felt the pull of the moon and welcomed the start of the change.

Of course, when he'd asked the question, he'd known the guy wasn't lycan. He smelt 100% human and slightly of mulled wine.

Having always tried his best to be safely locked up at home when the moon was full in the night-time sky, there was, inevitably, the occasional blip. As the metamorphosis took hold, bones breaking, black fur shooting through pores, fangs replacing teeth, he howled in glee and embraced his wolf.

The snowman screamed as the Were-Cam brought down its maw and ripped out his throat, chomping through his neck and amplifying its blood lust. Once the oozing liquid no longer bubbled from the male's decapitated body, the beast broke through the carriages and ate the driver.

He did take a moment to admire the cab's festiveness. The driver even had a small tree in there with silver bells.

Nice.

His wolf laughed as he took just a moment to piss on that tree.

Fuck your silver bells.

In wolf form, he was able to race home faster than the train would have taken. Changing back to human, he was glad there had been no one to buy a ticket from or CCTV at the ancient station.

He'd gotten away with it again, for now.

Just as he had for the last 100 years. The Beast of Glenn-ville lived to tell another tale.

And this had been the Christmas edition.

Dead Man's Tree

Christopher Stanley

Shortly after midnight, the Toyota Avensis crunches onto the gravel driveway and stops in front of the bungalow. Adam Donahue switches off the engine but leaves the high beams on so the building glows red against the night sky. He tips his head from side to side to stretch the stiffness from his neck, feeling every one of his forty-two years. His tongue is furry from the mince pies he washed down with successive cups of service station tea. Everything else is good. Good-*ish*. He hopes he remembered to pack his toothbrush.

Sarah Donahue snores lightly in the passenger seat. In the back of the car, their eleven-month-old son, Max, is also asleep.

Adam reaches under his seat to retrieve the bundle of folded cloth he hid there before they left. He slips the flashlight from the door pocket and climbs out of the car as quietly as he can. Outside, the December air is chilly enough to fog his breath. Waves roll and crash beyond the dunes. He zips his jacket up to his chin and pulls a green-striped beanie over his bald head.

The doormat says *Please Leave the Beach on the Beach.* Adam enters the bungalow through the side door and shines the flashlight into the corners of the kitchen. Everything looks clean. The dishwasher door is open enough to see that it's empty, and the fridge-freezer is switched off at the wall. The clock above the sink has stopped ticking.

The kitchen leads to a large lounge/diner, which smells of old rug and wood polish. The Toyota's headlights shine through the windows, partially illuminating a sofa, a pair of armchairs, a boxy television, a circular dining table, and the spiky branches of a Christmas tree. French windows overlook a small patio, while the other internal door leads to a hall, from which it's possible to access the remaining rooms: a bathroom, a linen closet, and two double bedrooms.

Adam shines his flashlight on the three-seater sofa, revealing several freckles of dried blood about the size of chocolate coins. He unfolds the cloth he carried in from the car—a white cotton throw decorated with autumn leaves—and uses it to cover the stains. When he hears his wife dragging a suitcase along the narrow path at the side of the bungalow, he tucks in the throw around the arms of the sofa and steps back to admire his handiwork.

"No phone signal here," says Sarah, struggling to lift the suitcase through the backdoor. "And I swear it's colder inside than out." She's dressed for the season in a purple hiking jacket and bobble hat, with a knitted cream scarf that's similar to the one she was wearing when they met at an 80s revival concert. He told his friends she looked like Margot Kidder from the *Superman* movies, only prettier, with large eyes, long black hair and bangs. He liked her smile, her self-confidence, and her no-nonsense, no-fuss attitude. She said his receding hair-line made him look wise.

He slips the beanie from his head. "I can't do anything about the phone signal, but I'll put the heating on for you."

Sarah wheels the suitcase into the lounge and takes in her surroundings. "Is that a Christmas tree?"

"I know! Stroke of luck, right?"

"It's creepy."

"Creepy?"

"It's your uncle Howard's tree. It must have been up since he passed away."

"It's not like he died in the bungalow. And he would have wanted us to have it. Well, probably. It's better than nothing."

Sarah finds the wall switch, and the room lights up obligingly. "Oh my God, it's beautiful."

The Christmas tree is draped with heavy garlands of silver tinsel, like scarves meant to protect it from the seasonal chill. Its branches are laden with bells, bows, and baubles of burgundy and gold. The tree itself has a gnarled, woody trunk with rich green needles. It looks real, although it must be fake to have survived the year.

"It'll do," says Adam with a bounce in his voice. "Let's bring Max in from the car."

Sarah stands on tiptoes to kiss him on the lips. "I'm glad we came here. I'm sure it'll all look better in the morning."

Adam watches her walk back to the kitchen and wishes he'd had the courage to tell her the truth.

* * *

Sarah dreams of things with legs. She's distantly aware that she's in bed—*a* bed, not her own—and she's convinced the bed is slowly sinking in a pool of syrupy blood. Her mother paces back and forth in the lounge, hair in multicolored curlers, cigarette dangling from the corner of her mouth. She's ranting again, saying Adam's not good enough, that he's hiding something important. She urges Sarah to find out what it is, but Sarah is too preoccupied with the legs to pay attention. They tickle her feet, scurry over her knees and brush against her thighs. Too late, she realizes her mouth is open. She can feel them on her lips and tongue. Crawling down her throat

Choking, she kicks her way out from under the duvet and clambers off the mattress.

"Honey?"

It's too dark. She gropes for the light switch, finding everything else on the bedside table first.

"Are you okay?"

With the room lit up, her eyes focus on the beige carpet, the mirrored closet doors, and the bed with Adam sprawled naked under the blue-gray covers. Before he can stop her, she pulls the duvet from the bed and shakes it.

"What the fuck?"

She finds her phone and thumbs on the flashlight, dropping to her knees to shine the beam under the bed.

"They were here." Her voice is croaky. "I swear they were."

"Who?"

"Spiders. Lots and lots of spiders."

As she says it, she realizes how ridiculous she sounds.

On the bed, Adam says nothing. The color has drained from his face.

✳ ✳ ✳

The next time Sarah wakes up, she takes her dressing gown from the suitcase before heading to the kitchen to warm a bottle of milk for Max. The Christmas tree shimmers in the darkness as the fairy lights bloom and fade. She wishes they'd had room in the car to bring their own decorations from home. There's something not right about having a dead man's tree in the living room.

After Sarah's father moved out, her mother didn't have the energy or inclination to put on a fancy Christmas. Sarah remembers the quiet joy of opening her gifts—a new coat or lunchbox for school, and a variety pack of assorted chocolate bars. Following a dinner of turkey burgers and chips, she would cuddle up with her mum on the sofa and watch *Home Alone* or *The Wizard of Oz*. Their Christmas tree was three feet tall, with silver branches and green and red baubles. It wasn't much, but it made the room sparkle.

Adam's childhood Christmases involved a stocking by his bed, a pyramid of presents in the lounge, and enough food on the table to feed Santa and his merry elves. His Christmases were an event, with friends and relatives visiting from all over the country to play bingo and board games after eating roast turkey. Their tree was always fresh and lavishly decorated with silver bells and sapphire bows.

Sarah would happily say goodbye to the tree in the bungalow, but she knows Adam will want to keep it. It's a connection—however tenuous—to his family and the Christmases of his youth.

As she opens the kitchen door, she hears the jingle of baubles bashing together. She turns around, half-expecting to see the spiders from her dream scuttling between the tree's branches—spinning their webs, weaving their nests, luring their prey. She's never been fond of spiders, but the creatures from her imagination are monsters.

"Just a draft," she whispers to herself.

She remembers the rest of her dream and her mother's urgent warnings. For weeks, maybe months, Adam hasn't been himself. He's been quiet in the mornings and late home in the evenings. If she phones him while he's at work, there's always a meeting he needs to attend or a client he's promised to call back. They've stopped going to bed together, and she can't remember the last time they made love. Maybe it's Max. Maybe Adam regrets their decision to start a family. She doesn't think he wants to leave her, but the thought may have crossed his mind. In her darkest moments, she wonders if he's found someone else.

Max is giggling when she arrives with his milk. His bedroom door scrapes against the carpet, and light spills in from the hall. "Morning, sweetheart," she says. She places his sippy cup on the dresser and steps forward to lift him out of his crib.

Then she stops.

In his hands, Max holds something he shouldn't have, something that shouldn't even be in his room. He waves it in the air and chuckles at the distorted reflection of his face.

It's a burgundy bauble from the Christmas tree.

* * *

"We can't put the tree in the trash," says Adam.

They walk north, following the steps that form part of the sea defenses between Sea Palling and Happisburgh. Max is in his stroller, leading the way. On their left, the inverted curve of the concrete defenses is badly chipped and cracked. On their right, the sea roars before crashing against the boulders at the top of the beach, sending spray high into the sky. Above them, heavy gray clouds are every bit as threatening as the sea.

"But it gives me the creeps."

Adam doesn't want to fight with Sarah about something so trivial. Not on Christmas Eve. Not on their way to lunch. She thinks their impromptu holiday is an elaborate plan to avoid seeing his mother-in-law on Christmas Day, but it's more than that. He hasn't told her he's losing his job, that he'll return to the office in January to work his notice with no hope of reprieve. Since Max was born, every other conversation they've had has been child-related—whose turn it is to feed him or change his diaper. Adam needs time to unwind and think about how to tell Sarah the bad news without worrying her. He knows she'll be annoyed that he kept it a secret, but he's confident she'll understand, and then they can have a sensible conversation about what to do next.

"Adam? Did you hear me?"

"The tree was a gift from the neighbors. I don't want to upset anyone."

Spots of rain splatter on the stroller's canopy, and Adam adds this to his list of disappointments. He really hoped it would snow for Max's first Christmas.

"We should turn back," says Sarah. "I can fix us some lunch."

"We're closer to the café than the bungalow. See the cart gap up ahead? It's just through there. Let's keep going."

The Spring Tide café is a small, red-brick building not far from the Happisburgh Lifeboat Station. Icicle lights glow above windows frosted with spray-on snow. An elaborate holly wreath with bells and berries welcomes customers at the door. Inside, the walls are decorated with tinseled photographs of Happisburgh's candy-striped lighthouse. Steam hisses from the coffee machine while Doris Day sings "Here Comes Santa Claus" over hidden speakers. The counter display is a shrine to Christmas cakes and chocolate logs.

The waitress, who looks about fifteen, steps out from behind the counter. She has thick, black eyeliner, silver bauble earrings, and an expression that's as cold as the season. "Are you sure you should be here? We don't care for troublemakers."

Adam waits for a punchline, which isn't forthcoming. "I beg your pardon?"

"Do you have a reservation?"

"Oh. Yes."

The waitress shows them to their table and leaves to fetch a highchair for Max.

"I just don't get it," says Sarah, handing Max a biscuit from her handbag. "Why would the neighbors buy your Uncle Howard a Christmas tree?"

"Because it's Christmas."

"But why?"

Adam remembers their wedding and the weeks they spent agreeing on the guest list, finding a suitable venue, writing the speech, organizing the rings, the outfits, the gifts. Howard refused to respond to the RSVP, saying it was a lot of fuss over nothing. Then he refused to buy a gift—a point that Adam and Sarah were happy to concede. When the big day arrived, he missed the service and was drunk when his taxi arrived at the venue. He spent most of the afternoon asleep in his room.

"I hate to speak ill of the dead," says Adam, "but Uncle Howard was a miserable old bugger. There's no way he was going to buy his own Christmas tree."

The waitress returns with a highchair, which she scrapes across the hardwood floor until it crashes into the side of the table.

* * *

By the time they've finished their lunch, the rain has eased off, and the clouds are beginning to thin. Instead of walking back along the beach, they decide to follow the road inland, where the gardens of the ramshackle bungalows are cluttered with rowboat planters, marble dolphins, and other sea-themed ornaments. Adam makes racing car noises as he weaves the stroller around deep, water-filled potholes, and Max chuckles as though it's the funniest thing ever. Sarah spots movement in one of the windows and sees the owner, an elderly woman, leaning on a walking stick. A few bungalows down, a husband and wife stand in their front window, dressed in Santa hats and matching Christmas sweaters. They're so still, she almost mistakes them for mannequins. On the opposite side of the road, she sees another face in the window—an old man with thick glasses. She waves at him, hoping he'll wave back or smile or do something to make the situation less weird. When he doesn't respond, Sarah hooks her arm around Adam's elbow and keeps her eyes fixed on the road.

Are these the same neighbors who chipped in to buy Adam's uncle the tree? She wouldn't be surprised.

Four years ago, council engineers unveiled plans to update the sea defenses between Happisburgh and Sea Palling. The proposal was cheaper than previous options, and the engineers were confident the government would provide the additional funding. For the Bush Estate residents, the work would see their properties protected for generations to come. With one exception, they urged the parish council to push forward with the plans. The exception was Adam's uncle, who argued the existing sea defenses would outlast him, so why should he care? He wanted the money invested in other community projects from which he might benefit or, better still, a reduction in his council tax. When the sea-defense proposal fell through, the residents of the Bush Estate felt aggrieved. They refused to speak to Howard and wouldn't even look at him when they passed him on the road. Instead, they left angry, anonymous notes in the letter box at the foot of his drive. On one occasion, they left the carcass of a dead bird—a headless, red-breasted robin. Then Christmas came around, and the season of goodwill prevailed. Howard's neighbors wanted to apologize, so they bought him a tree.

Adam told Sarah the whole story in the café, between mouthfuls of homemade steak and ale pie. When the waitress brought them the bill, she'd overcharged them.

❅ ❅ ❅

Sarah feels an enormous sense of relief when they arrive back at the bungalow. Adam says he's tired after the previous night's drive and retreats to the bedroom for a nap. Sarah leaves Max in front of the television and heads to the kitchen to phone her mom on the landline. Before the phone starts ringing, she hears the Christmas baubles banging together again. Max must have crawled over to the tree to play with the decorations. She returns to the lounge, but Max is still in front of the television, exactly where she'd left him.

Except there's tinsel wrapped around his waist.

"Sweetheart, you mustn't pull the decorations off the tree."

That's it. She's had enough. She isn't going to wait for Adam to wake up; she's going to dispose of the tree right now. If Adam complains, she'll invent some excuse about Max trying to climb it. He won't argue if their little boy's safety is at stake.

As she reaches through the branches to lift the tree, a sharp pain shoots through the back of her hand. She jerks away, almost tripping over the leg of a dining room chair. Her hand throbs. Blood trickles between her fingers. She searches the tree for sharp edges, half-expecting to find a length of barbed wire amongst the tinsel, but all she sees are decorations.

She sits down heavily and examines her hand, which feels fat and alien. There are two angry, red puncture wounds about an inch apart. Her stomach grumbles like pebbles shifting in the sea. Her mouth tastes like copper pennies. The spiders from her dream crawl back into her thoughts, and she can't seem to shake them off. The more she looks at her hand, the more she thinks she's having an allergic reaction. She pulls herself to her feet, and everything is wrong. The room tilts and twists without warning, and her legs don't move the way they're supposed to. The journey to the kitchen is a hellish fairground ride, and she only just makes it to the sink before she throws up. Thankfully, the medicine cabinet is well stocked. She drops the contents to the counter as she rummages in search of painkillers, antiseptic cream, and a blister pack of antihistamines. Her hands shake so badly she can barely lift the glass of water to her lips. Her tongue feels numb, and she finds it hard to swallow. She needs to sit down before she falls over.

Back in the lounge, she collapses on the sofa. She wants to wake Adam to show him her injury, but the bedroom is too far away. Max will be okay if she closes her eyes for a few minutes. She tips her head back against the armrest as the room starts to spin in a muddle of thoughts about decorations and dead birds and long-legged spiders with giant fangs and —

She opens her eyes.

There's no way she can let herself fall asleep without first covering the tree to make sure no one else hurts themselves. A trash bag would rip on the spiky branches. The spare blankets are all in the bedroom with Adam. She searches the room for inspiration and realizes she's sitting on the solution.

The throw on the sofa.

❋ ❋ ❋

Adam can't remember what he was dreaming, only that he woke up tangled in the bedclothes and sweating. The room smells fusty. He shoves the covers onto the other half of the bed and flips his pillow over so he can lie on the side that isn't damp, but it's too late. He's awake.

He opens the curtains to see if the weather's improved. The sky is pale gray with no hint of snow.

At the bottom of the garden, beyond the weather-beaten shed, a man stands on the narrow footpath that leads through the dunes toward the beach. He looks to be in his late fifties, with thinning hair, a scruffy beard, and the same cheerless expression as the waitress in the café. Under his raincoat, he wears a strawberry-red suit with white trim. It's not uncommon to see people walking past as they return to their properties, but the man in the red suit stands motionless, staring at the bungalow.

Adam steps away from the window. How long has the man been there? And why? He's probably lost, but if that's the case, why isn't he moving? Adam raises his hand and waves.

The man turns sharply and walks back toward the beach.

❅ ❅ ❅

Sarah is curled up on one of the armchairs, head cradled in the crook of her arm, feeling like she's slept for a week. How long was she out? She blinks to clear her eyes and searches the room until she finds Max standing by her legs, holding onto the armchair for support. "How are you doing, handsome?" she asks, lifting him onto her lap. "You've been such a good boy for Mommy."

She sifts through her memories, trying to make sense of the afternoon. Was she really sick in the sink? Did she really pass out on the armchair? If it weren't for the bruising on the back of her hand, she'd happily believe she'd had another bad dream.

She wants to tell Adam about it. She wants to ask him about the sofa, too. He should have been up by now, so where the hell is he? The holiday was supposed to bring them closer together, but she's beginning to think nothing has changed. Adam is still absent, and she's still stuck in front of the television, cuddling their baby boy. She closes her eyes and decides she'll deal with everything later.

"Everyone okay in here?"

Sarah opens her eyes again when she hears Adam's voice.

"Sarah?"

"Sorry, I... I can't seem to stay awake. What did you say?"

Adam grins as though all is right with the world. "I asked if you're okay."

"I'm... No, not really. Tell me again how your uncle died?"

"He had a heart attack. In Great Yarmouth."

"That's bullshit."

Adam looks like he's been slapped. "Please don't swear in front of Max."

"I'll stop swearing when you tell me the truth. Why is there blood on the sofa?"

Adam notices the naked sofa and the dark stains on the cushions. He frowns at the throw draped over the Christmas tree. "Okay, okay, you're right," he says, scratching his elbow. "I haven't been completely honest. I wanted this to be a great holiday for us. For Max's first Christmas. After I lost my job, I—."

"You've lost your job?"

"I was going to tell you."

Sarah finally understands why he's been aloof in recent weeks. She has so many thoughts, so many questions, but her tired mind can't keep up. She takes a breath and forces herself to say on topic. "We'll talk about that later. What I want to know right now is what happened to Howard. What *really* happened."

Adam looks deflated, like a week-old party balloon.

"I'm afraid the truth is… Nobody knows."

"But he didn't die in hospital."

Adam shakes his head.

"And the blood?"

"Are you sure you want to discuss this in front of Max?"

Max is engrossed in a curious version of the nativity story that seems to be set in the coal shed at the back of an abandoned hotel.

"He's not listening."

Adam rubs his forehead, trying to massage his thoughts into some sort of order. "Uncle Howard died here. In the bungalow. He had…wounds. Bite wounds. Lots of them."

"Snakes?" Sarah wants it to be snakes because she knows there are adders in the dunes, and adder bites can be treated.

Adam shrugs. "He was a mess when they found him. Bloated and bloody. " He fingers a tear from the corner of his eye. "After all the business with the sea defenses, the police suspected foul play. They investigated, but it didn't make any difference. Nothing was proven. The pathologist couldn't even identify the venom in his blood. He said there was more than one type."

"And they never found the things that bit him?"

"Not a trace."

"But you thought it would be a good idea to bring your family here? To a crime scene? Without telling me?"

"I didn't think you'd come if you knew."

"All the more reason to say something."

"It was a year ago, Sarah. There's nothing here. The police said so. Pest control said so. My cousin had the bungalow professionally fumigated. We're safe. Whatever killed Uncle Howard is long gone."

Sarah holds up her hand to show him the puncture wounds. "Are you sure?"

* * *

Adam stands on the patio and stares up into the night. The clouds have dispersed, and the sky is full of stars—more than he could ever hope to count. It's beautiful. Overwhelming. He hasn't believed in Santa Claus since he was a little boy, and yet he wouldn't be surprised to see a dozen flying reindeer pulling a sleigh full of presents. To accept the impossibility of the universe while rejecting the existence of a jolly old man in a red suit seems foolish.

He thinks back to his conversation with Sarah and decides she was being unfair. Yes, the wounds on the back of her hand looked like bites, but they could have been caused by anything. Bee stings. Mosquitos. She was probably bitten on the way back from the café. There was no reason to believe it was the tree or some invisible monster living in its branches, and there was certainly no reason for her ultimatum.

"I'm going to make this easy for you," she'd said. "Either the tree goes, or I'm taking Max home."

She had him at a disadvantage, and she knew it. He'd lied about his uncle's death. He'd kept his redundancy from her. All he could think was: *What kind of first Christmas will it be for Max if we aren't all together?* Trying to stay calm, he'd argued there must be another way. A compromise. What if he put the tree in the loft instead of the trash? Wouldn't that be just as good?

Sarah couldn't even agree to that without rolling her eyes.

Adam unpacks the presents from the trunk of the Avensis and carries them through to the lounge, where he stacks them against the wall in the space where the tree used to be. Four big boxes and three bags of smaller presents wrapped in a variety of golds and glittery reds. Most of them are for Max, who probably won't have a clue what's going on, but Adam doesn't care. The thought of helping his son rip the paper from his gifts is all that's kept him going in recent weeks.

Once he's finished arranging the presents, he steps back to admire his handiwork and realizes he's failed. The pile of Christmas presents looks pathetic hidden in the corner of the room. He could move them to another location, but they're never going to look as magical as they would have done if they were stacked around the base of a Christmas tree—especially one as resplendent as the one he transferred to the loft. That's the image he wants Max to see when he wakes up: tinsel and sparkle and presents for all the family.

If only Sarah had been more reasonable. Would it really have made any difference if they'd kept the tree up for one more night? Well, *fuck* that. The tree didn't bite him when he moved it.

He has an idea. It's so simple, it's perfect. All he needs to do is wait until Sarah goes to bed, and then he'll get to work.

He heads to the kitchen to pour himself a celebratory sherry.

❆ ❆ ❆

Sarah dreams of things with legs. Her mother is in the hallway, hair disheveled, hurrying between the lounge and the bedroom. She pleads with Sarah to get out of bed before it's too late, saying she doesn't have time to sleep, that her only hope of salvation is to bag up the Christmas tree and toss it into the North Sea. Sarah can't listen, not now, not while things are crawling over her stomach, her chest, her neck. When she feels something on her face, she swipes at it. She knows there's nothing there, it's just a dream, and yet her fingers connect with something solid.

She sits up when she hears a loud *thock* next to the bed.

The room is dark and silent. She blinks the sleep from her eyes and checks her bedside table to see if she knocked something to the floor. Everything is where she left it. She rolls over to find out if Adam heard anything, but he isn't there. She climbs out from under the duvet to look for whatever made the noise.

At the foot of her bed, in the middle of the floor, is a burgundy bauble. Adam must have dropped it when he put the Christmas tree in the loft. She bends down to pick it up and the bauble rolls away from her. She steps back, startled. Is Adam playing a trick on her? The bauble's movement was so fast, so deliberate, it seemed like it was being tugged—although she can't see any thread. Maybe she caught it with her foot and kicked it across the floor. Again, she reaches down to pick it up. Again, the bauble rolls away from her.

"What the...?"

The bauble stands up on eight shiny legs. Its mouth opens to reveal great pincer-like fangs extending from its lower mandible. Sarah can't see anything resembling eyes, although the bauble appears to be aware of her presence. It takes a couple of tentative steps toward her. When she doesn't retreat, it scurries toward the bedroom door, its little legs clacking together.

She thinks it must be some sort of novelty gift. Adam's probably in the lounge, drunk, and grinning to himself, controlling the bauble spider with an app on his mobile phone. Something about the season always brings out the child in him. She feels the heat rising in her cheeks. Her fingers clench to fists. After everything that's happened, how can he imagine this is a good idea?

She ties her dressing gown around her waist and rushes into the darkness of the hall, only to be smacked in the head by something hard and sharp. She stumbles backward, lights flashing in her eyes, and buries her face in her hands. When the pain subsides, she wipes the tears from her cheeks and looks up to see what hit her. There's a gaping black hole in the ceiling, and the long tongue of a ladder reaches down to the carpeted floor of the hallway.

"Oh, Adam," she whispers. "What have you done?"

She opens the lounge door, and the first thing she notices is the Christmas tree in the corner of the room. It's back, and it's alive like a freshly disturbed ant nest. The baubles have all become spiders with paper-thin legs scuttling along the branches. Lengths of tinsel slither like snakes around the trunk. She stares in disbelief, searching for a rational explanation and finding nothing.

The second thing she notices is Adam, slumped on the sofa. Angry purple blotches cover his arms. His head has fallen backward, and saliva foams between his lips. His neck is swollen and riddled with bright pink puncture wounds. He isn't moving; he doesn't even appear to be breathing, but every time the bauble spiders sink their fangs into his body, he spasms as though he's being electrocuted. The worst thing is his hands, which lie limp in his lap, curled around an empty sherry glass. They tell the story of a husband sitting down at the end of a long day to relax and unwind with his favorite Christmas drink. Set against the chaotic carnival of the lounge, the sight of the sherry glass is so normal, so typically Adam, it hurts.

She needs to help him. If she's quick, she might save him. She's about to cross the room when she notices the trio of tinsel snakes sliding across the rug toward her. Like cobras, they rear their heads and fan their hoods wide. The way they move is exaggerated and unnatural, as though their brains haven't fully learned how to control their muscles. Their tinsel skin shimmers, making them appear even more dangerous. She hears them hissing. She sees their forked tongues flicking between glossy lips. She only just manages to close the lounge door before they lunge.

There's nowhere near enough oxygen in the hallway. Sarah stumbles away from the door, gasping for breath, her body trembling in shock. Shapes seem to move in the shadows, and something scuttles around the open lips of the loft. She falls against the ladder and digs her nails into her arms, hoping the pain will wake her from this nightmare, but her chest grows tighter until she can barely breathe at all.

And then Max cries out.

She rushes into his room and finds a burgundy bauble spider in his crib, its metal legs exploring his chubby cheeks, its fangs uncurling, ready to bite. Without hesitating, she bats the spider away from her son's head and smothers it with a knitted blanket. The spider tries to fight its way free, but its legs become entangled in the woolen weave until it can't move. She lifts it from the cot and smashes it repeatedly against the wardrobe door.

Max's body is warm inside his sleeping bag, and he doesn't appear to have been bitten. She holds him tightly to her chest, promising she'll never let him go. He coos, blinks drunkenly, and falls back to sleep against her shoulder.

There are two ways out of the bungalow: the French windows or the side door in the kitchen. Both options involve crossing the lounge. If she's going to stand any chance at all, Sarah needs something to protect her from the snakes. In the linen closet, she pulls flannels and pillowcases off the shelves, searching for anything that might help. And then she finds what she's looking for: a large beach towel. She's about to close the door when she spots a pair of wellington boots tucked under the bottom shelf. They're too big, but she stuffs the sides with flannels and pillowcases until they're snug around her calves.

With Max in one hand and the beach towel in the other, she returns to the lounge. Something has changed. The room smells different—acidic, noxious. On the sofa, Adam's head lolls forward. One of his eyes is swollen shut, and there's a large, lumpy, black stain down the front of his t-shirt where he's been sick.

Sarah whimpers as a tinsel snake sinks its fangs into Adam's calf. She imagines the snake's teeth piercing her own flesh and muscle before scraping against her bone. The thought of it makes her squirm.

Adam doesn't even stir.

The other snakes slither toward her, rearing up, ready to strike. The beach towel feels utterly inadequate—a poor choice of weapon against such deadly creatures. The snakes hiss when she steps onto the rug. Heart pounding, she takes a second step, and then a third. The Avensis keys are on the dining room table, almost within reach. She takes another step and the nearest snake lunges at her, its fangs ripping through the thick cotton of the beach towel. Sarah screams in surprise and throws the towel across the room, buying enough time to snatch the car keys from the table and open the curtains to the patio doors.

Outside, there are people. Lots of people.

At first, she thinks they're part of a rescue party. She counts five on the drive, two in the garden next door, and four more on the road. Instead of flashlights, they cradle tealights in their hands. By these slivers of light, she can make out their padded red suits with giant buttons and fluffy, white trim. On their heads they wear floppy Santa hats and fake bushy beards. She twists the handle but doesn't open the door. Something is wrong. From the way the Santas are standing, spread out to cover as much ground as possible, it looks as though they're waiting for her, ready to stop her if she makes a run for it.

Sarah feels beaten, paralyzed by fear.

Oblivious to the dangers around him, Max reaches out to stroke her face, his little hand soft against her skin. He stares at her with his large blue eyes, his lips curling into a smile. He looks so much like his father, like the man she'd hoped to spend the rest of her life with. This is what she needs. She's may not be a fighter, but she's a mother. She can't give up yet.

She runs back through the lounge. The tinsel snakes lunge at her, the first two falling short, the third managing to sink its teeth into her boot. She doesn't stop; she doesn't even slow down until she's safely in the kitchen. Then she slams the door repeatedly against the snake's body until it releases its grip and falls limp. With all the padding in her boot, its fangs didn't breach her skin.

She searches the kitchen for a weapon—anything she can use to hold the Santas at bay until she's made it to the Avensis. A saucepan. A rolling pin. Better yet, a knife. She pulls the knives from the rack and soon finds a chef's knife with a decent length and heft. The blade isn't as sharp as it could be, but that doesn't matter. It's only for show.

She unlocks the backdoor and steps out onto the narrow path that runs alongside the bungalow. A man emerges from the shadows, pulling his fake beard down below his chin. His face is pale and gaunt, his eyes lost in pools of shadow. "You should never have come here," he says. "Your family isn't welcome, not after what Howard did to us." He takes another step forward, and Sarah recognizes him as the man with the thick glasses she saw on her walk home from the café. His glasses are gone, and without them, he looks like Death in a Santa costume. "But now you're here, and I'm afraid we can't let you leave. You've seen too much. Please go back inside. Don't make this harder than it needs to be."

Sarah doesn't reply. She doesn't have the energy. Instead, she marches toward him, Max clutched tightly against her chest, the knife held low by her side.

The man raises his hands defensively. "Think of your child."

Sarah isn't sure what happens next. It's as though a barrier breaks in her mind—the one she built to contain her fears, her nightmares, and the reality of her husband's body slumped on the sofa. She feels herself rising high up into the night where the air is cooler and the sky is filled with infinite and incomprehensible wonders. Below her, she sees the residents in their ridiculous Santa costumes. She sees the man at the end of the path, his hands raised because he doesn't want a fight. He looks old and frail and vulnerable. She knows what she needs to do.

Before the man can utter another word, she stabs him in the stomach, driving the knife as deep as it will go. His eyes widen. His mouth opens and closes. A thin line of spittle falls from his bottom lip.

"I'm sorry," she says. "I'm so, so sorry."

The man doubles over, wheezing, his arms held around his torso. He backs away from her, trips, and falls to the ground, his breath leaving him in wispy white clouds.

"Bitch," he groans. "How…could…you?"

The other Santas surround him. In the light from the bungalow, Sarah recognizes their faces: the husband and wife with matching Christmas sweaters; the woman with the walking stick; the waitress from the café.

The waitress scowls. "I knew you were trouble. I knew your family was going to ruin Christmas. That's why I spat in your husband's gravy."

Without thinking, Sarah stabs the waitress between the ribs. The young woman stares at her, shocked and confused, and then falls face first into a flower bed at the edge of the drive.

Sarah holds the knife up to the remaining Santas. "You did this," she says. "You put those creatures in the bungalow. You killed Adam's uncle. You deserve to go to hell for what you've done." She edges towards the Avensis, sweeping the knife from side to side so no one will see how much she's shaking.

The Santas watch but don't move.

Sarah's nostrils fill with the scent of pine from the air freshener hanging around the rearview mirror. She locks the door behind her and drops the knife onto the passenger seat before transferring Max into the back. His sleeping bag is covered with long streaks of red. Sarah panics, thinking he's hurt, and then she sees the blood on her own hand—the one that held the knife. It isn't Max's blood. It isn't hers either. Feeling relieved and more than a little nauseous, she wipes her palms on her dressing gown and starts the engine.

The Santas in the road step forward to block the gate, but Sarah doesn't stop. The car shudders as it catches one of them on the hip. She clips another with the passenger-side wing mirror.

Once she's free, she bumps along the roads, driving as fast as she dares, turning right and then left until she can see the edge of the estate and the long, straight road leading out of Eccles. The first milestone on their journey to safety.

She doesn't see the pothole until the car has bounced up and crunched back down, concrete scraping the underside of the chassis, the whole vehicle lurching sideways before coming to a halt. Sarah's head collides with the window in the driver's door hard enough to leave a ringing in her ears. Everything else falls silent, as though the world is holding its breath, waiting to see what she will do next.

Sarah touches her fingers to the lump on her forehead and winces. Outside, the night shifts restlessly as hedges rustle in the breeze. In the back of the car, Max begins to wail. And there's another noise. Quiet, threatening. It's the sound of footsteps on gravel. Lots of them.

Sarah checks the rear-view mirror and sees half a dozen Santas marching around the corner, carrying forks, spades, *For Sale* signs, and rotary washing lines. Any makeshift weapon they've been able to liberate from the gardens they've passed.

"Shit."

The car's engine has stalled. She thumbs the ignition, muttering words of encouragement under her breath and praying she hasn't punctured a tire or crunched the suspension. The Santas move closer, their weapons raised. They don't seem to be in any hurry, and this scares her even more.

They think they've won.

They think they're going to drag her and Max back to the bungalow.

She thumbs the ignition again, and this time the engine catches.

"Fuck you," she screams at the reflections in her mirror. "Fuck all of you!" She slams her palm against the car horn and lets it scream into the night. Then she eases the car out of the pothole, over-revving, terrified she's going to stall again.

There's a sharp crack as one of the Santas strikes the roof of her car with the edge of a spade. He prepares to strike again, but Sarah pulls away. Seconds later, fields and hedgerows flash past as she races down the long, straight road toward Lessingham.

Lessingham is little more than a handful of red-brick cottages and a pub, all decorated with gaudy Christmas lights and figurines. It's too close to Eccles-on-Sea to be safe. She doesn't stop in the village of Ingham for the same reason. Instead, she presses on toward the nearest town.

Stalham High Street is lit from one end to the other with cheery Christmas lights. Sarah is appalled by how normal it seems. In a few hours' time, families across the country will come together to exchange gifts and carve turkeys. At the same time, she'll be stuck in the police station, trying to explain the impossible while waiting for her mom to rescue Max. So many people she loves are going to have their Christmas days tarnished because of her misadventures. They just don't know it yet.

She keeps driving until she sees the giant Tesco sign on the edge of the town. She doesn't want to stop because she doesn't feel safe, but she needs to call the emergency services and send help to the bungalow.

To Adam.

She knows he's dead. On some level, she hopes he's dead because then he won't be in pain anymore. She doesn't know how anyone could come back from all that suffering and ever be the same again.

She steers the Avensis to a halt in front of the supermarket. By the time she's freed her phone from her dressing gown pocket, her hands are shaking so badly she can barely dial 9-9-9. Behind her, Max chirps happily in his seat. She adjusts the rear-view mirror so she can watch him while she's on the phone.

And that's when she sees it.

In Max's little hands.

A burgundy Christmas bauble.

Y✷ANKEE S✷WAP

John M. McIlveen

"**L**✷eaving already?"

Damn it! Kat cursed inwardly, cringing as if pincers had claimed the back of her neck.

Randy Oberlein was the personification of "insufferable." The son of affluent socialites, he was born with a silver spoon inserted so far up his ass he could stir his pancreas. It meant nothing to him that Kat was engaged and very much in love. *And pregnant,* she mentally added, although it didn't show yet.

As assistant division manager, Randy was her superior, which put her in an undesirable position as a subordinate. She was a purchasing manager, a station she had been proud of… until she'd actually started the job.

Randy wanted her—had for months—and as far as he was concerned, she was his right…his entitlement. Evidently, "no" was a word he was not accustomed to and had difficulty acknowledging. She had considered reporting him, but he was as sly as he was arrogant, and the best offense she could present was a *he said/ she said* scenario she feared would cost her her job. Her lack of action or reaction only seemed to encourage him.

Randy was the primary reason she had dreaded attending the holiday party, but she'd felt obligated to show up. That it was held in the DoubleTree Suites ballroom had made her more apprehensive. The smug bastard surely had a room reserved and expected her to throw herself upon the mercy of his unhinged whims.

Unfortunately, Kat's fiancé, Vernon, was in Singapore doing whatever it was field engineers did, otherwise he would have been here with her and for her and for their baby. Kat could envision him, with his rugged gunslinger's confidence and overprotective daddy-swagger, planting a size-eleven boot against Randy's forehead. She calmed herself but didn't look at the greasy bastard, instead focusing on the memory of Vernon's glowing smile when Kat showed him the two thick, pink lines on the pregnancy test. His eyes shone as he joked about trading in the Harley for a minivan and designer diaper bag. He had posed like a fashion model and asked her if she'd still find him irresistibly sexy with a baby in a papoose strapped to his chest.

"Leaving already?" Randy repeated, as if she hadn't heard him the first time.

"Yes. I'm not a fan of crowds or loud parties," she said, knowing it sounded like the bullshit it was and that he saw right through it. She remained composed. What she truly wanted to do was embed the pointy toe of her Franco Sarto pumps into his grapes.

"I've rented a top-floor suite. We could go there if you'd like to be someplace quieter."

Bingo!

"No. I really have to go...somewhere."

"Are you okay to drive? I can give you a lift."

"I'm fine," Kat said. "I didn't drink anything." She clutched her dinner purse tightly between her arm and ribs and headed for the door. As expected, Randy fell into step beside her.

You fucking fatheaded snake, she thought, and realized that was exactly what he reminded her of, with his large forehead that tapered down to sunken cheeks, and those black beady eyes. He was a dangerous, cold-blooded serpent. He was a cobra.

Shaking inside and out with fear and anger, Kat stopped abruptly, her eyes locked on the floor before her. "Stop—following—me!" she said, assertively enough that a few heads turned toward them.

Randy noticed, too. He held his hands up and took a step away from her in a show of harmless submission, but his hostile eyes promised she would pay for her defiance.

Kat rushed forward, through the ballroom doorway and away from him. She claimed her coat from the check, walked past a bank of elevators, and shoved open the heavy steel door that opened into the parking facility. She was taken aback by the painfully frigid winds that sliced through the garage, unhindered it seemed, from the Charles River. With her notoriously poor sense of direction, she naturally was disoriented. By the time she found her car, her face and fingers were in agony, and she cursed herself for not bringing gloves and a hat...mussed hair be damned.

The blow that caught Kat on the back of the head was sharp and unexpected. She had not heard anyone approaching, and her single thought before she lost consciousness was, *Randy.*

❄ ❄ ❄

A rattling sound brought her around. When she tried to move her head, the pain defined her and owned her, radiating from the back of her neck, over the top of her head, and across her shoulders. A woman cried despondently from nearby, her sobs repetitive and shrill, piercing. Kat wanted her to shut the fuck up before the sound split her skull. She thought she might be in the hospital and tried raising her left arm to feel the small but reassuring swell of her belly, but something metal and unforgiving restrained her movement. She yanked, and there was a tightening around the front of her legs, and her other arm was tugged downward.

She opened her eyes to nearly complete darkness, except for a small red light that blinked about every five seconds. Although bright, it seemed distant and offered little help. She couldn't see what bound her arms, but it rattled like heavy, steel chains. She panicked and yanked, ignoring the nauseating pain that flared up her neck and into her skull, driving her to tears. She was seated, her hands tethered to each by a chain strung beneath her chair. Any movement of one arm was countered by pressure on the front of her legs and a pulling on the other arm.

"Ain't no use," said a man's voice, originating from a few feet in front of her. "Just going to fuck your wrists up, is all."

Kat tensed. Her nerves buzzed with anxiety, and she expected to be touched—or worse—at any moment and from any direction. *This is bad,* she thought.

"Randy?"

"No, ma'am."

"Who are you? What do you want?" she demanded with a fear-fueled bravado she wasn't feeling.

"I'm Shep. I'm not the one who did this to you, if that's

what you're thinking," he said. "Or I wouldn't be sitting here chained to a fucking chair, either."

"Who did this? What do they want? Why..."

"Whoa there, cupcake. I don't know any more than you do," Shep said. "I woke up like this a couple hours ago, I guess...hard to tell. Head's splitting. Last thing I remember was closing up my office. Fucker said 'excuse me,' and when I turned to him, he popped me good on the head. Sounded like Richard Simmons, the twisted little prick who did this."

Shep didn't sound scared, which had Kat suspicious despite his words. She was terrified, her breathing elevated, and she teetered on the edge of hysterics, though not like the woman still blubbering miserably somewhere to her left. She was incoherent, but her deep, hoarse cries made Kat think she was a mature woman of fifty or more.

"Hey," Kat called to her, "can you give it a rest?"

"Yeah, don't bother. She's zoned out," he said. "And if she doesn't stop carrying on that way, I'll be going over the fucking edge, too. By the way, if he strung you up the same way he did me, you should be able to free a foot or more play for your arms by lifting your legs over the chain. It's work, but it's worth it."

It took Kat a couple minutes, but Shep was right; the small freedom was nearly blissful.

"Christ, I have to go to the bathroom," said a young woman at Kat's near right. *Or maybe it was a teen, or maybe a boy.*

"That there's Gwen," said Shep. "Name's about all I could get out of her; I think she's in shock."

A man to Kat's right released a contemptuous chuff, startling her. He sounded near enough to touch.

"Who's that...? Is that him?" Kat sputtered, leaning away from where the sound had come.

"No. He's been fading in and out for a while, but that

snort sounded like derision. It's dark as unholy fuck in here, but there are five of us, maybe six," said Shep. "I tried centering in on the breathing."

The man near Kat moaned in agony. *"Mierda,"* he mumbled, a word Kat was familiar with. Chains rattled softly, and then more determinedly. "What the fuck? What's with the chains, man? This some kind of joke or something?"

"No joke, hombre. Asshole's got a bunch of us penned up here in the dark," said Shep. "Took my phone. Reckon he took the rest of yours, too."

"What does he want?" asked the man.

"Fuck if I know," said Shep. "You Mexican or something? What's your name?"

"Miguel. I'm Dominican, but why the fuck does that matter?" he answered, and then said, "Come on, lady, shit's bad enough without you squealing like that, you know?"

"Please?" Kat said. It was getting on her nerves, too. The woman kept at it.

"How about you? What's your name," asked Shep, and it took a while before Kat realized the question was directed at her.

"Kat," she said. "Katrina."

"You got an accent, too," said Shep. "Fucked if I can tell where from, though."

"Philippines," said Kat. "You like that word, don't you?"

"What word?"

"The F word," said Kat.

"Fucking right I do."

She actually smiled, not that anyone benefited from it.

"Seems we got us an ethnic smorgasbord… a Philippine, a Dominican, a Texan, a Gwen, and by the sounds of it, a banshee," Shep said. "Maybe he's putting together some kind of collection. A set. Any of it make sense to y'all?"

"I'm black," said a nervous voice to Kat's right, somewhere between Shep and Gwen. "If he's collecting..."

"That you, Gwen?"

"No. I'm Delanna."

"That's a new one on me. Well, howdy, Delanna. I'd shake your hand, but that ain't in the cards right now. How long you been eavesdropping?" asked Shep.

"Fifteen minutes or so. Trying to evaluate the situation," she said.

"Any luck?" asked Shep.

"No," she admitted.

"HOLY FUCKING CHRIST, LADY, SHUT UP!"

The room fell into a dead hush; even the keening woman became silent. What was more unexpected than the sudden shriek was it had come from the one named Gwen.

"Amen," Miguel whispered gratefully.

They sat for an immeasurable amount of time, appreciating the quiet, when the room burst into blinding light. They all cowered, lowering their heads and covering their eyes as much as their fastened hands would allow. Although it seemed to Kat as if a bank of stadium lights were turned directly on them, by the time her eyes adjusted, it was difficult to believe that only six standard incandescent lightbulbs on a wagon-wheel chandelier and two or three strands of Christmas lighting could provide that brilliance.

They sat in matching chairs around a large, round, distressed-wood table. Each of them was equally distant from each other and the table, but all beyond reach due to their manacles and chains. The room was rectangular, with double windows on either side. An opaque material covered the glass, making it impossible to determine whether it was day or night. Kitschy Christmas decorations festooned the place, beneath which was a Southwest decor. Kat wondered how far they were from Boston and if Shep, Southern accent and all, was as innocent as he professed.

At the far end of the room was a door, but no windows. To the left of the door—behind Shep—was a sideboard with a lamp and a nativity scene, complete with baby Jesus and the full cast of characters. Beside the manger was the source of the blinking red light—a small desktop cam, the likes of which you could purchase from Best Buy for fifty bucks.

Kat looked at the five people who sat around the table and saw that they were all just as screwed as she was. Facing her from across the table, Shep was easy to recognize with his blue denim shirt and thick mustache on a weathered face that might have been handsome if he hadn't been so gaunt. Wholesome Delanna sat directly to Shep's left, staring back at Kat with frightened but intelligent eyes. She looked barely old enough for college.

Miguel, directly to Kat's left and across from Delanna, leaned forward, only his wavy black hair visible as he searched beneath his chair, trying to decipher the mechanics of his confinement.

"Son of a bitch," he said. "Chains trapped by the support rails. No slipping out of this, man."

He had intense black eyes, a rugged body, and thick arms, both of them sleeved with intricate tattoos. He intimidated Kat. Although she hated to admit it, he was the kind of man she would not meet eyes with in public and completely avoid in a dark alleyway.

The familiar, high keening emanated from the woman to Miguel's left. She lowered her head and managed to fan herself with one hand, a generous hammock of fat swinging loosely beneath her upper arm. Probably in her late sixties and easily two-fifty, Kat would have wagered a week's pay that the woman had twin teacup poodles named Mitzy and Fitzy at home that yipped incessantly at nothing in particular. Her eyes were red and swollen above bloated cheeks covered with a patina of tears and snot.

"Oh, don't fucking start that shit again," said the petite woman to Kat's right.

It was intriguing, such aggression coming from such a tiny woman with so adolescent a voice. If Gwen broke ninety pounds, Kat would have been surprised. Alabaster skin, hair dyed coal black—with matching black fingernail polish and lipstick—she was a teen Goth dream come true. Yet on closer inspection, Kat detected lines near her mouth and eyes that gave evidence of someone years older.

"Agreed," said Shep. "How about telling us your name there, Buttercup?"

The keening woman didn't answer, only carried on sniveling.

Fear dominated the table, but Kat saw something underneath the others' terror that kept her from dissolving into a hopeless, blubbering mess like...well, like "Buttercup."

Shep looked like a doer, constantly scanning the room for answers and a means to escape, as did Miguel, but Miguel also was a mover, pulling at the chair arms, trying to manipulate the chains. If they were to get free, Kat figured she would follow his lead. Delanna looked as confounded as Kat felt, though sentient, and Gwen just looked utterly pissed off.

Kat turned in her chair as far as the restraints would allow and looked behind her. A large Christmas tree, heavily swathed with lights and ornaments as generic and tacky as she had ever seen, stood to the right of another door. Beneath the tree, presents of various sizes lay across the floor in a haphazard offering. Further to the right, cornered with the windowed wall, was a small side table on which was set another camera that winked ominously.

"We're being watched," Kat said.

The far door slammed open, crashing heavily into the side-board. A figure leaped into the room and flung its arms sky-ward. "Correctamundo!" he blurted, and then took a moment to look at each one of them. "Oh, look at you all...so adorable!"

He wore a red mid-length jacket with a white fur collar, green tights, and a wide black belt that cinched his middle. On his head was a pointed red cap that bent to the left a third of the way down. The Santa's helper getup might have been cute and even disarming, if not for a hideous rubber goblin mask, which made the whole display terrifying. Butter-cup crescendoed into a completely new level of wailing.

"What the fuck?" Shep said upon seeing this display.

"Oh, we're going to have so much fun!" The masked odd-ity skipped closer to them. "I'm Flea...get it? Backward it's A-E-L-F, a elf." He sounded proud of himself.

His voice was high and did have a Richard Simmons in-tonation to it, as Shep had mentioned, but Kat thought it sound-ed contrived.

"An elf," Gwen corrected, her lip slightly lifted in a sneer.

Flea's grotesque face snapped in Gwen's direction, and he scuttled behind her.

"Oh, are we *an* English teacher?" Through unseen eyes, he watched her intently, swaying slightly. "No, honey, you're *a* tattoo artist and I'm still Flea because I said so...so there."

He touched Gwen lightly on the head with his index fin-ger and hurriedly moved around the table to Buttercup's side. He leaned close to her, their faces inches apart. His circus clown theatrics gave him unsettling stop-motion intensity.

"What's wrong, my blubbery, blubbering butterball?" he asked, his tone syrupy sweet.

Buttercup stared at the grotesque mask, quivering and snif-fling, her fingers fumbling nervously among themselves.

"BOO!" Flea screamed in her face and then pranced off, giggling maniacally.

Buttercup squealed childishly and managed to squeeze her girth deeper into the chair.

"Why are you doing this?" Kat asked.

"Oh, isn't that obvious? 'Tis the season, sweetheart." Flea spun, raised his arms in a less-than-impressive pirouette, and sang, "It's the most wonderful time of the year."

"Pardon me there, amigo, but what the fuck are you talking about?" asked Shep.

Flea stopped spinning and faced Shep. "Christmas, silly! It's the season for giving, and I've got gifts for all of you to open!"

He clasped his hands together and dashed to the Christmas tree, squatted, lifted three of the gifts, and carried them to the table. He set them neatly at the center and repeated the process.

"There! Isn't this fun! We're going to have a Yankee swap!"

He patted Miguel atop the head. Miguel recoiled, and Flea, unperturbed, skittered around the table. He situated himself behind Gwen, grabbed ahold of her chair, and slid her closer to the table. He repeated the process with the five remaining chairs and their occupants. To Kat, it seemed he moved Shep's, Miguel's, and Buttercup's chairs just as easily as Gwen's.

Stationing himself behind Delanna, he merrily clapped his hands together. "So...does everyone know the rules for a Yankee swap?" he asked and waited. "Come *on*, people, somebody answer me!"

"Fuck you," Shep muttered.

"Oh, I don't think so."

Flea quickly maneuvered behind Shep and ran a hand affectionately over his head. The Texan's eyes widened, and his entire body began convulsing as a rivulet of drool ran over his bottom lip and fell to his shirt, forming a dark blue Rorschach pattern.

Buttercup amped up her squealing, and Miguel let out a dismayed "fuck," trying to scoot backward in his chair. They all stared at Shep in dismay, and then at Flea, when he proudly displayed a black device to them.

"Nothing inspires cooperation like one of these...they're stunning, if you'll pardon the pun. Whether you want to or not, you're *all* going to cooperate." He put the stun gun in his coat pocket; his left one, Kat noted.

"Okay, sunshine, time to come back. You need to hear the rules," Flea said cheerily, as if speaking to a toddler. He slapped Shep's cheeks lightly. Shep groaned and glared at him. Flea cocked his head disturbingly to one side and then righted himself.

"Good!" he said dismissively. "So the rules *are*...the participants—that means all of you—draw numbers." Flea drew a handful of papers from a pocket on his jacket, removed his cap, and pushed them inside. "I *love* this! Okay! Whoever draws number *one* goes first and opens a gift from the pile. Number two then opens a gift. If he or she prefers the gift number one opened, he or she can *trade* for that one instead." He paused thoughtfully. "You know what? Fuck it; I'll tell you the rules as we go."

His masked face regarded each person seated around the table, moving from one to the next with a jerking motion that reminded Kat of a bird, especially with the black hollows of the mask's eyeholes that betrayed nothing of the man inside. The goblin face abruptly jolted and faced Kat, and with a flourish of the wrist, he pointed at her.

"You first!" he said. He bounced to her side and held the opened cap toward her.

Kat looked at the faces of the others seated around the

table. In their eyes, she encountered terror, hatred, anger, and hopelessness, but not the salvation or inspiration she thought she'd seen earlier. That he had chosen her to go first was a terrible omen that seemed to validate her fear of not leaving there alive.

"Ka-at, pick a number," Flea said in a singsong voice, bisecting her name into two syllables.

She was frozen. She couldn't move or speak but only stared at the collection of gifts centered on the table and Delanna's countenance in the hazy background, slowly shaking her head in fearful denial. Seeing no alternative, Kat slowly reached a shaky hand into the hat and pulled out a square of paper. The rest of them followed suit as Flea moved clockwise around the table.

"Okay, kiddies, unfold your papers and tell me who has number one." He rubbed his hands and shuffled around the table. "Who is it? Who is it? Oh, who is it, already, or do I have to get zap-happy?"

"I do," Delanna whispered.

"Ooooh, hooray!" Flea said with delight. He capered over to her and plucked the paper from her fingers. "Okay…pick a gift!"

Delanna stared at the colorful packages, saying nothing.

"Come on!" Flea cajoled.

Silence.

"PICK A FUCKING GIFT!" Flea erupted. It started as a shriek and ended as a throaty growl. Everyone around the table started, and Buttercup recommenced her soggy sniveling. Kat heard insanity in his words, but they resonated in the back of her mind, as if they had awakened something familiar yet out of reach.

"The blue one," Delanna said, her voice no more than a whisper.

"Snowflakes or *Frozen*?" asked Flea.

"Snowflakes."

Flea grabbed the chosen package and tossed it to Delanna, who mechanically caught it, her chains rattling with the quick movement.

Half-crouched, rapt, and looking ready to bolt, Flea watched her. "Open it," he said with childish impatience.

Delanna cautiously pulled at a silver ribbon as if afraid it would explode. Within the wrapper was a small box. Delanna opened it and removed some tissue and a small prescription bottle.

"Whatcha get—whatcha get?" Flea asked excitedly.

"Pills?" Delanna said cautiously, sounding more like a question.

"Yes! Well, capsules actually, but not just any capsules... those are special *Jesus* capsules. They'll take *all* your pains and worries away," said Flea. "And there are six of them, in case you're in the giving spirit. Sharing is caring! What a wonderful gift! I'll even open them for you."

He did so, setting the bottle and cap on the table before her.

"I really have to piss," Gwen said again.

"Me, too," added Miguel.

"Be my guest," Flea offered amiably, dismissing them. "Okay, who's next?" After a short silence, he patted his left pocket. "Number two-ooo. Zap zap!"

"Yup," said Shep. He crumpled the paper and tossed it to the center of the table.

"I'm so looking forward to you!" Flea gushed, enthusiastically clapping his hands.

"I'm sure you are," Shep muttered.

"All right, cowboy, make a choice."

Shep sneered at their twisted host and said, "The flat one."

"Ooooh!" Flea brought the chosen gift to Shep and set it down.

Shep slowly opened the package and from inside the slender box withdrew an old hacksaw with a black Bakelite handle and a rusted blue blade.

"Oh, what have we here?" Flea said. "It looks a little worn. I doubt it would cut metal, but in a pinch, it could still work for you."

Flea grabbed the saw from Shep and dragged it across the man's exposed arm, leaving an angry red gash. Shep recoiled and hollered in pain. He pressed his wounded arm against his abdomen, leaving a bloody streak on the denim. His jaw tightened and his face darkened as he defiantly tried to compose himself. Buttercup, in contrast, launched into another bout of squealing cries.

"Such a *handy* gift, if you catch my drift," Flea said.

Buttercup's wails escalated, and Flea's head dropped and his shoulders sunk. He set the hacksaw down before Shep and walked purposefully around the table to stand behind the squealing woman.

"You are ruining our *fun*," he admonished her. There followed a high-pitched report, like the snapping of a dry branch. They all jumped, and Delanna yelped in surprise at the gunshot. Buttercup's body went rigid as her right eye blossomed red, then she slumped to her side, silent and still. Eyes wide, mouth agape, Kat watched Flea switch the small pistol to his right hand and pocket it. Despite her shock, she had the absurd realization he was left-handed.

"Why the fuck you do that, man?" Miguel demanded, disbelieving.

"She was such a party pooper," Flea said with embellished pathos. Recovering quickly, he clapped his hands. "Look at the bright side! We have an extra gift!"

Kat couldn't take her eyes off Buttercup. They had turned a corner. Reality shifted. She knew the potential of death was present, but she had wrapped herself safely within denial until then. A series of panicked thoughts scrolled through her mind and the awareness that they had never found out her name.

"So, cowboy, are you keeping your gift, or do you want to trade with Delanna for her capsules?" Flea asked.

Shep stared coldly at him. "I'm good," he said. His arm was still pressed against his shirt, but judging by the stains, he wasn't bleeding much.

"Now we're back on track! Who's number three-eee?"

"Yo," said Gwen, holding the paper loosely between thumb and forefinger, trying to appear unfazed. The fast rise and fall of her chest betrayed her terror.

"Yo-ho-ho, Gweno!" sang Flea. "Pick a gift, sweetie pie."

Something in the way he said her name troubled Kat.

Yo-ho-ho, Gweno!

Gwen's eyes shifted to the goblin face, and Kat thought she saw recognition in the other woman's eyes. "*Frozen,*" Gwen said, suspiciously watching the demon mask, searching.

"Adorable!" Flea clapped again, a frenzy of hand pats.

Gwen… Gweno, Kat thought.

Flea delivered the box to Gwen, his hip brushing Kat's arm. She recoiled impulsively, as if his corruption could leach through her clothing and flesh and contaminate her. Flea's head jerked toward her, and Kat hoped he felt threatened, if only for two seconds. She sensed—or more so, smelled—a faint whiff of cologne. It was one she recognized…one she both loved and hated. It was so manly and stimulating on Vernon, so cloying on Randy, but downright nauseating on this piece of shit.

"Lacoste," Kat said.

"What?" Flea asked.

"Lacoste," Kat repeated. "Your cologne. You're wearing Lacoste Essential."

He froze for a moment, and Kat knew she had shaken him and wished she could see his face behind the mask.

"Open your gift," he said to Gwen, a little less vibrant. She accepted the package, her frightened eyes never leaving the mask. He seemed to notice the scrutiny.

"Yes?" he asked her with a tilt of his head, his voice chipper yet wary. Gwen didn't answer. "Open your gift," he repeated, his voice deeper under the gravity of threat.

Gweno. Gwen the Ho, Kat thought. *Gweno... tattoo artist... Lacoste Essential... left-handed.*

Gwen opened the package and removed a small Igloo cooler, inside of which was a single box cutter that, like the hacksaw, had a rusty blade.

Flea, returning to form, gasped with glee. "Isn't the cooler delightful, sticking with the *Frozen* theme that way? And a box cutter! It would work great on those pasty white wrists of yours. Now all three of you have an easy way out... if you so choose!" He compellingly put his hands to his chest. "See, I'm not a bad guy. You can't deny there's an element of generosity here."

"Oh, my God!" Kat said with a sob. "You're supposed to be in Singapore!"

Shep looked confused, and Delanna studied Kat like a scientist awaiting a chemical reaction. Kat's reality swooped and spun. The room seemed cavernous and then tiny, fading and sharpening, echoing and then stuffy, and Kat sensed she was on the verge of passing out.

"Excuse me?" asked Flea.

"You called her Gweno," Kat said. "Gweno the Ho. Gwench the Wench...the unfaithful ex. I know it's you, Vernon!"

"Vernon?" Gwen said in disbelief. A parade of emotions crossed her face, starting with shock, then confusion, anger, disgust, and settling on fear.

Flea's shoulders fell, and he pulled off the mask, revealing his handsome face. Delanna's eyes widened, but she remained silent. Somehow, she knew him, too.

"You miserable prick," Shep said.

"You always have to fuck things up, don't you?" Vernon said to Kat, his eyes cold and feral.

Gone were the elfin voice and ostentatious gestures and any sign of the tender man who had asked for her hand six months earlier, the man she had kissed in E terminal of Logan Airport four days ago. Kat felt as if she were detached from her body, trying to make sense of the unexplainable.

"Vernon. Oh, Jesus Christ, how could you?" Kat asked, her words choked with emotion and snagging on her confusion.

"I didn't get on the plane. I didn't go to Singapore, you idiot...I've never been there," Vernon said.

How could that be? He left for a week every two months, had been doing it since she met him more than a year ago.

"You fucking killed someone!" Gwen said, not comprehending. "You need help."

"She was a piece of shit. My asshole landlord. She deserved it." He gave a dismissive *oh well* shrug. "I planned to let one of you live. Not you," he said to Kat. "But since you let this cat out of the bag," he said, jacking both thumbs toward his chest, "no one's going home."

Disbelieving and fearful glances passed around the table, most pausing on Buttercup's still form. With surprising reserve, Shep asked Delanna, "So, what did *you* do to cross him, sweetheart?"

Delanna's lip curled as she spoke. "We worked at Hastings.

He kept asking for a blow job. He tried to drag me outside one night. I started screaming and he got fired."

"Hastings?" asked Kat. As far as she knew, Vernon had never worked there, but it seemed there was quite a bit she didn't know.

"In Waltham. We make heat sinks," said Delanna.

"*Made* heat sinks in your case, you frigid bitch," Vernon said with a mocking laugh. "Should have just done it—you wouldn't be here. You're still going to give me one... maybe more."

"So this is a grudge-fest?" asked Shep. "Punish those who hurt your little pussy feelings?" His reckless defiance concerned Kat.

"Exactly. They might be little pussy feelings, but who has the upper hand now?" asked Vernon. "Not a thing even a piece-of-shit Texas lawyer like you can do."

"What the fuck I do, man?" asked Miguel.

"Sorry, guy, wrong place at the right time. I needed six players, and you were convenient. Sucks to be you."

Players? Kat wondered. *This is all a game to him.* Who was this stranger? He was insane... evil. How had she planned a life with him? How had she slept with him, been intimate, and gotten pregnant by him and not seen this?

"I'm pregnant...with *your* baby!" Kat said.

He glanced at her abdomen and released a single, quick snort. "Number four," the man who looked like Vernon demanded.

"Are you fucking serious?" asked Gwen.

"Yeah, I'm fucking serious," mocked Vernon. "Number four. NOW!"

"I want to trade," Gwen said quickly, her scared eyes wide. "You said we could trade."

Vernon stared at her acidly. "Fine. With whom? How

about Delanna's capsules? I'd love to watch you take one."

"Fuck your capsules," said Delanna. She flicked the bottle with the back of her hand, sending it spinning and scattering its contents across the table.

Rage contorted Vernon's face. He reached into his right pocket but stopped and forced composure. He smiled at his former coworker, and Kat could see it took every iota of his strength.

Disregarding Delanna, Vernon instructed Gwen to slide the box cutter to Shep, which she did. He then told Shep to slide the hacksaw to Gwen. Staring blankly at Vernon, Shep gave the hacksaw a quick push, and it caromed over the edge of the table. With barely bridled reserve, Vernon bent to retrieve it, his eyes locked on Shep's. Kat's eyes moved to the cutter.

"Watch yourself," Vernon said.

Kat wasn't sure if the warning was for her, Shep, or Gwen, but decided she'd rather not have any more of his attention than necessary. Vernon placed the hacksaw in front of Gwen and held her gaze. Kat saw the dare in his eyes, but they shifted warily, and she thought, *He's scared, but he has to go through with this. He can't leave any of us alive, and he knows we're desperate.*

"Number four!" he demanded.

Staring blankly ahead, Kat set the paper face-up on the table.

"Pick!" Vernon immediately responded, discharging the word like a bullet.

"The white box," said Kat.

Leaning close to Delanna, Vernon reached for the gift and slid it in Kat's direction. It fell over the lip of the table and dropped solidly into her lap. It was heavier than she had expected.

"Open it," he said impassively.

From inside she withdrew a wooden cigar box, the name *COHIBA* printed in thick black letters on the cover. A small metal latch held the box closed, and Kat preferred it that way.

"Go on. Open it," Vernon said.

Kat considered throwing it at him, but she'd never had good aim and it would only piss him off further. She slowly lifted the latch, opened the cover, and gawked at the box's contents. She quickly placed it on the table.

"That's a Ruger SR9C, but of course, you wouldn't know that. It's also ironic you picked it since you're too goddamned prissy to use it. For what it's worth, it's fully loaded, but I'm not concerned. How many times have you told me you'd never take a life, even to save your own? I guess we'll find out now just how honorable you really are."

She was confident he'd never give any of them a loaded handgun unless he was suicidal. He couldn't have known she'd be the one to pick that gift. But he'd already surprised her on a few accounts, so she couldn't really know. The bitch of it was that he was right. No matter her own shock and horror, she wouldn't kill. Couldn't kill.

"You're lying," she said.

"The clip holds seventeen rounds; check it out. Give it a try."

"Do it! What do you have to lose," hissed Miguel. "Shoot the motherfucker, man."

Kat couldn't. She didn't have it in her, but she could trade with someone who did. Maybe if...she again glanced at the box cutter.

"I want to swap with Shep," she said, and prepared to slide the box.

"Hold it!" Vernon said. Kat stopped and Vernon grinned. "Cowboy, slide the box cutter to Kat."

Kat's bleakness increased. She had planned to slide the gun over the edge of the table and divert Vernon's attention so Shep could use the box cutter on him, but Vernon was too attuned.

I'm so stupid! Kat thought. *Now I have a blade I'm afraid to use and Shep gets a likely useless gun.*

"Slide the box to the cowboy. Gently."

Kat did.

When Shep reached for the box, Vernon aimed the Beretta at him. "I'm watching your every move," he said. Shep slowly settled back, the chains rattling against his chair.

The gun might actually be loaded, Kat thought. Vernon's reaction seemed authentic. Vernon rounded the table and stood behind Buttercup's corpse, to Miguel's left. His eyes stayed trained on Shep.

"Two presents left, thanks to your neighbor, here," he said to Miguel. He patted Buttercup atop her head.

Kat looked at the presents and then saw Gwen to her right. She sat with her head slightly lowered, breathing rapidly as if she had sprinted up a series of stairways. Kat wondered if it was a form of meditation to alleviate the discomfort from having to piss, but Gwen looked up, displaying the terror in her eyes.

"Oh, God!" Gwen gasped and then snorted, desperate for breath. She tried to rise, but the chains caught. She dropped back into the seat and started convulsing.

Is she epileptic? Kat wondered. A milky froth coated Gwen's lips, and Kat understood what she had done. "No! Help her! She took the pills!"

All heads turned toward the struggling woman, and pleading voices rose. Kat's attempt to rise also succumbed to limits of the restraints.

Vernon walked slowly toward Gwen, watching her with profound interest. He squatted near her and studied her horrified eyes as she searched the room, her now-shallow breaths creaking into and out of her.

"Not as quick and painless as you were hoping, is it?" he asked her impassively.

"Help her!" Kat said.

"Come on!" said Miguel.

Silent, Delanna watched Gwen, her eyes wide with shock.

"Nothing I could do if I wanted to," Vernon said, his eyes still searching Gwen's as if looking for some cryptic truth. Finally, gratefully, Gwen fell unconscious.

To Kat's right, Shep snagged the box from the table. Vernon sprawled to the floor and scrabbled behind Gwen as Shep wrestled the gun free of the box and clicked off the safety.

"Stupid move, cowboy!" Vernon said.

Shep aimed for Vernon's voice and the reemerging arc of his head as it maneuvered to either of Gwen's shoulders, popping up for a fraction of a second and then disappearing.

"He's got his gun out, bro!" warned Miguel. The words no sooner left his mouth when a shot snapped, and a red star blossomed on Miguel's left cheek. He jolted upright in his chair, as if posing for a portrait, and then slowly slumped forward.

"You fuck!" screamed Shep, steadying the Ruger with both hands.

Vernon feinted to the right and then lunged left, putting Kat between them. Shep tried to draw a bead on him, but Vernon repeatedly bobbed from left to right over Kat's shoulders.

"Shoot him!" Kat, sure she'd be the next to die, surprised herself by slapping hard at Vernon's gun hand. The little gun cracked a shot off before careening across the room and settling beneath the Christmas tree.

Taken off guard, his expression unreadable, Vernon stood with his hands slightly raised. Shep held the Ruger steady, aimed at Vernon's head, and pulled the trigger, but no shot rang out. Instead, Shep yelped in pain, threw the pistol to the ground, and brought his hand to his mouth.

A smile spread across Vernon's dementedly handsome face. He walked toward Shep and stooped to pick up the gun. Holding it with the handgrip toward the ceiling, he pressed the trigger, and a silver needle protruded from the handle directly behind the trigger.

"I'm proud of this one... an old trick, making the trigger a syringe, but I machined it myself." He patted Shep on the shoulder, though keeping safely behind him. "You're in store for an ugly, painful death, cowboy, which really kind of pleases me after the screwing you gave me. Ever hear of an Eastern Brown Snake? Australia has the best critters. The venom is available on the black market, if you're willing to cough up the cash. I was willing, so you'll be dead within an hour." He set the Ruger on the table.

Gwen's body released a shuddering paroxysm, and Kat hoped it was her last, for Gwen's sake.

"Three dead. Soon to be four. Two to go," Vernon said.

"They'll find you," Delanna said. "They'll make the connections."

"No, they won't," Vernon said.

His smug confidence disgusted Kat. She couldn't believe she had once found it appealing. She recognized the certainty of her death, but she couldn't accept the unfairness that her child would be cheated of a life. When she had told him of her pregnancy three months earlier, he had seemed so pleased and comforting. Beside her, Shep jerked in his seat. A fine sheen of sweat had formed on his brow.

"Won't you help him?" Kat asked.

"Nope."

"And you're willing to let your baby die?"

Vernon gave a scoffing laugh. "That's the reason you're here...well, it was the final straw. I don't want no fucking kid, and I know you wouldn't let me walk away like I wanted to. You'd demand money and other shit and make my life miserable, like the rest of these pricks have."

"Who are you?" Delanna said, the thought contorting her face. "You evil bastard. I hope you burn in Hell forever."

Vernon snorted. "Maybe if I believed in Hell."

"So you feel nothing," said Kat.

"Nada." He gave a sarcastic *sorry* shrug.

"And for me?" Kat asked.

"Especially not for you," Vernon said.

"Prove it," said Kat. "Kiss me."

"What?" asked Delanna, unbelieving.

"I can't even stand looking at you; why would I want to kiss you?" asked Vernon.

"If you really don't love me, kiss me and prove it has no effect on you. You know you still care."

Vernon searched her sad eyes and looked behind him. Gwen was no threat. Shep sat across from them, staring blankly forward, his chest rising and falling rapidly. On the table, out of either Shep's or Kat's reach, were the Ruger and the box cutter.

"Fine," Vernon said, too arrogant to refuse the challenge.

Vernon pressed his lips to Kat's, and she spit heavily into his mouth. She simultaneously dropped her left hand and drove her balled right fist into his throat. Even though the chains enfeebled the blow, it worked. Vernon stumbled backward, the impact of her small fist causing him to swallow both her spit and the little capsule she had popped into her mouth.

Vernon recoiled, shocked, disgusted, and clutching at his throat. He collided with Gwen, swerved around her chair, and staggered away from Kat, trying to cough. Leaning his left hand on the back of Gwen's chair, he glared at Kat, who was spitting repeatedly onto the floor, praying she would be able to get rid of at least most of the residual poison.

Vernon reached to gain his balance, but Shep, rattlesnake quick, grabbed his wrist and yanked, pulling him onto his lap. The Texan wrapped his arms tightly around Vernon, trapping him.

"Can either of you get to the blade?" Shep asked, his face contorting with the effort, his body shaking.

"Just hold him! He swallowed cyanide!" Kat said.

"No shit?" Shep asked, managing a grin despite his struggle.

"He's reaching for the stun gun!" Kat warned, noticing Vernon's fingers working at his jacket pocket.

Shep clamped his teeth into Vernon's shoulder and bit down hard. Rewarded with an agonized wail, he clenched harder and held Vernon until his breath became labored, his limbs twitched, and ultimately his body went limp. Shep let him slide to the floor.

"How in the hell did you pull that off?" he asked.

"I was counting on his ego and that he'd look to see if he could reach the box cutter, and he didn't disappoint. That's when I popped the pill." She spat on the floor again.

"I think you'll be okay. Those were capsules and the poison's inside," Delanna said.

Kat looked at the inert form of her fiancé sprawled on the floor and spit again. The betrayal, the emotions, and the utter horror of what had transpired finally grabbed hold of her and she burst into tears.

"Shep, oh my God, are you okay? Is it starting to affect you?" Kat asked, guiltily pulling herself out of her grief and back to the present.

Shep flexed his hand. "Got the nervous sweats and a little

burn where the needle bit me, but feeling no worse for wear. I'm thinking Vernon got played by his black market friends. Either that or I'm nastier than that old snake. 'Course, he said an hour, so maybe it just hasn't set in yet."

Kat pitched forward, bouncing her chair and herself toward the table in diminutive increments.

Shep watched her for a moment, then asked, "Where you off to?"

"The hacksaw," Kat said. "Might not cut metal, but if it'll cut a bone, it'll cut wood. We got to get out of here and get you to a hospital."

The saw lay on the table in front of Gwen's slumped form, but at the rate Kat was moving, it would remain there a while longer.

Shep took up after Kat's lead, bouncing forward in small hops toward the table.

"Don't! You'll speed up your circulation!" Delanna warned him, and started bouncing toward the table, too, but Shep was quickly within reach of the box cutter and Ruger. Delanna and Kat both stopped bouncing.

"I'm going to try to knock the saw closer to you," Shep said to Kat. He took aim and slid the box cutter across the table. It careened off the side of the hacksaw, only managing to nudge it closer to Gwen. Delanna rolled her eyes, and despite the nightmare they had endured, Shep laughed aloud.

"Well, that wasn't worth its weight in shit," he said. "Hang on."

"You the one needs hanging on," Delanna said.

"I'm good," Shep said. He repeated the process with the gun, which again missed the mark. "Fuck!" he shouted as the Ruger shot across the table, knocking the hacksaw even farther to the left.

The gun plunged over the edge of the table, but Kat

hooked the trigger guard with the tip of her ring finger in an impressive display of athleticism. She was saved from tumbling to the floor by the arm restraints, but not without a substantial dose of discomfort to right herself. Shuffling a bit closer to the table, she set the gun flat, aligned her sights, and pushed. The gun hit the intended target squarely, and the hacksaw ricocheted perfectly into Shep's waiting hands.

"Show-off," said Shep.

* * *

The saw was indeed dull. By the time Shep made the four cuts necessary to free him from the multiple binding points on the chair, his arms and hands shook and throbbed, and a clammy sweat covered his brow. He sat back to rest a moment.

"Still feeling all right?" Kat asked.

"Yeah." He flexed his hand again. It felt weak and was still vibrating, but he attributed that to the sawing. "Maybe Vernon's venom was a dud, after all."

"Clearly, after exerting like that," Delanna said. "You're a lucky guy."

Shep rose, flipped his chair, and freed the chain. Fighting a bout of vertigo from rising too fast, he gathered the restraint over his shoulder and asked, "Who next?"

"Forget that! See if you can find a phone," Kat said. "Call the police."

"Maybe there's a better saw around here somewhere, too," said Delanna.

Shep looked at them and huffed. "Smart ladies," he said.

He headed for the kitchen; if there was a phone, it would be in there, he figured. Legs numbed from sitting too long, he stumbled through the doorway and scanned the room, which was cluttered in a haphazard way that was indicative of intrusion, not of residence.

A computer backpack lay open on the counter beside an opened laptop. To the left of the laptop, near the door, a land-line phone was mounted to the wall, and to the right, two open clamshell containers, one of them still half full of Chinese takeout food, an empty bottle of Corona, and a mostly full bottle of Diet Coke. Shep found this especially disconcerting.

Dinner for two.

He stood silently still and listened for evidence of another soul, then decided the best action was to get help as quickly as possible. As he reached for the phone, a sudden dizziness washed over him. He staggered to the counter, knocking the laptop's mouse to the floor and awakening the computer dis-play to a disturbing split-screen image of the dining room from either end, one facing Kat, the other facing Delanna. The cam-eras were black-and-white, which gave everything an ethereal, indistinct hue. The women's eyes shone silver, and Shep was taken by their vulnerability, chained to the chairs as they were.

With a shaking hand, Shep lifted the handset, which slipped through his numbed fingers and fell to the countertop. His left leg defied him next, folding beneath him and drop-ping him to his knees in front of the laptop. The strength in his legs had diminished with unsettling speed, but it wasn't his legs that stopped his effort to rise.

On the small computer screen, Shep watched as a mono-chromic Delanna stood before Kat. Short lengths of untethered chain dangled from both of Delanna's manacles, dragging across the tabletop as she picked up the box cutter.

Shep corralled the phone handset closer to him and jabbed the break button. Once he heard the dial tone, he managed to depress 9-1-1 with barely responsive fingers.

Ringing…

On the screen, Delanna moved toward Kat. Shep's chin hit the counter, and as he fell to the floor, awkwardly clutching the phone to his ear, Kat's screams emanated from the dining room. He heard a voice that sounded miles away.

"Nine-one-one, what's your emergency?"

☀On the ☃Night ✦Before ☃Christmas ☃They ✦Arrived

Niko Hart

Denver Skinner rocked in his creaky old rocking chair. Logs popped and crackled in the fireplace. His little cabin smelled of spiced cinnamon schnapps thanks to the blackened tea kettle boiling away on the woodstove. Outside, the Northern Michigan Gods of Winter dusted the world with snowflakes. There'd be another three feet of it by morning, the weatherman on the radio had said. But the radio was dead now, and Denver was too comfy to get up and wind it back to life.

"Christmas Day, gonna be a bloodbath," Denver sang, every bit as excited as a kid tap-dancing on an ant hill. He leaned forward in his chair and squinted in the candlelight to check his grandfather's grandfather clock. Five minutes to midnight. *Boy, how time flies when a man has nothing but time,* he thought.

An owl screeched. He imagined a snow mouse being eviscerated by a big, ol' snow owl somewhere out in the dark winter wonderland abyss.

"Welp, the boys can let themselves in; I'm right tuckered out," he told the bottom of his mug as he sipped the last of his cinnamon drink. He pulled the flannel blanket a bit tighter around his neck and prepared to doze.

A crashing on the roof ripped him back to wakefulness. Denver had always considered himself a brave man, but on this night, his body disagreed. He sat petrified in his chair, as stuck as those dinosaurs down in the Los Angeles tar pits.

A great hiss echoed through the room as water pouring down the chimney doused the fire, followed by something that went *plop!*

When the smoke cleared and his coughing stopped, Denver found a flaming brown paper bag in the fireplace. For reasons unknown other than reacting to the great surprise of its sudden appearance, he rushed over and squatted down to beat out the flames with a log. He gagged and lurched back as the unmistakable stench of sizzling poo filled his sinuses.

"Yippee-ki-yay, motherfucker!" cried a high-pitched voice an instant before the front door splintered into pieces. A frigid wind swept through the cabin. At the doorway stood a six-foot, 500-pound reindeer with pupils the size of pinpoints and whisky on its breath. It lowered its massive velvety horns and charged, screaming "On Blitzen! On Blitzen!" as its hooves *click-clacked* across the wood floor.

Denver closed his eyes and prepared to die. A crashing in the kitchen bought him enough time to crawl behind his chair and gawk at the massive creature slurping up a puddle of boiling hot cinnamon schnapps.

"Damn, that's one stout animal," Denver whispered.

A second reindeer burst into the cabin in a flurry of *click-*

clacks and Ricky Martin Latin dance music. He was smaller than the first and far leaner. No beer gut on this caribou, no sir. It wore heeled dance shoes. An old-school boombox was strapped around its hip. "She's livin' *la vida loca!*" it sang as it *cha-cha-cha'ed* into the room.

"Dancer, turn down that horseshit!" roared Blitzen as he thrashed about, trying to unstick his antler from the handle of the refrigerator. The appliance made jagged gouges across the floor as it was yanked several feet in each direction.

"No way, it's party time!" squealed a third reindeer as it entered the cramped cabin, taking quick, dainty steps over the mess of wood splinters Blitzen had made. He wore a halter made of fine green velvet with brass fastenings that reflected the candlelight. His green cashmere sweater spelled *Prancer* in flashing red Christmas lights. He stopped and sniffed the air with a frown. "Dang it, Vixen. You drop another bag of excreta down the chimney or what? It STINKS!"

A burst of delighted honks and grunts echoed down the chimney. "Yep, yep! Special delivery of flaming doggy turds. A classic trick indeed!"

Blitzen managed to rip off the refrigerator door and frisbee it into the wall as countless bottles of Coors shattered across the floor. He was on the lake of beer at once, lapping it up with his long purple tongue and chewing bits of broken glass without pause.

"Damn stout animal," Denver muttered a bit too loudly. Blitzen snorted and then was standing over him, his wet, crusty snout inches from Denver's face, breathing hot, boozy breath all over him.

"Ohhh, what did you find?" asked Dancer.

"A human," Blitzen replied.

"Does he like to dance?"

"Or party?" Prancer said as he moved over for a closer

look.

"He smells like Christmas," Dancer said, taking a big sniff of Denver's head. "And the sea, like fish. You sure it's a human?"

Blitzen pressed a thick spike of antler to Denver's collarbone, making the old man squirm. "That's cinnamon booze you're smelling on him. And fish sticks. He's not a Christmas Thing."

By now, Vixen had scrambled down from the roof and was pushing into the cabin. "So do we deliver him presents then?"

"Better-smelling presents?" Prancer said. Then he and Vixen squealed with laughter.

Blitzen cocked his head at this. "Maybe..." He removed his antler from Denver's chest. "Hey, human, we might have a wrapped present with your name on it if you can boil us up some more Christmas hooch."

"Ohhh, and we can use candy canes as stir sticks!" Prancer cried. He reached over and cranked up the volume knob on Dancer's radio with his teeth. "Ignition" by R. Kelly. He began to spin and prance, smashing lamps and knocking over a shelf of books and magazines across the floor.

A copy of *Alpine Bowerhunter* slid into Blitzen's hoof. On its cover was a husband and wife pair squatting over a big, dead, bullet-riddled hog, their pistols as big as their grins.

Blitzen, the intoxicated caribou, snorted and sideswiped Denver with a full rack of his antlers. "You...A HUNTER?!" he thundered.

Denver toppled sideways with a dislocated shoulder. "Ahhhhh!" he cried out. Thankfully, the agony of the blow cleared his head like a gust of wind blowing a rain cloud apart. "Me, a hunter? Gosh, hell no. I love animals. All of God's creatures—and Santa's, too—are like kin to me. And those fish sticks I ate were veggie—vegetarian. Plant-based it's called, I think."

All the reindeer relaxed. Vixen said that Blitzen had issues managing his anger.

Blitzen hung his head in shame, then took a mouthful of Denver's sweater and helped lift him to his feet. "Sorry, buddy," he said.

"Sure thing," Denver replied through clenched teeth.

Blitzen honked in approval, and all the other reindeer bounced about in joy. Then a silence fell over them as the *tinkle-tinkle-tinkle* of bells reached the cabin.

"Oh, goody gumdrops, it's the ladies ready to get down!" Dancer said.

Two more reindeer appeared at the gaping entrance into the cabin. With a mouthful of mistletoe sprigs and a coat polka-dotted with heart-shaped spots, she was unmistakable.

"Cupid," Denver blurted out.

"Yes, sir!" she said.

The reindeer behind her carrying a big, red Christmas stocking and a roll of duct tape in her mouth wasn't so easy to identify. She stood there in the doorway, silent but for the rhythmic *ting-ting* of her belled collar as she shifted her weight from hoof to hoof. Denver found this troubling, maybe even a bit terrifying.

Cupid approached him. "Sit down, mister; we need to talk." Her voice was sweet as snickerdoodle dough, and her big dark eyes radiated love, understanding, and innocence. He trusted her at once.

She got in close and watched Denver with a careful expression. Her coat smelled of eucalyptus, and she had honey on her breath. "Now," she said, "I'm going to ask you this once and only once, okay?"

Denver's stomach began to churn. He blamed it on his

poor supper choice of a family-sized box of fish sticks and a quart of schnapps, but on a deeper level, he knew the hurricane in his stomach heralded danger. "Sure, yeah, okay. I'm all ears."

"Are you a hunter?"

Don't stutter. Don't you stutter!" he told himself. "Ugh—well...why, why do you ask? I mean, nope!"

Cupid watched him a moment more, her expression flat and unreadable. Something dark passed over her eyes. She gave a quick nod and stepped behind Denver. His anxiety was rising. He tried to laugh it off, but clearly, he was in bad company.

The other reindeer stepped forward with her duct tape and her red stocking. Her eyes gleamed with sadistic mirth. As he sat transfixed by those eyes, Cupid popped her neck, then headbutt Denver. He was out before hearing the *crack!*

✳ ✳ ✳

He woke slowly. The scratchy wool of his favorite chair against his arms was comforting. The warmth of a fresh fire. Slippers hugging his feet. "Just a strange dream..." he yawned. So why couldn't he scratch his nose? He went to shift in his chair. Duct tape pulled at the hairs on his forearms.

"Oh..." he said.

Maniacal laughter boomed in the small cabin. His eyes shot open, and he saw all the reindeer standing in a circle around him. They had kitchen knives clutched in their teeth. And that one holding the stocking, she was still there, front and center, her eyes smiling with bad intentions.

On the kitchen table was his deer rifle. *Bad.* And next to it, the trophy buck's head he had mounted in his bathroom last season. Chunks of drywall hung from the screws where the deer had ripped it off the wall. *Very bad.* On the ground was a little cardboard circle; they had used the entire roll of tape to secure every inch of his body to his favorite recliner chair. *Very bad, indeed.*

He squirmed and cried out, "My—my boys are gonna be here any minute and—and they are gonna have the best Christmas they ever had when they see all this meat and horn waiting for 'em in my cabin! When it comes to man versus nature, man wins every time, so ha!"

The one with the stocking let it drop from her mouth. Eight bloody big toes rolled out when it struck the floor. They were sloppily severed. Chewed off was the best way to describe them. "Your boys already came," she told him. "And Donner and Dasher were hunkered down in the bushes having a smoke when they pulled up."

Denver felt bile slosh up his throat. "This ain't happening. It just ain't," he mumbled like a prayer.

"Is too!" said the one who had brought the tape and the big toes.

"Who the hell are you supposed to be anyway!" he spat at her.

"I'm Olive," she replied, grinning.

Denver was pleased to find his terror changing into anger. "Olive! Exactly who in the hell is that?" He laughed the laugh of a madman at the end of his rope. "Ain't nobody singing about no *Olive!*" He said her name like it was rotten milk.

Anger flashed in her eyes. She moved in, her lips an inch from his ear, and brayed, "*Olive, the other reindeer, used to laugh and call him names!!*" With her mouth still open, she latched onto Denver's cheek and began chewing.

Denver bucked against the duct tape, his cry sounding anything but human.

After some wet smacking, Olive stepped back. Denver

appeared to be smiling because his back teeth were visible through the gaping hole in his cheek.

Denver's flash of anger shrank back to fear. He moaned. Then wept. Then pleaded. "I only hunt 'cause I love nature. I'm a sportsman. Deer overpopulation is a real thing. Please, Santa's Reindeer, show some mercy."

A look passed between the reindeer. Dancer turned his boombox toward Prancer, who used his teeth to mess with the knobs.

All at once, "Jingle Bells" was blasting. The reindeer danced around Denver, taking turns jabbing kitchen knives into his groin.

"A man no more! A man no more!" they sang.

Outside, the snow continued to fall. A wolf howled. An owl screeched. And all the woodland critters were hunkered down in their dens on this early Northern Michigan Christmas morning.

THE SEVENTH CHRISTMAS
Jacqueline Moran Meyer

verything Peter had dared to dream had come true—a beautiful family celebrating Christmas together under one roof in a secluded country home smelling of pine and cinnamon, with twin ten-year-old girls and Miranda by his side. He resisted the urge to pinch himself. How had his solitary life turned into a Christmas movie with Peter in the lead role? He was the man of the house.

Peter glanced toward the fireplace, where four stockings hung. The logs crackled, bright flames slowly devouring wood and turning it to ash. By firelight, Miranda's features softened. By firelight, Miranda's features softened, and dancing shadows played across her face, partially concealing the angular slant of her jaw, and her nose's sharp edges. The fire's glow bounced off her blonde hair as she sat on the braided rug, wrapping the last of the presents.

Miranda slumped forward as she worked, her long, toned body hidden under the pink bathrobe she had been wearing for days. She smoothed out the wrinkles in the used paper decorated with fat, cheerful Santas, but she took little joy in wrapping Claire's Barbie and was now cutting corners. It was not like their first Christmas Eve together, when all the gifts had been new, perfectly wrapped, and placed under the tree with precision. The sparkling smile he'd admired when they had met at work was gone, replaced by rigid lips and bitterness. That first one had only been seven Christmases ago. Or had he only imagined that?

Peter caught a glimpse of himself in the mirror placed over the feather tufted green sofa across the room. Although he wore expensive clothes, they fit poorly. Miranda had carefully selected the crisp white shirt peeking through the neck of the crimson cashmere sweater stretched taut about his ample frame. Peter's beer belly hung over the button of his gray flannel slacks. The expensive clothing also did little to disguise Peter's rough life. His graying hair was long and stringy, in need of a cut. Deep wrinkles under his eyes and across his forehead made him appear older than his forty-two years, and the broken blood vessels on his nose suggested he had seen the bottom of too many whiskey bottles.

Peter drained the rest of his eggnog and hummed "Santa Claus is Coming to Town." The song had been playing on an endless loop for the last seven days. An enormous Christmas tree, complete with ornaments, fairy lights, and presents, stood before the house's lord and master. He took a few steps back, admiring his work, but noticed how brittle the tree had become. Several days ago, the evergreen had appeared fresh and lovely. Now, the branches drooped, and the needles carpeted the old, wide-plank maple floor. Peter gingerly placed the few remaining pieces of tinsel on his tree, one by one. The tinsel had become solely Peter's job days ago because Miranda and the twins, Claire and Jamie, couldn't be trusted with the task. Earlier in the week, he had caught Jamie throwing a fistful of the delicate silver strands at the tree, although he had explicitly instructed her to apply them one at a time.

The ungrateful brat.

However, a few holiday hiccups did not dampen Peter's Christmas spirit. This Christmas was still an improvement over past ones—those non-existent, abusive Christmases of his childhood. Peter had moved from foster home to foster home, where there had never been a present left for him under a Christmas tree. Santa Claus had never come. Believing he had earned a permanent place on Santa's Naughty List, Peter had blamed the other foster care kids who had dared him to do naughty things. Young Peter had complied with the other children's requests for two reasons: he wanted friends and he enjoyed doing naughty things.

Miranda had always treated him kindly from the moment they met, which was the biggest reason he'd fallen in love with her. She was too good a person to ever ridicule anyone. Today was their seventh Christmas celebration together. But today, Peter vacillated from worshiping Miranda to being filled with rage because of David.

Miranda watched Peter from the corner of her eye. Peter stretched his chubby arm above his head and stood on his tippy-toes to reach an upper branch in need of decorating, exposing his stomach in the process. Miranda's eyes widened when she spied the gun at Peter's waist. She hoped for a chance to catch him off guard and steal the weapon or to at least be able to hit him over the head with something, knocking him out, or better, killing him, but she hadn't gotten a chance all week.

"Dearest," Peter said.

Miranda flinched at the sound of his voice and kept her head down. She tried to still her shaking hands.

"Look at me, darling," Peter said, his voice gentle.

Miranda's heartbeat increased. Sweat glistened on her upper lip. She was exhausted and worried after being unable to sleep or eat for days, but she slowly lifted her gaze to meet his.

"Why the fuck is the doll out of its box? It's crap. Used. Garbage." His voice had filled with rage.

When he noticed Miranda's eyes filling with tears, he smirked. But then he cringed when he saw the swollen left eye and ruined mascara streaking her face. He was disappointed by her attitude. He preferred the cheerful, relaxed Miranda, the one who had greeted him every morning at work.

Her face was so beautiful when she was joyful.

"I'm sorry," Miranda murmured, her voice barely audible.

Peter clenched his fists as he approached her. Miranda cringed and closed her eyes, holding her hands up to protect her already bruised face.

"I'm sorry. I'm sorry. I'll try harder," she replied.

Peter raised his fist but immediately became disgusted with himself at the thought of once more hitting the woman he loved. His features softened, and when Peter placed a hand on Miranda's shoulder, she sobbed.

"Good girl. Christmas is a wonderful holiday. We're so lucky."

Miranda went back to her project, and the king of the castle sat in the recliner, warming himself by the fire. He hummed while keeping a watchful eye on Miranda.

Crash.

Thud.

The noises came from below them, which comforted Miranda. Sound meant that David was still alive.

146

Miranda lifted her gaze and stared at Peter's face. Her stomach lurched when she brushed his leg, but she was desperate. She would do anything to save David, and maybe if Peter thought she loved him, he would set David free.

"Please, Peter. Don't hurt him," Miranda pleaded.

When he answered her, his voice sounded like a barking, snapping dog. "Isn't it enough I have forgiven you? I'm even wearing the clothes you bought for *him*. I'll decide what to do about him when the holidays are over."

"When will that be?"

"When...Darling. When will that be...Darling?" Peter said in a high, mocking voice as he corrected her.

"When will that be, darling?" Miranda asked.

"Too soon, I'm afraid. Hey, it's midnight, time to wake the girls. Merry Christmas!" Peter giggled and rubbed his hands together, enlivened, anticipating the children's excitement.

"Okay, dear."

Miranda prayed tonight would be the night she could wrestle his gun away. She was prepared to kill Peter. David could not last much longer in the basement.

Peter helped Miranda stand and followed her up the winding staircase toward the children's room. He retrieved the keys from his front pocket when he reached the door and fumbled with them before inserting it in the lock and giving it a twist. Peter turned the doorknob.

The room was dark. Quiet.

"Jamie? Claire? It's Christmas. Time to get up." Although Miranda tried to sound happy, she failed.

Peter turned on the light.

The girls were awake and clinging to each other in one bed. The room reeked of urine from the girls' inability to leave their locked room for most of the week. Miranda choked back tears.

"No. Not again, Mommy," Jamie said. "Every day is the same."

"Shh," Claire whispered. "Play along."

"Aren't you excited, Jamie?" Peter asked through a tight, menacing smile.

"Yes." Jamie's voice was flat, empty.

Peter smiled and clapped. "Come on, silly heads. Your presents are waiting."

Miranda and the twins descended the stairs with heavy limbs and hearts and took their places by the tree.

"Now, who wants to open the first gift?" Peter asked.

Claire raised her sister's hand for her, which prompted a loud groan from Jamie.

"Okay. Jamie's first." Peter grinned and took out his phone to film her.

"I'll open the Battle—" she abruptly stopped and then quickly added, "I mean the one next to you, Mommy."

Miranda handed her the ripped and crinkled package. She anxiously bit her nails, praying her daughter would act surprised.

"Oh, thank you. Battleship! Just what I wanted," Jamie said with mock surprise and delight before throwing the present over her shoulder.

This was the seventh day Jamie had opened Battleship. This was the seventh Christmas they had celebrated this week. Seven days since the doorbell had rung. Seven days since Miranda had opened the front door, surprised to see Peter, the security guard from her office. He'd been holding a shovel with a red bow attached. Peter had entered the house and had pointed a gun at David, Miranda's husband and Claire and Jamie's father. Peter had swung the shovel at David's head, and David had collapsed. Peter had dragged David to the basement door and pushed him down the stairs to the cement floor below.

"I want my daddy," Jamie whimpered, wiping tears from her eyes.

Peter's pinched face became red, and his body shook with anger. No one spoke for several long minutes until Peter broke the silence. He bent down in front of Jamie and lifted her small chin, forcing her to look at him.

"Jamie, I'm not enjoying you or your spoiled, bratty, ungrateful tone," Peter hissed. Each word spewed from his twisted mouth, spraying vile spit at his prisoners.

Jamie cried, and Peter let go of her. He briefly cupped his head in his hands, regretting his outburst. Miranda used his moment of distraction to reach behind her and grab the brass lamp off the end table. She brought it around and bashed Peter over the head. The blow did not knock Peter out, but it did open a deep gash in Peter's head. And it did make him angry.

With blood running down his face, Peter lunged at the stunned Miranda. He pushed her down, pinning her to the coffee table, which collapsed beneath their combined weight. Miranda heard a crunch before red-hot pain radiated from her shoulder.

Peter wrapped his obese hands around Miranda's slender neck and squeezed. Hard. Miranda clawed at his face and hands with the one arm that still worked. Her daughters' pitiful screams started to sound far away.

❄ ❄ ❄

When Miranda came to, Jamie was patting her face. Peter lay completely still next to her, with a second gash in his head, and Claire stood over him, holding the brass lamp.

"Girls, Mommy's okay." Then she called out, "David, can

you hear me? David?"

Claire and Jamie, splattered with blood and traumatized, fell on top of their mother and wailed. Miranda's shoulder throbbed.

Peter had smashed their phones and cut the landline. She would need to get the keys from his pocket, unlock the basement door to rescue David, then drive to the Martins' house to call the police. The Martins, Miranda's nearest neighbors, lived five miles away.

A rattled Miranda transferred her keys from Peter's pocket to hers. When she held his gun in her uninjured hand, she felt safe for the first time since this nightmare had begun. Miranda kicked Peter in the arm to make sure he was dead. He didn't stir.

As they walked to the basement door, each of them called out.

"David?"

"Daddy?"

"Daddy!"

No one answered.

Claire put the gun in her pocket and unlocked the door. The foul smell that assaulted them terrified Miranda.

"David?"

"Daddy?"

David didn't answer. The only sounds Miranda could hear were her daughter's whimpers and that damned Christmas music.

"We all need to go down together. Daddy may be tied up, and I'll need your help to untie him."

The girls nodded and grabbed hold of Miranda's bathrobe.

Miranda flicked on the lights, leaving the keys in the lock, and steadied herself by grasping the railing. They descended the creaky wooden stairs.

"David? David, we're coming," she yelled.

When they reached the bottom of the staircase, she hesitated.

"David?" Miranda called out.

Silence.

"Girls, listen to me. Promise me you will do exactly as I say."

They nodded.

Miranda hoped for the best outcome, but she had no idea what she was about to see when she turned the corner and had a full view of the entire basement.

"Close your eyes and do not open them until I tell you to. Do not open them."

The girls nodded again. They closed their eyes and clutched Miranda's robe. Miranda braced herself to remain calm for her children's sake, no matter what she was about to see.

She turned and stifled a gasp as her heart dropped and her dreams shattered. David swung by a rope in the middle of the room. Peter had David's hands behind his back and had wrapped her husband's head with duct tape, leaving two slits where his nostrils would be so he could breathe. His head rested unnaturally on his shoulder. A chair lay nearby on its side.

Miranda could not imagine the suffering her husband had endured while she and her daughters were locked in their rooms or celebrating Christmas for days on end. She wondered if David had given up and knocked the chair over on purpose. Or had he kept struggling until his body gave out? It sickened her to think the noises she'd heard earlier were David's final moment.

"Mommy?" Claire asked, worried.

"Keep your eyes closed, girls. Daddy isn't here, but..." Miranda could not finish. She didn't get the chance to lie to her daughters. She would have told them their father had escaped and was looking for help. But like telling children not to touch a hot stove and curiosity getting the best of them, the girls had, of course, opened their eyes. They screamed at the macabre sight.

Miranda broke down as well. Somehow, she managed to turn the girls around. They started to drag themselves back up the stairs.

"Do you smell smoke?" Miranda asked midway.

Thick, black smoke billowed through the doorway, roiling over the silhouette of a man.

Peter.

He rubbed the back of his head with one hand and held the set of keys in the other.

Miranda had left them in the lock.

She and the girls froze.

Peter snapped the basement light switch off and slammed the door.

She heard the lock catch.

❆ ❆ ❆

Peter started his car and watched the fire. He drove off when he was sure the house would burn down. Fire engines passed him, heading toward the house. He felt dizzy, and his head hurt, but he had a week of vacation left to heal. Peter was pretty sure his hair would hide his wounds.

With "Jingle Bells" blasting from his car radio, Peter began to relax. As he let his thoughts drift, an image of Sophie, the paralegal who worked on the eighth floor, popped into his aching head. Sophie wore cute cat-eye glasses, had freckles, with no wedding ring to complicate things. Peter was in love, and Valentine's Day would be here before he knew it.

T✸RISTAN AND S✸AM
Jude Clee

ap. Tap. Pause. *Tap.*

Sam's signal, Tristan thought when she heard the knocking on the wall.

"Can I go upstairs?" she asked Gran, who was perched on the rocking chair by the Christmas tree. It was an artificial one, dragged up from the depths of the basement and bathed in Pine-Sol to give it a natural tree smell. Tristan couldn't complain. It gave the house that authentic Christmas-y feel, just like Tristan's kindergarten crafts and the carols on the radio.

It helped her pretend that things were normal.

"I don't know, can you?" Gran said without looking up from her crocheting.

"May I?" she said. It took all of her self-restraint not to roll her eyes.

"Only if you stay in your room. I don't want to catch you

153

on the roof, you hear me? I don't care if it's technically within the boundaries; it's still dangerous. Mind you, I don't want you talking to that Santini boy at all. He'll grow up to be a crook like his father, you mark my words, but that's another matter."

"Yes, ma'am," Tristan said. She ran up the stairs before Gran could change her mind. Her bedroom—the smallest in their twin house—was directly above the kitchen, facing the backyard. The window gave her a glimpse of the woods just beyond the fence, her only slice of the outside world.

Deftly, like the stray cats that sometimes teetered on the fence, Tristan eased herself out of the window, untangling one of her flyaway curls caught in the latch, and climbed onto the kitchen roof.

Sam was already waiting on his side.

"Finally," he said. "My ass fell asleep waiting for you."

"I couldn't help it. Gran started lecturing me."

The rooftop was their meeting place ever since they were little. Back in elementary school, it brought them sheer joy knowing they were doing something naughty, something secret. Now, it was a lifeline. For the last month, it was their only way of going "outside," if you could even call it that.

"Whatever," Sam said. "Think fast!"

The ball came right at her face, and she caught it one-handed. It was almost insulting, really. Tristan was the best female athlete in their middle school—she could beat a lot of the boys, too, not that Sam would ever admit it.

"Watch it, stupid," she said, tossing it back. "You want to lose another ball?"

A red rubber ball lay uselessly in her backyard, propped up against the roots of the oak tree.

"Speak for yourself. I'm not the one who dropped it last time."

He's never going to let me live that down, she thought wryly as they settled into their routine of pass and catch. It wasn't much as far as exercise went, but after a month stuck inside, they'd take what they could get.

"Christmas is gonna suck this year," Sam said.

"Yeah," she agreed, catching the ball. "But maybe they'll have presents in the next drop-off."

"Yeah, right. They barely got any good food or supplies. If there's anything extra, it'll be something lame like socks. If we even get it in time. The drop-offs are always late, so we probably won't get it 'til New Year's."

"There's still..." Tristan's voice faded away with the wind.

"What?"

"Santa," she mumbled into her knees.

Sam threw back his head and laughed, his blond curls bouncing back. Sam's laughs were usually playful and a tad mischievous. This one was pure cruelty.

"I can't believe you still believe in friggin' Santa Claus!"

"I don't really! I was just saying. Shut up! I hope you fall and break your stupid neck!"

Instant silence. They both know what falling outside of the boundaries meant, and it was a lot worse than breaking a stupid neck.

Tristan squeezed the ball in her hand. "I'm sorry, Sam."

"Forget it," he said, shaking his head. "I was being a dick, anyway. I wish I could still believe in something like Santa. Maybe that would make this whole crappy deal a little better."

"My dad says it won't last forever. He says they'll get sick of us eventually and move on. That's what happened in, like, Canada, I think. They got bored, so they moved down here."

"Hope so," Sam muttered, but he didn't sound convinced. Tristan wasn't, either. Even at the wise old age of thirteen, she still clung to the childish notion that her dad's word was gospel. Yet as much as she wanted to believe him, she couldn't help suspecting that it was just one of those things adults told kids to make them feel better.

A sudden howl shook the treetops. The hairs stood up on the back of Tristan's neck.

"Don't worry about it," Sam said quietly. "It's just passing through, same as always."

There was another howl, louder this time. The mild winter day suddenly turned freezing.

"It was just the wind," he said.

"Yeah, that's what I'm afraid of," she muttered.

"The regular wind."

"Seriously? You know that, like, every time someone says that in the movies, they get killed."

"Oh no, I jinxed us! Oh wait," he smirked, "this isn't a scary movie."

"If it was, I'd be dead in like a second," Tristan said, making an effort to joke along with her friend. If she could joke, then she wasn't really scared. "Black people always die first."

"Not always. They didn't in *Us* and *Get Out*."

"So basically, I'm safe as long as it's a Jordan Peele movie."

"I kind of wish it was a movie," he said. "Then we could just shoot 'em. That always works in movies."

"You don't even know how to use a gun."

"I'd learn. Anyway," he said, his voice turning serious. "They can't get us. We're technically still in our own houses. They can't get you in bounds."

That's what everyone said, anyway. She didn't understand it, but she'd heard it plenty over the last month. Whether it was the news or an Internet forum, they all agreed: you're safe if you don't leave the house. Sometimes Tristan read those forums on her tablet late at night to reassure herself as she tried to fall asleep. It was better than those videos of the people who ventured outside in the early days—those still gave her nightmares. Zombies is what everyone said back then, and the guys at school talked about survival kits and getting bitten. But it was so much worse than zombies. At least there were rules for zombies. At least you could see zombies. No one saw this new thing, or if they did, they didn't survive long enough to tell. All they left behind was a mess of blood and meat that didn't look remotely human anymore.

"I heard it's the smell," Sam said as he caught the ball.

"What smell?" she asked. All she could smell were the piles of decaying leaves overtaking the backyard and the roast chicken cooking in the kitchen below. From the Santini side of the house, she heard laughter and music. If she closed her eyes, she could pretend it was a normal Christmas Eve.

"Smell is how they get you. They can't smell you when you're inside your house, but once they get a whiff of you outside, they got you. That's what my brother said."

"Derek's full of crap."

"Brian said it," Sam shrugged. "If they're really from a different dimension or whatever, it makes sense that their rules are different than ours."

"My dad says that's why we can't see them. That our dimensions have, like, blended together, but they haven't completely crossed over. That's why they can only see us sometimes, and we can't see them at all."

She didn't understand it, but she trusted Dad. He said it was like catching static between TV settings or overhearing someone else's conversation during a video chat. Here but not here, seen but unseen. Whatever it was, Dad said, they needed to avoid it just like she needed to avoid the deer that once ventured through their open gate into the backyard; a cornered, wild animal was dangerous.

Sam shrugged again. "You're probably right."

Tristan tossed the ball back. It must've been too quick for him, or maybe he just wasn't ready yet, because his reflexes were too slow. He fumbled for it, but it only brushed the tips of his fingers, bouncing off and rolling down the roof.

"No!"

Sam dove after it. He didn't think, just like when he slid headfirst to steal a base. This time he slid and kept going.

"Sam!"

For a moment, she thought he'd fallen off of the roof. He didn't, though it wasn't much better. Sam clutched a tree branch, legs dancing in the air like the cat posters she sometimes saw at school.

"I'm okay," he panted. "I got it, don't wor—"

Snap!

"Sam!" Tristan cried. Sam's face turned pale, his eyes widening. Without thinking, she plunged headfirst after him. Her arm stretched out for any part of him, desperately, while still trying to keep her feet firmly planted on the roof. Sam's clammy hand latched on to hers.

"I got you," she said, pulling him up slowly.

SNAP!

Tristan caught a fleeting glimpse of Sam's wild green eyes before they both went plummeting to the earth.

It knocked the wind out of her, just like that time Charlie Barton tackled her in football. It hurt like hell, but it wasn't excruciating. Nothing was broken.

She sat up.

The damp earth soaked her jeans. She was looking up at the two houses, hers and Sam's, the rooftop hovering above. She was outside. She was outside for the first time in a month—and out of bounds.

The wind howled again. She didn't turn back to look. She couldn't, not yet.

"Sam!" Tristan said.

Sam groaned and sat up. Mud splattered all over his yellow curls. "I'm okay. You?"

"Sam, we're out of the house!"

"Oh, shit!" he said. They stared at each other. Tristan felt like there were a pair of eyes glaring down at the back of her head. They practically burned.

She didn't want to turn around. If she kept her back to the woods, facing the safe, familiar houses, she could almost pretend that she didn't hear the whoosh of the wind picking up, the faint rattle of crumpled leaves swirling around.

But she couldn't help it. She craned her neck to see the little tornado forming mid-air, faster and faster until the spirals of wind and debris formed four long, spindly fingers, ending in sharp, narrow triangles that dug into the closest tree, splintering the bark.

She jumped when Sam's hand clamped onto her forearm.

"RUN!"

The Santinis' back porch was closest, so that's where they went.

"It's me!" Sam shouted, pounding his fists on the door. "It's Sam!"

No one came to the door. Something was wrong here, something terribly wrong, but Tristan couldn't figure out what.

"Come on!" he bellowed. "Open up, you assholes!"

It hit her: the house was dead silent. Earlier, there had been Christmas music, the sounds of adult laughter; now there was nothing. The Santini family should be able to hear them. They should come running. But they didn't.

"Come on," Tristan said, pulling her friend away. "Let's try my house."

Hand in hand, they darted across the driveway, past Mr. Santini's prized Chevy, to the Blackwell side of the twin house. Tristan ran up the familiar wooden steps, the middle one creaking like it always did, until she reached the front door, where an evergreen wreath hung.

Tristan wasn't ready to give up hope, not yet. They've only been out of bounds for two minutes. That was practically nothing. Surely, it wasn't too late.

She banged her fists on the door, rattling the wreath.

"Daddy?" she called out, loud and clear against the silent street. "Gran? Open up! It's me, Tristan."

The curtain lifted. Tristan's father peered out at her, face framed by the wreath. His eyes widened.

He stared at the two children on his porch, and Tristan didn't want to read the expression written clearly on his face.

"Daddy, please!" she cried.

He shook his head, mouthing the words, "I'm sorry."

The curtain fell.

"Dad!" Tristan screamed, pounding on the door. But the house was still. No one moved.

"What are we going to do?" Sam whispered.

Tristan barely heard him. She stood on the porch, staring at the door like it might somehow give her a different answer if she waited long enough.

The howl behind them almost sounded human. Almost like footsteps coming, just out of sight.

"It's just the wind," Sam said with a smile as phony as his words.

She pretended to believe him.

Making My Rounds:
Tales of the Christmas Troll
Chisto Healy

The troll rubbed his thick green hands together excitedly. His short, squat legs led him in a joyous dance, and his bulbous wart-covered nose snorted his happiness. This was the occasion he waited for all year. This was his time to play.

Christmas was a time of miracles, or so everyone seemed to believe. They also all believed in elves and Santa's helpers. It wasn't hard to get them to believe in him and what he offered. Every year, starting with December 19th, the beast allowed him to grant one wish per day, the results of which would be displayed on Christmas morning.

The troll had tried to bargain with the beast for more, but he was insistent. Six was his number, and he said that too many would ruin it because it would make people stop be-

161

lieving in the good of Christmas, and it was that very belief that allowed the troll to fool them. So, it remained six. It was always six. He had been playing this game for centuries, and it never ceased to excite him. The thrill of it made him giddy, and the beast was always proud of his work. When it was all done, on Christmas morning, the beast would reward his efforts by giving him a child. Children were his favorite food. He waited all year for his chance to play his game, to make the beast proud and earn his delicious Christmas dinner.

December 19th — Daniel

The troll smiled at the young blond boy. He danced from side to side, allowing the bell on his hat to flip back and forth and jingle as it did. The boy still gave him a troubled look. "What are you, again?" he asked.

"I'm Tum Tum, the Christmas elf," the troll said gleefully, showing his gnarled teeth when he smiled. "Every year, my boss allows me to grant six wishes to lucky boys and girls like you. You make the wish now, and when you wake up Christmas morning, it will have come true. Is there anything you would like to wish for, Daniel?"

The young boy scrunched his face and thought hard. "You sure you work for Santa?"

The troll smiled. "Positive."

Daniel thought some more. "My parents are divorced," he said. "Christmas stinks now."

The troll rubbed his hands together. "So what is it you would like?"

"I want my parents to be together for Christmas," the boy said.

The troll smiled. "And so they shall be." He touched his bulbous nose, and sparkling dust sprinkled in front of him.

He snapped his fingers. "Merry Christmas, Daniel."

The boy looked excited and jumped on his bed. He watched the magical elf disappear, and it really made him believe. His mom and dad were finally going to be together again.

December 25th — Daniel

Daniel awoke on Christmas morning, and he bounced with excitement. He didn't even care about the presents that waited for him downstairs. He remembered what the magical elf had told him. His parents were going to be together again. He ran down the steps as fast as he could. He could see his mom in the kitchen. He wondered if his dad was there, too. He always liked to drink his coffee on Christmas morning.

Daniel ran into the kitchen and stopped in his tracks. His mouth fell open, and his small body trembled. His mother and father were both there, all right. They were attached to each other, the skin stretching between their faces. They each had one arm and one leg; the others were half-formed and melded between them. Their eyes drooped where they connected and bulged on the other side. "Please help," they said in unison. "Please help us."

Daniel screamed.

Outside the kitchen window, bells jingled as the troll danced back and forth, clapping his hands at a job well done. The beast would be proud.

December 20th — Sarah

Sarah rolled her eyes and kept playing on her tablet as she laid on her belly across her bed. "I thought Mom and Dad were Santa. You're saying you're an actual Christmas elf?"

"Why, of course, I am, Sarah," the troll said. He sprinkled

magic dust from his thick, little fingers, and her tablet floated up and away from her, landing safely on her desk nearby. "I have Christmas magic, and I can grant you a special wish. Is there anything you would like?"

Sarah huffed and sat up, turning to face him. "I'd like my tablet back."

The troll smiled, showing his rotten teeth. "You will have that as soon as I leave. I just needed your attention for a moment. You make your wish now, and on Christmas morning, it will come true. You can wish for anything, Sarah."

The young girl rolled her eyes and huffed again. "Fine," she said. "I don't want to go to my grandmother's house for Christmas. It's boring there, and there are no devices. I don't want to be there on Christmas. That's my wish."

The troll smiled and bowed. "This year, I will make sure that you don't go to your grandmother's, Sarah. Merry Christmas."

In a blink, he was gone. "Whatever," Sarah said, getting up from her bed. She stalked across the room and snatched her tablet off her desk.

December 25th — Sarah

Sarah stormed out of the house, pouting. That stupid elf had said that she wouldn't have to go to her grandmother's house this year, and not only was she still going, but her mother wouldn't even let her bring her tablet. She growled as she got into the back seat of the car.

"You'll live," her mother said, climbing in the passenger seat. Her father started up the car, and the radio began playing carols. Sarah groaned with annoyance in the back.

Then they were on the road, headed towards grandma's, just like every other boring year. Sarah hated that lying elf.

She knew Christmas was crap. Her parents bought her presents. There was no Santa.

The car swerved, and Sarah was thrown across the backseat. She looked scared and tried to see what was happening. Her mother was screaming. Her father was jerking the wheel and yelling to hold on. He slammed on the breaks and they screeched, but the car didn't stop before crashing through the guard rail, where it tumbled and rolled down an embankment.

At the roadside, by the broken guard rail, the troll bowed once more. "Your wish has been fulfilled, darling," he said with a chortle.

December 21st — Craig

"Can you think of anything you'd like to wish for this Christmas?" the troll asked the small freckled boy who sat on his floor playing with action figures.

"A new skateboard?" Craig asked thoughtfully.

The troll bent his thick, little body over and met the boy's eyes with a smile. "Oh, Craig, you can do better than that. Think beyond toys. I can grant you anything. Something magical. What will it be?"

The boy put his toys down on the rug before him. He put his finger in his mouth and thought hard. Then he looked across the room at the empty birdcage. He looked over at the strange, little elf then and said, "My bird, Oscar. I want him to be alive again. He died, and it made me so sad. I wouldn't let Mommy take his house."

The troll nodded and mussed the boy's orange hair. "Christmas morning, Oscar will be alive again, my friend. Merry Christmas." With that, he was gone. Craig looked at the empty cage and thought for a moment about his friend. Then he smiled and went back to playing with his toys.

December 25th — Craig

Craig selected a box from under the tree. His father looked at his mother with curiosity. "What is that one?" he whispered.

She just looked at him with a confused expression and shook her head.

When the boy ripped off the paper, the box started to make a lot of noise. It even moved. He shook with excitement. Could it be? Craig tore the lid off of the box, and there was Oscar, alive and well. He was agitated and afraid from being in the box, and he fluttered and flapped. "Oscar!" the boy shouted. "You're back!"

The bird flew out of the box, and the boy whooped with joy. His mother gasped, and his father just stared at the bird, slack-jawed. They watched the bird flap around and fly straight up into the blades of the spinning ceiling fan. Craig screamed and ran to his bird, who had died all over again, on Christmas morning. His parents looked on in horror. Outside the house, the troll watched through the living room window, chuckling to himself. He jumped in the air and clicked his heels.

December 22nd — Mary

The troll sat beside the little girl who was already crying on her bed. He brushed her hair with his thick, little hand. "Why are you so sad, little Mary?" he asked her.

She sniffled and looked at the little man with his greenish skin covered in warts and thinning white hair. "Are you an elf?"

"I sure am," he smiled. "I can fix whatever is making you sad. You just wish for it now, and on Christmas morning, it will be so."

She wiped at her eyes with the backs of her hands, and then she sat up. "I don't want my Daddy to hit my Mommy anymore. He drinks a lot of that bad juice, and it makes him really mad and mean, and then he hits Mommy and hurts her. It happens every year."

"Not this year," the troll assured her. "You have my word." He snapped his thick, little fingers, and then he was gone. The small girl just blinked at where he'd been and rubbed her eyes some more.

December 25th — Mary

Mary watched nervously as her father selected another present. He had already had a lot of the bad juice, and she was afraid. Her mother looked just as nervous as she did. He ripped open the box aggressively. He pulled the tie out of the box like it was something dead and disgusting. He turned towards Mary's mom and glared at her. "What the hell is this?" he demanded to know. "This isn't what I asked for."

"There's more," his wife said. "I just thought it was nice."

"You thought it was nice," he said, throwing the box down. He got to his feet and grabbed up a bottle of liquor. He took a big sip and stared down at his wife. "You know what would be nice? If you ever damned listened," he snapped.

Mary started to cry as her father stalked towards her mother. It was going to happen again, and she really didn't want it to. Then her mother lunged. At first, she didn't even see the knife in her mother's hand. Neither did her father. She stabbed him over and over, plunging the knife into his torso and then pulling it out violently, only to plunge it back in elsewhere. Mary screamed, and the blood splattered the Christmas tree.

When it was over, Mary's mother dropped the knife and

looked at her own bloody hands with terrified eyes. "What did I do?" she said, shaking and crying now. "I don't know why I did that. Oh, God, I don't know why I did that."

"It was the elf," Mary said quietly. In the kitchen doorway, the troll waved his little fingers. Then the flashing lights showed up outside the house, accompanied by blaring sirens, and the troll blinked away.

December 23rd — Rory

"Wake up, wake up," the troll said to the sleeping boy. "I'm a Christmas elf, here to grant your wish."

The boy opened his eyes and squinted into the dark at him. He reached over to his nightstand, grabbed his glasses, and put them on. Then he looked again. "You really are a Christmas elf," he said.

"At your service," the troll said with a bow. "You can wish for anything you like, and on Christmas morning, it will come true."

"Are you magic?" the boy asked.

"I am magic," the troll said. He wiggled his fingers, and shiny lights danced about. "What would you like to wish for, Rory?"

The boy pointed past the troll. He turned to look at where the child was pointing. There was a wheelchair sitting there. "I want to walk again," the boy said.

"And so you shall," the troll said. Then he spun in a circle. There was a flash of light, and he was gone. Rory scratched his head, wondering if he had been dreaming. Then he took his glasses off, put them on the nightstand, and went back to sleep.

December 25th — Rory

Rory woke up Christmas morning, and he stepped out of bed. His feet touched down, and he started to walk across the room. He couldn't believe it. The elf hadn't been a dream. He was real, and he kept his word. He couldn't wait to show his parents this Christmas miracle. He ran down the stairs and into the living room.

His mother screamed. "How the hell did it get in here?" his father yelled. Rory didn't know what they were talking about. Then his father was hitting him with a broom and his mother was yelling at him to shoo. What was happening?

The broom smacked the Christmas tree, and ornaments fell to the floor. A silver ball rolled and landed in front of Rory. He looked at it and saw his reflection. He was a raccoon. *No. Oh no.*

His mother had opened the front door. He took the exit while it was there because he didn't know what else to do. Then Rory ran down the road on his new working legs, all four of them. Behind him, a short, squat troll went skipping along, singing a merry tune.

December 24ᵗʰ — Tonya

The troll stood next to the girl doing her homework at her desk in her bedroom. "Why would there be schoolwork? Are you not on winter break? That seems cruel," he said to her.

Tonya put her pencil down and looked over at him. She smiled when she saw him. "Hey, little guy. I'm just working on stuff so I don't forget it when I go back to school. I like to get good grades."

The troll smiled. "Oh, well, that is wonderful, my dear. My name is Tum Tum. I'm a magical Christmas elf. I get to grant six wishes per year, and I've already granted five. You are my last one, so think of something really special."

"Oh, Tum Tum! I already know what I want," she said with a gleaming smile. The troll clapped excitedly and jumped up and down to match her enthusiasm. "What's it going to be?" he asked.

"A while ago, my mom fell down the stairs and she broke her leg real bad. It's been weeks, and she's still in so much pain. She's a really good mom. I want you to fix it so she's not in pain anymore."

"Your wish is my command," the troll said with a smile. He blew her a kiss. "Merry Christmas, Tonya." Then he was gone. Tonya clapped her hands happily and then went back to her work.

December 25th — Tonya

Tonya rubbed her sleepy eyes and stumbled out of her bedroom. Her father was sitting on the couch in front of the Christmas tree, sipping a cup of hot coffee. Tonya shuffled over and sat next to him. He leaned over and hugged her and placed a gentle kiss on the top of her head. "Merry Christmas, baby," he said.

"Merry Christmas," she said back. "Where's Mom?"

He looked at her silently for a while. She just looked back, waiting for an answer. "Dad? Where's Mom?"

Her father put his hand to his mouth. His eyes filled with tears. "Honey, why are you doing this on Christmas?" he asked her.

Tonya shook her head. "Doing what? What do you mean?"

Her father wiped tears from his eyes. "Tonya, your mother died when she fell down the stairs weeks ago. You know that. I know it hurts, baby, but it's important to remember that your mother isn't in pain. She's in a better place."

Tonya stared at him in horror. Her own eyes filled with tears and quickly overflowed. A wicked, little troll leaned over and whispered in her ear, "Merry Christmas."

Then he was gone, and Tonya and her father were left with their grief.

December 25th — Christmas Night

The troll sat in his cave, content after another fine year. He was proud of the tricks he had come up with, proud of the way he distorted the children's wishes this year. He felt especially clever. He was already thinking of ideas for next year when he heard the sound of the beast coming to see him. He would recognize the clapping of those hooves anywhere.

He looked excitedly toward the opening of the cave, and the beast was there, entering on his goat legs, with his muscled torso, red flesh, and thick black horns. He carried a sack over his shoulder like Santa Claus. The troll smiled and clapped at the sight of him.

"You really outdid yourself this year, my little friend," the beast said. "I am always grateful for you. You are consistent, reliable, and so deliciously wicked."

The troll got to his feet and started bouncing in place. He knew what was coming, and his stomach grumbled. "Thank you so much," he beamed. "I love to make you happy."

The beast laughed. "You love the reward," he said. "But that's okay. You deserve it." He pulled the sack over his shoulder and dropped it on the ground. Something inside was violently trying to get out. The troll looked at the sack with hungry eyes. He could hear the muffled whimpering from within, and it made him salivate. The beast smiled. "Enjoy your candy," he said. "I'll see you next year, troll. Merry Christmas."

Then the beast turned and left the cave. Even he didn't like to be around when the troll was eating. The sounds were sickening.

⊛VER THE ℍILLS OF S⊛NOW
Patrick Barb

Bundled in winter coats, woolen caps, and fuzzy mittens, the children marched through the streets of town. After leading them from the meadows where he'd been brought to life, the creature, that golem molded from their compacted snow, switched places and trailed behind.

"Stop!"

The traffic cop hollered at the procession even as he felt his legs give out and his sanity depart at this glimpse of the unnatural and profane. The heel of his boot slipped on an icy patch covering black asphalt. Before he knew it, the officer lay prone—a snow angel draped across the empty intersection. With snowflakes on his eyelids and lips, he watched the children marching forward. Faces pressed into the screaming wind.

They did not look back.

Only the creature, bringing up the rear, turned back to regard the fallen man. It moved its ice-thickened arm up to touch the brim of a black top hat perched atop its spherical head.

(To say the creature was the same as you and me would be, at best, a stretch. Still, it was as alive as it *could* be.)

Along with the hat, the creature wore a long scarf wrapped around its neck like a hangman's noose. The red woolen scarf moved with a lewd gracefulness, bouncing against the otherwise opaque nakedness of the entity's exposed body. As it moved to catch up with its children, its ghost-white body parts seemed to dance around, thumping along to a forbidden rhythm that only it could hear.

Thumpity-thump. Thump.

Thumpity-thump. Thump.

When they arrived at the square, the creature's youthful acolytes broke ranks, running here and there. Passing adults, those brave enough to stand up to the monster, tried to grab for the children, hoping to free them and melt away whatever madness had worked its chilled and clutching fingers into their minds. But the children laughed, fleeing from their would-be saviors screaming, "Catch me if you can." Just as it had taught them.

Later, the surviving children—those whose mad ramblings could be understood—would claim that the creature's source of power must have been the old silk hat they'd found, its red band dusted with tiny white mitten prints from where they had placed it on its head. Whatever eldritch magic emanated from that cursed garment, it seemed certain the snowy humanoid would sooner part with one of its coal-black eyes than lose the showman's crown placed with jaunty defiance upon its smooth, corpse-pale head.

As it neared the altar prepared by the village's children, the wind whistled through the holes in the creature's button nose. The abomination kneeled in solemn observance of the children's efforts. Leaning toward the flame of one of the make-shift torches they'd placed around the altar, it lit whatever foul substance filled the corncob pipe jammed into a mouth of slate-gray, granite teeth. Never mind that the creature had no lungs from which to draw breath or to exhale the smoke that curled around its hat, those who would perish at its altar would die thinking only of its "voice," spreading across their brains like mental frostbite.

"Now, let's have some fun."

* * *

When it finished feeding, the man of snow looked upon the children who remained. Still under its spell, their bluish-white, chill-bloated faces were streaked with tears hanging frozen from their faces. They mourned the fact that they had not been chosen. They stood together, shivering. They waited to be a part of its unholy sacrament. The blood of the chosen dribbled from the creature's face. Droplets of blood and water sizzled when they hit the ground. The creature gazed up at the sun. The glowing red-and-orange sphere had emerged from behind the clouds and now hung above the frosty blue sky.

The left half of the creature's face slid off, splattering on-to the exposed earth. The creature sighed. With its snowy "flesh" falling away like leper's skin, it raised what was left of its arm and waved. Then it pushed back the black hat from its melting brow and let it fall to the ground. It rolled on its brim across a gray and soupy slush before stopping at the feet of the children left alive. As the last winds of winter screamed a final note of defiance, the creature's whispered words fluttered by like forgotten snowflakes confronting spring flowers already bursting forth from impatient soil. "Don't you cry," it said.

"I'll be back again...*some* day."

175

Twas the Night Before Christmas or Hengar's Story: *A Tale of Terror & *Mus *Musculus *Vengeance

Carl E. Reed

Twas the night before Christmas, when all through the
house
Not a creature was stirring, 'cept Hengar the mouse;
He'd consulted old grimoires with attention and care
To summon foul nightmares to slaughter the pair

Of aged accountants who stalked his quaint home
With curses and shrieks, lamentations and groans.
Bob and Jo Thompson didn't play nice:
They were wicked and ruthless in rooting out mice.

Hengar lost triplets to treacherous bait:
Bright Eyes, Burnt Whiskers, Thin Limbs—but eight-

Months-old when sounded a series of cracks—
Brittle necks snapping on cheese-baited traps.

Hengar vowed vengeance; the monsters would pay!
If not now, then next hour—nightfall—or next day.
Saddened, grief-maddened, he honed his dark art:
In fury he chanted, tore dimensions apart.

When out on the lawn came a crash and a clatter
An electric blue flash of other-dimensional matter!
Creatures poured in from a world sere and dark
Mayhem and murder steeling brute hearts.

A full moon shone silver on new-fallen snow;
Ice particles skirled; the temp was twenty below;
When what to wondering eyes should appear
But a pride of vile demons: eight slavering pain-fears!

And driving them on, so lively and quick
The Arch Fiend of Hell: face tentacled and slick;
More rapid than comets his coursers they came
and he whistled, and shouted, and called them by name:

"Brain Dasher! Skull Masher! Pain Dancer and Vex Him!
On, Vomit! On, Thunder! Putrid and Hexen!
To the top of the porch! To the top of the wall!
Now dash away! Smash away! Crash away all!"

As battle flags ripple 'fore hurricane blast
And foul flaming cats yowl and claw at their ass;
Up to the slant housetop the demon pride flew
Howling and shrieking—haint Prickle Mass, too!

And then in a twinkling, Hengar heard on the roof
A stamping and stomping of hell-romping hooves;
He squeaked in joy, looked madly around
As down the ol' chimney haint Prickle Mass bound.

Dressed in green fur from slime head to foot—
Spattered with blood, bits of bone, and black soot;
Eyes crimson pools of demon-dark fire
Wreathed in white smoke, kindled from pyres

Blazing in space alien and far-
Off where elder gods rumble and roar:
A dimension of savagery, of unending war,
A nihilist null-void of cracked bones and hot gore.

Hengar and haint Prickle Mass charged down the hall
Followed by pain-fears: eight demons in thrall
To blood lust, and fury, and maniacal glee;
They fell upon humans who'd no time to flee.

Bob and Jo Thompson were tucked in their bed—
SLASHITY! STABBITY!—now woefully dead!
Haint Prickle Mass spoke not a word as they worked;
All sundered in silence, took heads with a jerk.

And when they were done the horde chortled and danced;
Haint Prickle Mass frolicked; eight pain-fears pranced!
Then back down the hall this carnival of hell
Pounded *en masse*: a demonic pell-mell.

And laying a talon aside of his nose
With a wink and a nod up the chimney they rose
To the rainbow portal that flickered and strobed

Out in the white-drifted, moon-glowed snow.

Thus demon horde vanished into time and black space
Leaving nary a trickle; yea, nary a trace
Of their passing. Haint Prickle Mass cried, "Teeny friend—
Meepy-weep no more; thy dead are avenged!"

The Story of the Goblins who Stole a Sexton

Charles Dickens

In an old abbey town, down in this part of the country, a long, long while ago—so long, that the story must be a true one, because our great-grandfathers implicitly believed it—there officiated as sexton and grave-digger in the churchyard, one Gabriel Grub. It by no means follows that because a man is a sexton, and constantly surrounded by the emblems of mortality, therefore he should be a morose and melancholy man; your undertakers are the merriest fellows in the world; and I once had the honour of being on intimate terms with a mute, who in private life, and off duty, was as comical and jocose a little fellow as ever chirped out a devil-may-care song, without a hitch in his memory, or drained off a good stiff glass without stopping for breath. But notwithstanding these precedents to the contrary, Gabriel Grub was an ill-conditioned, cross-grained, surly fellow—a morose and lonely man, who consorted with nobody but himself, and an old wicker bottle which fitted into his large deep waistcoat pocket—and who eyed each merry face, as it passed him by, with such a deep scowl of malice and ill-humour, as it was difficult to meet without feeling something the worse for.

A little before twilight, one Christmas Eve, Gabriel shouldered his spade, lighted his lantern, and betook himself towards the old churchyard; for he had got a grave to finish by next morning, and, feeling very low, he thought it might raise his spirits, perhaps, if he went on with his work at once. As he went his way, up the ancient street, he saw the cheerful light of the blazing fires gleam through the old casements, and heard the loud laugh and the cheerful shouts of those who were assembled around them; he marked the bustling preparations for next day's cheer, and smelled the numerous savoury odours consequent thereupon, as they steamed up from the kitchen windows in clouds. All this was gall and wormwood to the heart of Gabriel Grub; and when groups of children bounded out of the houses, tripped across the road, and were met, before they could knock at the opposite door, by half a dozen curly-headed little rascals who crowded round them as they flocked upstairs to spend the evening in their Christmas games, Gabriel smiled grimly, and clutched the handle of his spade with a firmer grasp, as he thought of measles, scarlet fever, thrush, whooping-cough, and a good many other sources of consolation besides.

In this happy frame of mind, Gabriel strode along, returning a short, sullen growl to the good-humoured greetings of such of his neighbours as now and then passed him, until he turned into the dark lane which led to the churchyard. Now, Gabriel had been looking forward to reaching the dark lane, because it was, generally speaking, a nice, gloomy, mournful place, into which the townspeople did not much care to go, except in broad daylight, and when the sun was shining; consequently, he was not a little indignant to hear a young urchin roaring out some jolly song about a merry Christmas, in this very sanctuary which had been called Coffin Lane ever since the days of the old abbey, and the time of the shaven-headed monks. As Gabriel walked on, and the voice drew nearer, he found it proceeded from a small boy, who was hurrying along, to join one of the little parties in the old street, and who, partly to keep himself company, and partly to prepare himself for the occasion, was shouting out the song at the highest pitch of his lungs. So Gabriel waited until the boy came up, and then dodged him into a corner, and rapped him over the head with his lantern five or six times, just to teach him to modulate his voice. And as the boy hurried away with his hand to his head, singing quite a different sort of tune, Gabriel Grub chuckled very heartily to himself, and entered the churchyard, locking the gate behind him.

He took off his coat, set down his lantern, and getting into the unfinished grave, worked at it for an hour or so with right good-will. But the earth was hardened with the frost, and it was no very easy matter to break it up, and shovel it out; and although there was a moon, it was a very young one, and shed little light upon the grave, which was in the shadow of the church. At any other time, these obstacles would have made Gabriel Grub very moody and miserable, but he was so well pleased with having stopped the small boy's singing, that he took little heed of the scanty progress he had made, and looked down into the grave, when he had finished work for the night, with grim satisfaction, murmuring as he gathered up his things—

Brave lodgings for one, brave lodgings for one,

A few feet of cold earth, when life is done;
A stone at the head, a stone at the feet,
A rich, juicy meal for the worms to eat;
Rank grass overhead, and damp clay around,
Brave lodgings for one, these, in holy ground!

"Ho! ho!" laughed Gabriel Grub, as he sat himself down on a flat tombstone which was a favourite resting-place of his, and drew forth his wicker bottle. "A coffin at Christmas! A Christmas box! Ho! ho! ho!"

"Ho! ho! ho!" repeated a voice which sounded close behind him.

Gabriel paused, in some alarm, in the act of raising the wicker bottle to his lips, and looked round. The bottom of the oldest grave about him was not more still and quiet than the churchyard in the pale moonlight. The cold hoar frost glistened on the tombstones, and sparkled like rows of gems, among the stone carvings of the old church. The snow lay hard and crisp upon the ground; and spread over the thickly-strewn mounds of earth, so white and smooth a cover that it seemed as if corpses lay there, hidden only by their winding sheets. Not the faintest rustle broke the profound tranquillity of the solemn scene. Sound itself appeared to be frozen up, all was so cold and still.

"It was the echoes," said Gabriel Grub, raising the bottle to his lips again.

"It was NOT," said a deep voice.

Gabriel started up, and stood rooted to the spot with astonishment and terror; for his eyes rested on a form that made his blood run cold.

Seated on an upright tombstone, close to him, was a strange, unearthly figure, whom Gabriel felt at once, was no being of this world. His long, fantastic legs which might have reached the ground, were cocked up, and crossed after a quaint, fantastic fashion; his sinewy arms were bare; and his hands rested on his knees. On his short, round body, he wore a close covering, ornamented with small slashes; a short cloak dangled at his back; the collar was cut into curious peaks, which served the goblin in lieu of ruff or neckerchief; and his shoes curled up at his toes into long points. On his head, he wore a broad-brimmed sugar-loaf hat, garnished with a single feather. The hat was covered with the white frost; and the goblin looked as if he had sat on the same tombstone very comfortably, for two or three hundred years. He was sitting perfectly still; his tongue was put out, as if in derision; and he was grinning at Gabriel Grub with such a grin as only a goblin could call up.

"It was NOT the echoes," said the goblin.

Gabriel Grub was paralysed, and could make no reply.

"What do you do here on Christmas Eve?" said the goblin sternly.

"I came to dig a grave, Sir," stammered Gabriel Grub.

"What man wanders among graves and churchyards on such a night as this?" cried the goblin.

"Gabriel Grub! Gabriel Grub!" screamed a wild chorus of voices that seemed to fill the churchyard. Gabriel looked fearfully round—nothing was to be seen.

"What have you got in that bottle?" said the goblin.

"Hollands, sir," replied the sexton, trembling more than ever; for he had bought it of the smugglers, and he thought that perhaps his questioner might be in the excise department of the goblins.

"Who drinks Hollands alone, and in a churchyard, on such a night as this?" said the goblin.

"Gabriel Grub! Gabriel Grub!" exclaimed the wild voices again.

The goblin leered maliciously at the terrified sexton, and

then raising his voice, exclaimed—

"And who, then, is our fair and lawful prize?"

To this inquiry the invisible chorus replied, in a strain that sounded like the voices of many choristers singing to the mighty swell of the old church organ—a strain that seemed borne to the sexton's ears upon a wild wind, and to die away as it passed onward; but the burden of the reply was still the same, "Gabriel Grub! Gabriel Grub!"

The goblin grinned a broader grin than before, as he said, "Well, Gabriel, what do you say to this?"

The sexton gasped for breath.

"What do you think of this, Gabriel?" said the goblin, kicking up his feet in the air on either side of the tombstone, and looking at the turned-up points with as much complacency as if he had been contemplating the most fashionable pair of Wellingtons in all Bond Street.

"It's—it's—very curious, Sir," replied the sexton, half dead with fright; "very curious, and very pretty, but I think I'll go back and finish my work, Sir, if you please."

"Work!" said the goblin, "what work?"

"The grave, Sir; making the grave," stammered the sexton.

"Oh, the grave, eh?" said the goblin; "who makes graves at a time when all other men are merry, and takes a pleasure in it?"

Again the mysterious voices replied, "Gabriel Grub! Gabriel Grub!"

"I am afraid my friends want you, Gabriel," said the goblin, thrusting his tongue farther into his cheek than ever—and a most astonishing tongue it was—"I'm afraid my friends want you, Gabriel," said the goblin.

"Under favour, Sir," replied the horror-stricken sexton, "I don't think they can, Sir; they don't know me, Sir; I don't think the gentlemen have ever seen me, Sir."

"Oh, yes, they have," replied the goblin; "we know the man with the sulky face and grim scowl, that came down the street to-night, throwing his evil looks at the children, and grasping his burying-spade the tighter. We know the man who struck the boy in the envious malice of his heart, because the boy could be merry, and he could not. We know him, we know him."

Here, the goblin gave a loud, shrill laugh, which the echoes returned twentyfold; and throwing his legs up in the air, stood upon his head, or rather upon the very point of his sugar-loaf hat, on the narrow edge of the tombstone, whence he threw a Somerset with extraordinary agility, right to the sexton's feet, at which he planted himself in the attitude in which tailors generally sit upon the shop-board.

"I—I—am afraid I must leave you, Sir," said the sexton, making an effort to move.

"Leave us!" said the goblin, "Gabriel Grub going to leave us. Ho! ho! ho!"

As the goblin laughed, the sexton observed, for one instant, a brilliant illumination within the windows of the church, as if the whole building were lighted up; it disappeared, the organ pealed forth a lively air, and whole troops of goblins, the very counterpart of the first one, poured into the church-yard, and began playing at leap-frog with the tombstones, never stopping for an instant to take breath, but "overing" the highest among them, one after the other, with the most marvellous dexterity. The first goblin was a most astonishing leaper, and none of the others could come near him; even in the extremity of his terror the sexton could not help observing, that while his friends were content to leap over the common-sized gravestones, the first one took the family vaults, iron railings and all, with as much ease as if they had been so many street-posts.

At last the game reached to a most exciting pitch; the organ played quicker and quicker, and the goblins leaped faster and faster, coiling themselves up, rolling head over heels upon the ground, and bounding over the tombstones like footballs. The sexton's brain whirled round with the rapidity of the motion he beheld, and his legs reeled beneath him, as the spirits flew before his eyes; when the goblin king, suddenly darting towards him, laid his hand upon his collar, and sank with him through the earth.

When Gabriel Grub had had time to fetch his breath, which the rapidity of his descent had for the moment taken away, he found himself in what appeared to be a large cavern, surrounded on all sides by crowds of goblins, ugly and grim; in the centre of the room, on an elevated seat, was stationed his friend of the churchyard; and close behind him stood Gabriel Grub himself, without power of motion.

"Cold to-night," said the king of the goblins, "very cold. A glass of something warm here!"

At this command, half a dozen officious goblins, with a perpetual smile upon their faces, whom Gabriel Grub imagined to be courtiers, on that account, hastily disappeared, and presently returned with a goblet of liquid fire, which they presented to the king.

"Ah!" cried the goblin, whose cheeks and throat were transparent, as he tossed down the flame, "this warms one, indeed! Bring a bumper of the same, for Mr. Grub."

It was in vain for the unfortunate sexton to protest that he was not in the habit of taking anything warm at night; one of the goblins held him while another poured the blazing liquid down his throat; the whole assembly screeched with laughter, as he coughed and choked, and wiped away the tears which gushed plentifully from his eyes, after swallowing the burning draught.

"And now," said the king, fantastically poking the taper corner of his sugar-loaf hat into the sexton's eye, and thereby occasioning him the most exquisite pain; "and now, show the man of misery and gloom, a few of the pictures from our own great storehouse!"

As the goblin said this, a thick cloud which obscured the remoter end of the cavern rolled gradually away, and disclosed, apparently at a great distance, a small and scantily furnished, but neat and clean apartment. A crowd of little children were gathered round a bright fire, clinging to their mother's gown, and gambolling around her chair. The mother occasionally rose, and drew aside the window-curtain, as if to look for some expected object; a frugal meal was ready spread upon the table; and an elbow chair was placed near the fire. A knock was heard at the door; the mother opened it, and the children crowded round her, and clapped their hands for joy, as their father entered. He was wet and weary, and shook the snow from his garments, as the children crowded round him, and seizing his cloak, hat, stick, and gloves, with busy zeal, ran with them from the room. Then, as he sat down to his meal before the fire, the children climbed about his knee, and the mother sat by his side, and all seemed happiness and comfort.

But a change came upon the view, almost imperceptibly. The scene was altered to a small bedroom, where the fairest and youngest child lay dying; the roses had fled from his cheek, and the light from his eye; and even as the sexton looked upon him with an interest he had never felt or known before, he died. His young brothers and sisters crowded round his little bed, and seized his tiny hand, so cold and heavy; but they shrank back from its touch, and looked with awe on his infant face; for calm and tranquil as it was, and sleeping in rest and peace as the beautiful child seemed to be, they saw that he was dead, and they knew that he was an angel looking down upon, and blessing them, from a bright and happy Heaven.

Again the light cloud passed across the picture, and again the subject changed. The father and mother were old and help-less now, and the number of those about them was dimin-ished more than half; but content and cheerfulness sat on every face, and beamed in every eye, as they crowded round the fire-side, and told and listened to old stories of earlier and bygone days. Slowly and peacefully, the father sank into the grave, and, soon after, the sharer of all his cares and troubles fol-lowed him to a place of rest. The few who yet survived them, kneeled by their tomb, and watered the green turf which cov-ered it with their tears; then rose, and turned away, sadly and mournfully, but not with bitter cries, or despairing lamenta-tions, for they knew that they should one day meet again; and once more they mixed with the busy world, and their content and cheerfulness were restored. The cloud settled upon the picture, and concealed it from the sexton's view.

"What do you think of THAT?" said the goblin, turning his large face towards Gabriel Grub.

Gabriel murmured out something about its being very pretty, and looked somewhat ashamed, as the goblin bent his fiery eyes upon him.

"You miserable man!" said the goblin, in a tone of exces-sive contempt. "You!" He appeared disposed to add more, but indignation choked his utterance, so he lifted up one of his very pliable legs, and, flourishing it above his head a little, to insure his aim, administered a good sound kick to Gabriel Grub; immediately after which, all the goblins in waiting crowded round the wretched sexton, and kicked him without mercy, according to the established and invariable custom of courtiers upon earth, who kick whom royalty kicks, and hug whom royalty hugs.

"Show him some more!" said the king of the goblins.

At these words, the cloud was dispelled, and a rich and beautiful landscape was disclosed to view—there is just such another, to this day, within half a mile of the old abbey town. The sun shone from out the clear blue sky, the water sparkled beneath his rays, and the trees looked greener, and the flowers more gay, beneath its cheering influence. The water rippled on with a pleasant sound, the trees rustled in the light wind that murmured among their leaves, the birds sang upon the boughs, and the lark carolled on high her welcome to the morning. Yes, it was morning; the bright, balmy morning of summer; the minutest leaf, the smallest blade of grass, was instinct with life. The ant crept forth to her daily toil, the butterfly fluttered and basked in the warm rays of the sun; myriads of insects spread their transparent wings, and revelled in their brief but happy existence. Man walked forth, elated with the scene; and all was brightness and splendour.

"YOU a miserable man!" said the king of the goblins, in a more contemptuous tone than before. And again the king of the goblins gave his leg a flourish; again it descended on the shoulders of the sexton; and again the attendant goblins imitated the example of their chief.

Many a time the cloud went and came, and many a lesson it taught to Gabriel Grub, who, although his shoulders smarted with pain from the frequent applications of the goblins' feet thereunto, looked on with an interest that nothing could diminish. He saw that men who worked hard, and earned their scanty bread with lives of labour, were cheerful and happy; and that to the most ignorant, the sweet face of Nature was a never-failing source of cheerfulness and joy. He saw those who had been delicately nurtured, and tenderly brought up, cheerful under privations, and superior to suffering, that would have crushed many of a rougher grain, because they bore within their own bosoms the materials of happiness, content-ment, and peace. He saw that women, the tenderest and most fragile of all God's creatures, were the oftenest superior to sor-row, adversity, and distress; and he saw that it was because they bore, in their own hearts, an inexhaustible well-spring of affection and devotion. Above all, he saw that men like himself, who snarled at the mirth and cheerfulness of others, were the foulest weeds on the fair surface of the earth; and setting all the good of the world against the evil, he came to the conclusion that it was a very decent and respectable sort of world after all. No sooner had he formed it, than the cloud which had closed over the last picture, seemed to settle on his senses, and lull him to repose. One by one, the goblins faded from his sight; and, as the last one disappeared, he sank to sleep.

The day had broken when Gabriel Grub awoke, and found himself lying at full length on the flat gravestone in the church-yard, with the wicker bottle lying empty by his side, and his coat, spade, and lantern, all well whitened by the last night's frost, scattered on the ground. The stone on which he had first seen the goblin seated, stood bolt upright before him, and the grave at which he had worked, the night before, was not far off. At first, he began to doubt the reality of his adventures, but the acute pain in his shoulders when he attempted to rise, assured him that the kicking of the goblins was certainly not ideal. He was staggered again, by observing no traces of footsteps in the snow on which the goblins had played at leap-frog with the gravestones, but he speedily accounted for this circumstance when he remembered that, being spirits, they would leave no visible impression behind them. So, Gabriel Grub got on his feet as well as he could, for the pain in his back; and, brushing the frost off his coat, put it on, and turned his face towards the town.

But he was an altered man, and he could not bear the thought of returning to a place where his repentance would be scoffed at, and his reformation disbelieved. He hesitated for a few moments; and then turned away to wander where he might, and seek his bread elsewhere.

The lantern, the spade, and the wicker bottle were found, that day, in the churchyard. There were a great many speculations about the sexton's fate, at first, but it was speedily determined that he had been carried away by the goblins; and there were not wanting some very credible witnesses who had distinctly seen him whisked through the air on the back of a chestnut horse blind of one eye, with the hind-quarters of a lion, and the tail of a bear. At length all this was devoutly believed; and the new sexton used to exhibit to the curious, for a trifling emolument, a good-sized piece of the church weathercock which had been accidentally kicked off by the aforesaid horse in his aerial flight, and picked up by himself in the churchyard, a year or two afterwards.

Unfortunately, these stories were somewhat disturbed by the unlooked-for reappearance of Gabriel Grub himself, some ten years afterwards, a ragged, contented, rheumatic old man. He told his story to the clergyman, and also to the mayor; and in course of time it began to be received as a matter of history, in which form it has continued down to this very day. The believers in the weathercock tale, having misplaced their confidence once, were not easily prevailed upon to part with it again, so they looked as wise as they could, shrugged their shoulders, touched their foreheads, and murmured something about Gabriel Grub having drunk all the Hollands, and then fallen asleep on the flat tombstone; and they affected to explain what he supposed he had witnessed in the goblin's cavern, by saying that he had seen the world, and grown wiser. But this opinion, which was by no means a popular one at any time, gradually died off; and be the matter how it may, as Gabriel Grub was afflicted with rheumatism to the end of his days, this story has at least one moral, if it teach no better one—and that is, that if a man turn sulky and drink by himself at Christmas time, he may make up his mind to be not a bit the better for it: let the spirits be never so good, or let them be even as many degrees beyond proof, as those which Gabriel Grub saw in the goblin's cavern.

S*NOW *ANGELS

R. Michael Burns

enry Piper stared into the drifts beyond his mullioned window and felt his blood go slushy in his veins.

It was absurd, of course, to be so frightened by such innocent things—childish figures impressed in the fresh-fallen snow. But when he flicked on the red-and-white fairy lights trimming his little Queen Anne house for the first time that Christmas season and saw them—three tidy snow angels adorning the buried lawn—a chill went through him that froze him to the marrow.

He took a shuddering breath, and another, to settle his stumbling heart. Nothing but kids playing games, he told himself, harmless mischief amplified by an old man's empty-house jitters and too much deep-winter quiet.

Except...

Except he was dead certain those false angels hadn't been

there as he'd clipped the last of the lights in place and climbed off his stepladder just minutes ago, twilight dimming away to night as he shuffled inside. And if there *had* been children around, he surely would've seen them or at least heard their chatter, their boots crunching the snow. They couldn't have sneaked in and made those shapes and tromped off without him catching them at it. *Couldn't* have. And where would they have come from in any case? The nearest neighbor lived a good quarter of a mile down the road, the closest with children at least twice that. What kids would bother playing here? It was much too far to go for a prank.

Henry grunted at himself, shook his head. "'Course it was kids. What else?" His voice, familiar, strong enough, made him feel slightly better, steadier on his feet. Not quite so alone for a moment.

And yet...

The more he looked at those innocent shapes, the less he trusted them. It wasn't just the impossible suddenness of their appearance; it was...something else, something so fundamental he couldn't quite grasp it.

He forced himself away from the window even as his breath began to fog the glass, turned, and stared aimlessly into the living room.

Grief threatened to rise in his throat, and he bit it back, hard.

He'd done what he could to cheer the place up—a neatly trimmed tree in the corner, pine boughs along the mantel, red and green candles marching like pilgrims along each little table. But he lacked Teresa's simple flair for it, her light hand, and none of it could disguise the room's essential emptiness. There ought to be the fragrance of sugar cookies fresh-baked, or spiced cider sending up curls of steam. All the little things she'd done, so simple, the details that could still stir in him memories of his own long-faded childhood, when he'd believed in the magic of Christmas without a flicker of doubt.

But his gentle, good-hearted wife was gone now, and all those past Christmases with her as distant and unattainable as the stars.

Henry snorted. No point indulging in sentimentality. No point in reminding himself of all he'd lost, of how meandering and echo-filled the house felt with only him to inhabit it. No point in losing himself in that darkness that seemed so present in every hall and neglected room…or the darkness drawn up close beyond the windows.

A deep shiver ran through him despite the fire he'd kindled in the fireplace; he hugged himself against the chill.

Hot cider. That'd do the trick. A nice, steaming mug of spiced cider, improved with a shot or two of rum. He'd warm himself with some eighty-proof holiday cheer, watch whatever sports he could find on TV, and forget about lonely rooms and too-long nights and anything he might have seen out there in the drifts.

✳ ✳ ✳

Wednesday, January 5th, 1881

Truly, it is a yuletide miracle! I know that dear Edward wanted a son, as men always shall, but in my heart, I had yearned and prayed for a daughter, a rosy-cheeked child whom I could drape all in lace, whose hair I could comb and dress in ribbons, whose secrets I could share. A child whose heart I could know to its depth and breadth. For what can a woman ever honestly know of the masculine heart, even if it is the heart of her own son?

And now I am blessed—and not once, nor even twice, but thrice! Three tiny, pink girls, beautiful and delicate as porcelain dolls! The Christmas gift I'd dreamt of has been delivered at last, if somewhat belatedly, and I could scarcely be happier. Edward tries for my sake to conceal his disappointment in me for failing to provide him with the son he so ardently desired, but even his dissatisfaction cannot ruin my joy. In any case, I am certain he shall come to adore them soon enough.

Doctor Perkins tells me I am fortunate to have come through such a difficult ordeal so well, and even more so the girls themselves. Surely, they had angels helping them into the world—surely they *are* angels, three perfect Christmas angels, heaven-sent to fill my life with activity and noise and cheer.

As I write, they are asleep and every bit as quiet as dolls. Annie, their nursemaid, sits among their bassinets, now and then giving a gentle rocking to whichever one might be inclined to stir, soothing them back into a contented drowsing. I think that I, too, shall sleep now. I feel my strength ebbing and am surprised that it has lasted me so long, after all I've given to the girls. I shall sleep and dream bright dreams of my three angels.

❄ ❄ ❄

Somewhere in the deep of night, Henry trembled himself half-awake, senseless murmurs crawling over his skin like spiders.

"Teresa," he muttered, twisting himself around under the sheets, "wha—"

But her side of the bed was cool and empty, of course, and for a moment, that merciless fact drowned out everything else, and his heart felt as cold and heavy as lead. After a minute, just looking at that abandoned space got to be too much, and he shut his eyes against the sight.

The instant he did, the whispers came back, senseless yet

urgent, and he sat up and groped for the lamp beside the bed, flicked it on.

Darkness withdrew all around, slunk into the corners, crept back under the bed.

The room was silent.

The voices had come from outside—he felt sure of it, although the only murmur now came from the wind whispering in the eaves, sighing through the trees at the edge of the property.

He tossed back the thick bedcovers and instantly regretted it. The room had gone as cold as a stone cellar, as if he'd left a window open all night. Shivering, he crawled out of bed, stuffed his feet into the slippers that had been Teresa's last Christmas gift to him, and shuffled toward the window.

If it hadn't been for the icy glow of the moon, he might have missed the figures in the yard. But the pale blue illumination picked them out with perfect clarity—three crude images stamped in the snow. Three mock-angels laid out there as if meant to be seen from just that angle, in just that light.

Henry's fingers clutched the windowsill with arthritic stiffness; his heart jackhammered in his chest. There was something strangely *lost* about those shapes, yet vaguely malicious, too, some dire warning written in a language he couldn't quite read. He had the crazy urge to run out there just as he was, an elderly fool in slippers and baggy flannel pajamas, and stomp them out, obliterate them in a frenzy of angry kicks...

But, of course, he would do no such thing. He hadn't lived the better part of eight decades by following childish whims, indulging foolish impulses. And why should such innocuous things fill him with such revulsion anyway? There was no sense to it, no reason at all to be so shocked and repulsed by those harmless depressions in the snow. He couldn't even call it vandalism.

All the same, a few minutes passed before he could bring himself to stop staring at the snow angels as if he half expected them to move or vanish as inexplicably as they'd come.

A violent shiver went through him, shaking him out of his reverie, making him aware all over again just how chilly the house had gotten while he slept. He turned from the window without letting himself look back out there, pulled on a tattered robe, and shuffled out into the hall to give the thermostat a tweak. He moved slowly, suddenly uncomfortable with the darkness in the narrow hallway, the stairwell gloom as impenetrable as brackish water. It shouldn't be so black down there, even with the curtains all drawn tight against the cold. There ought to be some hint of snow-brightened moonlight creeping in. That gloom felt treacherous—no way to be sure he was alone with so many shadows around, no way to be certain they hadn't gotten in—

Again, whispers—the ones that had tickled him awake, tiny senseless voices murmuring from the dark places of the house. And there were so many dark places. . .

He slapped the light switch at the top of the stairs, and at once the hallway was just a hallway again, the stairs only stairs, everything familiar and comfortingly banal.

Henry shook his head, pursed his lips. He could only imagine how Teresa would have scoffed at him, in her patient way, for being such a child. "Just turn up the heat and come back to bed," she'd mutter, rolling her eyes but smiling just the tiniest bit.

He bent close to the thermostat, squinting. The little red arrow already pointed at seventy-three degrees. Should've been enough to keep the house plenty toasty throughout. But even as he made the observation, he felt himself shivering once more. He nudged the dial up near eighty, heard the furnace rumble to life, the vents exhaling warmth.

That'll keep 'em out, he thought—and frowned. Keep *who* out, exactly?

"The cold," he told himself. "I only mean, that'll keep the cold out."

As he settled back into bed, he found he could almost believe himself.

❄ ❄ ❄

Monday, March 20th, 1882

How quickly the days and months fly past! It seems just yesterday that the girls, almost as one, learned to crawl about the nursery, wandering wherever their plump limbs might take them. And now, all at once, they are walking, all three of them! It is almost as though they conspired in the night and reached the decision together, knowing how they could challenge their tired mother and their good-hearted nursemaid by becoming ambulatory as a group. Now they totter about the room hither and thither, scattering neatly arranged dolls, toppling towers of wooden blocks, making it well-nigh impossible for we two adults to clean up after them while keeping them within our sight. I dread to imagine how things will be when they are quick enough and clever enough to escape the nursery and lose themselves in the rest of the house! It isn't as if our house is so large, but it is dark and meandering enough, with wandering hallways and staircases that rise as sheer as the Himalayas, and countless little rooms and closets where a wayward angel could hide herself and not be found for hours—for days!

Edward, of course, is little help. He has his duties at the firm to attend to, as always, but I know well enough that he has taken on extra work of late so that he might avoid coming home any sooner than he absolutely must.

I had hoped and believed that he would come to love the girls, but he merely tolerates them, as a man with a club foot comes to tolerate it out of necessity. He has tried aggressively to plant a son in my womb, but the more forcefully he exerts himself, the less successful he is, and his frustration on this score has turned him into something as cold and hard as a figure carved from ice.

Annie does all she might, but frankly, I believe that she is oftentimes too indulgent, too delighted in my three angels to correct them when they behave badly. And when she is retired to her room for the evening or gone on one of her many errands, I am too tired to do much more than watch them as they stagger and stomp about, undoing any semblance of order I've managed to create, poking into every corner and shadow of the room, asserting themselves upon every inch of my existence.

But I adore them, of course. I must love them all the more because their father isn't able, and all the better because their nursemaid is too careless with her affections.

If only it didn't all make me so very tired...

Henry closed the mailbox and sighed, watching his exhaustion drift away in a ghostly puff on the frigid air. No mail again today—not so much as an insurance ad or a phone bill. A man could only go so long without his phone ringing, without some sort of mail with his name on the envelope, before he started doubting his own existence. But that was his reward for outliving friends and family, it seemed—watching himself slowly fade out of the world's consciousness until, like Schrodinger's famous cat, he might be reduced to a state of non-being, neither life nor death, locked up in a black box of indeterminacy.

He wanted to laugh at the idea, to mock it, but found he couldn't quite.

Puffing, he kicked his way along the snow-swept curve of his driveway, back toward the house. Later, maybe, he'd drag out the snowblower, clear some of it off, as long as the sun stayed out. Teresa, of course, would've objected—"Get Teddy Ellison to do it," she'd say, referring to their neighbor's college-age son, a nice enough kid, but a little too eager somehow, a smidge more gracious than Henry could trust in a man that age. Besides, for all her advice on how to live a long life, Teresa had preceded him into the Hereafter, so maybe her wisdom was worth about what he'd paid for it.

He let out a little laugh, thumbed tears from the hollows of his eyes.

He could pretend as much as he liked that life went on, but that was half-true at best. Since the late-spring afternoon when the stroke had felled her, his own life had simply been winding down, tracing a similar path into oblivion. It would've been nice to dream he might meet her again on the other side, but nothing in life had ever led him to believe that death was anything other than an ending, a complete dissolution of all a person was: no pearly gates, no lashing flames, not even darkness.

The notion had always struck him as strangely comforting, at least for his own sake. He didn't see much need for a life beyond this one, modest as it was. But Teresa had deserved better. He supposed lots of people did.

He rubbed his cold-stung eyes with a gloved hand and took a slow, deep breath.

Nearby, someone spoke—murmured, really, a papery senseless whisper with a distinct edge of cruelty to it, as if his grief were someone else's cheap entertainment.

Anger flared in his chest, and he took a few stomping

steps in the direction the sounds seemed to have come from, determined to catch the little spies who found the pitiful old man so funny, sure they must be the same brats teasing him with the shapes in the snow.

He glared left and right, chasing hints of movement that flickered at the edges of his vision. But the snow-draped pines stood innocent all around, no trace of any intruders.

Rage threatened to erupt in furious shouts: *Stop it! Stop playing games and leave me the hell alone!*

But no—*no*. He wouldn't be that man, the crazy old coot standing in his yard hurling insults at the blameless snow.

Shaking with fury and cold, Henry turned back toward his too-quiet house—and stopped, heart stumbling as if it might quit on him.

All around lay fallen angels, their shapes fresh and clear, surrounding him like a gang of inquisitors. He forced himself to breathe, to slow his heart to a safer rhythm. He'd over-looked them, that's all, had stumbled into their midst too full of self-indulgent melancholy to notice them. They couldn't have simply *appeared* there, no matter how much vision and memory insisted they had. Such things just didn't happen in the dull-as-ditchwater world he inhabited.

He crouched down as best as his aching muscles would allow and stared at the angel at his feet, as if his years work-ing for the U.S. Postal Service had given him some incidental training in criminology and this was his crime scene. The shapes were smaller than he'd expected—not the size of kids who might be out for a prank, but of their much younger siblings, maybe. Somehow, that idea struck him as all the more inexplicable, all the more chilling—almost loathsome.

And even as this new revulsion surged through him, an-other realization came on its heels, that detail, the obvious one he'd missed the first night he'd seen the fallen angels, so simple, so basic…

The only footprints in the snow around the splayed shapes were his own.

✳ ✳ ✳

Thursday, February 1st, 1883

They've learned to get out, as I knew they would. All three of the girls, whispering to one another in that strange language which seems to belong uniquely to them. They nod together and conspire and smile—never laughing, never giggling like playful children are meant to, but murmuring all those senseless sounds, keeping their secrets, speaking only to one another. All three of them, so alike in every way, both in feature and mannerism. It upsets me sometimes, as if I had been cruelly tricked, delivered one daughter three times over and not three unique little girls. At times, they act so much in concert that I imagine I'm seeing one child surrounded by mirrors—except that even images in a mirror will ape their subjects in reverse, raising a right hand when the subject raises its left, and so forth. My precious angels refuse to show even that much variation amongst them.

Annie finds the whole thing charming, naturally, as if it were some adorable game. And Edward can scarcely be troubled to notice what his offspring are about. So it is left to me to chase them all around the house, upstairs and down, as if I am not frail enough from simply bringing them into the world. Doctor Perkins may have congratulated me on my excellent health at the time, but he either refused to admit or hadn't the wit to see the damage that had been done. After all, how could it not have taken a great deal out of me to produce three children all at once? My flesh, my blood, my bone. They took it for themselves and left me hollow, fragile as an empty glass vessel. I sometimes wonder if they don't mean to break me with their antics. Oh, to be sure, their smiles are full of innocence, and they look angelic enough in their white dressing gowns and tightly curled tresses. But I know better. How innocent can they be, these children who ruined my womb, made it impossible for me to bear Edward the son he demands? How gentle can their hearts be, they who sabotaged my marriage, and who now conspire against my delicate health?

Nonetheless, I shall try to love them, for that is my duty. I shall give myself to them — body & soul, if that is what is required of me. I can only hope that they shall be touched by some tiny fraction of their mother's love, for to imagine them growing up as they seem to be, three cold female expressions of their father, is too much for me to tolerate. I shall make gentle, loving beings of them yet, or...

❋ ❋ ❋

He jammed another log into the roaring fire and stood watching as it began to blacken and burn.

And still, he shivered.

It seemed no matter how much he turned up the heat, the place just wouldn't get warm. Must've been the furnace, although he and Teresa had replaced the thing not that many years ago. He'd cranked the thermostat up past eighty, but the vents remained silent.

Splendid.

He could only imagine what it would cost to get a repairman out here this time of year, Christmas just a couple of days away and snow piled deep all around. Might as well warm himself over a stack of burning cash.

He cupped his hands around his steaming mug, feeling the warmth creep into his flesh, his arthritic joints loosening some.

Another swallow of the heavily spiked cider helped a touch more.

He'd seldom indulged in such things when Teresa was around, if only because she'd never really had a taste for booze and he'd finally fallen out of the habit of drinking. Just about now, though, it seemed only reasonable. He turned his back to the fire, gazed out the windows. Beyond the red-and-white lit eaves, plump snowflakes came down, thick and steady, as if all the stars of heaven had burned to cinders and fallen from the firmament, burying the world in ashes. Had such evenings really made him feel cozy once? Perhaps—inasmuch as a man like Henry Piper might indulge in such sentimental emotions. But cozy, if that sort of thing existed, was something a man had to share with the one he loved. It couldn't be experienced alone.

Henry swallowed the last of his cider in a blazing gulp, but the chill that came after it seemed deeper than ever despite his thick wool sweater and the shirt under that. He'd be wearing a coat and gloves if the night kept on like this.

Grunting with old man aches, he abandoned his empty mug on the hearth and wandered to the nearest heating vent, an elaborate gilt thing set into the wall. It made him imagine days when the place probably had a big coal-fed furnace complete with a grimy wooden hopper and chute. Now only the feeblest breath of warmth came from beyond the brass grate, barely a sigh.

Well, maybe the Ellison kid could make himself useful after all. Lord knew Henry Piper wasn't up to stooping around the low-ceilinged cellar trying to determine what had gone wrong with the expensive hunk of hardware that was supposed to keep him from freezing to death in his own living room. And he wasn't about to pay time-and-a-half to get some middle-aged schlub from the manufacturer out here at this hour, even if the damn thing *was* still under warranty.

He flicked on the kitchen light, relieved to see only the falling snow beyond the window over the sink, as if he'd expected something...else...out there. Still, he didn't care much to be in the kitchen these days. It didn't feel right, didn't *smell* right since the odors of his own cooking had replaced Teresa's. He'd always been just a guest in that room, there by her permission, and now he felt like an intruder all over again. The sensation gave him a sort of aching satisfaction—lonely as they were, at least these feelings kept her alive here in some tiny measure.

Shivering again, he plucked the cordless phone from its base and scrolled through the stored numbers until the name ELLISON popped up. He jabbed the DIAL button, waited.

A quiet ring, a click. And silence.

Henry cleared his throat. "Ah... Hello? David? Teddy? Hello?"

The phone remained silent in his hand. Something in that quiet made him sure the line was open, but...*empty*, somehow...as if he'd dialed the furthest regions of the universe instead of the next house over. Or reached into the past...

Somewhere at the unthinkably distant other end of that line, someone murmured—a childish, senseless noise. The sound crept over his flesh like the touch of raw insanity, a contagion trying to burrow its way into his mind.

Henry slammed the handset down and stepped away, staring at the phone as if it were some venomous thing waiting to strike. He couldn't bring himself to turn his back on it, to stop watching it even for an instant.

He didn't dare.

"Be *sensible*," he told himself out loud, trying to hear it in Teresa's reassuringly logical voice but not quite able to do it.

The phone rang. Once, twice…

Teeth gritted, he put a hand on it.

Three times.

He forced himself to pick it up before the answering machine could intercept the call. He was an adult, for God's sake, and far too old to be frightened of prank calls…or whatever he'd just experienced.

He put the handset to his ear and opened his mouth to mutter, "Hello," but the whispers cut him off, left him mute. He heard an undertone of cruelty in those mutterings, but something pathetic as well, something deeply pitiful that was worse even than the viciousness.

"That's *enough!*" he heard himself say, sounding far braver than he felt. "I've had enough of your games! Leave me alone, or so help me…" He stammered, stopped, bankrupt of threats, feeling suddenly very old, impotent.

For a second, the silence resumed.

Then a voice came, tiny and broken and strangely choked, but somehow still tinged with spite: "We're *cold.*"

Henry's fingers went instantly numb, and the phone slipped free, hit the floor with a dry *crack*. The batteries went scudding across the parquet and vanished beneath the refrigerator like startled roaches.

The mere thought of crawling around after the damn things sent aches crackling through his back, and anyway, why give those nasty-spirited pranksters another chance to disturb his peace? The phone could rot where it had fallen for all it meant to Henry Piper, and so could the little brats who'd concocted these mean, petty, little stunts. Didn't they know it was damn near Christmas, time to shape up and show a little kindness?

Henry closed his eyes, massaged his temples with stiff, bony thumbs. How long had such old man thoughts occupied his mind? For years now, but mostly since Teresa left him. It had only been eight months, but he'd aged a few years since then, becoming the man his own father might've been had he lived as long, face scrawled with wrinkles, head full of silver hair…and old man thoughts.

He shuffled back into the living room, tugging his robe tight against the chill. For a time, he stood by the fire, watching the dying flames lap halfheartedly at the logs, the bank of ash beneath growing ever deeper. When had he last cleaned out the fireplace? He couldn't recall. Sometime while Teresa was still alive, no doubt, she being the one who always wanted a blaze going during the winter months. Perhaps if he cleaned it out, the fire would burn higher, maybe even warm the living room some. Of course—the ashes were choking the flames, smothering them. The whole thing needed to be swept clean… But not now. He'd do it in the light of day, when the world felt a few degrees safer, a few degrees saner. Just then, with the night pressed close against the windows and the winds sighing over the rooftops, he only wanted to keep the flames awake and dancing, fighting back the cold shadows with whatever heat they could muster. He couldn't snuff those flames, even to make the fire stronger. The thought of it filled him with a vast, irrational grief, as if once he let the flames die, he could never conjure them back. As if light and heat themselves would fade out of the world if he let this meager blaze die.

Nonsense, he told himself, almost whispering the word aloud, not quite daring. *You're thinking like a superstitious child terrified of stepping on a crack. Rattled by a load of ridiculous stunts and pranks. What you need is a good night's rest in a warm bed. When the sun's out, all these notions will seem every bit as foolish as they really are.*

But the instant he turned away from the faltering fire, panic washed through him, icy and enveloping, never mind how irrational. Perhaps he *was* cracking up, feeling the first sly effects of Alzheimer's or some other brand of senility. He'd deal with that tomorrow, too. For now, he had a fire to protect, his last defense against the deep gloom and the creeping cold.

He dragged an armchair out of its corner and parked it at the edge of the hearth, the tinder pile at his fingertips, and settled in for a long, long night. The darkness crouched all around, shuffling its silent feet at the edges of his vision, waiting for its moment.

❄ ❄ ❄

Thurs September 13th, 1883

Edward has left me, & he has not left alone. Annie, too, is gone, her little closet empty, her carpetbag vanished from her room.

I am not surprised.

Dear Edward imagined that I was somehow blind to the long gazes he gave her, the shameless hunger in his eyes. And darling Annie... She never guessed that I saw how she looked upon my children as if they were her own, as if her body had paid such a dear price to bring them forth, as if her soul had paid out so much of itself to make their hearts beat, their eyes shine so. Like the glass eyes of three cold porcelain dolls. No doubt Annie would have taken them had Edward allowed it. He, though, would never accept such a burden, even to please his trollop. I can only guess at the pleasure he took in placing that load entirely on my shoulders.

They scamper all over the house at their will now, lurching about like mechanical toys, their actions guided by clockwork gears and tightly coiled springs—like machines built by some cunning puppeteer to drive me to distraction. Constantly they murmur & mutter to one another in that language no adult could hope to penetrate, then scatter about the house, making noises at me from above & below, slamming doors & stomping over wooden floors and then hiding, sometimes for hours, or even days, until I can scarcely recall how many of them there are. Does the number even matter? Should I care at all if there are three of them, or a dozen, or only one, scrambling around the house? They are all the same, my angels. But it frustrates me deeply that however many of them I chase down, it always seems as if there must be another hiding somewhere, mocking my efforts, sending me on errands that always prove fruitless, even dangerous. Just yesterday, I came within inches of taking a terrible fall when I stepped on a toy one or other of them had left on the stairs. It was hidden in the shadow of the second step from the top, and when I unknowingly put my foot down on it, my ankle turned and I stumbled. Had I not caught myself on the railing as I fell, I am sure I would have ended up in a heap at the bottom of that tall staircase, my neck and frail limbs all snapped like the poor twigs they have become. And I am certain—yes, quite certain—that as I grasped the rail and strained to catch my breath, I heard one or more of them giggling—a mean, hateful, tittering sort of sound.

Indeed, I hear them now, two or three of them clustered in the hall just beyond where I sit writing

this. Plotting again. Murmuring. Crafting treacherous schemes to confound & exasperate & perhaps do
true harm to their mother, just as their father
and nursemaid must have plotted & schemed. They
won't get the better of me! I will not be defeated
by ice-hearted children scarcely out of diapers, no
matter how angelic their appearance. I am weak,
yes, & harried, but I am no fool. With Edward gone,
this house is mine, and mine alone, & I shall be
certain that my three angels understand this. I am
hurt & lost; yes, of course, what woman wouldn't be?
But I am not and will not be defeated.

* * *

The pounding jolted him out of his sleep like a blow to the chest, and for an instant he sat blinking, trying to make sense of where he was, of the jagged pains prodding at his back, stabbing at every joint, his whole body catgut-stiff.

Again, pounding, someone pounding on the front door, and Henry Piper staggered out of his chair even as his brain registered where he was: living room, camped out near the lifeless fireplace, the flames gone, not so much as a glowing ember or a curl of smoke left there.

Doesn't matter, he told himself, feeling wildly triumphant at the sight of white sunshine pouring in through the living room windows. *I made it! See... I made it!*

213

As if in answer, the thuds from outside grew louder—then ceased.

Halfway to the front door, Henry paused. The pounding was bad, but the sudden quiet was worse—expectant, like a trap baited and set.

"No more games," Henry muttered and stomped to the door and swung it wide and stared into the dazzling expanse of freshly fallen snow.

At the edge of his vision, a vague gray shape flitted off toward the trees marking the property line. No, not one shape, but two—or were there three? Kids, sure, the nasty little things that had left those absurd snow angels everywhere, the ones who'd somehow tinkered with his phone and left him feeling so old and dull-witted and unsure of himself.

Rage blazed through him and he loped out into the snow, sinking up to his knees and following the vague shapes anyway, each slippery glimpse of them between the trees spurring him on. Snow clotted on his flannel pajama pants, wrenched off first one house slipper then the other, but even the brutal cold stinging his feet didn't matter just then—adrenaline and righteous fury overwhelmed the pain. Ahead, the maze of pines opened on a clearing and he stumbled forward, sure he'd catch them there, out in the open with no place left to hide—

But the clearing lay empty, nothing more than pristine white snow all around...except—

"Oh, Lord—"

Scarcely five feet beyond where he stood, the wind had swept the snow away, exposing a bleak expanse like grayish glass—a pond, its surface glazed with a sheet of treacherous ice, its edges indistinct beneath the drifts. And in the center, three dark splotches, almost like shadows, where the ice was broken through.

It took very little imagination to make those pits in the

ice take on distinct shapes, shapes that had become so mockingly familiar to him over the past few days. . .

* * *

December 11, 1883 — Tues —

Their birthday grows near, and I find myself unable to sleep.

They are young, yes, I know this very well, but they grow sharper, more cunning every day, always conspiring together, keeping their numbers a secret from me. And I am certain that if they celebrate their next birthday, some unthinkable threshold will be crossed, some dangerous territory entered & the way out barred forever. Three is a magical number to them, after all. Why else would they pretend to be three? Three turning three. No one could doubt the dangerous power of such mathematics! The multiplications which might occur are simply too horrible to contemplate.

I find myself slipping into the nursery in the dead of night, counting them over & over, sure that

one or more must be missing, must be awake & creeping about, perhaps even spying on me as I attempt
to spy on them, or planting another trap. Their
numbers never reassure me. I count three, but I know
that number can no longer be trusted, was never
the truth. I can only guess at why Edward & Annie &
even Doctor Perkins lied to me about how many
children I'd given birth to that day, what evil
agenda they were perpetrating with their false-
hoods. It hardly matters now that I've seen through
the deception.

The girls are very excited about Christmas, of
course. As I write, several of them are out flopping
in the snow, making snowmen & angels & such as
children will do, playing as if their innocence were
genuine, & not some cunning ploy to lure me into a
false sense of comfort. Their father has sent along
gifts (by post, naturally—he hasn't the courage to
show himself in person, even to see his daughters) &
although the curt note that accompanies the presents does not say so, I see Annie's hand in their

selection. Edward would never have had such clever taste—indeed, one doubts he would have troubled himself at all had Annie not insisted. He has even sent along a fir tree, which stands now in the corner of the parlor, as our previous Christmas trees have. Another of Annie's guilty offerings, no doubt. But I have not had the heart or the strength to decorate it, & the little ones aren't to be trusted with the glass baubles, so the tree stands naked in its place as if it were some intruder from the woods beyond the house.

I see by their eyes that the girls know what lies ahead, or sense it as I do, that with the celebration of their birth will come some new power, some strength I shall no longer be able to deny or even keep in check. They yearn for it perhaps even more eagerly than they yearn for the Yuletide merriment.

They expect some great surprise from Saint Nicholas, I know, as children their age do at this time of year. And surely some tremendous surprise is in order for my clever little angels.

I must see to it that they are not disappointed.

✳ ✳ ✳

His feet stung fiercely, but he felt fairly sure he'd managed to get back inside fast enough to prevent frostbite. Not that the house was too much warmer than the great outdoors—it seemed the winter chill had taken over the whole place, fierce and clinging. At least the floors were dry and solid under him.

He collapsed into the chair he'd set beside the fireplace and grabbed a handful of kindling, eager—almost desperate—to get a new fire going. Only the fire could banish the cold in his house, in his veins. Only the fire could keep the shadows back, could keep the angels from creeping inside with him.

Henry laughed, or maybe it was a sob. He'd lost it, that was clear enough, lost his mind—not all of it, but some component vital for clinging to the slippery surface of reality. He'd lost his grip, as the saying went, but that seemed far less important than getting his fire going and banishing the shadow angels from the house. As long as they couldn't get in, couldn't get *close*, he would be fine. He stuck another piece of split wood on the pile he'd built, then snatched up the matchbox and shook out a wooden match—the *last* match. Dammit—hadn't the box been at least half-full just last night? He couldn't be sure, couldn't quite trust such simple memories anymore. They didn't matter anyway. What mattered was that he had one shot at getting this little project right.

He gave the match a flick over the hearthstones—and watched it flip from his numbed fingertips and vanish into the heap of ash he'd never gotten around to clearing away.

A ridiculous, childish cry escaped him even as his hands

plunged into the filthy, crumbling heap, groping for that vital stick of wood, everything turning to dust in his grasp. Then his fingers snagged something, a brittle sheaf of paper that had somehow gone unburned under it all.

The neatly folded pages looked ancient, their corners curled and black, but the rest was shockingly intact, as if they'd been plucked from the fire rather than lost for who-knew-how-long in the ash pile.

Impossible, the rational voice in him insisted. *You've cleaned this fireplace dozens of times. How could this little bundle have slipped past you every time?*

It couldn't have, of course, not in any world that obeyed rational rules. But somehow, some time ago, he'd drifted outside of that world, wound up here in the penumbra between reason and insanity, this place where the shadows could leave impressions in the snow and things that should have been long lost might return, in one form or another. After all he'd seen in these dark days creeping toward Christmas, he could no longer hold so tightly to the idea that all of existence followed strict, quantifiable laws. Sometimes the barriers broke down, the universe buckled under the frequently irrational freight of the human heart until even reality got tangled up in itself and dream-logic ruled the day. And here he held the proof, a missive from another age sent by unknown hands, left among the ashes for him to find on Christmas Eve day. Even without opening the delicate pages, he could sense their author—some long-forgotten resident of the old house he and Teresa had chosen to retire in. A lost wraith reaching across the abyss to him.

Fingers trembling, he gingerly unfolded the pages and began to read.

✻ ✻ ✻

Dec 25th—Christmas—1883

It is done, & weren't the girls surprised! Oh, the expressions on their tiny round doll faces, oh the way they screamed & cried out! For the first time in far longer than I can recall, they seemed truly like little girls, sweet little innocent angels such as any mother must simply adore. And I—I could but watch them with the deep satisfaction of a mother who has given her girls precisely what they de-served. Precisely what was needed.

Tempting them out onto the frozen pond in the woods beyond the house proved far less difficult than I'd feared, & of course the ice held the box with its bright ribbons well enough as the box was empty & weighed very little. I'd placed it with great care in the dead of night when I was confident the ice would be at its strongest, using a broomstick to push it out as far as I dared, so that it sat neatly over the deepest part of the pond.

One of the girls had wit enough to ask why Saint Nicholas would leave their special present out in the snow, but I simply winked & told them all that it was a secret, & for all their cunning & cleverness, they trusted me. Or else their greed simply overwhelmed such concerns.

In any case, they ran to it, just as I'd imagined they would, in a tight cluster—thick as thieves, one might even say!—the crisp snow crunching under their tiny boots, their breath puff-ing in the air like smoke from a chugging steam train.

The ice gave way all at once—it was almost comical to see! Three little doll figures bundled in cloaks & mittens, there one moment & vanished the next! Then came the splashing & screaming, all of them clawing at the useless snow, their eyes so big & shocked, their voices imitating fear, crying for me.

I knew better, of course. They weren't afraid, not in the least! They were simply angry that I'd bested them, beaten them while yet I could. I saw the fury behind their false terror, the hatred they'd learned from their father showing through the feigned innocence they'd copied from Annie.

The flailing & splashing & cracking of ice didn't last

long at all.

Later—

I should be pleased, happy that it is finally done & I can rest. And yet—I cannot chase away that fear, that fear of numbers. Are they *all* gone, those false angels? Are they all growing sodden & cold in the modest depths of the pond? Or—have I missed one? More than one? Are there others, other copies running about even now, hiding in closets & attic shadows & basement trunks? They are so like mice, like rats—how can one ever be certain that they have all been gotten rid of? I pause, & listen carefully, & the house—at last!—seems per-fectly silent. But they are tricky, those false angels, & might yet be lurking, biding their time, until—

I won't sleep—not a wink—if that's what's required of me. I will remain vigilant at all times, & if there are any of them left, or if they try to creep back in, I'll know—they won't catch *me* unawares!

❄ ❄ ❄

By the time Henry Piper finished reading, snow had begun to fall again, steady and silent and deep. His hand shook as he lowered the brittle pages, his fingertips numb, as if the crazy woman's narrative had stung them with frostbite.

He shuddered, chilled from the inside. How far gone, how completely stark, raving insane did a woman have to be to act out such paranoid madness? He stared into the living room, taking it all in yet seeing none of it—the tree (done up as Teresa liked it, as if she might yet show up for a glass of eggnog), the pine-garland trim, the little knickknacks (candles, wooden nativity scene, all of it set out because she would have expected it). The whole lonely imitation of Christmases past faded to invisibility before his eyes, swept away by a single, devastating image: the iced-over pond and the three dark, familiarly shaped pits in its frigid surface. He could imagine only too well the helpless girls thrashing and crying, screaming, too young to comprehend what had been done to them, knowing only that the icy water had sunk its claws into their flesh like a monster from their worst nightmares, dragging them down into a smothering darkness—and Mommy wasn't trying to help them. She was there *but not trying to help them.*

Had the three of them carried those thoughts with them into death, that terror and abandonment? If so, they could hardly be blamed for sleeping so restlessly.

Henry laughed, a raw, harsh sound in the snow-deepened silence. Not a week ago, he would've snorted at the very idea of ghosts or any continuation of a person's identity beyond death. But now, on this night when much of the world celebrated the birth of a man who, it was said, had returned from death, Henry Piper felt he could no longer trust what he'd come to think of as the Basic Rules of Reality. The world was far more slippery, far less clearly defined than he'd allowed himself to believe. Or else... Perhaps it was his mind that had slipped a cog or two. Perhaps hunkering here in his little house under the snow, alone, alone, all all alone (as some poet had once written), he'd simply drifted into a bleak fantasy full of ghosts and madness. Why on earth he would dream up a psychotic mother terrified of her own daughters he couldn't guess, but the notion that all of this was the product of some sort of senility struck him as strangely comforting. After all, which was better, easier to believe, and maybe even live with? That his mind had broken down, or that reality itself had cracked?

From somewhere nearby came a childish murmur, very like what he'd heard on the dead phone line.

With shuddering slowness, he looked up at the mullioned window.

Three dead-gray faces gazed back at him, round and blank, eyes shiny, black pits above prominent ivory cheekbones.

Henry flinched, heartbeat pounding in his throat—and then the window was empty, as it surely had been all along, those ghostly faces just another amusing little prank his crumbling mind had played on itself.

But... He could see muddy, wet smudges on the glass, freezing there in the brutal cold like after-images.

Why now? he thought, and the question had a sharp edge of bitterness to it, of something like desperation. *We've been in this house for—what?—twelve years? Twelve years of peace and not so much as a whisper, no hint of ghosts or things that go bump in the night. So why now?*

But the answer was right there for him, in his own question. *We've been in this house...* Except there was no "we" anymore—not this Christmas. Just him. Henry Piper, a man alone. No more "we," no more buffer against the world's darker things.

The temperature in the living room seemed to dive another few degrees toward freezing, the lights to dim, as if the chill itself had cast a shadow over the whole house.

Gotta get that fire going, Henry chided himself, and the imperative had a note of urgency in it. *Gotta keep the cold back...the shadows...*

Matches—a match. He ignored the empty box and searched the kitchen, dug through every drawer and cabinet, sure he'd find something—a Bic lighter abandoned by some houseguest, a matchbook taken from a long-forgotten motel or restaurant. But by the time he collapsed in front of the dead fireplace, he felt as if he'd rummaged through every drawer, ransacked every room, and come up empty-handed. It was crazy. Any house that had been occupied for more than a year or two was bound to have acquired that all-American detritus: take-out menus, random keys, stray postcards—and matchbooks. Not as popular as they'd been in his younger days when bars and hotels and the like expected you to smoke and always made sure to give you a light, but still... It was almost as if...as if...

Henry laughed again, a raw, unhealthy sound, every bit as cheerless and fatal as the hacking cough of a lung cancer patient. But how could he *not* mock himself for having such an idea, for thinking that it was almost as if someone had sneaked in and swiped every last matchbook? As if three innocent little girls, dead for over a hundred years now, might creep into his home (yes, his now, regardless of any family history they might have here) and sneak off with every source of flame. As if three drowned-like-kittens little girls could be so calculating, so malicious...

* * *

December —?? 18—

I've failed.

I thought I had rid myself of them all, or at

least the original three, for weren't there only three at first? And surely the others would wither to dust if I destroyed the first? Or perhaps I was wrong from the start about their numbers. I can no longer recall—so many things I cannot recall, memories as inconstant as tallow, melting & running together in a senseless mess.

It doesn't matter. They are still here. I hear them at night, making the floor planks creak, making the windows rattle, thumping doors open & shut. I catch glimpses of them at the edges of my vision, their eyes dark, their hair lank, skin ghastly pale. And when it is dark & the wind falls still, I hear their whispers, that strange language they speak amongst themselves.

And this morning—is it Christmas morning still? can it be?—I saw in the fresh snow all around the house deep impressions such as children make, flapping their arms & legs in imitation of angels. Fallen angels, outside every window.

I've no idea how many are in the house with me now—one for each of those impressions in the snow? More? An industrious few? That, too, doesn't matter. I shall not let them have their way, their revenge, whatever it is they want of me. They won't destroy me!

I discovered the arsenic among the clutter in the cellar, almost as if someone had left it there for me to find. If the dime novels I thieved from my brothers as a girl are to be believed at all, I am confident that it will do for me what must be done. I can only guess at what reward may await me in the next life, but I find that hard to imagine or even concern myself with. All that matters now is finishing this dreadful business on my own terms. Even as I write these words, I know well that I must burn these pages lest they ever be discovered & misunderstood. But quickly now—I hear their voices in the hall, & they mustn't be allowed to stop me—

❄ ❄ ❄

Henry Piper blinked himself to wakefulness and instantly started to shiver. Before him, the fireplace sat dead-breathless, the furnace vents silent all around. Snow had painted over the windows, casting the whole house in shades of gray, turning everything the color of ash. What time was it? What day?

At the thought, a voice echoed across his mind from some old movie, one version or another of Dickens's creepy *Christ-*

mas Carol: "Why, it's *Christmas day*, sir!"

Was it? Christmas Eve? Christmas morning? In the feature-less gloom, the question seemed almost meaningless. Did time even matter anymore?

Oh, but it matters. Of course *it matters*, a stern voice spoke inside him—not the voice of an actor from some half-forgotten film, not even quite Teresa's gently firm get-things-done voice. Some *other* voice, distant and pitiful, so feeble despite its passion that it seemed like a sad joke. But the voice spoke on: *How could you... How could you forget? You have company coming today! Guests!*

The idea jolted him, but still he couldn't quite rouse himself from the chair in front of the dark fireplace, could hardly stir at all except to tremble violently against the cold.

What company? His mind turned a lazy circle around itself, too cold, too lost in the gloom to find the answer, to catch hold of anything meaningful at all. If only he could get warm, just a little, the slow sap of his thoughts might flow a tad more freely, and he could touch all these stray, dark puzzle pieces together into an image that meant something...

So cold here, he thought, with a shudder that was nearly a convulsion. But of course: it was *their* cold, the clutching, cease-less chill of his guests, a deep-freeze set here in their old house like a neatly laid table. To make his visitors feel at home.

From somewhere upstairs, footsteps, tiny and muffled but unmistakable. The padding of little girl-feet, the soft whining of old floorboards as his visitors made their way down the stairs. Each footfall a shade heavier as they came nearer, sounds made by things that had long since forgotten how to walk, things that had maybe never known innocence at all... Henry Piper sat shivering in his icy chair and waited. At least he wouldn't have to be alone today. And, after all, what was Christmas without children?

Norma and the Elf
Dan Foley

Ten-year-old Norma had the red hair, blue eyes, freckles, pug nose, and smile of an angel. She was anything but. Norma was pure trouble. She was also the big sister, which had its advantages and privileges. For now, she was willing to let her little brother, Dickie, believe in Santa Claus. Not for any altruistic reasons, but it made her feel superior knowing the truth.

"Don't worry," she assured her mother. "I won't tell Little Dickie Santa's not real."

"Please don't call him that. I told you it's not nice," her mother answered.

"Why not?" Norma innocently asked, even though she knew why it wasn't nice. "It's his name, and he's little, not big like me."

"Just don't," her mother insisted, not willing to explain

229

why.

Her mom almost turned away before telling her, "And don't spoil the Elf on the Shelf for him either. He's really excited about it."

"Don't worry, I won't," Norma assured her. *Not right away anyway,* she added to herself.

❄ ❄ ❄

Dickie's stupid Elf on the Shelf was named Phillip.

"Phillip is one of Santa's helper elves. The book says so," Dickie told her for the umpteenth time. "He comes every year in December and watches us. He flies back to the North Pole every night to tell Santa if we've been good or bad. I'm going to be extra good so Santa will bring me lots of toys for Christmas."

Norma laughed to herself. She knew there was no Santa Claus. Had known it for two years. And the Elf was just a stupid doll. She'd tell Dickie on Christmas Eve.

Norma drew her mother aside after dinner and asked, "Can I be in charge of moving the elf every night?"

Her mother gave her a puzzled look. "The elf moves itself. You know that. It said so in the book."

"Oh, come on. I know Santa isn't real, and the elf is just a doll. But if Dickie thinks it's real, it would be fun to play along. Like a game, you know?"

"All right," her mother agreed after a moment. "But make sure your brother doesn't know you're involved. And don't make it so hard he can't find it. It has to be where he can see it."

"No problem," Norma agreed.

❄ ❄ ❄

"Well, Phillip, it's just me and you now," Norma told the

elf that evening after Dickie went to bed. The elf just smiled back at her with its stupid grin. The thing was about a foot tall, and its body was clad in red with a white collar. It didn't have feet, just legs. The ends of the arms were white to simulate mittens, and the hands were sewn together. A red hat with white trim sat on its head. The whole thing was ridiculous, but it was the face that pissed off Norma. Neat brown hair, big blue eyes with black lashes, cherubic cheeks with a blush of red, a tiny nose, and pursed red lips. Most people would think it was cute. Dickie certainly did, but Norma thought it was ridiculous. To her, the smile looked like a smug little grin because it knew a secret she didn't. That's what upset her the most.

"Where should I put you?" she asked it. "How about on the mantle over the fireplace? Dickie would be sure to see you there. You like that? Okay. But first, you and I are going to have some fun."

Norma's idea of fun was a sadistic little game of "Torture the Elf." "How's this feel?" she asked as she bent its right leg forward at the knee. Then she did the left. Of course, the elf didn't answer; not even the smile on its face changed. Norma knew she couldn't *really* hurt it, but she could imagine she felt bones breaking and tendons tearing. When she was done, she placed the elf on the fireplace mantle where Dickie was sure to see it.

❄ ❄ ❄

"There he is!" Dickie cried as soon as he entered the living room. "I'm going to be really good so he can go back to the North Pole and tell Santa." Then he turned and looked at Norma. "And you better be good, too, because he's watching you, too."

"Yeah, right," Norma told him.

"Norma," her mother cautioned.

"Don't worry, Little Dickie, I'll be good," she assured her brother. And she was good during the day. She saved all her naughtiness for the elf at night before she moved it to a new location. Dickie found Phillip on top of a window, on the bathroom sink, hiding under the tree, even in the fireplace. No matter where Norma placed it, Dickie always managed to find it within minutes.

"There he is," he would shout and then proceed to tell the elf how good he had been. Norma wanted to puke listening to him.

Over the following weeks, Norma twisted every one of the elf's joints, stuck a needle into its chest where its heart would be, stuck the same needle in each eye (you could hardly see the holes unless you looked closely at it), and threw it on the floor and stomped on it. All that effort and the damn thing still had that stupid grin on its face. And every morning, the first thing Dickie would do was scour the house until he found it.

"Just wait until Christmas Eve, Phillip," she told the elf as she slammed it against the floor. "You'll be leaving all right, but not for the North Pole. I've got other plans for you."

* * *

When Christmas Eve finally came, Dickie spent a full half-hour saying goodbye to Phillip and telling him to be sure to tell Santa how good he had been. Norma listened to her brother prattle on and wanted to puke. She couldn't wait for Dickie to finally go to bed so she could have her turn with the elf. She was so excited about what she had planned that she forgot to tell Dickie that Santa wasn't real and the elf was just a stuffed doll.

Norma was careful not to let anyone see her grab the elf on her way to bed. As soon as she was in her room with the door closed, she sat on her bed and propped the elf up in front of her.

"This is it, Phillip, the night I've been waiting for. Want to see what I've got for you?" The elf didn't move, of course; it just stared back at her with its stupid grin.

Norma grinned back, reached under her pillow, and drew out a large pair of scissors. She had to stifle a laugh as she used them to cut off Phillip's head. In the morning, she'd hide the doll and then get rid of it. Hopefully, in the excitement of opening presents, no one would miss it.

* * *

Something, some movement or noise, woke Norma. She glanced at the clock. It was 12:01, Christmas Day. She closed her eyes to go back to sleep but was startled by a tap on her forehead. When she opened her eyes, she was staring into face of a six-foot Elf on the Shelf. Phillip sat on its shoulder, holding his severed, grinning head in his hands. Dozens… hundreds of smaller, grinning elves filled the room. Norma tried to sit up, but the giant elf pushed her back. The smaller elves swarmed over her and lifted her out of bed. Before Norma could even scream, they were rocketing through the night on their way to the North Pole.

* * *

"Well, Norma, the elves tell me you've been a very naughty girl," Santa said. "What you did to Phillip was very, very bad. I was going to put coal in your stocking, but the elves insisted I give you to them."

Norma started to protest, but her protests turned to screams when the giant elf snapped both of her legs forward at the knees.

S*anta Claus versus *Anti Claus

Peter Caffrey

'Twas the night before Christmas,
And all through the house,
Not a creature was stirring,
Not even a mouse…

r a hamster. He lifted his boot off the flattened animal, picked up the mish-mash mess of fur, blood, and guts, and threw it back into the cage.

"That'll teach them to keep vermin as pets," he muttered with contempt.

Creeping into the living room, he spotted the Christmas tree and placed the wrapped presents underneath it: a personalized bottle of single-malt whisky for father, a designer-label crocodile skin handbag for mother, the latest virtual reality

235

game console for little Johnny, and a robot cat for Susan. There was one more box. He shook it and listened to the rattle, sniffed it, recoiled, and dropped it under the tree in disgust. Bath salts? There had to be an old bastard in the house. Those old ones were the worst, always preaching goodwill to all men.

Moving stealthily upstairs, he opened the first door. There was Johnny, tucked up in bed. He went to the second door and peeked in at the dozing parents. The third door revealed Susan in a deep sleep. The fourth door had to be Granny. No, it was the toilet. He thought about taking a shit, but he had too many houses to visit.

The final door opened, and on the bed lay Granny, asleep, with her teeth in a glass on the bedside table. Her slack mouth hung open as she noisily sucked in air. He tiptoed across the room and gently removed the pillow from under her head before clamping it down on her face. She struggled, he thought, somewhat like a sparrow being crushed in his mighty hands, but eventually, her body went limp, lifeless like a spent husk. He waited to make sure her breathing had stopped before heading back down the stairs.

"That'll make their Christmas," he muttered. "I bet they're relieved, the bloody hypocrites."

As he headed for the back door, he spotted the fridge. Opening it and perusing its contents, he selected a can of beer. Cracking it open, he drank deeply. On the fridge door, spelled out in magnets, were the words "Hello Santa." He rearranged them so the message read "Hello Satan," then walked out into the cold, crisp night air.

Thumbing the starter button on the big Kawasaki-engined Skidoo, he roared off into the snow-filled sky.

Anti Claus was making his rounds.

* * *

Across town, on the corner of Misery Street and Depravity Avenue, Santa Claus brought his sleigh to rest. He had spotted something from above and wanted to make a stop to check it out. A small, crippled boy was rooting around in the snow with his withered limbs.

"Ho, ho, ho; merry Christmas, Tiny Tim."

The boy turned, smiled brightly at the sight of Father Christmas before gloom once more fell over his face like a morbid shadow. "Santa, Tiny Tim died last week. He was run down by a drunk driver in a hit-and-run incident. It's common at this time of year, with everyone celebrating Christmas. I'm his brother, Tiny Bob."

Santa rubbed his head and let his shock and confusion subside. How could he have forgotten? His elves had told him of the carnage as Tiny Tim was spread across three carriageways. He watched Tiny Bob continue to forage in the snow.

"What are you doing, Bob?"

"I'm looking for food, Santa; maybe the crust off a pizza, some dropped chips, or a dead rat."

Santa questioned why Tiny Bob didn't ask his parents for food, but the crippled boy shook his head and explained his mother had left with an itinerant trumpet player, and his father would give him a big, ol' punch in the kisser if he dared to ask for anything.

Tiny Bob and his late brother, Tiny Tim, were the illegitimate spawn of a clapped-up hooker named Veronica and Quentin Snide, a big, fat industrialist who was the epitome of all that was wrong with modern business greed. Snide was a tyrant who hated Christmas and anything good in the world. He saw the festive season as a simple reason to drink to excess and fornicate with intoxicated, low-paid single mothers who were desperate for extra cash to see themselves through the festive season.

Santa told Tiny Bob to sit on his sleigh, and he rooted in his sack until he found a large bar of chocolate. The little cripple smiled and munched his way through it.

"Tiny Bob, there are some evil people in the world, and they see Christmas as a time for excess, bad behavior, and greed," Santa said. "All they want are expensive consumer goods, rich food, strong drink, and sexual intercourse with ladies in tight, short skirts and bright red lipstick. They forget about peace and goodwill to all men. They forget the birth of the Savior. They forget the holly, the ivy, and the robin redbreast."

Tiny Bob tried to feed some of the chocolate to the reindeer, but Santa stopped him.

"Tiny Bob, you're too kind. Even when you have nothing, you want to share what little comes your way. That's the true Christmas message. You see, my sack is filled with gifts, but they are meager: apples, oranges, carpet slippers, table-tennis bats with balls attached on lengths of elastic, stuff like that. Christmas is changing, and the spirit of goodwill hangs in the balance. Tonight, I must deliver more of these simple gifts than the consumer goods most people crave if I am to save Christmas. I must rebuild the Christmas spirit, or I will be defeated, and Christmas will be lost forever."

Tiny Bob stopped chewing the chocolate and asked, "Who will defeat you, Santa?"

Santa Claus smiled, but even Tiny Bob could see the pain hidden behind his jolly posturing. Then he muttered through his dense white beard, "Anti Claus will defeat me. He is at large tonight, and unless I can spread joy faster than he spreads greed, Christmas will be lost forever."

Tiny Bob chirped up. "Santa, you will win, you will."

Santa shrugged. "He has power, power built upon greed. He has the X-Box One X, the PS4, the iPhones and Galaxy S20s, the iPad Pros, and the Bluetooth vibrating butt plugs. I have fruit and furry footwear."

Tiny Bob looked up at Santa, a tear rolling from the corner of his cripple-boy eye. "But Santa, you have love," he said.

Santa looked down at Tiny Bob and replied, "Yes, you're right, I do. I have love."

With that, he lifted Tiny Bob to the ground and climbed onto the sleigh. "Now, Dasher. Now, Dancer. Now, Prancer and Vixen. On, Comet. On, Cupid. On, Donner and Blitzen. To the top of the porch. To the top of the wall. Now dash away. Dash away. Dash away all."

The sleigh lifted into the wintry night sky, and Tiny Bob waved as Santa disappeared into the darkness.

* * *

Across town, Anti Claus looked around to check the coast was clear before driving his elbow through the small window. Reaching through, he opened the door and crept inside. In the corner was a small tree, where he quickly deposited the presents: a set of golf clubs for him, an umbrella stand made from an elephant's foot for her, and a Macbook for their one-and-only, Julia. He had time for a nose around, looking in drawers and cupboards, but found little of interest, so he headed upstairs.

In the bedroom, the husband slept soundly with his wife. Anti Claus lifted the bed cover to have a peek and spotted she was wearing crotchless knickers. Not only that, she'd shaved herself, too. All this, and a set of golf clubs? Anti Claus gently moved her leg so he could get a better view and dropped his trousers.

He went at himself quickly; after all, he had work to do. He edged closer to the bed as his pounding became more frantic, and then he exploded. She awoke and screamed, but he was already running down the stairs. As he fired up the Skidoo and sped into the stormy sky, he laughed, imagining her telling her husband it was Santa who'd spunked all over her. He'd have found another use for those golf clubs before daybreak.

* * *

Santa Claus moved silently through the house. He was placing a few pieces of fruit under the tree when he heard the little girl's voice.

"Who's there?" she asked.

He turned and saw her sitting on a stool. She was blonde and beautiful, about fourteen years old. She was innocence personified.

Santa smiled and said, "Ho ho ho. 'Tis me."

"Who?" asked the girl.

Santa replied, "Surely you know who I am."

The girl spoke softly. "No, I don't recognize your voice, and I can't see you. I'm blind."

Santa moved closer and knelt beside her. His role was to deliver presents, spread a little goodwill, and hopefully engender a bit of peace along the way. He knew it was against the rules to interfere in the ways of the world. He shouldn't change the circumstance, but he was powerless to resist the temptation.

Her beauty and elegance were stunning, but her pain cried out to him. He gently touched her eyelids, and a small sparkle of light illuminated her face for no more than a second.

She opened her eyes and excitedly said, "I can see, I can see. It's you, Santa. Thank you, I love you."

She threw her arms around him, and he felt the surge of love between them. The candles on the Christmas tree flickered briefly and then burned brightly. He knew that this family would have a truly happy Christmas.

* * *

Anti Claus held the puppy's head down in the toilet bowl and flushed again. After the third flush, it stopped moving.

"They keep being told a dog is not just for Christmas. Will they ever learn?" he muttered as he dropped the soggy canine corpse to the floor and walked into the next room. Picking up the decanter, he swallowed down the scotch in one long, continuous gulp and then urinated into the crystal bottle before replacing it.

He was going upstairs when the sleigh land outside. Santa had arrived.

The first bedroom was inhabited by a teenage girl. She looked like trouble. Delivering a hard jab to the ribs to ensure she woke up, he took off. If Santa had to confront someone, it would slow him down.

The girl awoke with a start, and hearing the receding footsteps, she climbed out of bed, donned a robe, and headed downstairs. Entering the living room, she came face-to-face with Santa Claus holding the dead puppy he'd found in the bathroom. He knew it was the work of Anti Claus and wanted to bring the dog back to life, but after the blind girl, he couldn't risk another case of interference. Spotting the girl, Santa hid the puppy behind his back.

She moved closer to him, eyeing him up. "Are you for real?"

Santa nodded, and from outside, a reindeer pressed its face against the window. The girl giggled.

"Bloody hell, you're the real thing, aren't you?"

Santa nodded again, and the girl smiled, slowly opening her robe. She walked toward him and asked, "Do you like what you see, fat man?"

Santa averted his eyes and mumbled that yes, she was quite nice.

"You can do me for a smart TV, okay?"

Santa tried to explain that beauty was a gift, not a commodity, but she obviously wasn't listening and added, "I'll blow you for a grand."

Santa tried to explain the benefits of humility, but still ignoring him, she leaned backward, pushing her hips forward, and said, "Okay, I'll let you finger me for an eBike."

Santa handed her an orange. She looked at it and said, "Final offer. For a ten-spot, I'll shove it up my…"

Santa missed the end of the proposition as he walked out into the night, shaking his head with sorrow and despair. As he climbed onto the sleigh, he muttered to the reindeer, "Some you win, some you lose."

* * *

As Santa's sleigh cut through the wintry sky, he spotted something out of the corner of his eye. Despite the thick veil of falling snow, he saw a Skidoo parked behind a house. The only person using such a machine on this holy night would be Anti Claus, and the fact the snowflakes were turning to steam as they landed on the engine meant he'd arrived recently. Santa steered the sleigh to the ground and sat thinking for a few moments.

This was it. Had it been a Spaghetti Western, this was the time when the silver watch would start to chime. No matter how it was dressed up, the face-off wasn't far away. The spirit of Christmas hung in the balance.

Santa Claus crept into the house. Beneath the tree was a pile of expensive-looking presents. Then Santa spotted torn wrapping paper. Someone was already unwrapping the gifts. He had to act fast to stop them; once greed took hold, the battle would be almost impossible to win. He moved into the hallway, and as he passed the kitchen, he heard tearing paper. Whoever was opening the gifts was on the other side of the door. He pushed into the room.

At the table, with his back to the door, sat Tiny Bob, the crippled boy. In front of him was a half-unwrapped present. Santa approached.

"Ho, ho, ho. How are you, Tiny Bob?"

Tiny Bob turned and, seeing Santa, grabbed a bread knife off the table. As Santa came closer, the boy lashed out, plunging the blade into the red coat and white fur, through the material and into Santa's chest. Santa fell back, clutching at the wound and trying to stem the blood flow, as Tiny Bob limped toward him, the knife still in his hand.

Struggling to rise, he pleaded, "Tiny Bob, it's me, the real Santa Claus. Look in my sack. Go on, take a look."

Tiny Bob cautiously opened the sack and pulled out apples, oranges, and slippers. He looked at Santa and smiled. "You are the real Santa." Then he leaned over the prostrate figure, and with one movement, he thrust the knife into Santa's eye socket, slicing through the eyeball and creating a spurting geyser of ruby-red blood. Outside, the wail of a chainsaw kicked in, contrasting with frantic animalistic screams, as Anti Claus butchered the reindeer.

Tiny Bob squatted down next to Santa. "Listen, you pompous twat, just because I'm a cripple doesn't mean I don't want a bloody X-Box One X. You want to take all the fun out of Christmas; you want to remove the shopping and expensive presents and overeating and drunkenness and shagging the secretary at the office party. You want people to be nice to each other even if they don't get them good presents. You'd rather give me an apple than an iPad, you tight-ass."

Santa lay there, the light fading in his eyes. The door burst open, and another bearded, red-coated figure entered.

Santa muttered, "Anti Claus, your evil works have won the day."

"Good, you utter shitwad," Anti Claus laughed. "Christmas is the true festival of capitalism, and we don't need nonces like you screwing it up for us."

Santa tried to speak, but his throat gurgled with the blood that was welling there. Then he spat out a large blood clot and rasped, "Who are you? Let me at least know before I die."

The figure removed his beard.

"Oh shit, it's big, fat Quentin Snide," Santa mumbled before his head fell back and his eyes closed for the very last time.

Tiny Bob struggled to his feet and shouted, "All right. Nice one, Dad."

Quentin Snide stood astride the corpse of Santa and roared to the heavens. "Don't come around here with your peace and goodwill to all men. Don't tell me it's the season to be jolly. Just buy me stuff and let me get drunk and touch up your wives. Bring me a turkey, a bloody big one, and make sure it was kept in a cage all its life. Free-range equals muscle; I want my meat milky and tender. What's more, I just want the breasts. You can send the legs to those starving chaps in Africa. I want glitter, tinsel, trees, mince pies, and that feature-length episode of *Sabrina, the Teenage Witch*, when she tries on the bikinis. Just don't tell me about the birth of the baby Jesus."

Tiny Bob shouted, "Yeah, fuck him, he's only an egg."

Snide looked at the cripple, shook his head with utter disappointment, and said, 'No, you twat, that was Humpty Dumpty...wasn't it?"

Here We Are, as in Olden Days

Stephanie Rabig

"Sooooo," Sadie drawled, sidling up to her best friend and bumping hips, "we're doing some ganj."

"Oh, my God."

"Smoking some Mary Jane."

"Nobody even says—"

"Going mad with reefer."

"I'm divorcing you."

"Can't divorce me; we're not married."

"Whatever the 'friend' equivalent of divorce is."

"There is none. You're stuck with me."

"I've got to start making better life choices."

"Starting tomorrow," Sadie said, watching as Harper crumbled up one of the buds. "Right now, drugs."

Harper laughed, then huddled down a little deeper into her coat. "I can't believe Charlotte made us come out here.

246

I'm freezing my ass off."

Harper had burst through their door about ten minutes ago, calling herself Santa Claus as she waved the baggie of weed. Normally, Charlotte would've been happy to join in—or at least ignore them as they went into one of the bedrooms to smoke. But she'd gotten a new job at a hardware store two weeks ago, and her paranoia over someone smelling it on her clothes had made her banish them outside, where they were currently huddling in the toolshed for warmth.

"Is it me, or is she acting a little weird lately?"

Sadie shrugged. "No weirder than usual. She's just super panicky since her old place shut down." It had taken her five months to find a new job, leaving her to beg her parents for enough money to make her share of their rent. Her parents had helped, but they had also taken every opportunity to lecture her about how if she'd just gone to nursing school like her mother and uncle and grandmother, she wouldn't have to worry about all this. "Pretty sure if her new boss asked her to donate a kidney, she'd do it."

"Ugh. Don't give that creeper any ideas."

"Yeah. Now *there's* a weird guy."

"I can't believe Charlotte took a job with an anti-masker," Harper said, passing her the joint.

"I mean, at least he's not one of those assholes who won't let his employees wear one."

"I'm not giving him any benefit of the doubt," Harper said. "You saw the bandage on Charlotte's arm."

"Yeah," Sadie said, taking a long pull from the joint before passing it back. Charlotte had come home from work around a month ago with a bandage on her wrist and a grumbled explanation that she'd been demonstrating how to use a power saw and it had slipped. She'd refused to let them look at it and refused any kind of workman's comp report, insisting that she was fine and it had just been an accident. "I bet OSHA would have a field day with that place."

"Never thought I'd be grateful to work fast food. You know, they—" Harper groaned as she heard high-pitched barking coming from the house. "Oh, come on, Goldie, I *just* took you out."

"Maybe Charlotte'll do it."

"Yeah, maybe," Harper said, opening the door just enough to drop what remained of the joint outside and grind it out with her foot. "I swear, that dog is all bladder."

A few seconds later, Goldie stopped barking, and Harper grinned. "Thanks, Charlotte!" she called.

A grumble was their only answer, and both of them laughed.

Then Sadie's phone chimed; she dug it out of her pocket, smiling when she saw it was a message from her girlfriend. "Laura's off work early."

"Nice," Harper said. "Want me to leave you alone so you can sext?"

Sadie laughed and elbowed her, and Harper stepped out of the toolshed, shutting the door behind her. She looked up, smiling as she saw a few snowflakes drifting out of the darkness.

If it kept this up, maybe they'd have a white Christmas day after tomorrow. Or at least a vague-dusting-of-powder Christmas, which was more than they'd gotten the past couple of years.

At least it would at least make for a pretty end to the miserable shit-heap that had been 2020, she thought. She'd been ready to write the year off back in February when Tim had broken up with her. Then had come March and with it, a modern-day plague.

Wasn't like we would've been able to have a huge Halloween wedding this year anyway.

She grinned and then opened her mouth, trying futilely to catch a snowflake on her tongue for a couple of minutes before heading back toward the house.

She'd taken only a few steps when her foot squished down into something, and her nose told her what it was an instant later.

"Oh, *gross*," she wailed, and she heard Sadie's voice from the shed behind her.

"Harper?"

"I'm fine, just stepped in a 'present' Goldie left."

"Ew."

"Tell me about it. I'm gonna go take a shower." *After I hose off this boot,* she thought. At least it wasn't summer; then she would've just been in her sandals or, worse, barefoot.

"Okay. I'll be in soon."

Harper started to wipe her boot off in the grass, then frowned and took out her phone, turning on the flashlight.

Goldie was a Pomeranian. What she'd just stepped in was about half the size of the little dog; it couldn't have been anything she'd left. And it was steaming in the cold air.

Don't freak out, she thought, as she heard a low growl from the darkness off to her left. The Alvarez's St. Bernard just dug his way out again. The dog growled and barked at everything that moved but was actually a sweetheart.

"Hey, Buddy," she called, shining the light toward where she'd heard the growl. "You need me to walk you back home?"

There was nothing there.

"Buddy?"

And there, there was movement, but from something much taller than Buddy. She swung her phone around and caught a glimpse of dark fur and yellow eyes and masses of teeth before the phone tumbled through the air as a swipe of claws cut nearly all the way through her arm.

Harper's mouth dropped open in an attempted cry, but all that came out was a high hiss of air, and then the creature was on her.

"Harper?" Sadie called, lowering her phone slightly and covering the mouthpiece, listening for an answer before she raised it back to her ear.

"What's going on?" Laura asked.

"Oh, I thought I heard Harper say something. She was calling for Buddy. I swear, they should've named him Houdini."

Laura laughed. "At least Goldie doesn't get out all the time."

"Not because she doesn't try. Every time I head out for work in the morning, she tries to dive past my ankles."

"Aw, she just wants to chase a few squirrels."

"Pretty sure the squirrels are bigger than she is," Sadie said. Then her phone beeped, and she swore as she looked at the screen. "Shit. I'm at two percent. I'll call you back in a few minutes."

"Okay. Love you."

"Love you, too," Sadie said, hitting "End" before opening the shed door. She circled around the general area where she'd heard Harper's voice coming from, hoping to avoid the poop.

It was starting to snow, and she frowned up at the sky as she hurried past the side of their small house. "My windows better not be iced up in the morning," she muttered, and then her frown deepened as she came within sight of the front door. It was standing open.

She'd known Harper was in a rush to get in the shower, but come on.

Sadie hurried in and shut the door behind her, putting her phone on the living room charger before calling out for Goldie.

Nothing.

"Dammit. Hey, Charlotte!" she called. "I think Goldie got out!"

No answer from her, either.

Maybe she'd stepped out with Goldie. It was a bit late to take her on a full walk, but if she'd seen one of their neighbors outside, she was probably talking with them. Charlotte rarely missed an opportunity to strike up a conversation with anyone.

Dodging the presents piled around the Christmas tree, she headed toward the kitchen, intent on grabbing a snack while waiting for her phone to charge. Then she hesitated.

Something was wrong.

The bathroom, she realized. The door was standing open; Harper wasn't in there.

Come to think of it, had her boots been on the porch? She'd been focusing on the open door, yeah, but she was pretty sure she'd remember smelling something if Harper had just kicked off her boots and run inside.

"Harper?" she called, heading into her roommate's bedroom. Also empty.

"What the hell?" she muttered. Neither of her friends were the pranking type. "Hey!" she called, walking back toward the kitchen. "Where are you guys?"

The fridge was standing open, too. Sadie shut the door, then yelped and scrambled back when that revealed a bright smear of red on the floor.

And was that a clump of fur?

She tried to draw in a full breath, tried not to hyperventilate, as she grabbed one of the kitchen knives. She could picture everything clearly in her mind:

Harper had come home, waving the plastic baggie of weed. She and Harper had headed out to the shed, leaving

Charlotte alone with Goldie in the house. Someone had knocked. Charlotte, surely assuming a neighbor, had grabbed her mask, put it on, and answered the door. The psycho at the door shoved his way in. Charlotte ran. Goldie barked her head off—which she and Harper had heard out in the shed—and the guy killed her, then went to find where Charlotte was hiding.

Maybe she hadn't hid, though. Maybe she kept running. Would she have had time to make it out the back door?

Warily eyeing her bedroom door and the open door to the bathroom, Sadie opened the back door and stared out into the night. The backyard looked ominous in the darkness, no light until the streetlamp in front of the Alvarez's house.

She wanted to call out, but her mouth felt too dry to form words.

Sadie turned and hurried back to the front room where she'd left her phone, her finger hovering over the "9" before she hesitated.

What if she was picturing this all wrong? Laura was always teasing her about her addiction to true-crime shows. Maybe the blood was from Charlotte; that cut on her arm could have opened up again.

That was it. She'd bumped into something and re-opened the cut and had been getting a bandage when Goldie started barking to go out. She'd taken her out, missing the latch on the front door in her hurry. There hadn't actually been fur on the floor; it had been something else and she'd misinterpreted that in her panic.

And what about Harper?

There's an explanation for that, too, she thought as she set the phone back down. What she wasn't going to do was figure that explanation out after she'd called the cops while she still reeked of pot.

Hell, for all she knew, it hadn't been blood at all. Maybe Charlotte had dropped a jar of strawberry jam, and she and Harper had seen how it looked and decided to prank her; maybe they were outside even now, giggling as Goldie growled at snowflakes.

Then go check, she thought. *You want to think that wasn't blood? You want to think you imagined the fur? Go check.*

She couldn't move.

Sadie squeezed her eyes shut, embarrassed and angry about the tears that dripped down her face when she did.

"Guys!" she yelled, startling herself with the loudness of her own voice. "This isn't funny!"

She opened her eyes again and found herself staring at a monster.

It filled the doorway to the hall, dark fur grotesquely illuminated by the tree's red-and-green blinking lights, its bloodied teeth bared.

Sadie didn't remember scrambling to her feet, didn't remember throwing the front door open, but she'd almost gotten out onto the porch before claws sank into her shoulder and dragged her back. The animal flung her across the living room, and she crashed into the tree, shrieking in pain as she landed on broken Christmas ornaments.

Tears blurring her vision, Sadie grabbed present after present, pelting the approaching creature with first the gifts and then some of the ornaments, praying she might get lucky and get some glass shards in its eyes. Then she saw something gleaming in the lights from the battered tree.

The knife. She'd dropped it when she'd landed; it had skidded across the floor.

Now she lunged forward, making a desperate grab for the weapon as the animal—werewolf, it was a goddamned *werewolf*—leaped.

She stabbed the knife into its chest as hard as she could.

The werewolf howled, staggering back, snarling as it re-grouped. Sadie pushed herself to her feet and grabbed the handle of the knife, intent on yanking it out and stabbing this thing again, but the werewolf darted its head forward and bit her hand. Sadie cursed and grabbed one of the creature's ears with her free hand, twisting it.

As soon as its mouth gaped open in pain, Sadie yanked her hand away and ran, vaulting down the porch steps and racing out onto the sidewalk. She kept going.

A moment later, another sound wormed its way through the gasps of her own ragged breathing.

Singing. Someone was singing.

There. On a more well-lit part of the next block where three houses in a row had neon light displays. The Alvarez kids were caroling.

Their mother and father were with them. All of them with masks on, staying on the sidewalk instead of going right up on porches like they had last year. They'd adopted three kids, had twins a few years later, and then adopted two more. The youngest was barely four, and her dad was carrying her. They'd brought over a giant tin of cookies to welcome the three of them to the neighborhood when they'd moved here a couple of years ago. If anyone could actually pull off the "everyone wearing matching outfits for the holiday photo" thing, it was the Alvarez family.

Shit. She couldn't lead this thing to them.

She turned, seeing the werewolf running down the side-walk toward her, moving far too fast for something that still had the handle of a butcher knife jutting out of its chest.

Weirdly, instead of being terrified, she felt a floating calm-ness come over her, as if she was cuddled down under a plush comforter watching a Hallmark movie—which was how she'd planned to spend the evening—instead of facing down a horror movie monster.

This was it. She was dead.

Fuck it. At least I'll die a hero.

Sadie charged forward to meet the monster, heedless of its teeth this time as she grabbed the knife handle and yanked the blade out, stabbing it in the throat.

The werewolf let out a gasping attempt at a howl, then collapsed against her, its weight sending her to the ground even as it scratched at her again, its razor-sharp claws opening up her sternum. She stared at the full moon, smiling at the sight of the snowflakes twirling down. Maybe the roads would be awful tomorrow, maybe her car would be iced up, but who cared? Not like she'd be driving.

With some effort, she turned her head to the side and saw the werewolf's massive form shrinking, the hair fading away, leaving brown skin behind. The matted fur on its head shifted, replaced by Charlotte's black hair.

It's a bite, she thought blearily, seeing the scar on her friend's arm for the first time.

"Power saw, my ass," she whispered. Might have giggled if simple breathing wasn't making her chest burn. Maybe the werewolf—Charlotte, maybe Charlotte—had gotten her worse than she'd thought. She didn't want to look.

Then she heard panicky voices approaching and let out a rattling sigh, trying not to worry too much about the bubble of blood that came up between her lips. It felt like a long shot, but maybe they'd get her to the hospital in time. Living as a hero instead of dying as one, that might be nice.

"What happened, Sadie?" Mrs. Alvarez asked, crouching down next to her.

Sadie opened her mouth, tried to explain, but couldn't get any words out.

"It's okay," Mrs. Alvarez said. "It'll be okay, I promise." She got to her feet and hurried over to her husband, and when she came back, she was holding his coat. She pressed it to her chest, hard, and Sadie winced.

"I know, sweetie, I'm sorry."

A whimper had her looking to Charlotte again, and she instinctively tried to get to her feet when she saw that her friend had reached up, was pulling the knife out of her neck. As soon as the blade was out, the fur began sprouting from her skin again, her teeth elongating as she grinned.

Stupid stainless steel knife, she thought hysterically.

"It's okay, look at me," Mrs. Alvarez said. "Stay with me, okay? We're getting an ambulance. Don't move; I've got to keep pressure on this."

Sadie realized that she'd already written Charlotte off as dead—why wouldn't she; she'd done her damnedest to decapitate her. She flopped back to the ground, unable to hold herself up any longer, her vision blacking out for a second from pain. "Run," she whispered.

"What?" Mrs. Alvarez asked, her gaze still focused sharply on the wound. Mr. Alvarez was several feet away, the kids gathered around him like ducklings. He was talking rapidly on the phone while cradling their youngest child in his free arm. None of them were looking their way.

Then Mrs. Alvarez *finally* looked past her, her eyes growing terror-wide as she looked up, and up. Sadie closed her eyes. She supposed she could try again to tell them to run, but it didn't matter. They'd never make it, anyway.

✱A Trailer Park Christmas
Joshua Marsella

Like every other Christmas Eve, Carl sat alone in his mobile home. December was a festive time in the trailer park, but this year, Carl's lot looked abandoned. His was the only trailer without colorful lights hanging from the roof. No holly, jolly wreath adorned his screen door. The corner of his living room did not have the customary tree decorated with glass bulbs, tinsel, or lights. Not a single holiday card was displayed on his refrigerator—or anywhere else, for that matter. The only evidence of the holiday season was the Santa hats worn by the polar bears printed on the cans of Coke he was mixing with his whiskey.

Don't get it confused; Carl was no Ebenezer Scrooge by any means. He used to love the holiday season. In the years prior, he would have been the first to decorate his home. It had been a tradition since he was a young boy to put up the decorations the week after Thanksgiving, no matter how much it annoyed his parents. Now, he did all he could to avoid any reminders of Christmas, which was no easy task.

This Christmas Eve, he had passed out drunk in his faux leather recliner watching *M*A*S*H*, wearing only his torn work pants and a stained tank top. As the hour approached midnight, the cable network switched to *It's a Wonderful Life* to the sound of Carl's sawmill snoring. Had he been awake, he would have immediately changed the channel. Even on Christmas, he had no interest in watching Capra's classic film.

As George Bailey contemplated suicide on the 12" television screen, a heavy *thump* sounded on the metallic roof above. This was soon followed by tapping noises muffled by the snow that had accumulated there. It wasn't a tapping like somebody lightly banging a hammer, nor did it sound like the prancing of eight tiny reindeer that one might expect given the occasion. It sounded more like the pitter-patter of little feet. Several sets of little feet, to be exact.

Carl, oblivious in his drunken slumber, had a syrupy bead of spittle hanging from his drooping bottom lip. His smudged glasses rested in the patch of chest hair sprouting from beneath his tank top. They were attached to a strap around his neck so he wouldn't lose them.

Outside, the *thumping* of small boots landing in the snow could be heard from the porch situated beside the trailer.

On the television, a twelve-year-old George Bailey is rescuing his brother Harry from drowning in the frozen pond when somebody knocked hard on Carl's loosely hung screen door.

Carl snapped awake. "What the...?" His blurred eyes darted confusedly around the dimly lit room, unsure of what had woken him up. He rubbed his eyes, then clumsily placed his glasses onto the bridge of his nose. As he became more fully awake, he reached over to the stack of milk crates he used as an end table and grabbed his drink. Taking a swig to wet his whistle, he heard another knock on the front door.

Carl was so startled at the sudden pounding that he spilled his drink into his lap. "Shit! Goddamn it! Who the hell is knocking at this hour?" he barked as he peered up at the clock on the wall. Five past midnight. "Christ, that better be a beautiful, young hooker."

Carl leaned forward in the recliner and set down his drink. Standing up, he noticed the television was no longer playing his favorite show, but a Christmas movie instead. *Bleh!* He grabbed the remote control that was jammed into the side of the recliner cushion and quickly changed the channel.

He was oblivious to the pair of glowing green eyes peering in at him through the window, nor the tiny fingers clawing at the screen, eager to get inside.

The knock at the door came again, but this time it was more assertive.

"Jesus, hold your horses," he called. Then added under his breath, "Probably those damn kids from next door."

The floor settled under his weight as he walked to the door. His head spun wildly from the booze. The rundown trailer was a sufficient living space for himself, but he never meant for it to become his permanent home. Last month, he had been in talks with the bank about using his Christmas bonus for a down payment on a two-bedroom ranch the next town over. He was also up for a considerable promotion. Unfortunately, this fell through following the company owner's sudden death, along with his wife and two children. They were killed in a hit-and-run after leaving the annual company Christmas party the last week of November. All the workers in the plant had been laid off. Over 100+ people left jobless just weeks before Christmas. Carl was devastated.

So here he remained, in the West Burnchester trailer park. A jobless alcoholic with no family. His minuscule military pension helped pay the bills and stock up his liquor cabinet, but it wasn't enough to get him into a new home.

He sluggishly made it to the door and flipped on the porch light. Snow was steadily falling. The hexagonal window in the door gave off the illusion that he was flying through space. He stood on his tippy toes and peered outside to get a glimpse of the intruder but saw no one.

"Who's there? Do you know what time it is?" he said. No response came. Carl opened the door and swung it open, expecting to see some nosey kids waiting with snowballs, but no-one was there.

In the snow, he could see several small boot prints heading in all directions. Someone had torn the screen down the middle. He noticed small, greasy handprints had been pressed against the glass on the bottom half of the screen door. A cold draft of snow pushed its way through the torn screen, sending a chill down Carl's flesh. Shivering, he folded his arms across his chest.

"Son-of-a-bitch. Who the hell is out there?" he called out." You show yourselves right now, you little pricks. I don't play games."

Poking his head through the door, he looked in all directions to see if he could spot anyone hiding in the shadows. Carl heard what sounded like the high-pitched laughter of children mixing with the whistle of the wind.

"I know you're out there. Shouldn't you be in bed waiting for Santy Claus, you little punks? Where are your parents?" Still, no response came.

He supposed the noise could have just been the wind blowing through the trees or the loose siding on the trailer, but something wasn't sitting right with him. Carl looked quizzically one more time at the small handprints, then slammed the door behind him.

"I'll be sure to call the landlord this morning. Christmas or no Christm—" Carl's words were cut off by the sound of breaking glass coming from the back of the trailer. A brisk wind howled through the broken window, bringing with it a gust of snow. "Are you fucking kidding me?"

He sounded infuriated, but the truth was, Carl was beginning to feel a little nervous. He wanted to believe it was kids just playing a prank on him, but this was getting out of hand.

After storming through the living room, he entered the kitchen. He eyed the 8-inch kitchen knife that rested by the sink and considered grabbing it. *It's just kids, Carl. Don't be foolish.* His thought was interrupted when he jammed his bad knee into a wooden chair beside the table. A surge of pain shot through his nervous system and sent him stumbling into the entrance to the hallway, hitting the wall hard with his shoulder.

Carl lost his breath and had to take a second to regain his composure. A sudden jingling sound caught his attention. He peered down the hallway in time to see something small dart by in the darkness. *Were those bells?* he thought, as he was now sure it was kids playing a Christmas prank on him. Too bad for them; he wasn't the playful type.

"Hey, kid! You better get the hell out of my trailer before I count to ten," he said, wincing in pain as he put weight on his injured leg. He placed a hand on the wallpapered paneling.

Through gritted teeth, the countdown began. "One. Two. Three." He started limping his way down the dark hallway. "You little shit… Better hope I don't get to ten."

He hobbled up to the first bedroom—mainly for used storage—and reached past the door frame to turn on the light. Nothing happened; then he remembered he'd forgotten to change the blown bulb. *Perfect,* he thought, then continued the countdown to Judgement Day.

"Four. Five. Six." His tone grew harsher with every number as the pain in his leg increased, "I'm warning you. I have a constitutionally protected right to defend my property."

He approached the door to the bathroom. His anger shifting to unease. *If this wasn't just some neighborhood kids playing a prank, what on earth could it be?* The wind continued to blow snow in through the broken backdoor window, which was forming a small snowdrift in the hallway. The frigid air sent another shiver down Carl's arms. *It's gonna cost me a fortune to fix that, sonsabitches,* he thought. A shimmer caught his attention on the broken. Thin strands of tinsel had caught on the broken shards of glass. *The hell?*

Flipping on the light to the bathroom, he was greeted by the bright glow of the halogen. He looked around. Nothing looked out of place. The shower curtain around the tub was pulled back, leaving nowhere for a kid to hide in the tiny room.

He turned towards the back room—his bedroom—and continued the countdown.

"Seven. Eight. You're cutting close. Last chance."

From the living room, he could hear an infomercial for a holiday CD playing samples of old Christmas tunes by generic pop artists.

Oh, the weather outside is frightful, but the fire is so delightful...

Carl looked toward the living room and let out an angry snarl. "I got your delightful right here," he said, grabbing his crotch.

Turning back to his bedroom, he pushed open the door a little bit. An unpleasant, high-pitched giggle—the sound of a child who also happened to be a heavy smoker—came from somewhere within the bedroom. He had them cornered; they had nowhere to go.

"Nine. You're fucked. You had your chance."

He reached in and turned on the light.

"Ten! Now you're mine!"

Elbowing the door, it swung open the rest of the way and slammed against his bed frame. His hand was still resting on the light switch.

Over his bed, he saw words crudely carved into the paneling.

WHEN JUSTICE IS DONE, IT BRINGS JOY TO THE RIGHTEOUS BUT TERROR TO THE NAUGHTY

"What the fuck? COME OUT NO—" His words were cut off by a searing surge of pain as the bones on his right hand were crushed by a blunt force. Carl let out a scream of agony as he pulled his hand back to look at it. Gripping his wrist below the wound, he saw it wasn't crushed, but something had pierced the center of his hand. Whatever it was had left a hole two-inches diameter straight through his hand. He could see the floor through the gore and pieces of broken bone protruding from the hole. The pain was unbearable. He looked down to see his attacker and wished he hadn't.

A short figure draped in a dark green hooded robe stood knee-high about two feet away from Carl. It wore scuffed black boots with a sharp metal spikes jutting from each toe. It was about the size of a child, but the facial features and wrinkled hands said otherwise. It pulled back the hood and rested it on its shoulders. Carl watched in horror as the thing licked the blood off the pointed end of the large candy cane it had used to puncture his hand. Its tongue slipped out between red, cracked lips that were enwreathed by a long, graying beard. Carl noticed it had pointed ears, except one of them looked as though something had bitten off half of it. Dangling from the ear lobes were earrings—strands of hair threaded through dangling human eyeballs.

Carl was in shock and disbelief at what stood before him, but the immense pain in his hand reassured him that it was all very real.

He opened his mouth to speak but stopped as another small, hooded creature rose from behind his bed. It held out defensively a set of sharpened reindeer antlers while it growled at Carl from the other side of the bed. This one looked more corroded, with pale green skin. Around its neck, it wore a necklace adorned with severed ears. The nose was a plump, purple thing covered in reddish spider veins. The rest of the attire matched that of its comrade.

Carl could hear someone on the television was singing, "*Let it snow, let it snow, let it snow.*"

"What is this? You some sort of demented gang? Look at my fucking hand!" Carl tried to sound angry, but fear was creeping into his voice. Speaking louder, he said, "Is this a robbery? Well, I don't have shit to steal, you jackasses. Look at me. I'm broke as a joke!" His words trembled as the pain in his hand shot up, making him weak in the knees.

The wicked pair just watched the man in the tank top stand there, blood running down his arm and onto the floor while he desperately pleaded for answers. They shot each other crooked smiles, flashing their jagged, rotten teeth, as if they relished his pain and suffering. The first one took another lick of the grotesque candy cane, savoring the taste of Carl's blood. The second one licked its lips, enticed by the pooling blood.

Carl's rage left him. Now he looked scared and despondent. There was no way he'd be able to outrun them with his injured knee.

His life was miserable and hopeless, but he didn't want to die. Not like this.

"What do you want?" he screamed. "Do you want me to beg? Is that what you want?"

The intruder took another lick, unbothered by the pathetic sight Carl presented.

Carl gave in. Using his good hand, he leaned against the doorframe and slowly lowered himself onto his aching knee. The pair approached him with menacing expressions, clearly not here to grant clemency.

Carl's eyes welled up as he began his plea for mercy. "Please, I beg you. Don't kill me. I want to live." This triggered no emotional response from the two, angering Carl. *"Please!* For God sakes, *it's Christmas—"*

His cries were cut short when a small, rough hand gripping his sweaty forehead and yanked his head backward. He felt pressure on his calf muscles as little boots stepped up onto his legs. A second hand swung around the other side and began to shove something into Carl's gaping mouth. Carl looked across the room at the standing mirror against the wall and caught a brief glimpse of what he was choking on: small, black cubes of coal. The taste was awful. He sucked in bits of dust, and loose pieces broke off as he desperately gasped for breath.

Please make it quick. Just let it be over with, Carl thought, hoping God would be listening. Some part of him worried it was far from over.

The two intruders joined their accomplice, bells jingled with each footfall.

Tears escaped from Carl's bloodshot eyes as a snippet of "Silent Night" played on the television. It reminded him of when his grandparents would bring him to church on Christmas Eve. He'd always loved the hymns.

Carl nearly forgot about the pain until the third intruder clobbered him on the base of his skull. Pain flared for a moment, then the world around Carl went dark.

Carl woke to find himself driving his car down a snowy road.
This was a dream. No—a nightmare.

The telephone poles were decorated with Christmas wreaths, and the trees were glistening with beautiful white lights through the freshly fallen snow. His head was heavy with drunkenness from the numerous drinks he'd had that night to celebrate his promotion. He knew he shouldn't be driving, but he didn't have any friends to stop him.

He tapped his hands on the steering wheel to the beat of an old-time Christmas song he'd always loved. As he approached a red light, his attention was pulled away by a Christmas display that decorated the front lawn of a beautiful two-story house. I'll own a house like that soon enough. It's what I deserve, *he boasted to himself.*

The lights made him feel nostalgic, and he got lost in the past. He remembered visiting his grandparent's at Christmastime and the warm feeling of sitting by the fire in front of the tree.

Carl blew through the red light and reality came crashing back when he clipped the rear end of a passing car, sending the other car into a tailspin, its tires skating over the icy road, out of control.

Carl slammed on his brakes and managed to skid to a stop and avoid slamming into a telephone pole. His head was spinning crazily as he rolled down his window to see what he'd hit. There was nothing in sight. He rubbed his eyes, unbuckled his belt, and stepped out into the snow.

Once out of the car, a jolt of pain shot up from his right knee. He was so intoxicated, he hadn't felt it jam into the underside of the dashboard. Limping, he returned to the point of collision and noticed a second pair of tire tracks. He followed them with his eyes until he spotted a gap in the guard rail.

He made his way over and peered down into the deep gulley below. What looked like a car had flipped onto its roof after smashing into several trees on its way down. From what he could see, nobody had crawled from the overturned vehicle. The falling snow softly landed on the exposed undercarriage of the car, melting as it touched the hot piping of the exhaust.

Carl was overcome with guilt. He fought the urge to vomit as he looked down at the car. The car he'd driven off the road and the people he possibly killed.

His entire future flashed before his eyes, and in an instant, he knew what he had to do. He glanced around at the roads and nearby homes and saw no witnesses.

Run, *a voice in his mind told him,* get out of here.

Carl stumbled back to his car, trying to ignore the pain in his knee, and drove home as carefully as he could. He hoped to make a clean escape and put this all behind him. For a while, he'd thought he'd done just that since the police never called him in for questioning.

He opened his eyes. It had just been a dream. He lay there for a moment in a state of confusion. He was in pain, and he was cold, and it helped to clear his thoughts. He was laying in the snow, staring up at the night sky. Snow was still falling. His jaw ached, and he gagged as he tried to take a breath. He lifted his hand to feel what was crammed into his mouth, and his palm erupted with pain.

It all came back to him. He had been home. It was Christmas morning. Someone had broken into his house. *There were three intruders,* he recollected, slipping into a state of panic, *little demonic things.*

The intruder holding the antlers kicked wet snow into Carl's face, and he shot up into a sitting position.

"Merry Christmas, murderer," a deep voice boomed from somewhere in the darkness. Puffs of breath escaped the darkness from whoever was speaking. One of the intruders hawked a loogie onto Carl's face. The thick wad of snot ran down his bristly cheek, but he didn't dare wipe it off.

Carl could not speak. His mouth was still full of coal. He struggled to breathe through his nose as he painstakingly followed the order.

I'm not a murderer, he thought, now on the verge of tears. *I'm not a murderer. It was just a bad dream.* He noticed all three intruders standing in front of him, the snow up to their thighs.

"I said, get on your knees!" the voice demanded. Carl squinted but could not see who was there.

Fighting through the pain, he did as he was told, afraid of the repercussions if he disobeyed. Finally on his knees, he settled into the snow.

Two of the intruders turned to face each other, and bowed their heads.

A looming figure at least a foot or two taller than Carl stepped from the darkness and into the light of a streetlamp. As wide as a refrigerator, it wore a black hooded cloak trimmed with what appeared to be human. The snow seemed to avoid the figure, blowing around but never settling on its large frame. It was as if its body was emanating an intense amount of heat. Thick steam rose off the cloak before dissipating into the air. Carl noticed as the figure took heavy steps forward that the snow around its boots sizzled and melted into a black puddle, staining the snow around it. Carl couldn't see it clearly, but the figure was dragging a heavy wooden object.

It stopped a few feet in front of Carl and paused. Tears streamed from Carl's eyes. Whatever he had done to deserve this meeting, he was now more sorry than ever.

With its free hand, the figure pushed back the heavy hood, revealing a man's face. He was practically bald. A fringe of black hair encircled his bare scalp and flowed down over his impossibly broad shoulders, and he sported a thick, bushy, black beard.

The man belted out a mock laugh, sounding like a lewd

Santa Claus. "You've been naughty, Carl. *Very, very* naughty."

Carl knelt in terrified awe, unable to speak a word.

The man spoke as if he was a father scolding his child, his voice reverberating into the night like distant thunder.

"You are one of the wretched few who was naughty enough to make my list," he explained, patting at his breast. The minions all hissed the word *naughty* at the mention of the list.

"Do you know who stands before you?" he asked, knowing Carl couldn't answer.

Carl violently shook his head.

"All you gluttonous, greedy humans know of jolly, old Saint Nick. My dollar-store whore of a brother." The three minions chuckled. "All because you believe he brings you presents and candy and all those material things you ask for. Garbage is what I call it." Spitting into the snow, it sizzled as it made contact. "Nobody knows of his younger sibling. That is until—as is in your case—it is too late. Carl Scottsdale, you are in the presence of Dominicus Claus, the Bringer of Christmas Judgement. I have not brought you presents on this Christmas morning. No candy. No; I have come to take something from you. Something that is rightfully mine." Dominicus's face lit up with a smile so wide his jagged, stained teeth were visible. "Your meaningless life."

Carl's eyes grew wide as a tightness balled up in his chest.

"They," Dominicus waved a hand towards the minions, "are my most loyal servants. There are many of them, but tonight, there are three. Think of them as the Three Wise Men if it brings you comfort."

Dominicus continued his monologue. "They were once Santa's elves, slaving away in his sweatshops for hours on end. Making toys for all the little boys and girls who didn't do *anything* to deserve them. That is, until my brother cast them out for having the balls to question his authority. You see, my brother is a bit of an authoritarian. Control over others is what truly brings him joy. What truly makes him... jolly. He thrives on the fact that he alone gets to pick which kids get presents and which get *nothing*." Dominicus growled the last word.

One of the elves let out a gravelly hiss through its gritted teeth and bounced his sharpened candy cane into his open palm.

"Now they humbly serve the one-and-only anti-Christmas. The yin to Santa's yang. Serving up the naughtiest of naughties on a platter to their beloved. Yours truly."

The elves chanted *naughty, naughty* in a taunting, schoolyard fashion.

"But enough of this," Dominicus roared, sounding indignant. The elves stopped their chants. "Now that I have enlightened you as to who we are, sentencing shall commence."

Carl mistakenly gulped, swallowing more bits of coal, and winced in pain.

Dominicus moved a step closer. Steam rose from the snow around his large boot. Reaching into his robe, he pulled out a large scroll, unrolled it, and began to read the text.

"*You,* Carl E. Scottsdale, are responsible for the untimely death of the Bartlett family. A loving mother, a supportive father, and their two innocent children. All of them died because you had one too many drinks. *You* drove them off the road. *You* ran home like a dog with its tail between its legs. *You* didn't even check to see if they were alive. Didn't look in the rearview mirror. Didn't even call for help." His judgmental voice now echoed like they were inside a cathedral.

The three elves growled as they slowly backed away from Carl, preparing for the oncoming judgment.

Suddenly, it all became clear to Carl what this was all

about. What the dream was about. It was no dream. He had killed his boss and his family. He was responsible for all his friends losing their jobs. Carl was overwhelmed by long-overdue remorse, knowing that, as impossible as it seemed, this was all really happening.

It was time to meet his maker, and he deserved no mercy.

Time as he knew it slowed. All around him, there was nothing but silence.

Dominicus Claus, Bringer of Christmas Judgement, lifted the wooden object he held in his huge hand. Carl tried to gasp as he saw the head of a mallet rise up out of the snow. Chunks of coal were wedged deeply down his esophagus, and he choked. It all made sense. It wasn't just a mallet; it was an enormous gavel. On the rounded end of the gavel, he could make out stains of dried blood mixed with chunks of flesh and broken bits of bone.

Time sped back up in time for Carl to hear Dominicus bellow out as he lifted the gavel high over his head, "When justice is done, it brings joy to the righteous but terror to the naughty. Peace be to the dead. Judgment to the sinner."

Carl took his last breath and closed his eyes. *I'm sorry*, he thought with self-pity. Sorry for those he'd unintentionally killed, but mostly for himself.

Dominicus brought down the gavel with all his might on top of Carl's skull. His head disintegrated in a spray of blood and gore while his collarbone collapsed in on itself. It sounded like somebody smashing a pumpkin. The crimson mixture of blood and brain matter sprayed out in all directions like a macabre tie-dye on the white snow. The elves cheered as they were showered in Carl's blood. They stuck out their tongues to catch the spray like children catching snowflakes. Carl's body continued to collapse under the weight of the blow.

The elves wasted no time cleaning up the mess they'd

made. It was their favorite part of the job, after all. They walked over to what remained of Carl and collected what parts they could find. They made their way back to the trailer, sneaking a nibble or two along the way. Climbing the stairs to the porch, they tossed the carcass onto the living room floor like a bag of trash.

Another infomercial was playing during the commercial break.

Dominicus made his way up to the porch. The wooden stairs nearly gave out under the weight of his gigantic body. He bit off the end of a large cigar, then, with a snap of his finger, lit the tip while admiring his work. He walked up to the door with his gavel resting on his shoulder. Cigar smoke billowed around his head like a halo. Peering in at Carl one last time, he paused. A song on the television caught his attention: *Here comes Santa Claus, here comes Santa Claus, right down Santa Claus Lane...* The upbeat Christmas tune celebrating his brother spilled from the TV's speakers. Dominicus flashed it a look of disgust.

"I fucking hate that song," he jeered, flicking the lit cigar onto the carpet. With a wave of his hand, the floor lit up like the 4th of July. Flames climbed up the curtains, spread to the ceiling, and swallowed the recliner. Carl's body was engulfed in violent fire. Within minutes, the rest of the trailer was ablaze, lighting up the trailer park.

The elves applauded from the lawn as they watched the roof slowly collapsing in on itself. Dominicus set down his gavel, clapped his massive hands, smiling. In a way, he looked almost jolly. The fire reflected in his dark eyes, making them twinkle.

"Let's go, boys," he called to the elves. They scrambled up onto the porch one by one, and without hesitation, their bells jingling merrily, they jumped into the blaze. Dominicus

Claus, the Bringer of Christmas Judgement, took one last look around. He removed the *Naughty List* and a quill pen from his breast pocket. Dipping the quill in the blood on the head of his gavel, he crossed out the name "Carl Edmund Scottsdale" before returning the items to his pocket. Finally, he followed the elves into the fire, where the four of them vanished without a trace.

Their work was complete. Justice was done.

That is, until next Christmas.

T✸HE S✸POOKY S✸EASON

Nick Chianese

Troy McClusky wanted a lot for Christmas.

He wanted—among other things—a pirate ship playset, the new Bulls-Eye pump-action paintball gun, and the glow-in-the-dark scooter he had seen advertised on his bedroom TV.

Mr. and Mrs. McClusky had purchased every gift for Troy (and his big sister, Katie) long before they drove to the Milwood Town Square. But on that frigid sunny day, two days before Christmas, his parents' hands were filled with bulging bags packed with gifts for their neighbors, cousins, and others whose names would slip their minds by New Year's.

"I'm hungry!" Troy shouted.

Promptly, the family of four pushed their way along the sidewalk, past the toy store and the tinsel-coated bookshop, and over to Hazel's Bakery for some chocolate reindeer doughnuts. The line to order was out the door, so the McCluskys waited their turn, shivering in the sun.

Troy's eyes impatiently wandered.

A few yards away, in the center of the square, he saw The Gingerbread Houses. At least that was what the towns-people called them: twelve 3-foot-high miniatures made of plywood, constructed each year and painted in greens and reds and covered with candy cane roofs.

But this year, Troy spotted an extra house.

It looked as if it were carved from a tree stump, growing out of the ground itself. The mini-home was complete with red tinsel on the roof, a perfectly shaped wreath on the door — and two eyes in the window.

The eyes, and the face they belonged to, quickly ducked down, but Troy knew someone was inside, watching him.

While Katie occupied their parents (insisting that their mom cut ahead because it just wasn't fair that they had to wait in the freezing cold), Troy walked toward The Ginger-bread Houses.

Standing outside the tiny structure, he read the wooden sign crookedly nailed above the door. In a childish scrawl, it read:

Spooky's Playhouse.

Then suddenly, in between blinks, it changed; now it read:

Sparky's Playhouse.

Before Troy could wonder how or why the words had changed, the Elf appeared.

He peered over the window ledge from the dark interior. "Do you want something?" he asked in a squeaky voice. He wore a green hat, much like the elves from Santa's work-shop. His ears, as pointed as bat wings, protruded from the sides of his wrinkled face, and his eyelids fluttered in the cold. And as they did, Troy noticed the Elf's unusual irises: one green, one red.

"Are you Sparky?" Troy asked.

The Elf grinned with paper-thin lips. "You can call me that, if you want." The Elf raised his right fist, clutching something in his palm. "And right now... I think you want to eat. Don't you?"

Troy nodded. "Yeah, I'm starving. Mom and Dad are getting me food."

"You don't have to wait on them," the Elf said. He thrust his arm through the open window and unfurled his hand, re-vealing the small gingerbread cookie inside.

But the cookie wasn't thin and flat like most gingerbread men. It was more cylindrical, with no frosting, no face, and no gumdrop buttons. If Troy were older, he might have thought the cookie resembled an ancient corn husk doll, baked to a golden brown.

"Take it," the Elf insisted.

The delicious scent of the cookie wafted into Troy's nos-trils, that ambrosial mix of cinnamon, nutmeg, and cloves, and the thick molasses baked right in.

"It's the season of giving. No one can give unless someone takes." The Elf's words hissed through the air. "You have to take..."

Troy nodded and grabbed the cookie, stuffing the whole treat into his mouth. He chewed, and he gobbled, and he loved every second. The cookie tasted so rich, so impossibly great; it was the single best thing he had ever tasted.

"Troy!"

He turned to see his father storming toward him. Mr.

McClusky grabbed him by the elbow as Troy swallowed the last crumbs of the gingerbread man.

"What are you doing over here?!"

"I was talking to the elf!" Troy whined.

But when they looked back at the little house, they found no one inside.

His father continued to scold him; yet, by the time they arrived at the front of the bakery, the McCluskys bought their children two reindeer doughnuts each.

Troy finished the last of his treats on the car ride home, just as they reached their driveway. He licked the chocolate from his sticky fingers, savoring every last drop, but his stomach kept on grumbling and growling.

"You're gross," Katie said, inching away from him in the back seat.

Troy turned to his sister, prepared with a snarky comment. But he said nothing. He was too distracted by the smell.

It was the scent of that delicious gingerbread cookie, the cinnamon and nutmeg and cloves. Troy sniffed the air, his nose twitching like a rat. He leaned toward his sister.

The smell was coming from her skin, like thick molasses baked right in.

"Mom!" Katie yelled. "Troy's being weird. Make him stop!"

But Mrs. McClusky ignored her as she put the car in park.

And Troy leaned in closer to Katie.

And closer.

Then he opened his mouth, and he bit into his sister's wrist.

"MOM!"

Katie's screech jolted both parents, and they turned their heads just in time to witness their son tear into Katie's skin, shredding through her muscle and tendons and into her bones.

Then with impossible strength, he ripped her hand from

her wrist—as easily as pulling a bow from a present.

And he kept on eating.

Overwhelmed by the smell of cinnamon and cloves that wafted off his whole family, he continued to consume, powering through the screams and the throes, until the seats were as red as Santa's suit.

When he finished, Troy leaned back and gazed out the window. In every direction he looked, the houses were lit up for the holidays, shining and sparkling and flaunting their Christmas spirit.

The season of giving was upon him.

And he was still hungry.

Home Sweet Home

Evan Baughfman

The voice came from inside the gingerbread house.

"Help," it said. "Please. Let me out of here."

Gwen stared at the little building on her kitchen counter. The voice emanating from within was barely above a whisper: raspy and reminiscent of entities from a thousand different horror movies.

"I already said no," Gwen replied. "Nuh-uh. No way in Hell."

The voice grew louder. Agitated. "Aw, come on! I need more leg room than this!"

"Not my fault. Isn't that right, Expo?"

Gwen's dog, a four-year-old Rhodesian Ridgeback, looked up at her with yellow-orange eyes. Gwen often asked him questions. He rarely answered them, however, and when he did, he usually only responded with nuzzles or hand licks.

At the moment, Expo stood on all fours, and from his vantage point, he couldn't see the gingerbread house, which Gwen had pushed up against the wall beside the toaster. But he could certainly hear the thing trapped inside as it begged for its release. And Expo likely smelled whatever-it-was, too, although Gwen's inferior nose only caught whiffs of icing and peppermint. Broken candy cane bits represented the house's asymmetrical windowpanes.

Expo's lips curled back on his dark snout. He growled.

"Yeah," said Gwen, nodding. "This isn't good."

"Why're you complaining?" asked the voice. "I'm the one breaking my back! Who makes a house this small? It's impractical!"

Expo snarled. Gwen held tightly onto his collar to prevent him from leaping onto the counter. Ridgebacks were originally bred to fight lions in South Africa, and Expo's protective instincts seemed to have taken over his brain.

Before now, he'd never done more than chase after a gopher in the backyard or stare down a raccoon from the other side of a sliding glass door, but Expo had the strength—and the teeth!—to do some real damage to anything he deemed a threat.

Years ago, Gwen had saved him from a shelter. Now, he seemed to be intent on protecting her from this mysterious intruder, going so far as trying to push past Gwen to attack the miscreant.

But she held Expo in place and scolded him for making the attempt.

Expo ducked his head and whined. Gwen didn't like yelling at him, but who knew if the thing in there, desperate and cornered, could hurt her Number One guy?

"Oh, God!" the voice wailed. "This is awful! Like a...like a coffin!"

John had left months ago, after six rocky years of marriage. He'd been the big holiday decorator in the relationship, not Gwen. All she'd wanted to do was give herself a little Christmas cheer. Hence, yesterday's construction of the lopsided gingerbread shanty. Admittedly, the structure was more a shack than a home.

"I didn't think it was possible, but this is worse than that damned ball! Feels like the walls are closing in! Help me, please!"

Gwen wanted to scream, though that would have only made matters worse with Expo.

How was she supposed to know that a garage sale ornament would house an otherworldly being? No wonder the glass baubles had been priced so cheaply!

Four minutes earlier, when Gwen had returned from her morning shopping spree, Expo immediately knew something was amiss. He leaped for the decorative spheres, nipping at the edge of the cardboard tray that held them.

The ornaments shattered on the hardwood floor, an explosion of glitter and gold.

From the wreckage sprang forth a puff of red smoke the size of carnival cotton candy. The center of the misty apparition held a pair of vibrant, neon-green eyes. Their pupils were vertical slits. Reptilian.

Demonic?

The thing floated there for three seconds, looking at Expo, at Gwen, and then back at Expo again when the dog started barking and snapping his jaws.

"Shit!" the smoke cried before taking flight.

Expo gave chase. Gwen followed after, dodging ornament shards.

The pursuit was brief and led directly into the kitchen. The crimson cloud zipped around in confusion, looking for a place to hide.

Expo was right under the thing and ready to lunge up-ward for a bite. Luckily, Gwen grabbed him by the collar before he could *carpe demon*.

The red mass had then dashed to the side of the ginger-bread house and disappeared through a left-leaning wall.

Whatever-it-was hadn't shut up since.

"Okay, this isn't funny! It's getting hard to breathe in here!"

Gwen snorted. "Weren't you just living inside an orna-ment?"

"You mean, 'suffering inside'? I wouldn't call that living, lady!"

"Want to tell me what you are?" Gwen asked.

"What I am is regretting my decision to solidify into my true form! 'Cause this sucks!"

"You really can't break out of there?"

"Once I choose a vessel, it's home sweet home until some-one sets me free."

That settled it. Gwen had to keep the gingerbread house together for as long as possible. Hold it steadfast with more icing, unless she wanted that thing flying around the kitchen again. But she couldn't apply any more of the stuff without first letting go of Expo.

"God, I chose poorly! Panicked!" Silence for a little while, then: "Seriously, no open windows? Nothing to let a draft come in? This is torture!"

Gwen shrugged. "Sorry, I'm no architect."

"No shit, lady!"

"What do you want, exactly?"

"Other than new digs? A friend, I guess."

"A friend?"

"Yeah, I'm lonely, you know? I was stuck in that ornament for who knows how long and only ever got to see people after Thanksgiving. When New Year's came around, I went right back in that moldy box in the attic!"

"Oh."

"Yeah. I'd like a companion, you see? Someone to talk to. You're the first person to say anything to me since last December."

"I don't...don't know that we can be friends."

"Why not?"

Expo growled. Gwen scratched him behind the ears in an effort to calm him down.

"Right," said the voice. "You've already got a pal. A mutt."

"Also, how do I trust a...whatever-you-are? This is crazy."

"What's crazier is talking to yourself for eleven months out of every year!"

"I...I need to...go do something."

"Like what? Hey, don't leave me alone for too long, now."

"Just stay put, okay?"

"Where am I going? This thing have wheels on it I don't know about?"

Gwen practically dragged Expo out of the kitchen. He kept his gaze fixed on the gingerbread house for as long as he could.

She brought the dog over to the front door. Expo's leash hung nearby. She clipped it to his collar. "This way, all right?" Gwen led Expo down the hall, toward her bedroom. Her plan was to lock him inside while she Googled "red smoke monster" and "exorcism for dummies."

All the while, Expo strained against his leash, yearning to return to the kitchen. Gwen struggled to stand tall in their tug-of-war match. Expo was eighty pounds of muscle.

"No, Expo!" she shouted. "No!"

She yanked back on the leash, hard, digging into the dog's throat. Expo yelped.

Instantly, Gwen regretted using such force, and she slackened her pull.

Expo suddenly charged in the other direction, pulling Gwen off-balance. She face-planted into a wall.

A lightning bolt of pain tore through her skull, and she surrendered the leash.

Dazed for a few moments, Gwen barely felt the framed photograph smack her on the top of the head. A picture of her and John at a friend's wedding, the glass now cracked down the middle.

"Bastard," she said, brushing it aside and staggering to her feet.

Growls in the kitchen.

"Expo, no!" she yelled. "Bad Expo! Bad!"

Gwen ran down the hallway, into the living room, listening to Expo's snarls and the crashing of pots and pans.

Once in the kitchen, she saw the dog on the counter, snout buried in the broken gingerbread house. He chewed on the scenery, consuming large chunks of the edible dwelling.

Also, between Expo's lips was a small, red, scaly figure, limp and soundless. Before Gwen could stop him, Expo gulped the creature down.

"Off of there!" Gwen shrieked, pulling back on his leash.

Expo skidded across the countertop, over the stove, and finally onto the floor.

Gwen knelt beside him, saying, "Open, Expo! Open!"

She used her fingers to pry apart his jaws. The fur around Expo's mouth was plastered with gingerbread crumbs, specks of icing, and splashes of blood.

Inside Expo's mouth, pieces of dessert were caught between teeth, as were bits of tattered flesh.

"Are you okay?" Weeping, Gwen hugged her Number One guy. "You're okay; you're okay. Thank God..."

"Yeah," said Expo. "I'm okay, lady."

Gwen recoiled, backing up against the oven.

Expo's eyes had turned a vibrant, neon-green, and he spoke with that thing's voice. "Now, this I can get used to." He chuckled. "Wasn't expecting an upgrade so soon, but I'll take it! My body might be dog food, but my spirit lives on!" He paused. "Weird feeling, tasting myself. To be honest, I could've used a little seasoning."

"Get out of my dog!"

"Like I said… Once I choose a vessel, it's home sweet home until someone sets me free."

"Get the fuck out of there! Let him go!"

"Sorry, lady, I'm not going anywhere. This vessel's mobile. He's got the run of a nice, big house. Already has you as a friend. This is great!"

Gwen lifted a pan from the floor. "Back the fuck up! I'm warning you!"

"Bullshit, lady. You wouldn't hurt your dog. You don't have the guts."

Gwen's hand trembled. She dropped the pan in defeat.

Expo then lunged forward, slamming his forepaws into Gwen's chest, pinning her in place. He snarled. "Now, you fucking listen to me, understand?"

God help her, Expo was gone. Buried deep. This was something else entirely. Something sinister.

Expo-ssessed.

"Fucking answer me!" The dog's breath was hot on her face.

Bleary-eyed, Gwen nodded. "Yes, I… I understand."

"Good. Take this fucking leash off of me! Now!"

Gwen complied. The leash fell, useless, beside the scattered cookware.

"Excellent. We're going to be a great team, you and I."

"No..."

"Oh, yes. You're going to do every little thing I ask of you, 'cause if you don't, I'll tear out your fucking throat. Let you bleed out right here on the floor, and then I'll feed on your corpse for days."

Gwen sobbed. "Please, don't..."

"And another thing: you bring anyone over to help you, I'll kill the sonofabitch. Or should I say, Expo will." The demon dog laughed. "If the cops should somehow get involved, I guarantee you, I will attack them, and they will not hesitate to shoot the fucking shit out of this mutt."

Gwen wailed. "Stop! Stop talking like that!"

"Fine. So long as you understand, I'm in charge. Me. Not you. I don't leave your side. Ever. Not for a fucking moment. You're my best friend, and I'm yours. Got it?"

"Y...yes."

"Fan-fucking-tastic! Christmas came early for me this year, didn't it? Now, show me the place, friend."

"You... You want a tour?"

"Yes. Get off your ass and show me how I'll be living."

Gwen reluctantly led the dog around the house. He stopped every so often to lift a leg and pee on something. Whenever he did this, he snickered and claimed the dripping object as his and his alone.

Soon enough, they reached the sliding glass door that separated the house from the backyard. Expo-ssessed gazed outside.

He said, "We're playing fetch."

"We are?"

"You know how long it's been since I've smelled fresh air? Since I've had room to run around?" He flashed his teeth. "Open the fucking door."

Gwen lifted the latch and slid the door to the side.

The dog looked up at her. "You first. In case you've got any ideas about locking me alone out there."

Gwen stepped onto a brick patio, into the sunlight. A pleasantly warm Southern California winter's day.

Normally, she loved taking Expo outside and watching him run around like a maniac. Now, though, that he was talking like an actual maniac. Gwen didn't feel a single ounce of joy.

The dog stepped onto the patio, too. "If you ever manage to trap me out here by myself, I will do one of two things," he said. "Neither of which you will like. I'll either slam this good ol' boy's body into that glass door over and over again until it's all mangled and bloody, or I'll hop that fence over there and maul the first little boy or girl I find walking down the street. Care to take a chance on what I'm telling you, lady?"

Gwen shook her head.

"Smart. Very smart. Now, pick up that ball by your feet. Toss it that way."

They played fetch for hours. Hours! The demon seemed to be in love with his new body and its treasure trove of energy.

The winter sun eventually began to radiate summer heat. Drowning in sweat, Gwen nearly collapsed from exhaustion.

Expo-ssessed let her lap water from his bowl so that she could regain her strength. Then he forced her to play some more.

When Gwen had to use the bathroom, the dog told her to squat in the grass.

She refused. "No fucking way," Gwen said, trying to sound firm. But there was an unmistakable quiver and crack in her delivery.

"Fine, but I'm right behind you."

The two of them re-entered the house. The place reeked of dog piss.

At the bathroom, Gwen told the demon, "Stay here."

He glared, eyes burning with verdant fire.

"Please?" she begged. "Please!"

"Don't try anything stupid. And crack the door."

Gwen did as she was told. She sat on the toilet, crying softly. What the hell was she going to do? She couldn't hurt the dog and risk permanently injuring Expo. She couldn't really test the demon's anger, either, in case he followed through with one of his many threats. But Gwen also couldn't let the monster at her door control her life forever.

She stood at the sink, washing her hands. In the mirror, she noticed the bruise on her face, a direct result of her earlier fall. She wiped tears from her cheeks.

She couldn't let that fucking thing hurt her anymore. She'd think of a way out of this. She had to!

When Gwen stepped back into the hallway, it was empty except for the broken picture frame. She cautiously ventured into the living room.

The dog lay on his side, breathing heavily. "Feel...like... shit..." he grumbled. "My...fucking...stomach..."

Then he began to dry heave.

"Fuck," he said between chest spasms. "Fuuuuuuck...."

Finally, he puked gingerbread onto the floor. Candy cane slivers. And a bile-covered, reptilian claw.

Wisps of red smoke expelled from his lips, too.

Of course! The little house she'd built had been loaded with sugar! With caffeine! Adorned with chocolate chips!

Gwen smiled.

All things that were enemies to canine digestive systems!

The fucking demon was as sick as a fucking dog!

"Oh, God," he moaned. "Help me... Please..."

More vomit came. More unprocessed food.

More exorcised demon smoke.

"Don't...look so...happy..." the dog groused. "You've... got to...clean up...all this...shit..."

Clean up? Okay! A small price to pay for an evil entity expunged!

Gwen grinned even wider.

Clean up? Holy shit! Great idea!

Clean up! Yes!

Gwen raced to the closet and removed a hand-vacuum, turning it on full blast.

The thing trying to stay inside her dog weakly protested, but Gwen drowned out the noise, crouching beside Expo and sucking up every last demonic tendril that curled away from his snout.

Soon, her Number One guy stopped vomiting. His eyes shined yellow-orange again.

Inside the hand-vac, a familiar and frustrated voice cursed Gwen. She didn't care.

"When I get out of here, I'm coming for you, lady! I'll slip inside you on your fucking breath! Take fucking control of you and make you do things you wouldn't fucking believe!"

Wiped out, Expo had fallen asleep right there, beside his own mess on the floor. He snored peacefully. His breaths undulated in a regular cadence.

When he awoke, Gwen would take him to the vet. But for now...

She looked at the little vacuum.

What to do with this vessel?

She toyed with the idea of giving it to John for Christmas. His new girlfriend, though, would probably find a gift from Gwen to be suspicious. And was it worth torturing both of them just for being happy together?

Gwen sighed and let that nasty idea dissipate.

She couldn't just throw the vacuum away, either, could she? That would be irresponsible. What if it broke open and released its contents inside a garbage truck?

A possessed vehicle of that size mowing down pedestrians left and right for miles and miles?

Nuh-uh. Gwen didn't need that one on her conscience.

So she did what was simplest.

She stuffed cotton into her ears and buried the screaming vacuum, deep, in the backyard.

It took a few days, but Expo recovered from the food poisoning. Soon enough, he was back to normal, playing, cuddling, and making Gwen feel good about her lot in life. She asked him questions, and thank God he never seemed to know how to answer them.

Weeks later, on Christmas morning, Gwen sipped hot chocolate on the back patio and read a novel she'd gifted herself. More than once, she pushed Expo and his curious tongue away from her drink. The goofy dog never learned, did he?

Still, it was a beautiful day. Very relaxing. And her new book... Well, unfortunately, it wasn't particularly gripping, and Gwen dozed off in her lounge chair.

"Wake up!"

Gwen sat up straight.

Who... Who said that?

Clumps of dirt and grass were piled high in the middle of the yard. A hole... God, no... A hole had been dug deep into the earth!

A hand-vacuum lay cracked apart on the patio floor.

Standing over his prize was Expo.

"You're mine, lady," he said, cackling, green eyes aglow. "All fucking mine."

Raw Materials
Liam Hogan

The wind whistled around the big man's legs as he slammed the door of the cavernous workshop, a drift of snow whirling across the ancient wooden floor until it finally succumbed to the warmth from the stove. Santa shuddered. It was *cold* out there, and the giant sack over his shoulder was only half full.

He'd have to go out again, one more time at least, but it could wait a while longer. There was still light, so there was still time. *Just*. He didn't like to cut it this close; the harvest had been delayed by a fierce storm that had left him snowed in, impatient and frustrated. It was only on the autumn equinox itself, the last day of the arctic summer, that conditions had improved enough for him to venture outside again. He had already made a dozen trips to make up for lost time; his back ached and his arms felt like they were carved from wood.

Such storms were getting disturbingly common. Climate change, perhaps. There was even talk that the North Pole would become ice-free in as little as two decades. Worrying times.

He shook his great bearded head. The window of opportunity had always been tight. He couldn't begin the harvest any earlier, and he certainly couldn't finish it later, in the dark, after the sun had finally set for the next six months. A week was all he would ever get, storms or not. But if there was no ice...

At his feet the sack wriggled. He untied the thick rope around its neck. Pale eyes peered drowsily up at him, blinking in the wan lamplight. He carefully tipped the sack so that the writhing, naked forms tumbled free, stretching and yawning, the ice that had encased them forming puddles around their little pink feet. Santa pushed forward brightly colored garments in an assortment of sizes, though he knew they wouldn't be interested in dressing quite yet. It took time for them to learn; right now they were as innocent as newborns. But it helped to familiarize them with the *concept* of clothes. Left too late they didn't bother, and that was a mistake he'd quickly learned to avoid.

The life-cycle of a North Pole elf was a peculiar thing that even he only vaguely understood. Harvesting them just before the equinox, before the arctic sunset plunged them into a deep state of hibernation, bringing them into the heated workshop, wasn't strictly natural.

But without them he wouldn't be here, up at the frozen summit of the world, freezing his ass off. Without them there would be no workshop, no Christmas tradition of long centuries standing.

He busied himself at the great stove, ladling red-stained bowls full of porridge, spiced with cinnamon and nutmeg, cloves and ginger. He couldn't abide the smell himself, not anymore, but it was all the elves would eat, at first. Later he'd add dried reindeer and seal blubber. They grew big and strong on the additional protein, quickly reaching maturity.

By the time he'd put down the last of the food—to a bow-legged runt he wouldn't have bothered digging out of the ice if he hadn't been in such a rush, and who kept tripping over his, or her, misshapen legs—a few of the elves were trying on the striped hats, giggling and laughing in their high-pitched voices. He stroked his beard. They seemed to be getting the gist of it.

Making sure the fireguard was secure around the stove (another mistake you only wanted to make once), he took up his spade. Checking how long it was until sunset (not long, not long at all), he grabbed his empty sack and went out into the fading twilight to dig up the rest of the elves.

By the time he returned, frozen to the bone, the previous batch was beginning to explore their surroundings, to pick up things, mostly cooking utensils, that might make good tools. He left the sack—filled to the brim on this, his last trip—and shooed the elves out of the kitchen toward the workshop proper, toward the cacophony of hammers and rhythmic chants, toward the rest of the elves. Despite the delays it had been a good harvest this year; there must be at least a thousand of them.

The wonderful thing about elves was that you only had to show one or two of them how to do something—how to make a Christmas toy, for example. They shared tasks and knowledge so that, even now, the new cohort was gathering around the elves he'd dug out of the snow at the start of the week, watching and starting to mimic their actions. Sometimes it looked like there were more elves than tasks, but somehow they worked it all out, two elves to a workbench, speeding through twice the work, movements coordinated by their earworm songs, even if what they were singing about was impossible for Santa to decipher.

Mindful of his latest charges, he dashed back to the kicking, punching, bulging sack, quickly releasing the cord and scraping the bottom of the giant porridge pot into the last of the red bowls, before scattering the remaining elf clothes.

Outside, the sun dipped below the icy horizon. Santa watched it with a small sigh. It would be a busy three months, the sunless days passing in a blur, as they always did. For three months he would be hard-pressed to keep the lamps lit, the kitchen stoves going, the elves fed. Hard-pressed carting supplies of raw materials from the outer stores and into the workshop as they ran low, refilling those stores with Christmas presents ready to be delivered.

Everything else, the toy-making, the painting, and the boxing, the elves would handle. Good, old-fashioned toys, the way they should be. No *digital* gadgets, nothing plastic, nothing short-lived or disposable. Dolls and carved animals, music boxes, and intricate puzzles. He wasn't sure where the elves got their designs from. Each year they were a little different, each toy unique and very obviously hand-made, a labor of love. Santa didn't really care that such toys were in diminishing demand, that he was only called upon to deliver them to the young of the Mongolian nomads who sent him his reindeer, to the Inuit, to a dozen other remote peoples who gifted him his oats and spices and a few other essential things the frozen North could not provide. He served a shrinking fraction of the world's children, but it was the *thought* that counted, the tradition upheld. The parents elsewhere would do the rest, in his name, as they always had, as they always would.

※ ※ ※

Christmas came round so damned fast. In the stables, the exhausted reindeer slept. But Santa himself had one big, onerous task to do before he too could rest.

The noise as he re-entered the workshop was deafening. It was always chaos when he returned with his empty sled. With nothing to do, nothing more to make, the elves were busy getting into mischief, clambering from the rafters, sticking their noses where they shouldn't. And these were *big* elves now, fully mature, fat and sleek on their rich diets and prolonged warmth, a state they wouldn't reach for at least a dozen years in the wild.

Banging an empty pot, Santa drowned out their squeals and the occasional scream when one of the elves slipped, waiting until there was silence other than a few broken whimpers. He gave the speech he always gave, never knowing how much of it they took in.

He thanked the elves for their tireless work, congratulated them on the ingenuity of their creations, assured them the children who received their toys would be truly delighted and would treasure them for years to come. He told them the elves deserved a day off, as a reward, and announced a feast, a grand Christmas celebration, and that any elf who wanted to help in the preparation of that feast was more than welcome.

Of course, they *all* wanted to help. In short order, the larders were raided and emptied, the workbenches cleared. A dozen elves stirred each of the great pots. The random, whatever-was-left ingredients made for a gray, unappealing mush, but thankfully he, Santa, would not have to partake.

Finally, when everything was as ready as it would ever be, he unveiled his secret Santa gift to the excited elves. Twelve huge barrels of potent, noxious liquor, a viscous, ruddy slop that bubbled even as it was decanted.

"Ho, ho, ho! Let the feast begin!" he called out, raising

his own, empty, tankard.

All day long the elves feasted and caroused, the impossible noise levels ratcheting even louder. As the barrels ran dry, elves squirmed through the openings to carry away the thick dregs. When the very last of it was scraped clean, the elves paired off in twos and threes. Rosy-cheeked, they staggered outside into the arctic darkness to do whatever the hell it was that led to the next generation of elves, that led to the strange shapes in the ice pockets that waited for the first touch of the polar sun before beginning to grow through the six months of summer, until they were finally ready for him to harvest as the sun once again set.

Arms crossed, his breath pluming in the bitterly cold air, Santa watched as they cavorted into the dark, waiting for the last elf to leave, the bow-legged runt he'd almost left behind, now naked and priapic. The cheeky sod gave him a wink as he passed, before he lolloped off to catch up with the rest. Santa kept the doors wide open, the heat quickly spilling into the insatiable cold. Pulling on his great red coat, he closed the air vents on the stoves, watched as the flickering flames died.

And then he set up his sharpening wheel, whistling as he worked. A tuneless, meaningless melody, but that didn't matter. There was no-one there to pick it up, to turn it into a maddening earworm that would come echoing back to him in a thousand high-pitched variations.

He'd be waiting, in the dark, by the cooling stove when the elves returned, flushed and giddy, skin red-raw from the cold. They'd lie down in messy piles of discarded clothes and fall into a deep sleep, their first in three months, exhausted by their orgy, drowsy from the barrels of intoxicating liquor, becoming even more lethargic as the temperature plummeted well below zero, until they finally succumbed to their hard-coded need to hibernate through the arctic winters.

It was a simple thing for Santa to visit each of them in turn, to place a wooden bowl beneath their necks, and with a wickedly sharp knife in hand, to quickly *slice!*

The air would soon be thick with the scent of their blood, but even that would fade as the elves froze solid. It was something that no-one ever seemed to ask, to wonder. What *did* children think Santa's presents were made out of?

Well, what *else* did he have? The only raw materials he had were the elves. Their mature bodies, carefully nurtured and replenished year after year. By the New Year, they'd be as dry and stiff as boards, ready to be rendered down. Every part of them would be used; Santa couldn't afford any waste, and he would be kept busy these next nine months. Nine months, Santa had, to process the cold corpses. Through the dead days until New Years, through the quiet months to the spring sunrise, where, across the snowy wastes, embryonic elves in their ice chrysalids would begin to grow in the startling sunlight, somehow taking enough from the air and the ice to finish the first stage of their development. Through those bright summer months, until the sun once again threatened to disappear.

Nine months to make soft leather from their skin, rope and string and braid from their sinews. To stack the bones by length, the skulls for carving, the limbs and ribs for structure.

And to make paint from their blood. The bright, glossy red paint that almost all Christmas toys sported. The same red that stained the elves' bowls. The same red that coated the corners of their mouths as they licked and shaped the paintbrushes. The hairs of which were also elf, of course.

There were other colors, acts of alchemy to be wrought from gall bladders and other internal organs, his large hands barely up to the delicate task.

Sometimes, in the dark thoughts that come to any man alone for so much of the year, he wondered if the elves knew what they made their toys out of. Surely, they must? Or did they think it was from some other animal, one they never saw? Did they realize what it was that was fermented in the huge barrels to make their alcoholic, celebratory, festive brew?

Santa put down the last of his sharpened knives, listened to the silence broken only by the keening wind. A silence he would have to endure for a long time after tonight. They'd be back soon, and the last deed of the year would begin, and then he could sleep, in his little hut separate from the by-then-frozen workshop.

He was so tired. So very tired. His thoughts strayed as they often did in this brief lull. It was the only downside to the whole magical annual cycle, that he could almost wish for some elves to assist him with the final stages of his work, the nine months of solitary duty that sometimes threatened to overwhelm the chaotic three with his thousand little helpers.

He thought about the runt, the cheeky one, but shook his head in sorrow. Another experiment tried and failed. Faced with dismembering his own kind, faced with the realization that he had drunk the fermented viscera of other elves, an earlier spared elf had run amok and Santa still had the scars to show for it.

No. Tradition was tradition, and duty was duty, even if it meant spending most of the year alone. Santa stepped into the shadows with his knives, listening intently for his raw materials to return.

B*ait

Mike Marcus

December 24

Dear Diary,

This year, the fat man is mine.

My plan is foolproof. In just a few hours, I'll have Santa Claus exactly where I want him. Finally, he'll have to answer for what he's done and all the lies he's told.

Everyone knows how Santa is supposed to do things. He's supposed to reward good kids with the presents they want, and bad kids are supposed to find only coal in their stockings on Christmas morning. That's the whole point of the Naughty and Nice lists. But I have to tell you... This is completely wrong. Santa and our parents have been lying to us because I can prove that bad kids still get presents and good kids like me don't get what they most want in the world. Plus, Santa uses his magic to do bad things no one wants us to know about.

I didn't know Santa was a liar and bad guy until Christmas five years ago. I had just turned six years old, and I was head over heels amazed by Santa. I believed all the stories and Christmas carols. I even had a teddy bear that wore a red Santa suit. I used to get so excited to get my picture with him at the mall. All that changed when I saw him in my living room.

It was Christmas Eve, and Daddy was out with the fire company delivering Christmas dinner baskets to the other farms around town. I just had my bath and was in my pajamas, the fun unicorn ones with the feet in them. I loved those pajamas. Mom and I put out a plate of homemade chocolate chip cookies and a big glass of milk. When Mom tucked me into bed, we talked about the pony I asked Santa for at the mall earlier that week. I was certain Santa was going to bring it for me. When I told him about it, he winked at me and smiled. And it wasn't one of those "that's so sweet little girl, now get off my lap" smiles that I saw him give kids who were crying or had wet their pants. I truly thought Santa knew how much I wanted a pony. My friend Allison got a brown-and-white pony named Maribel for her birthday that summer, and I wanted one just like it. Allison was lucky she got the pony for her birthday because there was no way Santa was going to bring her one. She was always mean to her little sister and threw rocks at her neighbor's dog. She definitely would have been on the Naughty list. Thinking back, I should have known better than to trust Santa—when I was on his lap asking for my pony, I couldn't help but notice that his teeth were yellow and he smelled like feet. Gross!

I was too excited to fall asleep that night and tried thinking of names for the pony I was sure would be in our living room the next morning. I was just starting to drift off when I heard whispering downstairs, then the sound of Mom giggling like she does when Daddy tickles her. I thought maybe he'd gotten home early, and I wanted to say goodnight.

I slipped out of bed and tiptoed down the hallway to the steps. Christmas carols played quietly on the radio as I crept down the stairs and peeked into the living room. That's when I saw him. It wasn't Daddy making Mom giggle. Santa was in our living room! He was sitting on the couch in his red suit, eating the cookies I left for him, and Mom was taking wrapped presents out of a big bag and putting them under the Christmas tree. Santa didn't look as big or old as I expected. His hair was short and dark like Daddy's, and the red suit hung loose on him. I knew it was Santa, but it was like he was wearing a disguise. I couldn't see his face, but his voice sounded familiar. He was leaning against a big pile of pillows on the couch, dipping the cookies in the glass of milk just like Daddy does. I was excited at first, but then I got a little scared. Daddy wasn't home, and there was a strange man in our living room. But when Mom snuggled up next to him on the couch and kissed him, I knew Santa was bad! They were whispering, so I couldn't hear what they were saying, but I'm certain Daddy would not be happy if he caught them. Is this what Santa does with all the moms when he sneaks into their houses?

I didn't know what to do. Mom was kissing another man in our living room while Daddy was out. I crept back to my bedroom and crawled into bed. It felt like hours later when I finally heard Daddy downstairs and I was certain Santa must have left. I finally drifted off to sleep that night, but I never forgot the image of Mom kissing Santa on our living room sofa.

The next morning there was no pony. I got lots of clothes and toys, but they were just okay and couldn't compare to the pony I really wanted. I was so mad. Not only did he not bring me the pony I asked for, but he had the nerve to kiss Mom in our living room. I wanted to tell Daddy about what I saw, but he loved Christmas so much. When he asked me if I got everything I wanted from Santa, he was smiling so big that I just knew if I told him no, and that I saw Mom kissing Santa Claus right where he was sitting on the sofa with his cup of coffee, it would have broken his heart. Kind of like mine did when I went downstairs that morning. So, I just smiled and said yes. I didn't like lying to Daddy, but I figured this one was okay.

All day I thought about what I saw the night before and the pony I didn't get. Even visiting Grandma and Pop at their house that afternoon, I couldn't stop thinking about it. I'm a good girl. I help Mom and Daddy around the farm. I feed the chickens every morning even though Tom, the old rooster, likes to chase me around the yard trying to peck at my legs. I even do pretty good in school. What did I do wrong that I didn't get my pony? I know lots of other kids who got what they wanted but were always misbehaving. Bobby Henderson pulls girls' ponytails, and at school, I've seen him eat paste, but that year he still got the puppy he wanted for Christmas. Kelly Myers got caught cheating on the spelling test, but she got the Barbie dream house she wanted. Even Jeff Wilson got the new baseball glove he wanted, and everyone knows that he steals lunch money from kids at school. That's when I realized the whole Naughty and Nice lists were a sham, and there was only one person who could answer for the lies. I needed answers from Santa.

I also couldn't explain why Mom kissed Santa until I realized it must be part of his evil magic. It's the only explanation. He must have cast a spell on her to let him act that way. How many other kids have had this happen to their moms and didn't know?

For the next two years, I tried to ask Santa about this when my parents took me to the mall to see him before Christmas, but he just ignored me, and after a few minutes, he had one of his elves take me back to my parents. I figured he couldn't talk about it in front of everyone else at the mall, so I tried to stay awake to catch him red-handed. On Christmas Eve, I'd get into my pajamas and sit on the couch across from the fireplace, right where he had been sitting. But the house was all warm and I'd get sleepy, and the next thing I knew, it was morning and I was waking up in my bed. It was only after I saw the movie *Home Alone* that I realized I needed a plan. I had to be smart and set a trap.

First, I tried to use my jump rope like a snare in front of the chimney. I tied it across the front of the fireplace and attached bells to one end. I thought that when he came down the chimney, his legs would get wrapped in the jump rope and the bells would wake everyone up. I was careful to tell Mom and Daddy to leave it alone so they wouldn't trip on it. I went to sleep that night hoping to wake to the sound of bells ringing and Santa struggling. The next morning, I found my jump rope wound up in a spool on the floor next to the fireplace. The jump rope was rolled up just like Daddy rolled it when I left it in the driveway. The bells were in a small pile next to it.

Last Christmas was warm, so there was no fire. I put a dozen mousetraps from the barn in the fireplace, plus the jump rope again. Somehow, he must have seen my trap. The next morning, the mouse traps were in a shoebox along with my jump rope. Again, he'd found a way to escape.

And that brings us to tonight. I've put in place a fool-proof plan to finally catch him. Last month, I was helping Daddy put out corn and salt licks for the deer on the farm. It was the first time he let me help him. I've known for a long time that he hunted the deer for the venison that we ate. But I didn't know that he used corn and salt licks to get the deer to come back to the same area over and over again. He said it was so he didn't have to chase them around the farm. While we were putting out the corn, Daddy also put bait in the groundhog holes in the orchard. Daddy said the bait made the groundhogs fall asleep in their nests, like when bears hibernate. That's when I got the idea for this year's Santa trap.

I had been going about catching Santa all wrong. If he was magical, regular traps weren't going to work. And if Mom was helping him, she might warn him or take away my traps before he even arrived at our house. I don't blame her since it was obvious that he was using magic on her. But I had to figure out a way to make sure Mom didn't interfere.

This afternoon I made the chocolate chip cookies for Santa all on my own. I convinced Mom earlier this month that I wanted to learn how to bake cookies, and for the past several weeks, we made cookies together. They were just small batches that Daddy took to work in his lunch or left at the firehouse for the volunteers. Daddy said they were the best cookies he'd ever had, and he couldn't stop eating them. I told Mom that I wanted to make Santa's cookies myself this year. She was surprised at first, but I knew that she's been busy lately. So, she let me.

What she doesn't know is that I added a special ingredient just for Santa. I followed the recipe card just like before. I mixed the butter, brown sugar, and eggs, then added the flour, baking soda, and salt. But before I dumped in the bag of chocolate chips, I put in a big scoop of groundhog bait from the barn. It all blended together perfectly. I couldn't even tell there was anything different about them. The cookies baked like normal, and just a few minutes ago, I left a plate of them and a big glass of ice-cold milk on the end table in the living room.

It's the perfect bait for Santa, and he'll never know!

Mom is downstairs listening to Christmas carols on the radio and Daddy is off with the fire company delivering the dinner baskets, just like every year. If Santa sticks to his pattern, he should be here soon, and he'll go for the cookies and milk. I just know I'm going to find Santa asleep on the couch in the morning, and then I can finally get the answers I deserve! He'll probably still have cookie crumbs in his beard!

God Rest Ye Scary Santamen
Nathan D. Ludwig

I wasn't exactly sure why, but at the very moment I embedded my ax into the bloated stomach of that obsequious, uncanny Kris Kringle look-alike, I felt compelled to finally confess to Derek my Santa Claus fetish.

Wait. I feel like I might have started a tad too late. Let me rewind a bit.

* * *

Derek and I had been planning our big hideaway vacation to Dover Beach in Maine for what felt like years. It was probably only eight months, but still. Perception is reality.

December in Dover Beach meant that the town changed its name to Jingle Beach and hosted its annual March of Santa Look-alikes Contest and Parade. They started doing it in the mid-80s as a gimmick to boost tourism, and the thing stuck.

People from all over the world came to celebrate the holidays and swelled the town's population to more than triple. At least for a few weeks. Santa cosplay enthusiasts from around the globe and every walk of life waited all year to descend upon the sleepy surfside hamlet and show off their yuletide stuff. Even Guy Fieri did an episode there once dressed as Santa. Not that that was a draw in any way for us.

I'd been with Derek for a few years now, and I was dying to share with him my love for all things Christmas by way of a picturesque, small-town escape filled with sleigh rides, spiked lattes, tacky sweaters, and lots of alone time. Our first year together, he was away on business a lot, and our second year as a couple saw me catch food poisoning from PF Chang's. Don't ask. Okay, it was the Bang Shrimp. Does me in every time.

This year, nothing was standing in our way. Both our families balked when we said we were going by ourselves this year. They thought we were eloping. After we talked them off that ledge, we reassured them that they would have us all to themselves next year. At least that's what we told them.

I always thought of Derek as a taller, slimmer, handsomer version of me. I called him my little aspiration. He claimed he thought it was funny, but he never actually laughed when I addressed him as such. Another reason I loved him so. The wherewithal to roll with my corny-ass punches.

About the Santa thing. I told you I was going to get back to that. For what seemed like forever, I've had a huge crush on the jolly, old fat man. Which is weird because I've never been into bears, per se. Come to think of it… I've never really had a preference. Except for Derek. And he's one helluva preference. Anyway, I think I can trace it all back to high school when my tenth-grade obsession, Matt Dinsmore, played Santa Claus at our holiday talent show. The whole thing was an ungodly dumpster fire, but when Matt came on stage and did his rendition of "Santa Baby" *as* Santa, it turned my whole world upside down. It marked me as a Kringle-fied chubby chaser for life.

Of course, I was terrified of telling Derek about it. What would he say? There was nothing more I wanted than to get him into a Santa suit and deck the goddamn halls, but I couldn't risk losing him over something so random. And weird. But hot. Really hot.

I pictured Jingle Beach like one of those towns straight out of a Hollywood movie. Clean, overly festive, bucolic locals galore, and lots of baked goods. Like way too much. Do they bake that stuff just for the movie, or do they just go to the store and buy it? How much is too much? I had to find out.

Our drive up there was uneventful yet deceptively pleasant. I tried to program the Christmas music like a celebrity DJ at Club Noel, but Derek had reached his limit of holiday tunes about halfway through our eight-hour trip. I couldn't blame him. Even I felt like I was forcing the issue. Oh well. It was nice while it lasted.

When there was a lull in his Spotify playlist of 80s new wave B-sides, he asked me, "Do you really love Christmas this much?"

"I mean, yeah, I love it. What's not to love?"

"Yeah, but *this* much?"

I understood what he meant immediately.

"Look, it's just a different kind of vacation. Something I've wanted to do for a while. After this week, we can mothball the whole North Pole mood and find some other adventure. I'm just happy we can get away together for a change. Just us. That's all."

It worked. Derek shifted into easygoing mode just as the next song was amping up. He reached for my hand, and it was the only thing I wanted at that moment.

"Sounds good. How about the running of the bulls?" Derek smirked as he glanced at me.

"Uh, let's find something in between those two extremes first. Jesus."

We both laughed it off, and I could tell he was really looking forward to this time away just as much as I was. Maybe even more. Maybe this could be it. I could finally tell him my secret desire. I was so excited at the possibility that I almost blurted it out right then and there.

Patience, Owen. Patience.

✳ ✳ ✳

We reached the former Dover Beach with stomachs full of hot chocolate and lobster rolls. A seaside eatery on the way up had really hit the spot. I almost told him about my Santa predilections there, but I choked a bit on my lobster roll and Derek had to step in and kind of save my life. You can't really blurt out a secret fetish after a near-death experience. Not when you have lobster breath.

Main Street was just how it looked in the photos on the website. They had a huge banner hanging from two vintage lamp posts on opposite sides of the street. Emblazoned on it was "WELCOME TO JINGLE BEACH—HOME OF THE MARCH OF SANTAS!" I loved it. It was comforting and tacky all at once.

People scurried here and there, up and down, and across the street as we rolled down Main at a snail's pace. Derek's eagle eyes scanned for our hotel.

"It should be just up ahead," he mumbled as he kept his eyes peeled on the advancing facades.

"There it is." I saw it first and stuck my tongue out at Derek with a playful chuckle. He smiled back and prepared to turn in to our accommodations.

The Surfside Inn. One of a handful of hotels on the main drag where we could have stayed. It had the most Christmas-y potential based on the photos I perused online. The only thing, though, was that it didn't have a single Christmas decoration on it. Not a one to be found. Like it was any other day of the year.

"Not too shabby," Derek admitted. Of course, he'd love the one sans holiday cheer.

"Same goes for you." I kissed him on the cheek, ready for this vacation to start in earnest. As he parked, I was already hopping out to go check in.

And then I saw the weirdest thing as I hurried into the hotel. A guy, clearly a Santa look-alike based on his white beard and approximate age, shuffled aimlessly down the sidewalk toward me. Empty eyes, mumbling something low and strange.

Thing was, though, he was skinny as could be. No bowl full of jelly to be found. Looked like a mummified member of ZZ Top. As I grabbed the door to go inside, his eyes met mine, and the stare he gave me raised my hackles more than a little. Maybe he was upset at himself for not being method enough to gain some legit Santa poundage. Whatever it was, I didn't really want to know. Those eyes. No thanks.

※ ※ ※

Inside was as normal and undecorated as the outside. I made a beeline for the front desk and caught the concierge just as he was getting off the phone. A tall, bespectacled man with a weird horseshoe mustache that bristled all over his face when he sniffed.

I thought I'd lighten the mood a little, even though I realized the mood hadn't even been defined yet. Vintage me. "How do you not sneeze all the time with that magnificent facepiece?"

The concierge, Marcello, if you believed his gold name tag, huffed up and bristled a bit. I could tell right away there'd be no witty banter to be had here. Oh well.

"Whatever do you mean, my good sir?"

Well, at least he was polite in his humorlessness. A plus. I guess?

"Checking in, please. Schmidt."

I hated my last name. It was so blunt. Schmidt. I mean, I had no complaints familywise. Except for that name. It never sat well with me. Now Derek, on the other hand, had a winner of a last name. Von Bargen. Derek Von Bargen. Owen Von Bargen. I almost reserved the room under Von Bargen. I was close.

"Will you be taking in the sights during your stay, my good sir?"

Huh?

"Are there…people who don't take in the sights…when they're on vacation here?"

"Everyone has a story, I'm sure, my good sir."

"O…kay. Sounds good. And yes, we will be taking in the sights. Any recommends?"

"If you find yourself out late at night, please do refrain from following any sounds of sleigh bells."

Was that a recommendation? What was happening?

"Wise advice, my good sir, wise advice indeed."

I harrumphed on top of that to a parodic level. I'm not sure if he fully appreciated it.

"We can have a bellboy take your bags to your room. Please have a pleasant stay here in the enchanted confines of Jingle Beach, my—"

"My good sir!" I bellowed with more than a little mock

zest.

And with that, I had had enough of the routine. I headed back outside to help Derek with our bags when that same guy, that emaciated Santa wannabe, was stopped dead in front of the doors, blocking my escape from this odd waystation in between Christmas and a random Tuesday in February.

"You're safe in here. No Christmas cheer."

The way the guy said it was both hopeful and terrified. I couldn't decide which one I preferred more. Instead, I just made for the door with a polite brush of my hand on his shoulder. It felt cold. Icy cold, like a fresh snowdrift. And he smelled like someone had dumped a giant box of gingerbread mix on top of him. Not an unpleasant smell under normal cir-cumstances, but this was not that. It smelled like he was try-ing to mask a much more insidious stench underneath it.

"You should probably bundle up. Layers help with the cold, you know. Excuse me."

"Safe! Safe inside where there's no cheer!"

This guy was annoying me and rattling my nerves in equal measures. As I made it past him and pushed open the front door, I could hear an employee trying to usher him outside and away from their establishment. I hurried extra quick so that guy and his eyes weren't directly on me as he left right behind me.

I made it to our car, and I think I scared Derek a bit with my abrupt return. He jumped in his seat and patted his chest gently. Rolled down his window.

"Jesus. You scared some pee out of me, I think. We good?"

I looked back to see where Diet Santa was. Nowhere to be seen. Not even shuffling down the sidewalk in the dis-tance somewhere. Just gone. I turned back to Derek and just nodded.

❋ ❋ ❋

After freshening up and settling into our room, we were determined to paint the town red. And green. Well, I was. Derek was a good sport and went along for the ride. I could tell he was tired and just wanted to nap, but I wanted to see all this legendary Jingle Beach cheer in the daylight. For posterity.

Our tacky sweater game was in full effect. Mine was a plum turtleneck with two reindeers nuzzling the crap out of each other surrounded by cheering elves. It was elaborate and sweet. Two of my favorite adjectives. Derek's was a bit more traditional. A fluffy sky-blue V-neck with Santa and Mrs. Claus joyriding in a sleigh in the middle of a winter wonderland. I picked that one out for him. It accentuated his nearly perfectly chiseled physique. Two great tastes that taste great together.

As we walked through the most decorated street I'd ever been on, I kinda sorta marveled at the intricacy of their decoration skills. Animatronic nutcrackers and elves greeted people walking into various shops, and a miniature train chugged around a massive track suspended in the air just above the streetlamps. It seemed to go on forever. The train whistle reminded me of trips to my grandmother's house for Christmas. She would blow her own little train whistle whenever cookies were fresh out of the oven for us kids to devour.

They even had a giant glass snowman filled with jellybeans. It must have been about twelve feet tall. You could guess how many jellybeans were in there and win what? All those jellybeans? It sounded like a pain in the ass of a prize. But still, very festive.

I was really getting into the seasonal mood, but I sensed Derek was still on autopilot, taking in the sights but refusing to let them affect him in any way. So, I tried the direct approach.

"Thank you for being here with me for this. It's beautiful, and so are you."

Okay, so that might have been a little on the nose. But I was being honest. Sometimes that's what needs to be said.

Derek just smiled and squeezed his arm around me even tighter. I was willing to take whatever I could get at that point.

Derek wanted a coffee, and I wanted baked goods. We split the difference and found a quaint cafe called Baker's Dozen that specialized in both. I ended up getting an apple turnover with cinnamon whipped cream. Just criminally delicious. And too big even for me to finish. Derek's spiked hot chocolate smelled pretty damn good from where I was sitting. I was never a huge fan of Bailey's in my sweet drinks per se, but I was willing to make an exception this time.

"Mind if I have a taste?"

You would have thought I'd just dug up the corpse of Derek's childhood dog the way he backed his whole body away from me while still seated in his chair.

"You can get your own, you know."

Wow. Okay. I wasn't going to let this morph into a public pissing match. I had to try another tack.

"Well, I can't finish this whole turnover myself. How about we share?"

"You never have a problem finishing too much food on your own. What's different today?"

Ouch. Sure, I wasn't exactly a Skinny Minnie, but I'm not a warthog, either.

"That's fine. I'll just bag this up and get my own drink. No worries."

Donnybrook averted. I knew he was just trying to start something as an excuse to go back to the room by himself. Not this time. I was in peak holiday mood, and nothing could bring me down right now.

Except for Diet Santa staring at us through the window. From across the street.

"Hey. Hey, Derek. Do you see that guy?"

"Where?"

"Across the street. He's literally staring right at us."

After a moment, Derek spotted him. And then said nothing. Just stared right back at him. To say it was unsettling was a gross understatement.

"What's with the staring contest?"

Derek was locked onto the guy and vice versa. I snapped my fingers in his face, and oh boy, did he not like that.

"Get your fingers out of my face." My snap caused him to snap. I'd never seen him that angry before.

"What is going on with you, babe?"

"He told me we're going to be his soon."

Excuse me?

"What the hell are you talking about?"

I looked out to where the guy was just seconds ago. Gone again. I was starting to get a truly uneasy feeling. All the spiked hot chocolate in the world wouldn't make it go away, I feared.

✳ ✳ ✳

Walking back to the hotel was more than a little awkward. The near fight, the scraggly Santa. All of it seemed dead set on ruining this trip. But I wasn't about to give up this early. Not on day one of all days.

"How about we rest up, and later we can go for a walk on the beach. I hear it's the perfect kick-start for some romance."

I thought Derek was going to respond with something snide again, but after a pregnant pause, he smiled and simply said, "Sure. I'd like that."

Trip saved. I was determined to make this work for me. For us. A little Christmas cheer can go a long way. Especially if there's beach sex involved.

* * *

Back at the hotel, I tried in vain to put the moves on Derek. All he was interested in was a big, fat nap. He was still down for the beach later, though. I called it a wash and decided to get some answers about the nagging feelings tugging at my subconscious. They were getting stronger now that my surroundings were quiet.

I made my way back down to the lobby and looked around with a puzzled frown. It couldn't have been later than four in the afternoon, and there wasn't a single person to be found. Except for Marcello. My old friend.

I tried to make eye contact with him as I approached the front desk. I even shuffled my shoes loudly on the carpet. Something to get him to look up. Nothing. Was he actively ignoring me?

"Ahem." I actually said the word "ahem" instead of clearing my throat. Very Karen of me, I will admit.

Marcello responded without meeting my gaze, like he was expecting me all along. "Mister Schmidt, how can I help you this time?"

This time? Was I that much of a pain in the ass? I could only remember speaking to this guy one other time. When we checked in. Hours ago.

"Got somewhere to be, my good sir?" I wasn't going to give up on making this stiff laugh. Hell, I'd settle for a muffled snicker at this point.

"I'm terribly busy at the moment, so if there's something I can assist you with, I would be delighted to do so immediately."

There was that polite rudeness again.

"What's with the lack of decorations for this hotel? Is the owner a Jehovah's Witness?"

"It's to ward off the blood curse that haunts this town. You chose the best hotel for your stay."

I heard what he said just fine, but my brain demanded a refund. "Pardon? Blood...blood curse...?"

"Absolutely, my good sir. Started in 1983 with a pagan ritual performed on the beach. Turned many townsfolk and tourists into demons. Ran amok. It was a whole thing. Quite the nasty aftermath."

This guy must have thought I was a real fucking asshole. I preferred the snide, condescending banter to this utter fuckery. I wanted to tell him to piss off and just head back to the room, but I had one more question, and I was damned if I wasn't going to ask it.

"What's with the dollar-store Santa roaming around town?"

"This town is host to a Santa look-alike parade and contest. You will have to be a bit more specific, my good sir."

"The skinny creep scaring the shit out of people and flexing his telepathy skills."

"Ah, yes...him. He is some sort of alchemist, I believe. A sorcerer, too."

"A what?"

"That is how he introduced himself, if I remember him correctly."

Huh.

"Well, thanks for the chat. You've got a fantastic imagination and I salute you."

I wanted Derek. I wanted a walk on the beach. I wanted away from this whacko loon.

"I would advise remaining in your room once the late hour arrives. Once you hear sleigh bells on the beach, it is already too late. Much safer indoors. Much safer in here, my good sir."

"I'll take that advisement under advisement. Thanks."

I tried to keep from rolling my eyes until I had turned away from him, but I had already started as soon as I finished speaking. I caught his mustache bristle a bit before my head was all the way around and facing the elevator.

Alchemist? Sleigh bells? Was this the roleplaying adventure nerd hotel? Did I pay extra for that? What the hell was going on? I knew Derek would be even less enthusiastic about this nonsense. I decided not to even mention I talked to Marstachio back there.

It was time for a romantic stroll on the beach. Come hell or high water.

❄ ❄ ❄

So, I may have oversold the beach a tad. Turns out, December sea breezes in Maine were like low-key Arctic winds. Even with our heavy sweaters and coats, it was a struggle to stroll with comfort and dignity. Even the thought of beach sex out here in this weather made my pelvis pucker.

It was beautiful, though. The moon was high and combined with the sand to create an otherworldly glow up and down the shoreline. Derek had his neutral face on, and it was really starting to annoy me. Sure, it was kind of inhospitable out here, but it was romantic, for God's sake. The rhythmic lapping of the tide said so.

We were basically dragging each other by the arm to keep moving forward so we could say we went for a walk on the beach when neither one of us had any desire to actually put in the work. After a day full of sneering and sniping and snapping, Derek was about to incur my full wrath. I was ready to unload on him now that we didn't have a captive audience.

"So, is this the part where you tell me what your deal is? Or do I have to hire a private investigator to find exactly where the bug that crawled up your ass is located?"

The look on Derek's face signified he knew this was coming. His opening salvo was surprisingly calm.

"You know I don't like Christmas. I'm doing my best."

"Yeah. But why? Why act like an asshole all day like it wasn't your choice to come here?"

"Well, it wasn't. You made sure of that."

"How the hell did you not have a choice? Are you an adult or not?"

Derek stopped. He still hadn't raised his voice or rolled his eyes yet. A record for this trip.

"You know what? Fine. Here you go. When I was fifteen, I was attacked by a mall Santa. I worked at the Orange Julius in the mall, and after my shift, in the parking lot, the fucking shopping mall Santa Claus tackled me, beat the shit out of me, and threw me in his car. He took me to his apartment and proceeded to drunkenly serenade me with all the Christmas carols he could half-remember in his blottoed state. Oh, and to top it all off, he puked his mall food court Chinese dinner all over me right before the cops showed up. Happy now?"

"How did you know it was Chinese food?"

"I'm out." Derek started back toward the hotel. My humor reflex had struck at the wrong time.

"Jesus, Derek. Why didn't you tell me this before? That's a pretty big detail to leave out before coming on a Christmas vacation to a Christmas town drenched in Christmas cheer!"

"I just wanted you to be happy. I know this trip means a lot to you. I thought I could do it. I really, really thought I could. But today was a struggle. I don't think I can do another day here."

Before I was able to respond, I could have sworn I heard sleigh bells further down the beach. "Do you hear that?"

"What?! Did you hear what I just said?"

"Sleigh bells..."

I have no idea why I followed the sound. Even after Marcello the Mustache Man warned me not to. Maybe it was my sense of adventure. Maybe it was my idiotic way of trying to keep our vacation going as it was crumbling around me.

Or maybe I was just trying to avoid processing what Derek just confessed to me. It meant my secret fantasy was probably going to remain a secret.

"Where are you going? Owen!"

His voice trailed off as I jogged toward the sound. As soon as I cleared a small dune, I could see a green bonfire up ahead. A holiday bonfire? Weird for sure, but I couldn't see any sign of sleigh bells even though they were still filling my ears.

As I got closer to the fire, I could see a figure. A man. And that's when it all fell into place and I realized I was the biggest fool in Fooltown. The mayor of Fooltown for life. There, throwing what looked like sand into the growing emerald bonfire, was him. The skinny, homeless, Santa-wannabe creep. I could hear Derek calling after me, his voice getting closer and closer. All I could focus on, though, was that man and his creaky, nasally chanting. I couldn't make out what exactly he was saying, but it didn't sound pleasant. Guttural, angry. Germanic? Something inhospitable, for sure.

"Owen, for god's sake—" Derek had caught up to me, and instead of finishing his sentence, he saw what I was fixed on and pulled on my arm. "Let's go. Now."

I wanted to go. I really did. But as soon as Derek spoke, the scraggly Santa wannabe locked eyes on us and smiled. It was the first time I saw his teeth. They were all pointed. He pushed his tongue out through his razor-sharp teeth, and it made a wet, squishy sound that made me gag.

"Hello, boys! You're just in time!"

As he was rubbing his hands together in excitement, another couple approached from the other direction. Probably from a hotel with a shitload of decorations. Yet, we were both in the same predicament. They were a cute, chubby couple with matching tacky Grinch sweaters. As if there were such a thing as a non-tacky Grinch sweater.

"Oh. Sorry to interrupt your—" The guy of the couple said, not really sure what they were interrupting. His girl was already backing away before he even began speaking.

"Oh, not so fast. This is perfect! Four for the price of two!" Diet Santa squealed.

And with that, he reached into the green flame of the bonfire and scooped some out like he was scooping up a snowball. Then he threw the fireball at the couple and shouted something that sounded like "Gin and tonic!" but in reality, it was more like "Gine ton!" even though I had no idea what language it was or what it meant.

As the fireball hit the stunned couple, they fell to the ground and writhed in what looked like agony. I wasn't sure.

"We. Have. To. Go. Now." Derek was trying to sound like the strong one, like he always does, but I could tell he was scared shitless.

I turned to run, but as I did, the couple started to change. Not like anything I would ever expect them to change into. At all. Their bellies expanded to a much larger size, ripping their clothes in the process. Their hair turned stark white and grew down to their shoulders. They both grew silver beards that reached their sternums. I could hear them making some kind of noise, but what I initially thought was howling or moaning was something else entirely.

"HO, HO, HO! HO, HO..."

They were bellowing like Santa Claus. Jolly and guttural. Deep, supernatural belly laughs. It was the most terrifying thing I had ever heard in my entire life.

Derek pulled on my arm hard, and I needed no other prompt at that point. We both turned and ran as fast as we could through the sand. Diet Santa's voice rang out behind us.

"Get them, my pets!"

The sound of ho-ho-ho-ing picked up and followed us the whole way as we sprinted across the beach and back to Main Street. I wasn't even thinking about where our hotel was. I just wanted off that beach, and I didn't have to ask Derek to know he was thinking the exact same thing.

As we reached the main drag and the sand had disappeared for good, I noticed the Santa belly laughing had also vanished. Were we safe? Was it only a beach thing? Limited range of control for Homeless Santa? I leaned against the storefront next to me and attempted to catch my breath. Derek was further out in the street. It looked like a ghost town. The place shut down earlier than any place I had ever been before. Almost right at sundown.

"Owen. Let's go. We should—"

Before he could finish, I felt a tight, strong hand close around my throat. Followed immediately by the sensation of being lifted several feet off the ground. And then, I was flying. For a few seconds, it felt nice, then my body met the plate glass window of the hardware store. I was pretty sure I caught the name of the store as I went through it. Samuelson's Hardware. When I hit the floor, I could hear Derek shouting my name, followed by the sounds of a scuffle. That's the last thing I remember before the lights went out.

* * *

I had no idea how long I had actually been out for. Seconds? Minutes? I knew it wasn't hours because I could hear Derek grunting and breathing hard just outside. He was still fighting off something out there.

I can't remember if I stood up first or reached for the ax that lay next to me in the mess of shattered glass and destroyed displays, but before I knew it, I was up and armed without even surveying the extent of my injuries.

Right away, I saw Derek fending off both of the…santa-men…weresantas? Why didn't the woman turn into a Mrs. Claus thing? Was that sexist?

They were gnashing their teeth, trying to bite Derek. Thick, white globs of saliva splashed off their thin, gray lips and onto Derek's arms and face. He was keeping them at bay with fore-arms and elbow shots to their bodies and faces. He was the very definition of a big, strong man, and he was showing it right there and then. Though as well as he was doing, I knew he needed my help.

I jumped through the now-windowless hole in the hard-ware store and charged at one of them. I wasn't sure which one was the guy or girl anymore. Like it even mattered. I swung my ax at the nearest one to me and planted it in its back. It definitely yowled in pain, but it didn't drop to the ground or die or anything. It just kept attacking my Derek.

"Hit it again!" I could tell Derek was getting tired; his voice was full of exhausted panic. I had to end this.

I yanked my ax out of the santaman's back, causing it to spin around to face me. Teeth out and gnashing. Chomping the air mercilessly. Its arms reaching toward me now. In a mo-ment of sheer panic and pure reflex, I struck out at the were-santa and hit it squarely in the stomach. My blade punctured it quickly and cleanly, like it was meant to go there.

The shouty groan that emanated from the Santa thing was sorrowful and accepting all at once. The other weresanta that was still attacking Derek stopped and howled in pain at the sound of its partner's death throes.

As my axed santaman dropped to the ground, I tried to yank the ax head out of its stomach, but it was a mighty struggle. I had to embed my foot into the bulbous tummy and pull mightily on the ax for it to finally come out, tearing the santaman's midsection from groin to sternum. Hot, steaming green jelly avalanched out and onto the street. The sheer audacity of the stench made me puke immediately.

I wiped away the vomit on my mouth with my sleeve, and I wanted to stammer *what the fuck*, but Derek beat me to it.

"What the fuck?!" He seemed more surprised than I did, which felt impossible given the circumstances.

"Heads up!" I tossed my ax to Derek, confident he'd know what to do with it. As he caught it, his attacking santaman grabbed his arm and took a chunk out of it with its pitiless, chomping pearly whites. Derek yelped in shock and pain but managed to bury the ax in the weresanta's stomach with one swift, quick thrust.

And so, another pile of steamy green jelly was on the pavement and another transformed jolly old fat man lay dead. Derek dropped to the ground, holding his bitten arm tight to his chest.

"How'd I do?" He was starting to lose consciousness and drooped over to one side, almost laying down on the pavement.

I knew what was coming next without having to see it. Before it could even begin to happen, I grabbed Derek and dragged him to the alley adjacent to the hardware store. I propped him up against the brick wall belonging to said store and checked his bite.

It looked like a deep bite from an average human set of teeth. There was blood but nowhere near as much as there would have been had it been some sort of wild animal.

Or a werewolf, Owen. Or a werewolf.

The region of surrealness and insanity I had found myself in was so extreme that my brain just shut it out completely and focused only on what I could do right then and there.

I ripped off a section of my sweater sleeve. The one not covered in my own puke. I wrapped it tightly around his bite and tied it off with all the strength I had left.

I looked into Derek's eyes and figured I had to say something profound. If not now, when? "I guess this would be a bad time to tell you I have a Santa Claus fetish."

Not exactly my finest moment, but it was on my mind. I expected Derek to dress me down even in his current state. Instead, he just laughed, ignoring the pain. His smile destroyed me inside.

"You're bleeding." I thought it was me talking to Derek. But it was him talking to me. "A lot."

I checked myself out and, sure enough, I was bleeding all over from the glass window I had unwillingly murdered moments ago. The adrenaline had masked the pain and even the awareness of anything amiss. Now that I was coming down from it all, I could feel slices in my skin all over my body.

"I'm fine. We need to get you to a hospital. Who knows if they had rabies or something."

"Rabies?" Derek coughed and laughed at the same time. A trickle of white liquid dribbled from the corner of his mouth when he coughed. It smelled like...

...*Milk?*

"Owen...you saw what happened. Saw what they became. Do I have to say it...out loud?"

"Weresantas. There. I said it. Look, Derek, I'm sorry. Sorry for all of it. We should never have come here. I'd rather spend Christmas at your parents for the next thirty fucking years. Let's get out of here."

Derek smiled and nodded. "It's okay. I feel pretty good.

I—" He coughed up what looked like half-digested milk and cookies. His breath stank of peppermint and cinnamon. And milk. I was immediately off desserts at that point.

As we looked into each other's eyes, I think we both knew that this was it. I took his hand in mine tightly and nodded. There was no going home. Not for the holidays, not for anything. He nodded back and it seemed like he was about to cry.

"Merry Christmas, Owen."

He tried to kiss me one last time, but the transformation had taken hold. His stomach bulged, busting out of his pants and sweater. His hair turned shaggy and silver, and a big, bushy, white beard started to grow on his clean-shaven face. I had never seen him with facial hair before. It was startling even out of context.

This was my fantasy *and* my nightmare come to life in the most inconsiderate way possible. I knew what I had to do, though. I leaned in and kissed him softly. My ax dug quietly into his expanding stomach. It was quick and easy as his stomach enlarged right onto the blade, popping it like a fleshy balloon. He died in the last throes of his transformation.

My sobbing sounded like someone else's. Someone who had been through a lifetime of tragedy and it was finally all coming out at once. It felt alien. It felt out-of-body.

"Don't cry, my friend. Your luck is about to change."

I knew that voice right away. It set the hairs on my skin aflame. I turned from Derek to see the scraggly, skinny, wannabe Santa standing in the alleyway. All around him were dozens and dozens of newly transformed weresantas. Locals and tourists ho-ho-ho-ing in their torn, ragged clothes with their distended bellies jiggling in the night air. Their white hair and beards glistened like shark's teeth in the late hour.

It seemed my moment had arrived. Certain death or the remainder of my life as a shapeshifting Père Nöel.

"Come over here and take your bite like a man."

I stood up. Feeling defiant, I raised my ax, ready to strike. Just a dozen or so feet away from Diet Santa and his army of Kris Kringles.

"And what do you think that will do?"

I stared at my ax. So far it was three for three. I liked my odds.

"Let me guess. Nineteen eighty-three. Blood curse. Pagan bullshit. Am I close?"

Diet Santa laughed. "Oh, indeed. But it seems I overestimated the amount of Christmas cheer in this godforsaken town. Too much of it. Much too much of it. Instead of raising an army of yule demons, it seems I had created something else entirely."

"Just say it. Santamen. Weresantas."

"You just said it for me. It's not exactly what I had been planning, but I suppose beggars can't be choosers. Especially around Christmas."

At this point, I was out of things to say. Out of things to feel. I felt like an empty husk waiting to be blown away by an indifferent gust of wind. The thought of being chomped to death by an army of weresantas took up all the real estate in my brain and blocked out everything else.

Then this waifish Christmas dick did something even a corpse would have thought was a bad idea.

He raised his arms to the sky and bellowed "Hail, Krampus! Hail, Belsnickel! Hail, Satan!"

Hmmm.

The throng of weresantas surrounding him, upon hearing those unholy words, those decidedly un-Christmas words, collectively gasped and proceeded to pounce on the alleged alchemist, gnashing teeth chewing on him posthaste. It was a disgusting sight. Poor guy was minced into mashed flesh faster than it takes to blend a margarita.

It took me a few seconds to realize that was my cue to make a quick exit. As the merry band of newly appointed gift-givers finished snacking on their former master, I quietly fast-walked back to the Surfside Inn. I was fully expecting to be body checked or bitten by an errant santaman, but eerily enough, all was uneventful. I made my way inside and rushed to the elevator, hoping to barricade myself in my room to wait for dawn.

* * *

Marcello was still at the front desk. Did this guy ever go home? I guess it was probably wise on his part that he didn't. He took one look at my bloody, frazzled frame and sniffed, that mustache blustering all over his face as he did.

"You'll be safe in here, good sir."

"No shit, Marcello. No fucking shit."

I didn't wait for a reply. Whatever he said wouldn't have mattered anyway. Derek was gone. I needed to get to my room and stay there. Even if it was safe in the lobby, as Mr. Mustache insisted.

* * *

Dawn came, and with it, no weresanta attacks. I had stayed planted firmly in the middle of my king-sized bed, knees to my chest and arms wrapped tightly around myself.

Had I done the right thing? Did I really have to kill Derek? Maybe we could have lived like that. Me and my Santa Derek. We could have just told everyone we were all in on the Santa mood and Derek wanted to look like more of a manly man. An elderly, overweight Norwegian lumberjack. Something like that. What if he had bitten one of our family members? *All* of our family members? How would I prevent that? Should I have tried? Did I really love Derek? I just killed him. It didn't take me long to even decide.

I forced my brain to shut its mouth and I got cleaned up, packed, and checked out without another word to Marcello. He knew. He didn't have to say anything and neither did I. Sleigh bells late at night. The beach. The whole deal. I just wanted to go home. I could hear him saying something about Derek as I left. Whatever it was, it wasn't going to bring him back.

As I pulled out of the Surfside Inn, I didn't see anything outwardly sinister in the streets and alleyways. But I looked closer. And when I looked closer, when I really tried to look for something, I could see people. People staggering in and out of view. Their tattered clothes and their big pot bellies. Men and women. No beards or white hair.

But I knew. I knew exactly what they were. What they would become again at night when the sleigh bells rang out in the distance.

I had the feeling that the town would clean up after itself. How else could they keep getting away with...whatever they were getting away with? Derek was gone, and it would probably stay that way. The curse of Jingle Beach was alive and well. Maybe just not in the way it originally occurred.

I had no interest in sticking around for the Santa Look-alike contest. It had pretty much already happened.

I sped up, trying to get the image of those staggering people with their fat bellies and torn clothes out of my head. I turned off Main Street and headed for the highway. For home.

The smell of cinnamon and gingerbread was still with me,

though. I had a feeling it would never go away.

Needless to say, I no longer have a Santa fetish.

T**HE** M**ONSTER** **IN** **THE** M**IRROR**
Scott Chaddon

ecember funerals were the worst, at least for William
Lamm they were. In a way, he felt lucky that there were
so few people in his life for him to lose. Yet, here he
was in the Mount Hope Cemetery, standing next to his Great
Aunt Sophia, holding her hand as she sat in her wheelchair.
Everyone was dressed in black as they surrounded his Grandmother Anna's casket. The two of them were the only blood
relatives present. The rest were her church friends, the eldest
of which was less than half her age. After the prayer was finished, Father Mills addressed the group.

"Anna's life was long and full. She was born in 1907 and
raised in Germany, living there until she was twenty-six. She,
her parents, her brother, and her sister fled to the United States
just before World War Two. Two years later, she met and married Hans Lamm, and together they raised three sons, two of

which gave their lives during the Korean War, the third passing away eleven years ago with his wife in a house fire. Despite a life filled with loss, Anna was always bright, optimistic, and full of life. She was an example for all of us. At this time, I invite each of you to share a memory you have of her life." He gestured to the lady on his left. She told the group about how his grandmother always gave good advice. As the stories moved around the circle, they were all about her church-related activities. Generosity, advice, wisdom, recipes, and knowledge seemed to be her hallmarks, but nothing was very personal.

William thought back to some of his earliest memories of his grandmother, and one specific recollection stood out: a story she told him every year at Christmastime. When his turn came, he cleared his throat.

"When I was young," began William, "my grandmother would always tell me a specific story at Christmas. Unlike *A Christmas Carol* or *The Night Before Christmas,* the story she told me was a cautionary tale she'd brought with her from the old world. It was about an evil man who hunted and ate children around Christmas." The expressions around the circle ranged from morbid curiosity to horror. "What she liked to stress," continued William, "was that he only hunted bad children, and as long as I was a good boy, I need never fear Hans Trapp." William paused to look around; the expressions had not changed. "I chose this memory because it demonstrated her love for me and honored family tradition, to caution me from making bad choices. She shared a piece of her culture and history with me, a piece of herself. The story does have a happy ending, of sorts. Trapp is struck down by a bolt of lightning from God and ends up assisting Santa Claus by frightening children back into good behavior." The group appeared to understand, and most of them smiled. Aunt Sophia seemed lost

332

in thought and simply squeezed his hand.

"Thank you all for coming," said Father Mills after a couple of minutes of silence. The group broke up and drifted apart while William and Sophia waited and watched as the casket was lowered into the ground. Sophia looked troubled but did not share her thoughts.

Instead of attending the reception right away, William made sure Sophia was safely in the hands of her caretaker and put on the medical transport back to the Shady Vale Retirement Home, the assisted-care facility where she lived in Miami. Her dementia was in the early stages, but he doubted that she would remember the funeral in two days' time. He kissed her forehead, bid her farewell, and waved as her transport left to take her to the airport.

The next day found Lamm back at work at the Valentine Police Department, despite his Lieutenant's offer of a few more days off for bereavement. Going through the motions of working the few cases on his desk allowed him to work through his grief. Later in the morning, William was contacted by Charles Webber, the lawyer handling his grandmother's estate. While most of the money had been set aside to care for his Great Aunt Sophia, he had inherited her house, land, and personal possessions. Because he had lived alone since his divorce, he really did not need such a large place. He arranged with Mr. Webber to donate her clothing, have her personal possessions boxed and delivered to his house, and begin the process of selling her house, land, and furniture. Mr. Webber arrived later in the day to have him sign the required documents.

Two days later, shortly after noon, the movers dropped off thirty-six large cardboard boxes, two full-sized file cabinets, and a large, antique chest. He imagined that roughly half of the boxes contained his grandmother's library. There were a handful of books that he remembered fondly and wanted to locate. The fate of the remaining volumes would be determined on a case-by-case basis. By the time he went to bed, he had sorted through five of the boxes and located two of the books he was after. William decided on a three-pile system: trash, sell, and keep. Much of his sorting time was spent online, researching the values of the items he was discovering. Using this approach, William expected to be finished in just over two weeks. He fully expected that the file cabinets would take a full day each.

By Thursday night, William had located the last of the books he was searching for, sorted a lot of trash, slated quite a few items he could sell for a tidy profit, and found a few trinkets here and there that he had decided to keep. All week long, he had been eyeing the big, antique chest and wondering what he might find inside, though he half suspected it contained his grandfather's secret porn collection. He chuckled to himself at the notion. Tomorrow, he would explore the chest.

The next evening, he discovered that the chest was not locked. When he opened it, it was filled to the top with small, ancient-looking items, each carefully wrapped in folds of decaying linen. The vast majority of the chest's contents turned out to be centuries old and very valuable. When he reached the bottom, he found a ceramic scarecrow. Unlike many of the other items, it was poorly crafted, and William could find nothing online about it at all. He had saved it for last because it was larger than most and had hoped that it would be something special. Instead, it turned out to be a dud. He gave it one last look, sighed, and tossed it at the trash can. It bounced off of the rim and shattered on the concrete floor.

Cursing under his breath, William set about cleaning it up, not noticing the tiny green bottle until he began sweeping up the smaller pieces. Curious, he picked up the little flask and examined it. The top was sealed with lead, and he could make out a few items floating in a liquid inside, but the dark color of the glass made a good look impossible. Shrugging, he dropped it in his shirt pocket and finished cleaning up the mess. Exhausted by his day at work and emptying the trunk, he went into the kitchen, microwaved a couple of corndogs, chased them down with a beer, and went to bed.

William started awake, covered in sweat, his heart pounding in his chest. He had a vague memory of the nightmare that had awakened him. It had had something to do with a dark figure in a mirror. It had said something to him that terrified him, but for the life of him he could not recall any sharp details. When his phone rang again, he almost jumped out of bed. By the fourth ring, he had calmed himself enough to pick up. Caller ID said it was work.

"Lamm here." He tried to fight his yawn but failed. "What time is it?"

"It's four-thirty, Will," said the voice of Officer Harding. "Everyone is being called in."

"What happened?"

"They found a kid's body." Harding sounded off. "Well, part of one..."

"Christ!" swore William. "I'll be right in."

"See you soon." Harding hung up. William did a fast cleaning, combed his hair, put on his uniform, and pushed the speed limits all the way to the station. The parking lot was packed, so he parked along the street and went inside. More than half of the officers called had not bothered to put on their uniforms, which explained how they had arrived so quickly. Most investigators tended to dress more casually, but William felt that the uniform gave him an air of greater authority. He checked in at the desk and was directed to the bullpen, where the other investigators were gathered.

"There he is," said Chris Mathers, "and in uniform. Pay

up, Malcolm." A twenty exchanged hands, and there were a few laughs until the Lieutenant cleared his throat.

"Everyone into the conference room." Lieutenant Red Cloud's voice was sharper than usual, and they quietly filed in. All of the chairs were taken, so William leaned against a wall. Silence reigned as the lights went down and the projector lit up the screen on the far wall.

The Lieutenant clicked the handheld and an image appeared on the screen. It was hard to recognize at first, some kind of mangled carcass. The next image appeared, showing a different angle. The face of a boy, no older than twelve, made it obvious that the remains were human. Quiet curses and horrified whispers filled the room as even the most hardened veteran paled. Image after image flipped by, flayed skin, stripped and shattered bones, torn limbs, and hollowed-out torsos, all on a lurid background of blood-soaked snow. William flinched at each new image and felt his stomach begin to churn.

"Who... What did that?" stuttered Robins.

"We don't know yet," said the Lieutenant. "What we do know is that the bones appear to have been gnawed on."

"Dear Lord!" gasped Hansen. She was the toughest lady he knew; that she was reacting like that made him feel better about his own nausea. "By what?"

"It may not be a 'what'," said Red Cloud hesitantly. He took a deep breath. "Preliminary evidence suggests a human assailant."

"Wait," Robins spoke up. "Scroll those pictures back." The images flipped back through the gruesome scene. "Stop there. Look at that thigh bone. There's a clear bite taken directly out of the bone. No human is strong enough to do that."

"Yeah," agreed Sanders, "about three hundred pounds of pressure, right?" A couple of the investigators nodded. "That's enough to bite through a finger, maybe, but not a thigh bone. It has to be an animal whose bite looks human; a gorilla or a chimp or something."

"We are already looking into that possibility," said the Lieutenant. "The Medical Examiner agrees with Sanders that humans don't possess the strength, but the only footprints in the area were human."

"When did this happen?" asked William.

"Medical Examiner says about midnight."

"What was a kid that age doing out at that hour?" asked Billings.

"As soon as we know who he is, we can find that out. Since Lamm is the only one who bothered to show up ready to work, I'm giving the case to him." The Lieutenant raised a hand, forestalling any complaints. "The on-duty investigators have already declined. Go home, get into uniform, and report back as soon as possible. Until the Medical Examiner rules out a human as the culprit, we will investigate both directions. Lamm, my office."

"Yes, Lieutenant." William followed Lieutenant Red Cloud into his office and closed the door.

"There was some forensic evidence left behind, but we need to compartmentalize it."

"The killer left something behind?"

"The forensics techs aren't done with the scene, so we don't know for certain about other footprints, fingerprints, or trace evidence yet. But I managed to confiscate something from the body before too many people showed up."

"What is it?"

"A handful of straw." The Lieutenant opened his desk drawer, removed an evidence bag, and handed it to William. A dozen stalks of dry straw smeared with blood rested within the clear bag. "There were fourteen stalks. I'm sending the other two off to an independent lab for testing."

"Straw?" William scratched his head. "That's strange. It's the middle of December. Where did the straw come from?"

"That's what I'm hoping to find out. Forensics will report to you when they're finished."

"Yes, Lieutenant."

"Work hard and work fast, Lamm. We have a jump on the press this time for a change. It won't last long, though."

"I'll do my best," said William.

"I know you will." The Lieutenant slipped the evidence bag back into his desk. "The file should already be on your desk."

"Yes, Lieutenant." William returned to his desk and found the file, flipped through the gruesome photos, and sighed. Who or what would or could do this much damage so quickly? Sitting down, he began organizing his notes while he waited for the forensics techs to give him their report. When he finished as much as he could, William decided to go and visit the coroner. The remains would have been there long enough for a preliminary report at least, and considering what little was left, possibly a full report.

"How's it going, Marc?" asked William as he entered. Marc Blankenship, the Coroner, looked up and waved.

"I've had better nights, Will."

"What can you tell me about the boy who was found to-night?"

"I've sent some samples off to the lab, but there wasn't much to go on." He handed Will his report.

"Can you determine what it was that bit into the body?"

"The jaw structure and tooth pattern appear to be human, though the teeth seem to have been filed."

"Human? Do humans have the bite strength to take a chunk out of a femur?"

"Not normally." Marc frowned. "The individual in question would have to be exceptionally large and strong."

"How large?"

"Compared to an average adult human, this one is at least seven feet tall and probably built like a tank."

"That's someone who should stand out in a crowd then?" William's brow furrowed in thought.

"Definitely."

"Did you get a saliva sample?"

"I think so," Marc looked down at his file with a frown, "but there's a good chance it was corrupted by local animal activity."

"I hope not." William grimaced.

"So do I."

"All right, thanks. Let me know when those tests come back, please." William shook Marc's hand.

"You can count on it. This monster needs to be stopped."

"I'll do my best." Will left the coroner's lab and returned to the Valentine Police Department. The forensics report was waiting for him on his desk. He had to read it twice. Except for the victim's, there was no foreign hair, blood, fibers, finger-prints, or DNA. The footprints in the snow were barefoot, and the steps were ten feet apart. Ten feet? What kind of creature was this? As he examined the photos of the crime scene, William noticed there were more bits of straw in the snow near the footprints that had not been gathered as evidence because of the dead grass under the snow. The prints were tracked back to a highway, where they were lost.

The coroner's report had as many mysteries as the forensics' findings. The bites appeared human, almost every bone the boy had left was broken and the marrow sucked out. There had been evidence of severe bruising on all surfaces. All of that damage had been done by hand. No weapons were involved. It just did not make any sense.

At the end of his shift, William gathered up his file and went home. After making himself some dinner, he sat and went back over everything, searching for any detail that might have been overlooked and making notes on anything that might provide a lead. By 10:30, exhaustion caught up with him, so he decided to get some rest and take another look at the case with fresh eyes.

When his alarm sounded, William practically jumped out of his bed, leaning against the wall with one hand to stabilize himself as his mind reeled while he caught his breath. His pajamas, soaked with sweat, were plastered to his body. As his breathing slowed, his mind clutched at the dregs of his dream. William could hear the deep, raspy voice laughing maniacally at him from the shadowy recesses of a bizarre mirror. A chill ran down his spine as he shivered uncontrollably in the dark. He switched on the lights, peeled off his pajamas, and stepped into a hot shower.

The laughter was still echoing in his head as he backed out of his driveway and started off to work. The Lieutenant called, and he put the call on speaker.

"Lamm here. What can I do for you, Lieutenant?"

"The bastard struck again last night."

Lamm's blood ran cold. "Another boy?"

"No. Two girls, roughly the same age, though." The Lieutenant's anger bled into his voice.

"Where?"

"The Valentine Senior High grounds, across from the United Methodist Church."

"On East Fifth Street?"

"That's the place."

"I'll be there in fifteen," said William as he took a right turn and headed for the east end of town.

"The media is already here." Red Cloud's voice was tight.

"Damn."

"See you in fifteen."

"Yes, sir." The Lieutenant hung up.

When William arrived, he pushed through the crowd of reporters and cameras, nodding at the officer guarding the crime-scene tape, and ducked under. The scene was so crowded that he could not get a decent look at the crime scene until he was practically on top of it. The remains of the two girls had been pieced together like a puzzle, forming one complete body with two heads. All the organs were gone, and the killer had combined their intestines and shoved them into the empty cavity, along with an assortment of bone fragments. The only way to tell one victim from the other was the difference in skin tones.

Lamm spent most of the morning working with forensic technicians and officers at the scene. A simple look and a nod exchanged between William and the Lieutenant was all he needed to know that they'd found more straw in and around the bodies. There were footsteps leading in at ten-foot intervals and bloody footprints leaving, meaning the killer had carried the girls, or at least the parts, to the site. The open locations of the crime scenes felt almost as though the killer was taunting them. When the remains were moved, it was discovered that the skulls had been cracked open and the brains removed. Considering the amount of missing flesh, William could only assume that most of the missing flesh had been taken away to be stored at another location. There was just too much for any one person to eat in a single sitting.

By noon, William had gathered as much information as possible from the site. He then made his way to the station and found updated reports in his "In" basket. The boy from the day before had been identified as Bradley Scott, a twelve-year-old poster child for truancy, with an impressive twenty-three offenses ranging from graffiti to theft and destruction of private property. His mother had called him in as a missing person at eight o'clock when she went to get him up for breakfast. At four o'clock, the two dead girls were identified when the mother of Adira Nazari called in to report her absence and that of her best friend, Shelly Myers. The girls had a habit of sneaking out at night, and they had been detained by police on six occasions for shoplifting, though no charges were ever filed because the merchandise was returned. The last part of William's day was spent breaking the bad news to three families. It was the worst Saturday he could ever remember. After conveying his deepest sympathies and explaining that the Valentine Police Department would not rest until the killer was found, William gathered his growing case file and went home. By ten, he was exhausted. He was asleep moments after his head hit the pillow.

The nightmare was clearer than ever. An ornately gilded mirror floated in the air before him, and the figure within was cloaked in deep shadow. There were no details except for the silhouette. The laughter he remembered from the night before was loud and clear. It was so cruel and malicious that it made William's blood run cold. Then it spoke, only two words, in a quiet, dangerous voice.

"I'm coming..."

"No!" William sat bolt upright in bed, soaked in sweat, his heart pounding in his chest, and the alarm blaring at him from his nightstand. He had just reached over and shut it off when his phone rang. It was Lieutenant Red Cloud. He picked it up on the third ring.

"Lamm," said William a little more sharply than he intended.

"We have another one." The Lieutenant didn't seem to

notice, but his voice was tinged with anger.

"Where?"

"The Raine Motel. The clearing along South Western Street."

"I'll be there as soon as I can."

"Sooner if possible, Investigator."

"Yes, sir." The Lieutenant hung up, and William climbed out of bed.

When he arrived at the scene, the victim's mutilated corpse had already been identified as thirteen-year-old Martin Cruz, a well-known juvenile delinquent. He had just finished taking his preliminary notes when the Lieutenant approached.

"This makes it serial," said Red Cloud. "We're going to have to bring in the Feds." William frowned.

"Four murders in three days certainly falls within their purview." William, like most police officers, did not care for including the feds in their investigations. They had a habit of taking over everything and alienating local law enforcement.

"Are we any closer to finding the murderer?"

"No. I'm sorry to say, we aren't. Did the labs turn up anything new?"

"Yeah, but it doesn't make much sense to me." Red Cloud shook his head. "The reports are on your desk."

"Thanks," said William. "No choice, huh?"

"Not without looking like idiots."

"Right." William's voice was bitter, and Red Cloud gave him a sympathetic look.

"I'll contact the FBI when I get back to the office."

"Yes, sir." William estimated that he had about twenty-four hours before the Feds arrived. If he could just get a solid lead, he could break the case wide open. The damage was consistent with the others, and the feet that made the prints were fourteen inches long, six inches wide, with long, claw-like nails. The impressions indicated that the killer was heavy, more than twice William's body weight. Anyone that big and that strange-looking should be easy to find, yet no one in Valentine fit that description. It would be a stretch, but he started calling the police departments in Crookston, Kilgore, Ainsworth, and the Native Tribal Authorities across the border on the Rosebud Native Reservation. He was able to get further than any other officer, except the Lieutenant, with the Lakota because his mother had been a full-blooded Sioux, born and raised on the reservation. In fact, one of his cousins served on the police force there.

When he hung up the phone after the last call, they had all promised to keep an eye out for anyone close to the description he supplied them with. The tones in their voices told him that there was little chance, but at least the surrounding towns were on the lookout. The saliva sample had been inconclusive, and all the blood belonged to the victims. The report on the straw contained strange results. The lab had tested it three times to be sure. The straw was over five hundred years old. The lab techs had left a note saying that the straw should have decomposed long ago. Also, they were unable to match the straw's DNA with any known database. It did not make any sense. Setting the file aside for a while, William made the trip to notify the Cruz family of young Martin's demise. Upon his return, he was directed to the Lieutenant's office.

"You asked to see me, Lieutenant?"

"Close the door and have a seat."

"Yes, sir." William settled down, expecting to be chewed out for his lack of progress concerning the cannibal case.

"You have three days," said the Lieutenant.

"Three days?" William cocked an eyebrow.

"The FBI is spread thin with other preexisting cases, so it'll be three days before they can spare any agents."

"I'll do my best, Lieutenant."

"I don't have to tell you that it would be a credit to the Valentine Police Department if the case were solved before the feds even arrived."

"If it's possible to be done, I'll do it." He paused. "I'd like to suggest tripling the police patrols at night. I know it'll mean a lot of overtime, but it'll increase the possibility of catching sight of the killer, if not catching him."

"That's a good idea." Red Cloud sighed. "I need to make a statement to the media, warning the public of the danger. Dismissed."

"Yes, sir." William left the office and returned to his desk to draw up patrol routes that would provide the best coverage. When he was finished, he turned it in to the Lieutenant's secretary, gathered his files, and went home to work on it there— and get some rest.

The mirror remained the same, floating in space, but the reflection changed in subtle ways. As it laughed and spoke, William thought he could just make out wide, moving lips and a hint of bulging eyes. When it spoke, William's skin crawled.

"I am coming, William." The voice sounded like he was gargling on glass and gravel. A rough, thick, liquid sound that was entirely inhuman. "And there is nothing you can do to stop me." More laughter burbled out of the mirror, long and loud. "Together, we will paint the land red with the blood of the wicked!"

"Never!" William yelled into the darkness as he sat up with a jolt. His legs got tangled in his blankets. His phone went off just as he fell onto the floor. Reaching up to the nightstand, he retrieved his phone, unsurprised to see it was Lieutenant Red Cloud.

"Lamm here."

"Get out to the community space across from the Lutheran Church on West Third Street."

"Another one?"

"This time we have a witness."

"We do? Who?"

"Officer Carlisle." His voice sounded tense.

"I'll be there in ten."

"The sooner, the better," said the Lieutenant. William threw on street clothes and a coat, then headed out. He reached the crime scene in eight minutes flat.

This time, the killer had made an effort to hang the body parts from the trees, using the intestines to tie the head, hollowed-out torso, and two limbs of a boy from the branches. The snow beneath was scarlet from the dripping blood. No wonder he was having nightmares. After making an initial assessment, he went to find the Lieutenant and the witness.

"Lamm," said the Lieutenant with a nod, "This is some strange stuff."

"Strange?" asked William. "In what way?"

"Tell him exactly what you told me, Carlisle," said the Lieutenant.

"Well..." Carlisle was shaking visibly, "I didn't see it actually hang the kid's parts in the tree, but I saw it flee the scene."

"It?" asked Lamm.

"Don't interrupt," said the Lieutenant. "Go ahead, Carlisle."

"It sure didn't look human to me." Carlisle shrugged. "It was over seven feet tall and almost as wide. It looked like a scarecrow. You know, straw coming out of its clothes and hat." Lieutenant Red Cloud held up a hand, forestalling the obvious question so the frightened officer could continue. "It had big, clawed hands and red eyes, and it moved so fast. It seemed to almost glide over the ground. I only got a good look at it when it paused before crossing the road to look around be-

346

fore disappearing again." Finished with his report, Carlisle took a shaky drink from his coffee cup.

William took the Lieutenant aside, out of earshot of the others, and whispered, "Do you think Carlisle was drugged somehow?"

"That was my first thought, too. We're going to test him, but his pupils are normal, and he hasn't hallucinated about anything else before or after."

"Do you think his report is accurate?"

"Until we know differently, we'll have to assume it is."

"Costume, maybe? I know those jumping stilts can give a person a hell of a stride."

"I don't know. I guess we'll figure it out when we catch him."

"I can't wait. I'm going to get back to work." The Lieutenant nodded, and William returned to the crime scene. Just when he thought this case could not get worse, the killer decided to try out his decorating skills. At least he was able to add a description and an artist's rendering to his file, even if it looked like it belonged on the cover of a horror magazine. By the end of the day, the local media had been given a formal statement, and they had issued a story on the air, warning the public to travel in groups and stay indoors at night. It would go national in two or three days' time. To Lamm's disgust, the media was calling him "The Christmas Cannibal."

Over the next two days, William began to feel like he was on a giant hamster wheel; a new child was found murdered each morning, while he exchanged maximum effort for minimal progress during the days and mind-rending nightmares every night. Only the murderer and the nightmares were making any progress. Despite the warnings, the killer had no lack of rebellious kids to choose from.

When the FBI arrived on the nineteenth, he was almost

relieved to hand the case over to them. They immediately took charge and redistributed manpower. William watched them take over the department with mixed feelings. He hated having the chain of authority being usurped, but he was relieved that the pressure of the case was no longer his. Despite his expectations, he was immediately disappointed with their methods. They assigned him, and eleven others, to extra day patrols. It was stupid; the killer operated at night. At least any screw-ups were on their heads now.

The morning of the twentieth was the first day he did not have to go straight to work after being jolted awake by a nightmare that had gotten increasingly macabre with each passing night. The mirror's gilding gleamed in the darkness, from which glowing red eyes burned, surrounded by a deep yellow, veined sclera. The mouth was filled with long, sharp, yellowed teeth, while a long, narrow tongue, the color of liver, kept licking the lips and leaving a thick trail of slime as it spoke.

"I see that you've brought me some new playmates, William." The monster in the mirror had laughed sadistically. "Oh, we are going to have such fun! And I owe it all to you."

"I haven't done anything," William snarled, though, on some level, it felt like a lie.

"Oh, but you have," said the silhouette with an unnaturally wide and toothy grin.

"You're just a dream," insisted William.

"If you say so," taunted the grinning shadow. "But we both know differently." The cruel laughter echoed, and William woke up just as he had taken a swing at the mirror in his dream.

He got out of bed, changing out the sweat-soaked bedclothes, just as he had for the past seven days, showered, dressed, and then headed to the office. The FBI was practically buzzing. The body of a fourteen-year-old boy had been found on the lawn of the Valentine Senior Citizen Center off of North

Macomb Street. The elderly woman who discovered the mutilated body had had a heart attack and died at the scene. The lead agent, Carlson, was faced with the feeding frenzy that was the media. William spent the day on his assigned patrols, feeling less like an investigator and more like a beat cop. During the day, he caught two kids spray painting the side of Young's Western Wear, investigated a break-in at Don't Rush Me Ceramics, and caught a thief who had held up Sharp's liquor store. At the end of the day, he filed his reports, picked up a couple of cold case files to look at over dinner, and headed home. That night, the silhouette in the mirror was tinged with red as its eyes glowed like coals. It said nothing specific to him but kept humming bits of a song. It was just enough that he recognized the tune but could not put his finger on it. Then the song changed. The tune was the same as "Ring Around the Rosie," but the words were different.

"Hunt around the precinct,
Feds blood makes the snow pink.
Slashes, gashes
They all fall dead."

The last word came out as a deep, reverberating growl.

"They were a lot of fun, not as filling as a child, of course, but fun just the same," the voice hissed with glee in its twisted, guttural tone. William sat bolt upright in bed, soaked to the skin, heart beating like a trip hammer. His phone was ringing. After getting his breathing to slow down, he picked it up and answered.

"Lamm here." His voice sounded shaky to his own ears.

"You need to get down to headquarters immediately!" snapped Lieutenant Red Cloud.

"Why? What happened? "

"Every one of the feds has been killed."

"Christ! How?"

"It looks like they found the killer," said the Lieutenant grimly, "or he found them." William had a sinking feeling in the pit of his stomach as he recalled his nightmare.

"Damn! How..."

"Just get here as soon as possible."

"Will do." The Lieutenant hung up, and William began to get the chills. He quickly changed out of his wet clothes and into a uniform before heading back to work. When he got there, the entire block surrounding the police headquarters had been cordoned off, and every way in was heavily guarded. News crews had gathered at each corner, and two officers were escorting one reporter off of the premises and into a patrol car near the blockade. William blew past the clamoring reporters, stopping fifty feet from the main entrance. His eyes widened and his mouth dropped open. The bodies of the four FBI agents had been broken into pieces and hung from the trees by sections of intestines like bizarre Christmas tree decorations.

"Dear God!" breathed William as he walked up to the Lieutenant. "How did he manage to get all of them and do this right in front of our headquarters without anyone seeing him?"

"The video cameras captured it. Time stamp shows that it happened just after midnight, and all of this took the killer under five minutes to complete."

"Under five minutes? How is that possible?"

"I don't know, but he did it. This is going to create a shit storm. We'll have FBI agents crawling all over the place."

"What do we do now?"

"Until they get here, you're the lead investigator, Lamm. But be quick about it."

"Quick?"

"I doubt you'll have access to their files after the reinforcements arrive." The Lieutenant gave William a grim smile.

"I'd agree." William nodded.

"Let's get to work."

"Yes, sir." They went inside while forensics worked the gruesome scene. Once they were inside, Lieutenant Red Cloud's demeanor shifted. He looked around the bullpen. William followed the Lieutenant's gaze around the room. When he was satisfied, Red Cloud nudged Lamm's elbow and tipped his head toward his office. William nodded; they went inside, and the Lieutenant closed the door behind them.

"You need to see the footage," said the Lieutenant in a low voice. He pulled down the blinds and turned on the plasma screen. A click of the remote started the video streaming. The images on the screen were a series of blurs and streaks. Body parts seemed to appear on the tree as if by magic. Red Cloud found two spots where the killer paused, giving them a clear image. He left the second of the two on the screen. The murderer was taking a bite out of what could only be a human liver, a sock-clad leg gripped by the ankle in the other hand.

"That thing is horrific," said Lamm. He choked as his stomach threatened to eject its contents. "How can anything like that go anywhere and not be noticed?"

They made copies of the FBI's files and had just finished reviewing them when the FBI arrived in force. Evidently, four dead agents got their attention faster than eight dead children. There were twenty agents and twice as many SWAT. William had a sinking feeling that they did not bring enough firepower—or manpower—to do the job. Anyone associated with the case was given new assignments, and the FBI took over the entire situation. Lamm was handed a stolen car case and sent about his business. As he went out to interview witnesses, he got a look at two huge vans filled with more technology than Silicon Valley. He collected his statements and searched the crime scene for clues. When he returned to the office, he had a BOLO put out on the missing car, filled out his report, filed it, and went home. He was not hungry, so he settled for a beer and then went straight to bed. Though he dreaded sleep, he was too exhausted to remain awake.

The shadowy figure in the mirror seemed clearer than ever before. It was as if a layer of shadow was removed each night, revealing more of the menacing thing each time he saw it. The eyes, teeth, and tongue were easily visible. Tonight, he could make out the hint of a hooked nose, high cheekbones, and dark hair in the features. Everything else was too overshadowed to make out. The silhouette laughed long, loud, and maniacal. No matter how many times he heard it, the deranged laughter always froze William's blood and chilled his soul. Tonight, it was worse than normal. There was a twisted sense of delight mixed with the madness.

"What to do, what to do," said the shadow with an impossibly wide grin. William could see elongated canines and rows of sharp, wedge-shaped teeth. It was as if they had been filed to points. "So many options, so many to kill, so much to eat," cackled the reflection. "I've had my fill of government meat, so I think I'll find something younger and tenderer."

"This is just a dream! You're not real. I want you to go away!" demanded William.

"You don't always get what you want, William," said the shadow. "Most certainly, you won't this time. You belong to me now, now and for all time!" The laughing resumed.

"No, I don't!" screamed William. "I don't belong to anyone!"

"Denial doesn't suit you, William. You're mine now." The gleeful laughter took on a sadistic tone. William turned from the mirror and attempted to run but felt as if he were running through mud in slow motion. When he glanced back, the mirror was just as close behind him as ever, and the laughter only got louder.

William sat bolt upright, soaked in sweat, pulse pounding in his ears, and clutching his bed sheets for dear life. After a while, he climbed out of bed and stepped into a hot shower, staying there until the hot water ran out. William felt nauseous, so he sat in the kitchen with a cup of tea in his bathrobe. When the phone rang, he was so startled that he almost flung the cup across the room. The remaining tea was sprayed across the room as he recovered the cup from the floor. The phone kept ringing until he picked up.

"Lamm here."

"Everyone's being called in," said Sergent Conners. "The Feds just got a nasty surprise in the lobby of the Niobrara Lodge."

"Damn! I'm on my way."

"Everyone is gathering at the lodge to help keep the media at bay."

"I'll be there." William hung up the phone, cleaned up the mess he had made, and went to get dressed.

When he arrived at the Niobrara Lodge, it looked as if every squad car was parked nearby. William added his vehicle to the blockade and made his way into the hotel. The Christmas tree in the lobby was decorated with the pieces of four children. Based on the dangling heads, they were the remains of three boys and a girl. Blood was pooling on the floor under the tree and had been spattered on every wall.

The night clerk's statement said that he had taken a few minutes to go to the bathroom. While he was using the facilities, he thought he heard laughter and a loud, harsh voice singing a Christmas carol: "Deck the Halls." When he returned to the front desk, he found the bodies. After he finished vomiting, he called it in. When the security camera footage was reviewed, it showed the same sort of activity that had occurred outside the Valentine Police Department. The FBI did not accept what they were seeing and insisted that the data had somehow been corrupted. They took the footage with them to see if they could clean it up while forensics worked the crime scene. William and the other officers spent the day taking statements from the hotel guests, including the FBI agents and the SWAT members that had been staying there. Between that and keeping the media at bay and writing reports, it was well after dark before William was able to return home. He was so tired that he was barely able to change clothes and climb into bed.

It seemed as if the laughter began almost as soon as he closed his eyes. It was gleeful in its insanity. The eyes were shining like burning flames now, and William could actually smell the fetid, stinking breath coming from the grinning maw of the reflection. When the figure in the mirror moved, he could hear a slight rustling sound that he could not pinpoint.

"Too late," said the reflection. William could almost make out skin color now. A chalky yellowish hue creased with lines and wrinkles. "Too late for them, too late for you; my work this year is almost complete."

"Your work?" asked William. "What is your work?"

"You could call it subsistence hunting. After all, a monster needs to eat."

"What exactly are you hunting and eating?"

"I enjoy the spice that evil brings to the meat," it cackled. "Of course, I consume both body and soul."

"That doesn't make any sense."

"Of course, it does; it makes sense to me," laughed the image, "and that's all that really matters."

The phone ringing jolted William awake. He wondered if this was going to be his life now; horrors during the day, nightmares at night. In the back of his mind, a tiny voice told him "not much longer." He shook himself, waking his brain and focusing his attention. William picked up the phone.

"Lamm here, what is it now?"

It was the Lieutenant. "The feds have taken another hit."

"How many bodies?"

"Five. Two kids and three FBI surveillance techs."

"Whose doorstep were they spread across this time?"

"No doorstep this time. The inside of one of their surveillance vans has practically been painted with blood and decorated with body parts and entrails. The usual organs and flesh is missing."

"That's going to piss them off." Lamm could not quite stop a snort of grim amusement.

"I think that the lead agent's head is going to explode. It's certainly red enough." Red Cloud's chuckle was just as grim.

"I'll come in as soon as possible."

"See you soon." The Lieutenant hung up.

William took a quick shower and put on his uniform. All during the drive, William could still hear the echo of that laughter in his mind. When he arrived at the surveillance van, it had already been taped off as a crime scene, and pissed off FBI agents were stalking around in their impotent rage. William wondered for a moment if that had been how he looked when the case was his responsibility. As usual, he was assigned to keep the media at bay and the perimeter secure. It did not help much, though, because the whole story went national on the news starting at ten o'clock in the morning.

His aunt's phone call was a surprise. When he saw her number on his cell phone, he expected her to be calling to wish him a merry Christmas; after all, it was Christmas Eve, and tomorrow would be filled with events at her retirement home. Instead, the voice on the phone was filled with panic.

"It's him!" she whispered harshly into the phone.

"Him?" asked William. "Him who?"

"It's Hans Trapp!" she sounded desperate. "I saw the news, the dead children, and the killings since the thirteenth. It's Hans Trapp, I tell you."

"Who is Hans Trapp, Aunt Sophia? The name sounds familiar somehow."

"Hans Trapp," said Aunt Sophia, her voice was raspy. "Your grandmother told you about him. You said so at her funeral."

William was stunned that she had remembered. "But that was just a Christmas story, Aunt Sophia."

"No, Hans Trapp was a real man. He was born Hans Von Tratha in 1450, in Krosigk, Petersburg, Germany."

"Wait, isn't your and Grandma's last name Von Tratha?"

"Yes, it is. Quit interrupting," she snapped.

"Yes, Aunt Sophia."

"He was a German Knight whose castle stood on the border of France and Germany. He was powerful, rich, and greedy, and when he wouldn't respect the local Abbot, he was excommunicated from the Catholic Church. Not long after, he sold his soul to Satan in exchange for superhuman powers." William had a sinking feeling in the pit of his stomach. "Satan told him that to maintain his powers, he must consume the living flesh of at least twelve bad people during the twelve days leading up to Christmas, and that children were better than adults." William's heart rate was rising. "Von Tratha was so selfish and greedy that he employed a powerful witch to help him compress his entire soul into the end bone of his right pinky. Then he cut the end of that pinky off at the joint, stripped it of flesh, and deposited the finger bone into a bottle filled with blessed silver and holy water so that Satan could never touch his soul. In this way, being denied Heaven and protected from Hell, he would become immortal." William began to feel ill. This was fitting his case a little too perfectly. "He stuffed his clothes and hat with straw to appear as a scarecrow whenever he went hunting. This inspired fear and superstition in the people. That fear gave him power over them, making them easy prey. For many years, he hunted and killed, and people dreaded the coming of Christmas, for no matter what they tried, they could not stop him. Convinced of his own invulnerability, Von Tratha abandoned caution and hunted during all kinds of dangerous weather. One very warm year, with five days until Christmas, he went hunting in a bad storm. Having surprised a disobedient boy out in the weather, he chased the child to the top of a hill where he caught him. Hans decided to begin eating the boy right there. During his meal, he was struck by a powerful bolt of lightning that reduced him to ash on the spot. Some say it was God's retribution for his unnatural evil, but his spirit endured because his soul remained protected and hidden."

"Where did he hide that bottle?" asked William. Maybe he could find that bottle, destroy it, and put a stop to this horror.

"No one knows," said Sophia. "If they had, they would have found it and destroyed it, sending him to the pits of Hell where he belongs."

"Thank you, Aunt Sophia," said William. "You've helped my investigation more than you know."

"Just be careful, William. Hans Trapp is very dangerous."

"I will. Thanks again, Aunt Sophia."

"If only I'd seen the news earlier, I could have told you sooner."

"It only started broadcasting the story today, Aunt Sophia. You must've seen the first airing before you called. You've done everything possible, and I am grateful." William was kicking himself; keeping the media from broadcasting had partially been his fault. If it had gone nationwide earlier, he would have more time to stop the monster.

"Such a sweet boy. You have always been such a sweet boy, William. You be careful. I love you."

"I will. I love you, too, Aunt Sophia." She hung up the phone. William had a lot to think about, but first, he needed to speak with the Lieutenant. He found Red Cloud in his office, but the door was closed and the blinds were down. William figured that he was probably meeting with the FBI. When the door finally opened and the feds filed out, he slipped inside. Lamm closed the door and repeated the story to Red Cloud exactly as his Aunt had told him. When he had finished, the Lieutenant's brow was knit and the corners of his mouth twitched downward.

"It sounds crazy, a folk tale killer brought back to life, but it does fit perfectly into the profile," said the Lieutenant.

"That was my thought, too," agreed Lamm. "I think we need to focus on finding that bottle and destroying it."

"Agreed." Red Cloud nodded his head. "Have you been through all of your grandmother's belongings?"

"My grandmother's things?" William felt confused for a moment. "Oh, yeah, I guess that makes sense why it would be here. You think her death may have triggered something?"

"It stands to reason."

"I was just over halfway through the pile in my garage when more important matters came up," explained Lamm.

"The killings?"

William nodded. "Do you think I might have unknowingly set it free?"

"It's possible. We need to go through everything you haven't yet and whatever you kept."

"What about the stuff I tossed?" William started to pace. "Everything is most likely crushed or incinerated at the landfill."

"Well, if we can't find it at your place, we'll start searching there."

"That sounds like a good plan. We'll need eight to ten more people to help go through the sheer volume of what's left."

"That's a lot of manpower," said Red Cloud.

"Yeah, but the bottle in question could be very small and easy to miss."

"True. We'll have to be careful and thorough." Red Cloud's voice was thoughtful.

"We'll gather at my house after shift change."

"What will we tell the officers helping us?" asked Red Cloud.

"Considering every bizarre thing we've seen on this case, why not tell them the truth?" suggested William. Red Cloud shrugged and nodded. "I'll spring for pizza."

"I'll offer them overtime."

"That should do it," said William. "Would you spread the word, Lieutenant? I'm late for duty."

"Will do."

"Thanks."

When the shift was over, William, Red Cloud, and ten officers converged on his garage. William ordered a stack of pizzas and three cases of beer, which they slowly consumed as the night wore on. By ten thirty, they had gone through everything thoroughly, and nothing resembling the bottle had turned up. After everyone else had gone home, Red Cloud stayed behind to talk.

"So, digging through the landfill on Christmas Day?"

"I'll be there, but I don't know how much help we can count on. Those off-duty officers will want to spend the time with their families, not digging around a junkyard looking for a bottle containing a finger bone."

"You're right. We'll have to wait for more help until the day after Christmas."

"So, tomorrow it's just you and me?" asked William.

"It's better than doing nothing and waiting for more bodies to turn up."

"Agreed. See you tomorrow at the dump," said Lamm.

"I'll see you there." The Lieutenant got in his car and drove away.

William went inside, cleaned up, and went to bed.

The image in the mirror was crystal clear. It was a twisted, evil-looking man with tanned skin, a hooked nose, high cheekbones, straight, black hair, liver-colored lips and tongue, glowing eyes, and sharpened teeth. The mouth was stretched into a wide, feral grin that reminded William of a vicious Cheshire Cat. His face was utterly nightmarish but disturbingly familiar. The laughter was different somehow, and he now recognized the tune the thing in the mirror had been humming bits and parts of over the last week: "The Twelve Days of Christmas."

"I know who you are now," said William. He felt stupid accusing a nightmare of being a killer. "Hans Trapp."

"You're a clever little puppet, I'll give you that."

"I'll find the bottle that contains your soul and crush it under my heel, you monster!"

"Oh, it's far too late for that. Especially considering all the children we ate."

"What do you mean by 'we'? I didn't eat any children! That's sick!" Lamm felt his gut wrench.

"Oh… But you did. Of course, I was in charge at the time."

"When were you ever in charge? How?"

"You found the bottle, a dozen days past. The moment you touched it, I had you. Sharing the same blood made things very easy. But I made you forget what it was you had." Images flashed through William's mind. He remembered finding the bottle and keeping it in his pockets for days until Trapp broke into Don't Rush Me Ceramics and made a new ceramic scarecrow. It was a much higher quality piece than the one William now remembered breaking. He watched helplessly as the bottle was sealed into the ceramic statue, which was set on his fireplace mantle until two days ago. Exactly where it was hidden after that remained a blank.

"No. It's not possible." William's mind reeled, rejecting the evidence before him.

"You've been the perfect host, my little lamb. In a few short hours, you will cease to exist at all, and there will only be me."

"I'm not the only one who knows about you!" The statement was out before he could stop himself.

"Don't worry, Will. Everything you knew, I knew. Dear, old Sophia is no threat to me. I will have to have a talk with your lieutenant, though. I won't need to eat for a year, but that doesn't prevent me from killing at will."

"According to the story, aren't you supposed to be helping Saint Nicholas by scaring kids straight?" asked William, grasping at any straw he could. The darkness around him seemed to be closing in, and he was gradually drifting closer to Hans Trapp and the mirror. Trapp laughed loud, long, and sadistically.

"A little lie to comfort the kiddies," said Trapp.

William's face was nose to nose with the monster, and the mirror was all that stood between them. Trapp's eyes burned like flames. With dawning horror, William realized why the face seemed so familiar.

"Santa Claus never existed, but I... I am all too real! And soon, very soon, I will leave this pathetic little town and wreak havoc on the world!"

All William could see were those burning eyes, and for

an instant, every nerve in his body burned like he was being tased a hundred times at once. He screamed in agony, and then it stopped. William looked around, realizing what had happened. A tear rolled down his cheek as he pounded on the inside of the mirror, trying to get out as he watched Hans Trapp's scarecrow-like figure drifting slowly away from him. The hideous laughter rang in William's ears, and he knew that he was not going to be waking up ever again.

* * *

Lieutenant Red Cloud wandered through the landfill. He had already had the manager locate the quadrant. It was not very long ago, so most of the trash was still near the surface. He checked his watch for the tenth time. Lamm was late. That bothered him. Lamm was never late. He dialed the investigator's number for the third time. It rang until voice mail picked up. Where the hell was he?

The FBI had their hands full with this morning's blood bath. The killer had taken the crew from the second surveillance van and eleven of the FBI's men; some had been agents, and some were SWAT. Then the killer arranged the remaining parts of the dead in a gory, bloody, fourteen-piece nativity scene set in front of the St. Nicholas Church Hall. It had been discovered by Father Mills. The Catholic Priest had vomited and passed out moments after seeing the abomination. Valentine was now the talk of the nation, maybe the world, and it was not receiving a good review.

Red Cloud saw a glint at his feet. He knelt to examine it. When he pulled it free, he put it back down. It was a small Seagram's bottle. A noise caused him to stand up and reach for his weapon. What was that? Some animal, perhaps? He scanned over the junkscape and saw nothing. The faint sound of laughter made him spin toward the noise. There was a blur of motion, and the Lieutenant felt like he had been hit by a truck. When he stopped spinning, he looked down to discover half of his abdomen was gone. He could see his ribs and intestines exposed for a couple of seconds before he fell into a pile of garbage. The darkness was closing in when Hans Trapp stepped into view. His eyes widened and he gasped painfully as the grinning monstrosity loomed over him. It was the enormous, inhuman shape he had seen on the video footage, but the face, twisted by the impossibly wide mouth and the burning eyes, was unmistakably Lamm's. That face came closer, and as the creature ravaged his body, he felt everything go cold before the darkness closed in and finally claimed him.

ABOUT THE AUTHORS

Patrick Barb is a freelance writer and editor from the southern United States, currently living (and trying not to freeze to death) in Saint Paul, Minnesota. His short horror fiction has appeared in *Twisted Anatomy* (forthcoming), *Shiver* (forthcoming), and *Hookman and Friends*, among other publications. For more of his work, visit patrickbarb.com.

Much of **Evan Baughfman**'s writing success has been as a playwright, his original plays finding homes in theaters worldwide. Evan has also found success writing horror fiction, his work found most recently in anthologies by Black Hare Press, Blood Song Books, and Soteira Press. Evan's first short story collection, *The Emaciated Man and Other Terrifying Tales from Poe Middle School*, has been published by Thurston Howl Publications. More about Evan can be found at amazon.com/author/evanbaughfman and evanbaughfman.com.

R. Michael Burns is an October child with a background in theater, philosophy, and other dark arts. He is the author of the novels *Windwalkers* and *Mr. Menace*, and more than two dozen horror, science fiction, fantasy, and other harder-to-classify short stories, including appearances in several "best of" anthologies. His essays on the craft of fiction have received accolades from Predators and Editors and have been used in college creative writing courses. A Colorado native, he taught English in Japan for nearly half a decade before returning to the United States in 2005. He currently resides in the deep dark swamps of Gainesville, Florida, with his feline familiar, Hermia, and the relentless voices in his head. More of his work, both fiction and non, can be found at www.rmichaelburns.com. Follow him on Twitter @RMichaelBurns1 and on Facebook at R. Michael Burns - Fiction Writer.

Peter Caffrey is a writer of fiction with an absurdist leaning. His novels include *The Devil's Hairball*, *Whores Versus Sex Robots*, and *The Butcher's Other Daughter*. His work has also appeared in *Underbelly*, *Infernal Ink*, *Horror Sleaze Trash*, *Danse Macabre*, *Close to the Bone*, *Frontier Tales*, *Terror House*, and *The Bumper Book of British Bizarro*, amongst others. He drinks too much, exercises too little and is unlikely to change. Website: http://petercaffrey.com

My name is **Scott Chaddon**. I was born and raised in Fairbanks, Alaska where cold winters tended to keep everyone indoors. I chose art, role playing games, and reading as my escape from the harsh weather, and ultimately I began writing so I could share my own thoughts, ideas and worlds.

Several of my stories have appeared in various anthologies, such as: *Occult Detective: Monster Hunter A Grimoir of Eldrich Inquests*, *Building*

Red:Mission Mars, Explorer One, The Dead Game, Spirit Walker, Colp Black and Grey, and *Gypsum Sound Jails.* My work has also appeared in magazines like *Last Line Journal, Sci Phi Journal,* and several issues of *Mad Scientist Journal.*

Nick Chianese was born and raised in New Jersey. He graduated from Vassar College in 2014 with a major in film and a minor in creative writing. His first published story, "The Tragedy of Longmorn" (written under the pseudonym Ramsey Wallaus Heath), was released by Rainfall Chapbooks in the U.K. in May of 2020. Some of his favorite writers include Stephen King, T.E.D. Klein, and H.P. Lovecraft.

Jude Clee is a writer and teacher. She is a contributor for the nonprofit blog Nueroclastic, and her short story "Notes from a Bathroom Stall" appeared in the Autumn 2020 issue *Black Petal.*

Charles John Huffam Dickens was a writer and social critic who created some of the world's best-known fictional characters and is regarded as the greatest novelist of the Victorian era. His works enjoyed unprecedented popularity during his lifetime, and by the twentieth century critics and scholars had recognized him as a literary genius. His novels and short stories enjoy lasting popularity.

Dan Foley grew up in Northern New Jersey. He has lived on the east coast, the west coast, the gulf coast and points in between, including two nuclear submarines. He has lived in Manchester, CT. since 1985. His genres of choice are horror and paranormal suspense.

Dan is the author of the novels *Death's Companion, Reunion, Abandoned, Alone, Witches,* and *Wolf's Tale,* the novellas, *Intruder* and *Gypsy,* and a collection of short stories *The Whispers of Crows.* All are available through Amazon and B&N. He has also published in various anthologies and magazines in the U.S. Canada, England and Australia. Find him on Facebook at www.facebook.com/dan.foley.31

Niko Hart writes horror and absurdist fiction that explores those days when things fall apart and reality bites back. He has been published in *Dark Gothic Resurrected, Vaulted Tails, Asylum Ink,* and *Sanitarium Magazine.* You can visit his lair at realityfails.com.

Chisto Healy has been writing since childhood, but he only started following his dreams and writing full time in 2020. On top of the award nominated self-published novels from his earlier days, he now has over 100 published stories. You can find out what is out to read at his blog (https://chistohealy.blogspot. com) or follow him on Amazon as there is new stuff constantly coming out.

He lives in NC with his fiancee and her mom, his daughter Ella who has inspired stories that have been published, his daughter Julia who has been published alongside him, and his son Boe who thinks the world is his drum.

Liam Hogan is an award winning short story writer, with stories in Best of British Science Fiction 2016 & 2019, and Best of British Fantasy 2018 (NewCon Press). He's been published by *Analog, Daily Science Fiction*, and Flame Tree Press, among others. He helps host Liars' League London, volunteers at the creative writing charity Ministry of Stories, and lives and avoids work in London. More details at http://happyendingnotguaranteed.blogspot.co.uk.

Nathan Ludwig is an award-winning screenwriter and filmmaker. He is also the founder and director of the highly acclaimed GenreBlast Film Fest in Winchester, VA. He lives with his wife and their two daughters in Richmond, VA.

US Army Veteran **Mike Marcus** is fascinated by fear and what it reveals about us individually and collectively. Mike lives in Pittsburgh, Pa., with his wife Amy, and their elderly Rottweiler mix Millie. Mike studied communications and political science at Frostburg State University in Frostburg, Md. Mike's short story "Ale for Humanity" appeared in *Second Round: Return to the Ur-Bar*, published in 2019 by Zombies Need Brains, LLC. His story "Moll Dyer's Revenge" appears in the 2020 anthology *From the Yonder: A Collection of Horror from Around the World*, published by War Monkey Publications, LLC. Follow Mike on Twitter at @MikeMarcus77.

Joshua Marsella is a Maine native. Married to his wife, Aryn, he currently works as a stay-at-home dad with his two sons. He is the author of his self-published debut novella, SCRATCHES. He has also written several short stories that will be published in upcoming anthologies. He's planning a solo anthology for sometime in 2021 as well as his second novella which will be a prequel to his debut.

John M. McIlveen is the bestselling author of the Stoker Award nominated novel *Hannawhere*, three story collections, *Inflictions, Jerks*, and *A Variable Darkness* (releasing Feb. 4, 2021). His novel *Girl Gone North* (nominated for the 2019 Wilber and Niso Smith Foundation Award in Unpublished Manuscripts) will release in late 2021.

He is CEO of Haverhill House Publishing, and works at MIT's Lincoln Laboratory. He lives in Haverhill, MA with his wife Roberta Colasanti.

Please visit him at https://johnmcilveen.com and www.haverhillhouse.com

Jacqueline Moran Meyer is a writer, artist and small business owner living in New York, where she received her master's degree from Teachers College, Columbia University. Jacqueline enjoys writing speculative fiction and mysteries. Her favorite author is Alice Munro and her favorite film… is…anything horror related. Jacqueline also enjoys hiking with her dog Molly and the company of her husband Bruce and daughters; Julia, Emma and Lauren. Connect with her at her website, www.jmoranmeyer.net; her Amazon author page, amazon.com/author/jacquelinemoranmeyer; and on Twitter, @jmmeyer64.

This writer, known as **Pi_Rational**, exists in the space between reality and fantasy, between light and dark, between rational and irrational. In this space, she writes her stories. Always dark and thought provoking, these are tales of men and monsters, stories of the best and worst of human nature and forces outside of our control. Check out more from Pi_Rational by following her Podcast "Stories from the In Between" at http://www.pirational.com/.

Janine Pipe is a horror loving writer and reviewer hailing from the UK. A lover of all things macabre, she owes a lot to her favorite authors, mentors and friends – Hunter Shea and Glenn Rolfe. You can find her work in several anthologies including *Graveyard Smash* from Kandisha Press and *25 Gates of Hell* alongside Brian Keene. She is working on her debut novella— think Buffy but with a lot more gore. When she isn't writing or reading, you can find her reviewing stuff on YouTube or podcasting with fellow Brit, Lou on *Cryptids, Crypts and Coffee*. She couldn't do any of this without her biggest cheerleaders, her husband and daughter. You may also see her spreading her love of horror as a reviewer for *SCREAM* magazine.

Stephanie Rabig tried to check out a copy of *Dracula* while in kindergarten: this was blatant foreshadowing. When not writing or reading horror, she can be found working on resin jewelry, collecting cryptid art, and mainlining Prodigal Son. Find her on Twitter @stephrabig.

Carl E. Reed is currently employed as the showroom manager for a window, siding, and door company just outside Chicago. Former jobs include: U.S. marine, long-haul trucker, improvisational actor, cab driver, security guard, door-to-door encyclopedia salesman, construction worker, and art show MC. His poetry has been published in *The Iconoclast* and *Spectral Realms*; short stories in *Black Gate*, *newWitch* and *Sci-Fi Lampoon* magazines. His most recent short story was published 2020 in the weird romance anthology *Down the Rabbit Hole*, vol. III.

Greg Sisco is a white male in his early thirties, approximately 6'4" and 270 pounds. He was last seen leaving a movie theater in Vancouver, British Columbia, unshaven, wearing a leather jacket, and driving a black Chevy Impala. He is believed to be unarmed and extremely non-dangerous.

Christopher Stanley lives on a hill with three sons who share a birthday but aren't triplets. His stories have been published by Unnerving Magazine, The Arcanist and in The Third Corona Book of Horror Stories. His novelette, The Forest is Hungry, was published by Demain Publishing in April 2019. Follow him @allthosestrings.

Matt Starr is a Best of the Net nominated writer and father of dogs in North Carolina. His second book, Prepare to Meet Thy God, is another title from Grinning Skull Press. You can observe him in the wild @illmattic919 on Twitter.

Steven J. Taylor is an Australian born author of all things scary and fantastical. Steven has always been passionate about writing, having contributed to music blogs and fantasy fan fiction sites in the past. From an early age Steven was obsessed with horror, growing up in a bedroom whose walls were plastered with '80s horror movie promo posters. And now, as an adult, he has found something dark growing inside. Stories. Bloody horror stories. Fantastical monster stories. And he can't hold them back any longer. They are bursting out of his mind and onto the page. They are coming…for you.

Grinning Skull Press Presents

DEATHLEHEM

Anthologies of Holiday Horrors for Charity

The Place where it all started

O Little Town of Deathlehem

Twas the fright before Christmas,
And all through the town,
Not a soul stirred,
No one dared make a sound…

Welcome to Deathlehem, where…
…Krampus, not Santa, brings the holiday cheer…
…the lights on the tree, so festive and bright, skitter and crawl and possess a lethal bite…
…malicious little elves, not a jolly one, know if you've been naughty—or nice…
and
…family gatherings often turn deadly.
So enter…if you dare.

A collection of 23 holiday horrors benefiting the Elizabeth Glaser Pediatric AIDS Foundation.

Return to Deathlehem

Slay bells ring,
Kids are screaming,
In the lane, snow is blood stained.
There's nowhere to hide,
Krampus has arrived,
There'll be feasting in a winter slaughter land…

Welcome back to Deathlehem,
…where the office Secret Santa proves more dangerous than a game of
Russian roulette…
…where trips to Grandma's house are fraught with danger…
…where a traditional Nutcracker poses a threat to a pair of would-be
thieves…
…where ghosts of Christmases past haunt and take vengeance against the
living…
…and many more!

Twenty-three more tales of holiday horror benefiting the Elizabeth Glaser
Pediatric AIDS Foundation

Deathlehem *Revisited*

You make this a Christmas to dismember,
Killing feelings in the middle of December,
Strangers meet, one unwillingly surrenders,
Oh, what a Christmas to dismember…

Welcome back to Deathlehem…again!…
where a mutated Christmas has a taste for human flesh…
…where a trio of trespassers are terrorized at an abandoned holiday-
themed tourist attraction…
…where elves thrive on the torment delivered to others…
…where holiday shopping drives people to commit extreme acts of
violence…
…and many more!

Twenty-three more tales of holiday horror to benefit The Elizabeth Glaser
Pediatric AIDS FoundationPediatric AIDS Foundation

The Shadow over Deathlehem

O little town of Deathlehem,
Within you death doth lie!
Beneath thy deep and rutted streets
Tormented souls do cry.
Yet in your dark streets shineth
A cold and ghostly light.
The fears and tears of all the years
Are met in thee tonight.

Well, here we are again, folks — Deathlehem ...
... where Krampus isn't the only creature to fear
when the holiday draws near...
... where holiday treats aren't safe to eat ...
... where not even the apocalypse will keep
people from celebrating the holiday ...
... where even Chanukah isn't safe to celebrate ...

Twenty-five more tales of holiday horror to benefit
The Elizabeth Glaser Pediatric AIDS Foundation

O Unholy Night in Deathlehem

Said the little child to his mother dear,
do you hear what I hear
Shrieking through the night, father dear,
And do you see what I see
A cry, a scream, blood coloring the snow
And a laugh as evil as sin
And a laugh as evil as sin

Well, folks, looks like we're back in Deathlehem, where...
...Santa's gift turns a mindless horde of bargain-hungry shoppers
into...well... a horde of hungry shoppers...
...defective toys aren't just dangerous; they're deadly...
...holiday ornaments prove to be absolutely captivating—permanently...
...those ugly Christmas sweaters are to die for...

Twenty-five more tales of holiday horror to benefit
The Elizabeth Glaser Pediatric AIDS Foundation

A Tree Lighting in Deathlehem

In Deathlehem, the masses hail
The Blessed one was born
They gathered in a manger
On that black December morn
Among the screams of Mother Mary
The Babe from her torn
Dark tidings corrupting hope and joy

So rest merry gentlemen
Let Satan's child play
Burning bodies light this Christmas tree
In Deathlehem today

Welcome back, folks. And for you newbies wondering where you are, that would be Deathlehem…
…where enemies meet on the battlefield to set aside their differences on this holiest of nights—only to be tormented by a legendary she-demon…
…where irons bars won't keep brothers from spending Christmas with their mother—much to her dismay…
…where the search for the perfect tree turns into a bloody nightmare…
…where an imprisoned evil has a young couple and their daughter wishing they'd stayed at home for the holidays…

Twenty-five more tales of holiday horror to benefit

The Elizabeth Glaser Pediatric AIDS Foundation

Made in USA - North Chelmsford, MA
1291566_9781947227583
11.22.2021 1210